What they're saying about Chris Well's first novel, *Forgiving Solomon Long*

Selected as one of the
Top 10 Christian Novels of 2005
by Booklist, *the magazine of the American Library Association*

⌒ ⌒ ⌒

"Here's a novel with the feel of real life—fast-paced and thought-provoking."

—Sigmund Brouwer, bestselling author and coauthor of *The Last Disciple, The Weeping Chamber,* and the Mars Diaries

"For lovers of crime fiction, *Forgiving Solomon Long* by Chris Well combines a taut, fast-paced thriller with a powerful message of forgiveness."

—CBA *Marketplace* magazine

"An intelligent thriller that combines sitcoms with Shakespeare, Froot Loops with coffee, and gunfights with church...anything but ordinary fare."

—Christian Book Previews

"A hard-edged, mean streets story—in which God's grace shines all the brighter...Heralds a new day in Christian suspense."

—Brandilyn Collins, bestselling author of *Web of Lies*

"Well's fresh voice makes this an enjoyable addition to faith fiction."

—*Publishers Weekly* magazine

"A-plus fiction...Will both surprise and delight you."

—*CCM* magazine

Starred Review "Well...serves up brisk dialogue and interjects references to pop culture into even his most violent scenes. This is Christian fiction, but Quentin Tarantino's *Pulp Fiction* comes to mind."

—*Booklist*, American Library Association

"So full of twists and turns, it keeps you guessing until the very end. An amazing story of suspense and grace."

— Tracey Bumpus, Managing Editor, FaithTalk

"A powerful tale of suspense and the power of mercy."

—*Infuze* magazine

"If this is what people mean by 'faith-based fiction,' then count me in."

—Jay Swartzendruber, editor, *CCM* magazine

"If there's one lesson I learned from *Forgiving Solomon Long,* it's that no one has fallen so far that he can't be redeemed."

—Crossings Book Club

"An excellent, untypical story...creative and compelling. Well mixes murders with messages and paints wonderful characters. A fun read."

—*Youthworker Journal*

"Filled with ironic twists and turns...action-packed prose for readers with a taste for bittersweet crime drama."

—*Romantic Times Book Club* magazine

"Enough hair-raising action, savvy laughs, and flat-out pulp punch to make me want to come back again and again. Stunning!"

—Matt Bronleewe, music producer for Natalie Imbruglia, Rebecca St. James, and others

"Tarantino-esque...ripe for cinematic adaptation."

—*HM* magazine

CHRIS WELL

Deliver Us from Evelyn

HARVEST HOUSE PUBLISHERS

EUGENE, OREGON

Cover by Terry Dugan Design, Minneapolis, Minnesota

DELIVER US FROM EVELYN
Copyright © 2006 by Chris Well
Published by Harvest House Publishers
Eugene, Oregon 97402
www.harvesthousepublishers.com

Library of Congress Cataloging-in-Publication Data
Well, Chris, 1966–
 Deliver us from Evelyn / Chris Well.
  p. cm.
 ISBN-13: 978-0-7369-1406-2 (pbk.)
 ISBN-10: 0-7369-1406-4
 1. Police—Missouri—Kansas City—Fiction. 2. Mayors—Election—Fiction. 3. Kansas City (Mo.)—Fiction. 4. Women publishers—Fiction. 5. Missing persons—Fiction
 I. Title.
 PS3623.E4657D45   2006
 813'.6—dc22   2005023977

Printed in the United States of America

06 07 08 09 10 11 12 13 14 /BC-CF/ 10 9 8 7 6 5 4 3 2 1

For Roberta,

*who wishes me to make clear to
the world at large that she is not the inspiration
for the character of Evelyn Blake.*

(Seriously, she isn't.)

Because the sentence against an evil deed is not
executed quickly, therefore the hearts of the sons of
men among them are given fully to do evil.

ECCLESIASTES 8:11

~ ~ ~

NEAR THE END.

BLOG

WHERE IS BLAKE #027
whereisblake.blogdroid.com

"Education is a progressive discovery of our own ignorance."

—Will Durant

My fault. My fault. If I had never started this blog, never started spilling company secrets, never come to Kansas City searching for my past, for my future, none of this might have happened.

But now a human being is dead. As dead as if I had aimed the gun myself and pulled the trigger. And now they're coming for me.

They're going to find me any minute. I know it. I must have been crazy, but then, that's how it always is, isn't it? You feel the thrill of secrets, the thrill of sharing from behind an anonymous mask, the power—and then you are caught. Napoléon was caught. "Hubris," I think it's called. Icarus. I would log onto a dictionary site and check the definition but I don't have the time.

Because they're coming for me. When my adoring fans log onto my blog tomorrow morning, I wonder whether my secrets will still be here. I wonder whether my "crazy theories" will have been proven.

I wonder whether I will have paid for my part in the death of Warren Blake.

But they're coming. These are not people who forgive. These are not people who forget.

All I can think is how it must have been for Warren Blake when his time came. Nobody deserves to go like that.

How will it be when my time comes? A shot to the heart? A knife to the back? A push into an open elevator shaft? Can a person ever know how it all ends for them?

NEAR THE BEGINNING.

~ 1 ~

Sunday night. April 23.

On his last day of this life, the Right Fair Reverend Missionary Bob Mullins checked the party dip. Just stuck his finger right in there, pulled some glop free, stuck it in his mouth, and sucked.

Hmm, good dip.

He wiped his saliva'd finger on his jacket, popped the top on a can of Pringles, shuffled a neat row of curved chips onto a Dixie paper platter.

There.

Setting the can down, he stepped back from the secondhand coffee table in the middle of the shag-carpeted office, looked at what his party planning skills had wrought. And he saw that it was good.

He went to the stereo system across the room, selected a CD. Personally, he would have preferred something by the Rolling Stones, maybe *Exile on Main Street* or *Beggars Banquet*—muscular, honkytonk rock 'n' roll you can get drunk or stoned to, depending on your mood. He could really go for the bluesy wail of "Tumbling Dice" right now.

But the music library here offered none of that. Besides, his marks—that is, the members of his "flock"—held certain expectations regarding what music was appropriate for a prayer meeting. Especially in a small armpit of a town like Belt Falls, Illinois.

(Who names a town "Belt Falls" anyway?)

The ladies would be here soon. Then Missionary Bob would use his people skills, honed from his years of "ministry," to good effect.

17

Would lead the group in a spontaneous (but carefully planned) evening following "the Lord's leading"—some Bible, some hymns, some ministry time. A carefully rehearsed prayer, a combination of wails and pleas, which experience had shown to be a very effective prelude to the passing of the offering plate.

Swept up by the rush of maudlin and spiritual emotion, the ladies would cough up plenty.

"Yea, but there are those who do not have it as comfortably as we do," he found himself practicing, fiddling with chair placement in the circle, maneuvering pillows on the couch. "Poor children who do not have the food or clothing or shelter such as we take for granted."

He double-checked the handy photos on the table. The orphanage in Mexico went by a lot of names. It would not do for the Right Fair Reverend Missionary Bob Mullins to get all weepy-eyed over JESÚS AMA LOS NIÑOS PEQUEÑOS and then whip out a photo showing a bunch of tiny brown faces smiling under a banner that said CHILDREN OF HER MERCY ORPHANAGE.

Following the fiasco in the last town, he'd played it cool once he got to Belt Falls. (Really, who brings a wagon train across the frontier, breaks ground on a settlement, and says, "From henceforth, this shall be known as 'Belt Falls'"?)

Ever since Andrea—his partner, his companion, his ray of light—had got Jesus, she'd stopped helping with the scams. Stopped helping him fleece the flock, so to speak. She laid it on thick enough—*It is appointed unto men once to die, but after this the judgment,* and all that.

He tried to smirk it off, tried the face that always brought her around, but it didn't seem to work anymore. Whatever had got hold of her wasn't letting go.

Missionary Bob would never admit it to anyone, least of all himself, that the dividing line between success and failure began and ended with Andrea. When she was working with him, the scams worked like butter.

But then she got religion, and the whole machine went up in flames.

Not that Missionary Bob got the clue. He kept working his games, town to town, each new gambit failing, each new town harder to crack than the last.

Once he set up shop here in Belt Falls (don't get him started again about the name of the town), he took his time getting to know the people. Found them to be a small, close-knit community, smugly going to their church services.

Smug, but not that pious—it did not take much effort to plant sufficient evidence that the only pastor in town was a raving drug user, maybe even a dealer. Not enough evidence to get the man convicted—even the hick sheriff saw it was a weak case—but the hapless pastor had to make only one phone call to the wrong deacon asking for bail money before word of his *unholy lifestyle* rushed through the congregation like wildfire.

In the eyes of God and the law, he was probably an okay guy. But once a congregation chooses to believe the worst, a preacher may as well pack his bags and move on.

Missionary Bob had even heard tell of one particular church, somewhere in the Midwest, where the members had booted the pastor because he'd had the temerity to wear *short pants* to a *church potluck*.

Yep, hell—if it existed—would be packed to the lips with smug, busybody churchgoers who ran their preacher out of town because he had worn shorts to a church potluck. Or, as in this case, had been the victim of circumstantial evidence planted on him by a traveling huckster.

He stood and straightened his dress jacket. Felt a bulge in his left pocket, was surprised to discover a coaster with the face of Jesus on it.

He looked around the office, befuddled. When had he picked this up?

You don't have to lift anything here, he reminded himself. *You've pretty much lifted the whole office already.*

Missionary Bob, in what used to be the hapless pastor's office, heard steps echoing from the foyer, somebody clomping up the stairs. *My, my*, thought the Right Fair Reverend Missionary Bob Mullins, *these ladies do need to lose some weight, don't they?* Whoever this was, she was pounding the stairs to wake the devil.

He stopped fidgeting with pillows and stood up straight, getting into character. Thinking of his plan, his mission, remembering the correct accent and speech patterns of a Right Fair Reverend Missionary, an accent as specific and undeniable as the drawl of New Orleans or the wicked blue-blood of Boston.

There was an insistent pounding on the door, a battering, really, if he had stopped to think about it. But he was too wrapped up in the character of a Right Fair Reverend Missionary. He slapped on a toothy grin and opened the door. "Welcome, child, to—"

It was a man. A. Large. Man. A grizzly bear towering over him, bloated flannel shirt cascading out of pants where they were almost tucked, tractor cap on his head declaring EAT ROADKILL. The grizzly bear pressed his flannelled beer belly against the Right Fair Reverend Missionary, leaned down from on high, and belched, "I'm Darla Mae's husband."

The Right Fair Reverend Missionary Bob Mullins broke character and cursed.

The rest of the confrontation was like a dream, a nightmare of slow motion, the bear smacking him, a freight train to the skull, tossing Missionary Bob across the room. Hitting the coffee table as he went down, elbow in the dip. The grizzly roaring, storming in, Missionary Bob on the floor, scrambling backward, away, fleeing in the only direction he could, farther into the room. The angry husband kicking the table over, party snacks flying, dip spattering across the bookcase.

As Missionary Bob kicked to his feet, always moving backward until the wall stopped his escape, one question kept flashing through his mind: *Is this about the fake antique Cross of James, or is this about the adultery?*

Either way, his back against the wall, this grizzly man bearing down on him, Missionary Bob was out of options. The giant man, his eyes red, had barrel fists clenched and ready to swing like sledgehammers.

There was a noise behind the grizzly, at the open door. "Missionary Bob?"

One of the ladies.

The enraged husband turned at the voice. Missionary Bob took his one and only chance, grabbed the stone head of Molière, clubbed the grizzly across the side of the head. The man stumbled backward and fell.

Missionary Bob, fueled by anger and fear and blind, stupid adrenaline, kept clubbing, again and again. The man on the floor now, blood streaming from his head. Missionary Bob clubbing him with the bust again and again. On his knees, on top of the man, clubbing him again and again and again.

Finally, adrenaline loosening its grip, Missionary Bob became aware the man was not moving. Clutching air in hot, painful gasps, he dropped the bust to the carpet. Felt something wet on the side of his face, wiped it with his sleeve, saw blood smeared on fabric. Not his own blood.

Gasping, wheezing, he looked up and saw the witnesses, ladies pooling in the doorway, staring agape at the Goliath on the floor, downed by the David with his stone.

- 2 -

Viktor Igorovich Zhukov took one last drag from his Lucky Strike, dropped it to concrete without stamping it out. Checked his watch. Sunday, 8:15 PM. While his comrades shared vulgar stories, Zhukov glanced around for the exits, planning his escape.

When Napoléon's army had foolishly invaded Mother Russia, he lost more soldiers in the retreat than in the attack. As a student of military history, Zhukov knew how important it was to have all the possibilities mapped out ahead of a battle.

Evil Duke Cumbee and his men would be here soon. Cumbee, and Zhukov's boss, Boris Amanovich Blokhin, had agreed to the location. This parking garage had been chosen as the meeting place, neutral territory, empty on a Sunday night. Zhukov did not know what sort of capitalist enterprises were conducted in the building during the week.

Blokhin pulled up the collar of his coat. "I do not know about this."

"Do not worry." Zhukov coughed, took another drag from his cigarette. "This should be good."

"We have men in place, yes?"

Zhukov smiled, showing crooked teeth. "Da."

Blokhin and Cumbee were meeting to discuss a truce. The two organizations had rushed in to fill the vacuum created by the downfall of Frank "Fat Cat" Catalano. The authorities watching over Kansas City, Missouri, had dismantled most of the long-running operations of the old families, and a new mob had rushed in to fill the vacuum. A mob less beholden to the old methods, to tradition, to any code of honor.

Catalano had come into power as a keen businessman, a capitalist who'd stitched together a patchwork of lucrative businesses to build his empire. Some legal but profitable, others questionable but extremely profitable.

But in a fast few months, something had happened. Fat Cat's empire had collapsed from within. Zhukov did not know the details, but by the time the authorities had swept up the debris, most of Fat Cat's family and inner circle were dead or in prison.

Which left Kansas City up for grabs.

Blokhin and Cumbee were the two strongest contenders to rise as the new power in Kansas City, a competition that led to regular friction between the two. Cumbee was aligning himself with high-society types, captains of industry, working from the top down. Blokhin, meanwhile, was amassing power from the ground up, starting with the street—working protection rackets and running drugs and arms.

Given the two opposite approaches, it seemed reasonable they might come to terms regarding the middle ground. Blokhin scoffed at the idea at first, had wanted to take the streets by force, line the gutters with blood. As mobsters raised under the KGB, intimidation and violence were their chief allies.

But Zhukov had convinced him. He had studied the glory years of the KGB. Had studied military history. Had learned the value of measured cooperation. Had learned the knife cuts most easily when it slides into the back.

He'd talked Blokhin into making nice. Try a face of honor, see where it leads. At best, they could reach a mobster's detente, and the two organizations would come out richer. Failing that, the Russian Mafiya could grab Cumbee by his neck and break it.

Blokhin was pacing, Zhukov watching. About thirty minutes after they had arrived, Zhukov heard the squeal of tires entering the garage. His men looked to him. He snapped out directions with his eyes, with hand gestures. The men took their positions.

The other car came in and pulled to a stop at an agreeable distance. The doors opened, and men in suits got out. Zhukov could not see their boss—apparently, Cumbee was staying in the car until it was deemed safe.

One of the men stepped forward, snapped off dark glasses, and said, "Hey, Russkies—how are things?" He flashed a grin. Something about it made Zhukov check for the exits.

A second car pulled in.

A third.

⌂ ▭ ⑦   ⊠

BLOG

WHERE IS BLAKE #001
whereisblake.blogdroid.com

"It is impossible to please all the world and one's father."
—Jean La Fontaine

My dad's favorite movie is <u>Last Train from Gun Hill</u>. Not that he could ever tell you that—he could never get the title right to save his life. He would call it everything from "Last Gun from Boot Hill" to "Last Call from Green Hall."

But make no mistake, he was always talking about *Last Train from Gun Hill,* just the same.

"Kirk Douglas and Anthony Quinn star in this 1959 Western thriller directed by John Sturges *(The Magnificent Seven, Gunfight at the O.K. Corral).* A U.S. Marshal (Douglas) vows to bring the young killer of his wife to justice—a task complicated by the fact that the suspect's father is the lawman's longtime friend. Suspense mounts as he finds himself trapped alone in town—with killers looking to hunt him down."

It's my dad's favorite movie.

I don't actually know why. He never told me, I never thought to ask him.

I wish I had. I've never particularly been a fan of Westerns. I started to like them only a few years ago. I started to watch them to get to know my father better. I enjoyed discovering The Magnificent Seven. I suppose it was my introduction to the world of Westerns. It was an easy enough initiation. I had already come to love two of its many descendents, A Bug's Life and Galaxy Quest, and had slept through the middle two hours of its epic antecedent, The Seven Samurai, in film class. So by the time I saw *The Magnificent Seven,* I pretty much had the backbone of the film figured out, which gave me the luxury of watching the individual characters, the individual performances.

My father never much cared for *The Magnificent Seven.*

I was fourteen years old before I found out he wasn't my real father.

That discovery began a journey that has lasted me the better part of a decade. It led me to Kansas City, Missouri, led me here to Blake Media Enterprises, led me to work for that awful woman Evelyn Blake.

Led me to work for Cruella D'Evelyn, the Wicked Queen of the Midwest.

Deliver us from Evelyn.

~ 3 ~

"This entire story is about stolen identity." Detective Charlie Pasch trying to explain the opera squawking out of the car radio. The digital readout said 8:17 PM. The Chevy sat at the curb across the street from the parking garage. Charlie and Detective Tom Griggs watching. Moonlight glinting on the wet street.

Earlier, the two had watched a carload of Russian Mafiya drive up, Boris Blokhin and his most trusted men. The car had entered the garage, empty this time of night.

Griggs and Charlie would soon be joined by Special Agent Martin O'Malley of the FBI. The three had spent a lot of time together lately, working shoulder to shoulder in the KCPD/FBI Joint Task Force.

Pooling their resources, they had punched a significant hole in Kansas City organized crime. Put away or dismantled the operations of several key figures, including Boss Joey Pratt, Big Ed Drake, Frank "Fat Cat" Catalano. Every time one rat came down, though, more swarmed in to take what cheese was left.

Griggs and Charlie were partners now, following a complicated series of events months earlier. In the process, Griggs had lost his former partner, Jurgens, who was now cooling his heels in prison. Charlie had almost been killed, and had a scar on his forehead to show for it.

Griggs felt responsible for the younger detective's brush with death and felt the need to look after the whiz kid. Play mentor. He liked the kid okay, but Charlie still made him uncomfortable sometimes. Seemed to know everything.

As the night wore on, Charlie fiddled with the radio and came upon the public-radio station. Griggs winced at the chaos that erupted. "How do you even acquire a taste for this stuff?"

"You study it a bit, I guess." Charlie cocked his head, thinking. "The harder you fight for it, the more rewarding it becomes once you grasp it."

Griggs glanced out the driver-side window. "I don't know."

"Like this here." Charlie pointed to the radio. "Mozart's *The Marriage of Figaro*. It's classic. A story of mistaken identity, jealousy, and betrayal. Lots of people in disguise. Class warfare. Hijinks ensue."

"Uh-huh."

Charlie sighed. Pandered. "They used the overture for the movie *Trading Places*."

"With Eddie Murphy?"

"Yup."

Griggs narrowed his eyes. "How do you know?"

"It's like you always say, Griggs—everything is connected. A detective always connects the dots."

They sat a few more minutes. Griggs, bored, turned and motioned to the radio. "*Trading Places*, huh?"

Charlie nodded. "Yep. Or, to think of it another way, it's sort of like the story of Jacob and Esau."

"Are they in the opera?"

"No, they're in the Bible."

Griggs made a face. "I don't like it when you talk religion, Charlie."

Charlie was going to answer but was cut off when the headlights came their way. About 8:30 PM, three more cars entered the garage.

Charlie checked something on the clipboard. "At least one of those cars is on the list." He looked over at his partner. "That car belongs to one of the guys who work for Evil Duke Cumbee."

Griggs made a face. "Evil Duke Cumbee?" The tipster had not mentioned the Russian mob was meeting with *him*. "I don't like this."

Charlie held his breath a second. A tap at his passenger window made him yelp.

O'Malley.

The Fed opened the back door and slid into the seat. "Miss me, Charlie?"

Before Charlie could assemble a non-awkward reply, Griggs was already turning. "You're just in time." Griggs checking his weapon. "We need to go in for a closer look."

Charlie nervously touched the scar on his forehead. Where Gino Catalano had shot him. "Don't you think we should call for backup?"

O'Malley grinned, chomping gum like a cowboy. "That's what you're here for, Charlie-boy." Checking his weapon too. Charlie saw Band-Aids around several of his fingers. "Ready when you are, Griggs."

Griggs turned to Charlie, placing a fatherly hand on his arm. "Stay in the car."

Detective Griggs and Special Agent O'Malley exited the Chevy, each with gun in hand, darted across the shiny, rain-swept street.

Charlie grabbed the car mic and called for backup. That out of the way, he needed to get out there, back up Griggs and O'Malley. Back up the two men who had gotten so close the past few months, fighting the mob together, hitting the batting cage together, fishing weekends together.

The scar on Charlie's forehead itched. He tried to ignore it. Unholstered his weapon, checked it. He was still useful.

He was getting out the passenger side when he heard the first shots. He ducked behind the car, heard more shooting, heard tires screeching loud as three cars roared out of the garage and up the street.

A black-and-white was approaching from the opposite direction. Charlie ran into the street, flashing his badge, telling the officer at the wheel to pursue. The black-and-white sped off, lights flashing, siren blaring.

Charlie, gun ready, raced for the entrance of the parking garage to search for Griggs and O'Malley. Fearing the worst.

He found Special Agent O'Malley inside, kneeling beside a car. The engine running, the doors open and accompanied by the telltale *ping-ping* of a door ajar. Several men fallen, draped around it. O'Malley checking for pulses.

Charlie didn't see Griggs. The garage was empty, except for the federal agent and the weird performance-art scene. "Where's Griggs?" Trying not to sound like a panicked kid.

O'Malley, grim, looked up, nodded toward the elevator. "Trying to catch whoever ran off."

The light over the doors indicated the elevator was still going up. Charlie ran to the stairwell. As he reached it, the door opened, stopping his heart in his chest.

Griggs. Panting. Shaking his head.

Charlie and Griggs walked back to O'Malley, who had given up on finding survivors. Charlie looked at the car, its headlights blazing, followed the light to where it bounced off concrete. Graffiti looked like spattered blood. It read, WHERE IS BLAKE?

- 4 -

Missionary Bob poured gas over the beat-up car. The one he had convinced the local auto dealer to donate to the "ministry." Barely aware of how he got here, how, in a daze, he had pushed through the mighty cloud of witnesses and must have walked the half mile to this abandoned barn on a patch of unkept land off the outskirts of Belt Falls, where he was staging his finale.

A homeless man was slumped in the front seat of the car, an itinerant Missionary Bob had transported from two towns over, a drunk intercepted in front of the local mission, lured with the promise of whiskey and salvation, then left sleeping in the car. Dead to the world. Soon to be dead, just dead.

All part of the plan. Missionary Bob had been planning his own demise all along. Of course, the plan had been to bilk the ladies of this town of all their valuables, their baubles, their trinkets, their cash, not unlike the way the children of Israel had ransacked their captors before they exodused out of Egypt ahead of the angel of death.

But this time, the angel of death was going to take the old man, the Right Fair Reverend Missionary Bob Mullins—who was to be resurrected at a later date with a new name. Sure, some nameless homeless guy would trade in his life in the process, all the better to fool the authorities into thinking scoundrel Missionary Bob had lost his life, no point in trying to find him anywhere else. It was a sacrifice Missionary Bob was willing to make.

But this plan was intended to cover his tracks after a major score—well, as major a score as you can get out of a place called "Belt Falls." The plan was not intended to cover his tracks after beating down a jealous husband with the sculpted head of a seventeenth-century French playwright.

Missionary Bob continued preparing the car for its fiery burial, barely aware he was humming "Street Fighting Man." Began to sort through his mental catalogue of possible aliases.

Malcolm Shake.

Ronald Shake.

Donald Shake.

Missionary Bob, not much longer for this Earth, did not know whether the man he'd left back on the floor of the office was dead. Who has time to check? It was a severe enough crime scene, in front of all his carefully cultivated marks. He needed to get out of town fast. Without the money.

Dropping the empty canister to the dirt with a hollow *ptang*, Missionary Bob stepped back, tried to think through his next move. His thoughts drifted, thinking how this was just the latest debacle in a string of bad luck. How he had gotten sloppy the past couple of years.

Donald Shale.

Ronald Shale.

Thomas Shale.

He was once a traveling king, a man who scored big payoffs, had the house, the cars, the friends to show for it. Until Andrea left him and it all fell to pieces. Until the local TV news crews swooped in like vultures, picking the bones clean.

In the two years since then, he'd never quite regained his footing. He'd lost his touch, each score a little less lucrative, each scrape a little narrower, each gig a little more desperate.

So here he was, in an abandoned barn on the outskirts of Belt Falls, Illinois, preparing to fake his death. No profit to show for it.

It was all spiraling out of control.

He could almost hear Andrea's voice. *Is this what it's come to? Torching a man to death to cover your tracks?*

Not now, Andrea, not now.

He tried to occupy himself, thinking of more possible names.

Shawn Thomas.

Shawn Malcolm.

Shawn Tate.

Missionary Bob felt in his jacket pockets, tried to remember where he'd placed the book of matches. He found his lighter, a Bible verse engraved on its side, the verse about how the tongue was a fire.

But a lighter was not the way to ignite a car soaking in gasoline. Get within arm's reach of that thing, the fire will ride up your sleeve and take your face.

After a few more futile minutes, he gave up on finding matches, had to think of a way to light the car with the drunk hobo still sleeping inside.

Malcolm Tate.

Tate Malcolm.
Tate Roberts.

He glanced around on the dirt floor, looking for rags, newspapers, anything to light and throw in the direction of the car. He saw bales of straw tucked in the corner, probably for insulation.

Well, Missionary Bob thought, *this place is going to get plenty warm, plenty quick.*

He went to one of the bales, bent, and clutched at thin wire crushing straw into a giant brick. The bale was heavier than it looked, the wire dug into his fingers. It hurt.

Maybe I should go back to the basics. Put together a name that exudes religious authority.

He dropped the bale, dropped to his knees. Checked to see if he could pull some of the straw free. Even a few strands would help.

It was more difficult to pull loose than you would think. He gave up and just kicked the bale. It rolled and he kicked with his heel again, angling it toward the car. With each kick and roll, he recalculated, determining how to position the bale by the wet car, gas evaporating by the second.

Abram.

He decided to make the bale stick out longways, giving him maximum distance from the car when he lit the straw. The bale in place, he bent on one knee, flicked open the lighter. He waved the flame, waited for the straw to catch. Any second now.

Saul.

Any second now.

Simon.

Any second.

The straw was too damp or something. Disgusted, he stood again and stepped away from the car, cursing, fishing in his pockets for the pack of cigarettes. He lit one and took a drag. Focused on the cigarette, a meditation that helped him relax. Then he noticed the end of the cigarette glowing.

Damascus.

He looked again at the beat-up car covered with evaporating

flammable liquid, mocking him. He looked again at the lit end of the cigarette. He smiled and prepared to flip the cigarette.

The hobo in the car stirred.

A pang of conscience gripped him. He strode to the driver-side door, dropping the cigarette before he set himself on fire, yanked open the door, grabbed the drunk by the collar. Pulled the man from the car, heaving, struggling, the man falling to the ground, dragged him across the bale of straw, across the dirt to the side of the barn.

He sat the man against the wall of the barn, checking him. "You okay, old man?" The drunk still dead to the world. Another few seconds and he would have been dead, just dead.

Damascus Rhodes.

He heard a crackling behind him, turned to see that the dropped cigarette had ignited the straw. Burning. Flames reaching toward the car.

Sonofa—

In a rush, he grabbed the old man by the arms, pulled him over his shoulders in that fireman's carry you see on television. No time to think, no time to plan, just carry and run.

Head for the barn door.

Ignore the weight.

Ignore the pain stabbing him in the side.

He did not get far out of the barn before the crackling gave way to a *whoosh* and a burst of hot air, fire lighting up the inside of the barn.

He got to the ditch, stumbling, tumbling, dropping the drunk on the ground beside him just as the car exploded. The whole barn on fire.

This far out in the country, he had no idea when the fire department might arrive, if at all. He could not take the chance of getting caught.

This night was just turning from one disaster into another—a major heist turned into a probable murder scene, and the murder he'd intended turned into a rescue operation.

Now he had no money, no faked suicide, just a pack of cigarettes and lighter with that Bible verse engraved on the side, the verse about the tongue being a fire.

And now a big flaming signal to lead the authorities right to him.

He had to leave. Now. On foot, through the woods, stay off the main roads.

So that is how The Right Doctor Reverend Damascus Rhodes came to leave Belt Falls, Illinois.

(And who names a town "Belt Falls"?)

⌂ ▭ ⑦   ⊠

BLOG

WHERE IS BLAKE #002
whereisblake.blogdroid.com

"I should like to think an irate Jehovah was pointing those arrows of lightning right at my head."

—Lord Byron, *The Bride of Frankenstein*

The blogosphere is spreading like a virus. According to reports, there are some ten million blogs in the United States already, with another twenty thousand or so new ones created every day. So my voice is just one of many.

For those of you just tuning in, a blog is just a journal kept on the Internet—a Web log, or "blog" for short. Ask Merriam-Webster, and a blog is a Web site containing "an online personal journal with reflections, comments, and often hyperlinks provided by the writer."

Some of them are as simple as news links, or daily journals about what's going on in Hollywood, or in fiction, or photos of the blogger's cat.

Me, I thought I was going to blog about my journey to meet my father and the other woman in his life—but it has turned into a blog about a woman who killed her husband.

Of course, I'm playing with fire. As soon as the wrong person sees this, as soon as the wrong person at the office figures out who is writing this blog, I could be history. Fired, I mean.

Because with the growth of the blogosphere, so grows the phenomenon of being fired for writing a blog about your workplace. Some of the fired bloggers complain about first-amendment rights, about their rights to divulge company secrets, their rights to slander co-workers.

Shut up, I say. This is not griping to a couple of friends over beer, this is broadcasting to a global audience. Because of the nature of blogs, this information becomes freely available to anyone, anywhere. Your co-workers, your rivals, complete strangers, everyone. Anyone might stumble across what you have posted.

Yeah, I am risking my job with this blog. But if I get fired, at least I'll have had my say.

If I am asked to leave, I will simply have to start looking for myself somewhere else. Find who I am. Find where I belong.

— 5 —

Assistant editor Dakota Flynn checked her watch and tapped painted nails on the conference table. The black polish flashed as they clicked against the polished grain of the surface. "I cannot believe she's late." Evelyn Blake. Her royal highness, Queen Evel. "She makes us come in on a Sunday night, and she keeps us waiting."

Managing editor Aubrey Burke, sitting to her right, almost snorted out her mouthful of white-chocolate mocha. "How can you say that? Cruella D'Evelyn?" She wiped her mouth with her sleeve and set her paper cup on a coaster. "Her clock is not as our clock."

"Yeah," nodded Flynn. "She has a lot more to worry about than a ninety-six-page magazine with her name slapped on the cover. A TV show, a book tour, speaking appearances—she has a lot of innocent people to terrorize."

"We should be honored that Queen Evel has time to meet with lowly ol' us."

From the end of the long table came a sarcastic, urgent whisper. "Pipe down, *ladies*." At the head of the table, by the door to the conference room—it was Dennis, receding hairline Dennis, bad-teeth Dennis, beleaguered publisher-in-name-only, his accent on the word "ladies" indicating he had a completely different word in mind—but God and the courts had intervened and he dared not speak that word in the office again.

Dennis followed his directive with a series of shushes, getting louder until he made eye contact with someone out in the hall, someone approaching. His nervous demeanor made everyone stop at once and hold their breath as the ice queen herself entered, ready to lord it over her underlings.

As soon as Evelyn Blake entered the conference room, Flynn was sure the temperature dropped three or four degrees. When Queen Evel looked her way, Flynn flinched and looked down at her black-nailed fingers on the table to avoid eye contact.

~ ~ ~

Forty minutes later, Flynn and Burke snuck out of the office to reconstruct the bloodshed that had followed and to decompress over margaritas and tortilla chips at Pedro's, the local Mexican restaurant. Eighties arena rock (Journey? Van Halen?) played in the background. Between them, they decided that a transcript of the exchange between Her Royal Highness, Queen Evelyn Blake, and Publisher-in-Name-Only Dennis Jung, All-Around Jerk, would probably read something like this:

QUEEN EVEL: [LOOKING AT PAGES LAID OUT ON TABLE] I do not like this. At. All.

DENNIS THE JERK: But this is...[PAUSE. CLICKING TONGUE. CALCULATING COST OF LIVING IF HE SHOULD SUDDENLY LOSE HIS JOB.] You were out of town, in Milan, but we had a lengthy conference call regarding—

QE: [STABBING FINGER AT PRINTOUT OF COVER.] What's wrong with this cover?

DTJ: I don't know what you mean.

QE: Who is this person on the cover?

DTJ: Excuse me?

QE: This person on the cover right there. [PAUSE, POINTING.]

DTJ: [SARCASM] That is the very famous actress Roberta Velvet Crocker.

QE: Tell me again, why is she on the cover?

DTJ: You were so inspired by her story that you interviewed her personally for a cover story.

QE: What else you got?

DTJ: We—we go to press tomorrow. We have been working on this issue for months. You knew the editorial lineup when we discussed—

QE: Are you calling me a liar?

DTJ: What? [TURNING TO ASSISTANT] Get me the notes from that meeting, now!

QE: Whose name is on top of the magazine?

DTJ: [PAUSE. PAUSE.] Your name, ma'am.

QE: I have a television show.

DTJ: I know.

QE: How about Darick Gold?

DTJ: What about him?

QE: There's your cover story.

DTJ:	But your newsstand readers would never pick that up. He is in a messy court case—
QE:	He's a famous sports figure. And a family man.
DTJ:	He's a retired, forgotten boxer who only resurfaced in the news when it went public that he beat his wife and then kidnapped his children when he lost custody.
QE:	He's a friend who could use some good press about now.
DTJ:	So…you want to dump this cover story, the one we spent five months planning and writing and editing and designing, this uplifting story about hope and survival—and instead put on this wife-beating, child-stealing thug, just to help him with his public relations?

(Well, Dennis the Jerk did not actually say that last part. He had more or less turned into a gurgling lackey by then, giving up altogether.)

It all started to go downhill after that. Which led to much scrambling among the staff to completely overhaul the issue. Poor Elsa Benitez was scrambling to write a new cover story on someone that, twenty minutes earlier, had not even been in the magazine.

Which led to Flynn and Burke sneaking out to the local Mexican eatery for quality time with frozen margaritas and chips and salsa. Flynn sipped her margarita and laughed. Scooped up salsa with a chip and shoved the whole chip into her mouth. No patience for manners tonight. "How soon before you think someone will miss us?" *Chomp*.

Burke frowned. "Let's see, poor Gene and Franklin are huddled way back in the art department, scrapping entire pages and redesigning, like, a third of the magazine."

"And searching frantically for a cover-worthy hi-res photo of that abusive freak."

Burke scooped more salsa with a chip. "And Elsa has to track down said abusive freak and interview him for an emergency cover story."

Burke checked her watch, saw where Mickey was pointing his gloves. "We're in the clear another thirty minutes or so."

Flynn sighed, dreading the unnecessary panic work waiting back at the office. "What's with Queen Evel, anyway? She doesn't have time for us when we're actually making the issue. She's too busy with her cable TV show or whatever—but when it's time to send it off to film, she shows up and makes a train wreck out of it."

Burke leaned in and whispered across the table. "It's like her husband isn't even missing."

"She's too busy to worry about him." Flynn smiled grimly. "What an inconvenient time for her husband to disappear."

– 6 –

Monday. April 24.

Detective Tom Griggs and Detective Charlie Pasch, back at the scene of the shooting. They had been out here late with forensics, out again bright and early as techs scraped blood off concrete, picked bullets out of cement block walls, and dropped evidence in labeled plastic bags.

The bodies were off to the morgue, the car towed down to the impound lot.

Griggs paced. Had no reason to be on site right now, except holding his breath in fear that the head of Homicide, Detective Robert Utley, might show up and throw his considerable weight around. Griggs and Utley had a history, and it was all bad. Nothing specific between them, just a general habit of fighting over jurisdiction, like kids fighting over territory on the playground.

Griggs wrung his hands. "It's times like these I wish I smoked."

"You don't want to do that." Charlie, leaning comfortably against the wall. Had already walked up and down the street outside the garage, found no useful witnesses. Apparently, Griggs, Charlie, and

Special Agent O'Malley were the only three who'd seen anything. And they had been outside.

Scratch that, Griggs thought. *There was one witness.* Someone had been here, had high-tailed it to the elevator. Had escaped the bloodshed.

"Does Carla still smoke?" Charlie asked.

Griggs stopped pacing, shrugged. "Off and on." He was watching one of the forensic techs intently.

"You guys still in counseling?"

"We still go every couple weeks."

"How's that going?"

Griggs frowned. "It's uphill sometimes. But, you know, worth it." Sighed. "I could have lost her, Charlie. Not every man gets a second chance like that."

He fidgeted, visibly nervous. Changed the subject. "You ever hear from Detective Hall?"

Charlie was surprised to hear the name. "Who, Jordan?"

"Yeah. Ever since she transferred out, I haven't heard from her." Griggs gave Charlie a knowing look. "I thought maybe you and she kept in touch."

He shook his head vehemently. "Nope." He rubbed his hands together. "She's engaged now."

"You were so cute together."

"Apparently. Everybody seemed to think we belonged together or something." Charlie shook his head again. "But we didn't belong together." It was Charlie's turn to change the subject. "You ever talk to Jurgens?"

"Why should I?"

"It's just…" Charlie trailed off, shrugging. "It seems like the right thing to do."

"With that weasel? What would I have to say to him?"

"I just—"

"He betrayed us." Griggs started pacing again, gesturing nervously. Distressed, searching for words. "Carla and I had him in our *home.*"

"He was your best friend." Charlie walked over to Griggs slowly. "And you cut him off, just like that. Doesn't seem healthy."

"Healthy? He told a carload of mob killers how to find my wife."

"He didn't know they would try to kill her."

"What makes you say that?"

"Jurgens told me."

Griggs stopped. Glared. "You talk to him? After what he did to you? After what he did to all of us?"

Charlie looked away. Shrugged. "Somebody should."

"No." Griggs pointed at his partner. "Nobody needs to talk to him. He's a traitor. He went to prison. He should die in prison."

He stomped off, trembling. Turned back and jabbed a finger at Charlie. "You have no business talking to him."

Charlie nodded slowly. Put his hands in his pockets. "We're supposed to forgive our enemies."

"Religion again?"

"You can find it in Luke," he said, trying to keep his voice low. Trying not to slip into his lecture tone. "*Love your enemies, do good to those who hate you, bless those who curse you, pray for those who mistreat you.* Back in Proverbs, it says that if you help your enemies, it's like heaping coals of fire on their heads. *And the Lord will reward you.*"

Griggs walked to another corner of the room to stew.

A few seconds later, Charlie followed him over. "I see that you and Special Agent O'Malley go and hit the batting cage together these days."

"Sure."

"You used to go to the batting cage with Detective Jurgens, right? Before everything went bad, I mean?"

"I guess so."

"You have a way of cutting people off, don't you? You cut your father off, you cut Jurgens off. You act like they don't exist anymore. So it's like you jettison one best friend and replace him with O'Malley. Is it a fair trade?"

"Charlie, sometimes you got a big mouth."

🏠 🗔 ⑦   ⊠

BLOG

WHERE IS BLAKE #003
whereisblake.blogdroid.com

"I have no special talents. I am only passionately curious."
—Albert Einstein

Lest you think the horrors inflicted by Queen Evel are limited to us pitiful wretches under her employ, a friend who works at another business recently shared a phone call she had with Evel. The woman was shocked—she had never been treated more rudely on the phone.

Apparently Queen Evel called about some business, and when the call was transferred to my friend, Evel demanded to lodge a formal complaint about the "hold music." According to my friend, Evel yelled, "[Your company] is laying off employees because of stuff like that!" And then she hung up.

"I don't know how you stand it," my friend remarked. "My blood pressure is up just from the one incident. I don't know how you can put up with that sort of behavior on a day-to-day basis."

If I didn't have a reason to be here, I wouldn't be.

🏠 🗔 ⑦   ⊠

NEWS

WHERE IS BLAKE?
KELLY VEITH. *Kansas City Globe*. Kansas City, MO: Apr 24, 2006.
pg. 001

Section: News
Word count: 700

Abstract: A recent mob shooting came with a timely reminder that

Kansas City's favorite son, Warren Blake, is still among the missing. Even though that fact seems to be lost on his wife, Evelyn Blake, still hard at work on her upcoming cable television series, *Evelyn4Life*....
<click for more>

LIBRARY PROJECT PUSHES FORWARD

KELLY VEITH. *Kansas City Globe*. Kansas City, MO: Apr 25, 2006. pg. 002

Section: News
Word count: 660

Abstract: Even as the authorities continue to search for Warren Blake, the library project he started several months ago presses on. Blake's wife, Evelyn, has stepped forward and made the project a priority, she says, for the good of the community. Notes one observer, "When Mr. Blake was nowhere to be found, Mrs. Blake did not seem to miss a beat. If anything, she used the opportunity to take over the library project that was his pride and joy... <click for more>

~ 7 ~

Tuesday. April 25.

Assistant editor Dakota Flynn, staring again at her black nails tapping on the table, heard Dennis the Jerk say, "What we have, Ms. Blake, is a slight public-relations problem." *Blake Life* publisher Dennis the Jerk, managing editor Aubrey Burke, and Flynn were meeting with Mrs. Evelyn Blake regarding a front-page story in the *Scene*.

Queen Evel stabbing a finger at the front page, Monday's edition of the weekly tabloid. A big photo splashed on the front, the crime scene from that shooting that happened over the weekend, under the graffiti WHERE IS BLAKE? "What I have is a public-relations *nightmare*," she shrieked, making Flynn wince, reminding her she had a hangover.

"I'm in the process of rolling out my own branded national-television series—"

"Cable," Dennis the Jerk offered, trying to be helpful. Poor sap.

"My own branded cable-television series," Evel continued, unfazed, "and all that those *journalistos* can focus on is the negative!"

Flynn looked up. Squinted. *"Journalistos?"*

Queen Evel did not hear the question. She was on a roll. "So maybe we are the subject of a few lawsuits…"

Flynn tuned her out. Queen Evel was, of course, the subject of two different lawsuits—one brought on by former employees, the other by former advertisers in *Blake Life*. The ex-employees charged that her employee policies were weird and discriminatory. The ex-advertisers charged that she and the magazine had defrauded the advertisers by millions of dollars with fake circulation numbers.

Both plaintiffs were, essentially, correct. And would probably win in court. But try getting the great and powerful Evelyn Blake to understand *that*.

Of course, today's front-page story was equally baffling to Queen Evel. And, frankly, Flynn wondered why it was made to be their problem instead of, say, being given to Queen Evel's own public-relations people.

Maybe her public-relations people had been beheaded.

Flynn had read the story. The reporter suggested there was a reason for the proximity of the shooting to the graffiti—this, despite the fact that somebody had actually been spray painting it all over the city, like some sort of cult thing.

The paper used the excuse to reignite theories that Warren Blake and reputed crime boss Evil Duke Cumbee might have been planning some sort of partnership. Before Blake disappeared.

The story also noted that Evelyn Blake had not shown much interest in finding her missing husband, was more preoccupied with her own public image. A sidebar detailed the lawsuits, the fact that her new book was rumored to have been rejected or sent back for rewrites or something, the fact that her new homemaking show would not exist if her husband did not own the network.

"It's like they're out to get me," Queen Evel continued. "Because I'm rich. It's *Citizen Kane* all over again."

Flynn covered her face with one hand, hiding rolling eyes. Poor, bitter, stupid Queen Evel. Much of her public-relations storm would lighten up if she only acted like she missed her husband.

Like she missed Warren Blake.

Evel said, "And what about these 'blogs' they keep talking about?"

Dakota jolted. "What?"

"In the news story here, they say they're getting inside information from these 'blogs.' What are they talking about?"

Dennis the Jerk furrowed his brow. "I-I don't know."

"Well, somebody here in the company is using these 'blogs' to share private information about the workings here." Queen Evel, ruffling the paper like a prop. "I need you to launch an investigation."

Dennis the Jerk nodding. "Yes." His face showed he had no idea what she meant. "What do you mean?"

Queen Evel pointing a finger. "Find who's leaking this information. These people say I don't care that my husband is gone!"

Dennis the Jerk, poor, poor Dennis the Jerk, did not answer. What could he say? He nodded. "Yes, ma'am."

Queen Evel threw the crumpled paper on the table. "Find who is giving away my private information. I want it dealt with!"

She stormed out, blind rage and blind stupidity and blind ego, leaving behind Dennis the Jerk and Burke and Flynn to consider why any of this was their problem.

Flynn would bet a week's pay Queen Evel had never even seen *Citizen Kane*.

- 8 -

The sun woke him. Missionary Bob was in his bed, sleepily feeling the warmth through the curtains. He could smell bacon frying from the next room. Andrea must have come to her senses. Must have left Jesus. Must have come home.

He found his slippers and robe, was tying the belt as he headed for the living room. There was Andrea, in the kitchen. He said, "You came back. I thought you were through with me."

Andrea turned, flashed those pearly whites, eyes twinkling. "I just came back for a visit. To see how you were doing."

Missionary Bob grinned. If he and Andrea were a team again, nothing could stop them for—

Missionary Bob awoke when the sun burned his eyes. No—wait, wait—he was no longer "Missionary Bob."

Missionary Bob was dead.

He was disoriented. His head pounding.

It took him a few moments to remember where he was. Lost in the wilderness, his back pricked by the bed of broken twigs.

He had abandoned his identity of "Missionary Bob," had burned his old self in a funeral pyre, to be resurrected out in the woods this blazing morning as the Right Fair Doctor Reverend Damascus Rhodes.

His eyes were glued shut, so dry it felt like spikes were being driven into them. He needed water, fast. In his eyes. Now.

He rolled, feeling his age in his back. Got up on his hands and knees. As long as he was blind, he dared not try to walk anywhere quite yet. Not now, not in these strange woods. For all he knew he was in spitting distance of a moonshine operation.

Not that he minded the thought of alcohol. It was the thought of the hick farmer with the shotgun that troubled him.

Like in the tale of Hercules and the lion, he crawled on hands and knees, the crackle of twigs and leaves on the ground, something sharp poking his palm as he pressed down. He suffered in silence—which is to say, he yelped, grunted, bit his lip, and whimpered. Remembered his fugitive status, held his breath, and listened.

He heard leaves rustling, a cool breeze blowing through the trees. Eyes squeezed tight, the blind man listened for signs of life: men with badges, dogs on leashes, wild animals that might rend him limb from limb. He thought of Daniel in the lion's pit, but remembered it as Samson and some sort of furnace and did not recall how the story turned out. All he remembered was that Samson was blind in the story.

Just like right now, he was blind, the Good Right Fair Doctor Reverend—what was it? Oh. Right. "Damascus Rhodes."

He needed to rinse his eyes. Otherwise they were no good. Ever since that time Andrea hit him in the eye with her hairbrush, he'd had this problem. Anytime the sun hit him in the face while he was sleeping. She said the hairbrush was an accident. She said lots of things.

Maybe it wasn't the brush. Maybe something else had messed up his eyes.

Whatever. He needed water in his eyes. Now.

He heard the breeze pick up. It rushed in his ears. There could be men crunching up behind him on the leaves, men with badges and guns, snarling dogs on leashes, and he would barely be able to hear them.

How was he supposed to find the water with all this wind rushing through his ears? A water pump, a well, a creek—heck, a puddle, if it wasn't too muddy.

But here he was, the Good Right Fair Doctor Reverend Damascus Rhodes, stuck on his hands and knees in the deep, dark woods, stuck with what felt like spikes in his eyes, stuck waiting for the drooling, snarling dogs on leashes, waiting for the men with hats and badges and guns, waiting for the wild animals to come tear him to pieces.

Lions. Tigers. Dogs.

Oh, my.

The Good Right Fair Doctor Reverend Damascus Rhodes was stuck. And then it began to rain.

BLOG

WHERE IS BLAKE #004
whereisblake.blogdroid.com

"We all stand between the jungle and the stars at a crossroads. I think we'd better discover what brings out the best in humankind and what brings out the worst. Because it's the stars or the jungle."

—Dr. Thomas Morgan (Rex Reason), *The Creature Walks Among Us*

You never know who's reading your e-mails. Your network administrator has a copy of every e-mail you've ever sent or received over the company network. She can view anything on your computer while it's on the network—your instant messages, your chat logs, even the window you have open on your screen.

Most IT departments are not staffed with voyeurs intent on reading your latest private e-mail or catching you at a dirty Web site. Their concern is with corporate identity, with security, with following the laws of the land.

Then again, sometimes you run across someone on a power trip. A woman I know (let's call her "Becky") got involved in what she thought was a discreet office romance. She began to date the network administrator, and the two used all the normal tools of a modern relationship: e-mail, instant messages, digital communications.

He began to brag to her that he could view any desktop on the network at any time, read any e-mail in the system. If he chose to, he could wipe out what someone was currently working on.

One day, after sending an e-mail to a friend in which she detailed her concerns about the relationship, "Becky" got a call from her boyfriend: He had read the message and forwarded it to his personal account for future reference.

How about that.

– 9 –

It was raining when Griggs got home. He was a little late, but he was still coming home better hours these days. Even just a few months ago, Carla would not know when or whether to expect him home.

He flipped through the mail on the table. Bill...bill...subscription offer...

A letter from his dad.

One of these days, he might open it, see what the old man had to say. Right now, just the appearance of it was like a brick to the head.

Maybe the old man had stopped with the lies. Stopped with the cheap shots.

Maybe.

He went to the closet door. Dropped the unopened letter in with all the others.

As he walked through the dining room, Carla entered. Threw her arms around his neck and kissed him. "How was your day?"

Griggs tried to smile. Grunted. "Hmm, okay, I guess." He knew he should elaborate—it was one of the relationship exercises the counselor encouraged.

But the kid—Charlie—had said some ugly things earlier. Still had Griggs steamed. For now, all he had the energy to tell Carla was, "I'll tell you about it later." He closed the closet door. Ran his fingers through his wet hair. "I need to dry off first."

Even after a change of clothes, his mood was still heavy as he sat at the dinner table. Carla had made lasagna, her mother's recipe. Griggs liked his mother-in-law well enough, but her lasagna recipe was nothing to write home about. Certainly nothing to write home and ask *for*.

"How do you like it?" Carla, chewing, made a sweet face.

He tried to match her sweet face. "Great." Tired of chewing, he gulped some lemonade to wash it down. He set the glass back on the table, gave a satisfied sigh. "How was your day? Did you teach today?"

She smiled gently. "I don't teach Mondays."

"Sorry. Forgot." He winced inside a bit. "As many times as you tell me that, I should start remembering it once in a while."

"That's okay, sweetheart. I know you're trying."

He stabbed the lasagna. Stabbing was too good for it.

Griggs often struggled with paying attention to his wife. Always had his job on his mind. Ridding Kansas City of the vermin, of the nefarious grip of organized crime, preoccupied him day and night.

"You said you'd tell me more about your day." Carla took another bite of her lasagna, maybe she actually liked it.

He set his silverware down and breathed through his nose slowly. Paused a beat. "Do you think I abandoned my dad?"

Carla, shoveling another forkful of lasagna, stopped mid-shovel. "Wh-what do you mean? What happened?"

He put both hands on the table, staring down. Shaking his head slowly. "Something Charlie said today. We were at the scene of that shooting again. At the garage, following up."

"Making sure Detective Utley didn't show up." She said it in a mildly disapproving *Boys, boys* voice.

He ignored the tone. "Yeah. So Charlie and I were talking. And you know the kid. Likes to talk."

"Sure." She grabbed the lasagna pan off the table, offered him another piece.

He declined. Knew better than to explain why. "He said I cut people off."

"What do you mean, 'cut people off'?"

"You know, somebody does me wrong and I just write them off. They don't exist for me anymore." He bit his lip, thinking. He looked up. "Did I do that with my dad?"

"You have every right to be upset with your father. He was the one who left. Not you."

"I know. He stole the family money, left Mom high and dry. When she got sick..."

There was a silence in the dining room. Carla said, "But it's been a long time. Maybe he's sorry. Maybe he finally understands what he did."

Griggs thought of the box of unopened letters from his dad. A new letter came in the mail every six or seven months. Each time, he tossed it, unopened, in the box with all the others.

He looked up at Carla with sad eyes. Felt like the rejected little boy again. "Do you think one of those letters is an apology? Finally admitting he's responsible for his own actions?"

Carla gave a little shrug. "Have you read any of them?"

"Not for a long time. I got tired of him playing the victim." He was silent. Carla watching him from across the table. "Do you think I should open them?"

Carla didn't have an answer.

They continued eating in silence.

⌂ ▭ ⑦   ⊠

╔══════════╗
║ **NEWS** ║
╚══════════╝

EVELYN GOES TO THE TOP MAN
KELLY VEITH. *Kansas City Globe*. Kansas City, MO: Apr 25, 2006. pg.
003

Section: News
Word count: 575

Abstract: Following an unflattering portrait in a rival newspaper, Evelyn
Blake personally visited the governor to demand that the authorities
"work harder" to find her husband, now missing for two weeks. "I cannot
understand how the media can be so cruel to a wife in her distress," Mrs.
Blake said. "It is clear that I have been driven to distraction since the
unexpected absence of my husband... <click for more>

– 10 –

Wednesday. April 26.

The Right Doctor Reverend Damascus Rhodes—his new identity, as
he carefully reminded himself—ended up at a truck stop. Did not know
quite where. He cleaned up in the men's room, rinsed his white button-
down shirt in the sink, had the presence of mind to put it on backward
to make it look more clerical, put on the soiled dinner jacket.

Threw some more water on his face, was ready to go.

Ready to go.

Walked into the diner, fighting a limp, but not fighting too hard—he
could use the limp in his favor. Inside, he glanced down and saw a
rack of Illinois newspapers. Asked the hostess for the table in the back
corner, told her it was for his "prayer and reflection time."

He could almost hear Andrea's voice. *You haven't prayed in your
life.*

The truth was, the back corner gave him the best vantage point to watch the room from. To find someone to pay for the coffee and eggs he was about to order. To watch for any members of law enforcement who might come looking for him.

The morning was largely uneventful. Rev. Damascus felt remarkably well, considering he had collapsed somewhere in the woods from exhaustion the night before and had slept until first light. Still, the whirl of events of the last couple days had taken their toll on him—his shirt, despite the rinse, felt sticky and gray. You would think being out in the rain like that would have been better for the clothes.

This was the longest he'd ever gone without a shower. Rinsing in the sink was horrible. This was why he could never take his dog-and-pony show out of the country; he was afraid to be without indoor plumbing.

Back when he first started to lose his game, he considered taking it somewhere else. Like a baseball player past his prime (as painful as the analogy was), he thought about heading for the bush leagues, where the audiences were probably less sophisticated, the competition less severe.

You know, maybe Mexico, South America, Guatemala. Maybe somewhere in Africa or Eastern Europe.

Do a *Heart of Darkness* number, go out to the native villages of the world, far away from the unsettling upgrades of American law enforcement (they kept finding new and sexier ways to catch bad guys), set himself up as a high priest. A shaman. A god.

But it always came back to the question of hot showers. That's where the whole system broke down.

The waitress came to the table, gripping a pot of coffee. Rev. Damascus slid his coffee cup and saucer toward the edge. She obliged with hot, steaming black liquid.

She smiled thinly and raised her eyebrows. He pointed to the plastic menu and rasped, "Eggs. Over easy, if you could, ma'am." Polite. Always paid to be polite.

She nodded and left the table. Rev. Damascus glanced through the metal window blinds.

Nothing. No sheriff, no deputies, no black-and-whites flashing up and down the highway. No state police. No dogs.

Nothing.

Rev. Damascus tore the corners off a handful of blue packets of Equal. Not sure what to think. Maybe Kismet—maybe Lady Fortune had changed her mind. Maybe his string of bad luck these past couple of years meant he'd finally accrued something going the other way for him.

The cops were scanning the countryside for a murderer and a con man, all right, but they must have been pointed in the wrong direction. Maybe something the vagrant said when they found him sleeping outside the hollow remains of the barn and the burned-out car.

Whatever had happened, Rev. Damascus was not going to let the opportunity go to waste. He was going to find someone to pay for his breakfast, then he was going to catch the first ride out of this hole and head somewhere far away.

He spent all morning sipping, keeping to himself. Anytime the waitress seemed to hover with the bill, he would bow his head again, close his eyes for more "prayer and reflection." Always keeping an eye out—through the blinds, across the room.

He was on his fourth cup of coffee after his second trip to the men's room. He wasn't jittery, though; if you drink that many cups all together, it cancels out the effects of the caffeine.

He was sipping again when he saw the big rig pull up, a diesel truck with big mud flaps that proclaimed REAL MEN LOVE ANGELS. The Right Fair Doctor Reverend Damascus Rhodes watched the driver climb down, took another sip of his coffee, and smiled. If he worked this right, he could get breakfast and a ride out of this.

⌂ ▭ ⑦　　　　　　　　　　　　　　　　　　　⊠

BLOG

WHERE IS BLAKE #005
whereisblake.blogdroid.com

"Crime brings its own fatality with it."

—Wilkie Collins

There is a new memo circulating about an office dress code. Only specific colors are allowed. Is this for real?

Lately, I have been wondering if Warren Blake was a victim of foul play. Sure, sure, I've suspected Evelyn Blake all along, but now there is the question of involvement of organized crime. For weeks now, there have been whisperings that alleged crime boss "Evil" Duke Cumbee has been seen around the offices at Blake Media.

Dennis the Jerk has been telling us that Warren Blake met with Cumbee, that maybe the two were discussing some partnership. Did Cumbee do something to Warren Blake? Did he have him "whacked" for some reason?

～ 11 ～

Detective Tom Griggs and Detective Charlie Pasch headed down the hall at Kansas City Police Department headquarters, each with a cup of coffee in hand. Griggs took his with cream, no sugar. Charlie took his with almond milk and Froot Loops. (Don't ask.) Headed for some emergency meeting in the war room.

Charlie could see Griggs twitching, anxious to get back to their case. Still trying to keep Utley locked out.

Griggs and Detective Utley had some sort of grudge between them, something Charlie could not quite understand. Charlie had worked in both divisions, had worked closely with both men—okay, perhaps he understood a little more than he was comfortable admitting. Charlie wanted to like everyone. Detective Utley made it hard sometimes.

As they reached the door of the war room, Griggs sipped some coffee and returned to their ongoing opera conversation. "So I guess if they did some kind of *Star Trek* musical opera, you'd just be in hog heaven."

"Funny you should say that—there's been talk about just that thing."

Griggs nodded. "So…" Shrugged. "…Are you in hog heaven?"

"If they do it right. But if they pick people who don't understand both worlds, we'll end up with some bad *Star Trek* and some bad opera."

"And…that would be bad."

"It sure wouldn't be good."

The room was wall-to-wall cops by the time Captain Hickman showed up, all bluster and papers. He rushed up to the front, flopped the file folder onto the podium, cleared his throat in that way he did, and launched into the spiel. He was not one for chitchat.

Charlie was the only one taking copious notes. Sure, some of the others scratched down the random comment or bit of information—but if you ever had a sick day, copying Charlie's notes was the next best thing to being there. It was true in school, it was true at the academy, it was true at the KCPD.

"All right, ladies and gentlemen," the captain grumped, "as you have all no doubt seen on the news, Warren Blake is missing."

Charlie knew about reclusive billionaire Warren Blake: as lauded as he was enigmatic. Had made—and blown—millions on a variety of ambitious schemes, from building a media empire to attempting his own commercial space-flight business. Frequently rumored to be running for mayor of Kansas City in the 2007 election.

Then, last week, he'd disappeared off the face of the earth.

"Detectives Kurtz and Carillo have been running the show. And, given the circumstances, have done an adequate job." (Captain Hickman was under the impression that "adequate" was a positive word.)

"However," he continued, "we are now in the middle of what you would call a media emergency. Mrs. Evelyn Blake has made a point to complain that the KCPD is not working hard enough on this, and has taken her complaints all the way up to the governor's office."

The captain paused, adjusted his glasses to read his notes. "Mr. Blake is considering a run for the mayorship—and would, as such, be running against our current mayor. Mrs. Blake has accused the mayor's office and the KCPD of dragging their heels so that Mr. Blake cannot be a threat to us."

A groan floated through the room.

Captain Hickman looked up from his notes, waved his hands in a conciliatory gesture. "I know, I know. But if we do not solve this Blake situation lickety-quick, it will reflect badly on the mayor's office."

Charlie chuckled, scribbling on his pad. Mumbled, "Not to mention reflecting badly on us too." He looked up, realized heads had turned. He must have said it louder than he meant.

Captain Hickman pushed his glasses up the bridge of his nose, scowled in Charlie's direction. "I'm talking here, Detective Pasch."

The captain looked down again, unhappy he had drifted off his notes. It took him a second to find his place again. "So in the interest of accelerating this process and reuniting Mr. Blake with his loving wife, we are reassigning many of you to help with the case. You will all coordinate your efforts with Kurtz and Carillo, who continue to answer directly to me on this."

The captain looked up from his notes again at the room of uncertain faces and sighed. Took off his glasses, leaned his elbows on the podium. "Look, I'm getting it from the commissioner, and he's getting it from the mayor's office, and they are getting it from the governor's office."

He stood again, regaining composure. Replaced his eyeglasses. "And now, you're getting it from me."

As the captain handed out the new assignments, each detective listened for his or her own name, grumbling if it was attached to the new assignment. Charlie, of course, was the only one keeping notes on them all.

Booker and Croteau, in addition to their full plate of robbery cases, were the first added to what Charlie now listed in his notebook under PROJECT: BLAKE. Detective Sammi Croteau—"Samantha" to her mom and, if it should ever come up, George Clooney—had a propensity for shouting "Book 'em, Booker!" Which drove her partner crazy to no end. Detective Leigh Booker, meanwhile, kept waiting for her *Cagney & Lacey* moment, when she could train her weapon on a perp and shout, "Freeze, sucka!" Last Charlie had heard, Booker was still waiting for her *Cagney & Lacey* moment.

Charlie noted the other reassignments. MacKenzie from Vice, Gainer from Homicide, several others—each already working full caseloads, which they no doubt considered to be the most important cases in the entire department at the present time. All now told to expand their plates to include their duties for PROJECT: BLAKE, to search for some rich playboy whose yacht had probably blown off course and run aground at Supermodel Island.

A man who probably did not even want to be found.

Charlie was relieved that only a few members of each division were pulled into this—at least the department recognized crime did not stop, not even for the great and powerful Warren Blake.

Charlie, paper on desk, nose on paper, focused on getting the details down, became aware of Griggs fuming. Of course—the shooting from Sunday night was neatly extricated from Organized Crime and put into the jurisdiction of Utley in Homicide.

Ooh, Griggs did not like that. He wondered whether Griggs was more frustrated because he was being stopped mid-case or because it was Utley who had the case now.

And with Charlie and Griggs added to PROJECT: BLAKE, that meant the entire KCPD half of the KCPD/FBI joint task force was now involved. The Organized Crime Division had been dwindling for months now, thanks to transfers and a shrinking budget. The irony of the team's success was that, with each new mobster in prison, the powers-that-be thought the team became more obsolete.

Charlie scratched in his notebook:

—RICH PLAYBOY MISSING

—ALL HANDS ON DECK

—MAYOR UP FOR REELECTION; WANTS
   RESPONSIBILITY FOR WIN

—COMMISSIONER WANTS TO FIGURE OUT
   BEFORE FEDS DO

He thought for a second, then added:

—SEEK AND YE SHALL FIND

He looked up from his notebook, blinking his eyes to focus. They were essentially breaking up the KCPD/FBI joint task force. This was not the smart thing.

Working under Griggs these past months, he had seen the value of police/Fed cooperation. The KCPD/FBI joint task force had brought down several key figures in organized crime in Kansas City, Missouri. But if the higher-ups wanted to make a horse race out of it, there was not much he or Griggs could do about it.

Captain Hickman finished the meeting, clapping his hands like a high-school coach. "Come on, people, many hands make light work! Let's find Warren Blake, and let's get him home safe and sound! Let's go, people!"

"Let's go, people" was his traditional way of ending powwows in the war room. It may not have been "Be careful out there" or "Avengers, assemble!" but it did the job. It abruptly ended the meeting, cut off questions—the chief hated going off his talking points in front of a crowd—and told the room of detectives it was time to go to work.

Of course, that did not stop the detectives from having questions. Not today. By the time Griggs and Charlie rushed up to the captain's office, a line had already formed at his closed door.

The captain was not taking visitors.

⁓ 12 ⁓

The Right Fair Doctor Reverend Damascus Rhodes watched big flat fields of crops pass as the truck zoomed down the Illinois highway. They would be crossing into Missouri soon. The driver had asked how far Rev. Damascus was going. The rev had replied, "As far as the Lord leads."

His first surprise, on entering the truck's passenger side, was that what he had thought was a chunky cross dangling from the rearview mirror was actually some sort of toy spaceship.

It was not long into the trip before Rev. Damascus realized he'd made an error in his choice of traveling companion. Sure, the trucker had paid for his breakfast and given him a ride. In the truck, though,

Rev. Damascus expected to sleep, hoped to sleep, desperately wanted to sleep, please, God, Dear God, let me sleep.

The trucker wanted to talk.

The trucker, of course, had a name (as most do): Riley Jones. And he seemed to have two deep and abiding loves—the open road and UFOs.

"Devil's crackers! It's like in Ezekiel there, man, where the UFO comes down and it has the face of an eagle or whatever, man."

Rev. Damascus leaned forward from the headrest again. If he had been at full strength, like when he was on top of his game a couple years ago—instead of this fugitive who just wanted to sleep and would strangle truck driver Riley Jones to get it, if he only knew how to drive a big rig—he could easily have deflected the conversation or turned it in a direction where he could pretend to be more knowledgeable.

However, in this condition, right here, right now, this was the best reply Rev. Damascus could manage: "Yeah?"

"Oh, yeah, UFOs are all over the Bible," the driver said, turning to look at Rev. Damascus as he spoke. Rev. Damascus would have preferred the man watch the road. They were pushing awfully close to that hatchback. "Like they built the pyramids in the Old Testament there, then killed the pharaoh's son."

"I thought that was the angel of death."

The truck driver turned to the rev again, smiled with brown teeth. "Who do you think was piloting the UFO?"

Rev. Damascus nodded in agreement in spite of himself. Such a unified theology had not occurred to him. "Angel of death piloting the UFO, huh?"

"Devil's crackers, yeah!"

"Like a sort of Red Baron from heaven?"

"What?"

"You know. The Red Baron."

The truck driver, pushing ever closer to that poor hatchback, turned to Rev. Damascus and frowned. Why couldn't he keep his eyes on the road? "You mean like in that Snoopy cartoon?"

Rev. Damascus smiled softly. "If you like."

Truck driver shrugged. "I don't get it."

Rev. Damascus nodded again. Apparently, trucker Riley Jones was juggling too many concepts at one time. "Doesn't matter."

Somewhere, he could hear Andrea laughing.

– 13 –

"Chocolate?" Professional thug Nelson Pistek offered a foil-wrapped treat to fellow professional thug Harry Cage. Pistek and Cage were on a gig. That's what Pistek liked to call it, "gig," as if they were playing a concert at Carnegie Hall or performing standup comedy at the Laffity Shack.

Of course, they were actually here to collect overdue money on behalf of their boss, Eddie Drake. Some guy had begged or borrowed a wad of cash, lost it on a bad investment or a slow pony, and now needed a stern reminder that you don't stiff Eddie Drake.

And with Evil Duke Cumbee breathing down Eddie's neck for his own payments, this was not the time to get behind with Eddie.

Standing in the fifth-floor breezeway of the apartment building, Pistek had reached into his jacket pocket, pulled out a gold-foiled square of dark chocolate. He'd held it out for Cage, who now shook his head.

Pistek unwrapped the square and shrugged. "Suit yourself." Looked at the message inside the wrapper. BE TRUE TO YOU. Crumpled the foil, threw it over the rail, watched it drop five floors to the concrete below.

He stepped over to the apartment door and pushed the bell. A few seconds passed, he made an impatient fist and pounded. "Come on!"

"Maybe he ain't here."

"He's here."

There was a rustling, and the door cracked open a bit. An eyeball saw the two men, and the door shut again quick, but Pistek had gotten the toe of his boot in, blocked it. It crunched hard on his foot, he swore, shoved his shoulder against it. The chain yanked taut, held fast.

He shifted his weight back, then shoved hard. Something gave way, splinters flying, the chain ripping the bracket off the jamb and dangling. Pistek stumbled in and fell to the carpet.

Behind him, Cage looked in and, eyes widening, cursed loudly. He darted over his partner, leaped toward the mark, who was holding the phone. "Drop that!"

The man threw the receiver down and ran deeper into the apartment. Pistek grinned. Where did this guy think he would go?

As Cage and the mark disappeared down the hall, Pistek grunted and pushed himself up. Stood and cracked his neck, then trotted toward the back. Heard lots of crashing. *Go easy, Cage,* he thought. *The guy can't pay Eddie if he's dead.*

But when Pistek reached what turned out to be the bedroom, he discovered the mark had teeth. The figure of Harry Cage came shooting out the door, slammed straight into Pistek. The two banged hard against the wall.

Pistek groaned, his breath knocked out of him for a second. He pushed Cage off, saw blood on the side of his face. "Dude, what—"

From inside the room came a shriek. "You stay away!" The man was swinging an aluminum bat wildly, must have connected with Cage but good. Of course, the fact his partner was still standing meant this guy didn't know quite where to swing.

Pistek pushed Cage aside. The mark had stopped swinging, was stepping backward toward the glass patio door behind him. Was now resting the bat on his shoulder. Big mistake. When he was letting the adrenaline do his thinking, he was dangerous. Now he would start to go cold, would start thinking about his moves.

Sunlight in his eyes, Pistek put a boot forward purposefully, held his hands out in a calming manner, began to speak. The aluminum death swung hard again, missed him, but he heard the *whoosh* as it passed, heard the ring as the bat collided with a lamp and smashed fragments against the wall.

He wondered whether an apartment like this came furnished.

The bat swung again. Pistek stepped back and let it pass, then leaped forward when its arc was farthest away. Tackled the guy, the bat bouncing across the room.

Pistek punched the guy hard under the ribs, knocking the wind out of him. Pressed his knee on the man's chest, pressed a solid arm across his windpipe. "Okay, I think we need to have a talk."

"I'll talk to him." Cage stumbled up from behind, spit on the mark, kicked him hard in the ribs.

Pistek was annoyed. He was trying to work here. He let go of the man and stood, turning to his partner. "Wait till get what we came for. Then you can do whatever you want."

There was a rattling behind him—the guy unlocking the door to the deck. They were both outside before he could grab the man by the shirt. "Nobody said you could leave."

There was still a fire in the mark's eyes. Nelson Pistek, at heart a coward, wanted to press his advantage before the other figured a way to turn the tables. "Harry, come on out here."

His partner in crime, dabbing the blood on his head with a towel off the desk, stepped out into the sunshine. "What?"

Pistek grinned. "Grab an ankle."

"What?"

The guy's eyes bugged. "Hey, wait a sec—"

Cage dropped the towel, leaned down to grab the mark's right ankle. The man squirming, Pistek socked him in the stomach again, bent to grab his left ankle. Took in a breath, then nodded. "Now."

The two thugs yanked. The guy slid over the rail. Suddenly Cage let go, and the weight was all in Pistek's hands. He staggered forward against the rickety wooden rail, yelled at Cage, "Hey! You let go!"

His partner bent for the towel. "I thought that's what you said." He began tenderly dabbing his head again.

"We're squeezing this guy for money!"

Below, the man was screaming, "Pull me up! Pull me up! I'll pay! I'll pay!" Saying everything twice, like it was a magic spell.

Pistek strained to pull the guy up, but the weight was too much. He turned to Cage. "Help me!"

Before the still-dazed thug could come over, Pistek's wrists got tired, and he let go.

Oops.

– 14 –

Nelson Pistek and Harry Cage on the deck of the fifth-floor apartment, looking over the rail at the body on the pavement below, watching for twitches. Pistek not about to go down and check for signs of life. Who knew whether a kid might be passing by on his bike? He tapped Cage on the arm. "Let's take off."

As they were walking through the apartment, Cage thumbed toward the big-screen TV. "How much you think something like that costs?"

In the car, Pistek was already calculating their story. How to explain why they didn't get the money. Once he figured a story out, he would need to rehearse it with Cage before they saw Eddie Drake. Ever since Evil Duke Cumbee had showed up in town, Eddie was scared, Eddie was jumpy, Eddie was unpredictable. No sudden moves around Eddie.

"We gotta hurry back," Cage said, looking out the window as scenery passed. "The Oz is on TV tonight, man."

Pistek swerved to avoid a car. Idiot. Gripping the steering wheel with one hand, he reached in his pocket with the other and pulled another foiled candy. "What, is *that* show still on?"

"Naw," Cage said, shaking his head vigorously. "You know, *The Wizard of Oz*."

Pistek unwrapped the square, popped dark chocolate in his mouth. The inside of the wrapper said DRINK IN THE MOMENT. Chomping, he turned toward Cage. "Really?"

"Yeah, what of it?"

"I just didn't know you had such classy tastes, man."

"A man can better himself."

Pistek turned his attention back to the road, back to his excuse. *You see, Eddie, it's like this...* Then he thought of something. He turned and squinted again at Cage.

"I know why you watch it. It's the hanged guy, isn't it?"

Now it was Cage's turn to squint. "What? You talkin' about that Pink Floyd shtick again?"

"No, the guy in the noose. Dorothy and them are all smiles and square dances, and there's this guy dangling by the neck in the background."

"You zoomin', man."

"No, it's the real deal. You see a shadow in the background at the end of the scene in the forest, just as Dorothy, the Scarecrow, and the Tin Man are square dancing off to see the Wizard."

"Oh, *that*." Cage relaxed his jaw, clearly in familiar territory now. "It's a bird."

"What?"

"A crane."

"You check with a bird doctor?" Pistek flexed his fingers on the steering wheel, agitated. "Why do so many people see a hanging man?"

"Most people today have never seen *The Wizard of Oz* on a big screen. On that little TV screen, they don't know what they see tiny in the background."

"No, dude, I heard about this. The hanging man was a stagehand or some guy who got tangled in some cables and fell into the scene while the cameras were rolling there." Pistek flicked eyes back to the street. He had bobbed into the other lane, a car had honked, and he flipped the driver off. Idiot should have been watching.

He de-pocketed another foiled square, opened it carefully while driving with the heels of his palms. This wrapper said GIGGLE. Chomping, he said, "We gotta get our stories straight."

"Look, Pistol, I have heard all the crazy theories. Trust me—you are *not* going to spring something on me by surprise."

"I had you goin' before."

"When?"

"Before."

"I was just surprised you brought that lame thing up. Nobody's tried that one in years."

Pistek pulled to the curb and parked the car. "Look, before we go up and see Eddie, we gotta get our stories straight."

"What, about The Oz?"

"No, about the guy who took himself a swan dive over the rail there. Remember?"

"What dive? You dropped him."

"No." Pistek leaned in, everything short of a wink. "Remember?

He was running and we were trying to catch him and then he jumped. Got it?"

Pistek reached for another chocolate, decided to check his fortune again. The foil said SHARE A SMILE. He popped the candy in his mouth.

— 15 —

When Detective Charlie Pasch had gotten with Detective Tom Griggs that afternoon, Griggs seemed to have finally calmed down. Charlie asked, "How do we play this?"

Griggs in that thinking pose: elbows on desk, hands clasped in front of his face, eyes scrunched closed. "How do we play what?"

"This Blake thing. What do we do now?"

Griggs put his hands down, made an innocent face at his partner. "You heard the man. We find Blake."

Charlie knew that look. The question was not whether Griggs was going to somehow circumvent his orders, it was *how* he was going to do it and whether he would share his plans with Charlie.

Griggs shot a glance at Charlie's notebook. "What you got there?"

"Just notes from the war room."

"Let me see." He reached out, and Charlie handed the notebook over. Pursed his lips, reading the notes. "What's this?"

"What's what?"

"SEEK AND YE SHALL FIND."

"It's in the seventh chapter of Matthew. *Ask and it will be given to you; seek and you will find; knock and the door will be opened to you. For everyone who asks receives; he who seeks finds; and to him who knocks, the door will be opened.*"

Griggs nodded, made no comment. Handed the notebook back. "So what do we know?"

"We got five members of the Russian Mafiya on slabs at the morgue. We got a car belonging to a member of Evil Duke Cumbee's gang, Myron Spangler."

"Myron? I thought he was one of Eddie Drake's boys."

"Ever since we got Big Ed on racketeering and little Eddie got left with the reins, the Drake organization is falling into a hole. They got rats leaving the ship left and right."

"So Myron is one of the Cumbee's boys now?"

"That's what our latest report says," Charlie said, checking the clipboard. "Of course, us not having access to FBI reports has left some holes in our database."

"Then maybe it's good to be disconnected like this," Griggs replied. "We depended too much on our friends in the FBI. We got lazy."

"Lazy? How can you say that?"

"You said we have holes in our database. We should get them patched up, dontcha think?"

"We're down to two guys in the entire office devoted to organized crime." Charlie put two fingers in the air. "Count 'em, two. It's not us that's dependent on the Feds, it's upper management. Two guys cannot handle organized crime alone. Not when we're reassigned to look for some eccentric Richie Rich."

"The man is missing."

"There are dozens of wives out there who don't know where their husbands are," Charlie waved his arms for dramatic effect, "but because this guy is rich he gets popped to the top of the list."

Griggs smirked, grabbed the baseball off the stand on his desk. "Charlie, we're looking for a connection between organized crime and the disappearance of Warren Blake. It's a reasonable request."

Charlie's anger was diminished somewhat by his sudden puzzlement. Why was his partner suddenly taking this so jake? He didn't have the nerve to broach the question. Instead asked, "Where do we start looking, then? I mean, without a crime, how do we follow a chain of evidence?"

"The Feds do it all the time."

"The Feds are trained for it."

"Cops are trained for it."

"*Other* cops are trained for it." Charlie started pacing. "Most of my experience is in homicide and now organized crime. We start at point A and then we follow it around the board."

He stopped. Turned to Griggs. "What do you think happened to the Russians?"

"What do you mean?" Griggs leaned back in his chair, casually rolling the baseball from one hand to the other. "They got popped."

"Yeah, but how?"

"I assume firearms were involved."

"No, I mean, the Russian Mafiya are the most vicious, most heartless group of criminals out there."

"They're all criminals."

"Yeah, but Evil Duke Cumbee at least pretends to have a code of honor."

"But you make him unhappy, he kills you."

"Yeah, but Blokhin—you make him unhappy, he slaughters your whole gene pool. It's a whole next level of butcher."

"The Russians were caught by surprise." Griggs stopped rolling the baseball. "On a level playing field, they would have dismembered Cumbee's boys."

"If they were, in fact, Cumbee's boys."

"What do you mean? We made the car."

"It's circumstantial. We didn't see any faces. We can't find the car, can't find Myron Spangler. We find him, maybe we got something."

"And the elevator."

"The elevator? One of Cumbee's goons? Or one of the Russians?"

"Maybe a witness." Griggs leaned back again in the chair, rolled the baseball again. Looked up and smiled at Charlie. "I guess that's the sixty-four-dollar question, isn't it?"

NEWS

EXTRA! (COPIES) - *BLAKE LIFE* MAG USED SHAM HAWKERS TO PUMP UP CIRC
MOLLY CARR. *Kansas City Globe*. Kansas City, MO: Mar 20, 2006. pg. 053

Section: Business
Word count: 657

Abstract: *Blake Life* magazine dumped bundles of its magazine at homeless shelters as part of an elaborate scam to fool auditors investigating the magazine's inflated circulation. The allegations are part of an ongoing investigation... <click for more>

CIRC CUT BY 300,000

BLAKE LIFE
MOLLY CARR. *Kansas City Globe*. Kansas City, MO: Apr 03, 2006. pg. 052

Section: Business
Word count: 527

Abstract: *Blake Life*'s monthly circulation will now be between 370,000 and 375,000, down from about 690,000 for the 12 months... <click for more>

MAG DEALS AD-ING UP

BLAKE LIFE
MOLLY CARR. *Kansas City Globe*. Kansas City, MO: Apr 10, 2006. pg. 043

Section: Business
Word count: 563

Abstract: Despite complaints, *Blake Life* mag is making headway in its efforts to settle with aggrieved advertisers. About 400 advertisers have signed settlement agreements. Blake Media set aside nearly $60 million to cover advertisers' claims... <click for more>

— 16 —

Somewhere in the middle of Missouri, the Right Fair Doctor Reverend Damascus Rhodes had his fill of truck driver Riley Jones.

Somewhere around the part where the truck driver started rattling off the secrets of Mormonism as found in *Battlestar Galactica*.

They came upon the green sign at the side of the Interstate alerting weary travelers to a state-sponsored rest stop. Rev. Damascus asked whether they could pull off. Jones's eyes flicked to the clock on the dash, weighing karma against his schedule.

After a few hesitant starts at a reply, he finally sighed and put one hand on the stick shift. "Heck, I guess'd b'okay."

At the rest stop, Rev. Damascus managed to switch rides, got himself in with an elderly couple in a Winnebago. He thought they would give him a break for some much-needed rest, but the old man behind the wheel was all smiles and questions.

"If you don't mind my asking, Father, how did you come to be hoofing it out here to a rest stop in the middle of the cornfields?"

Rev. Damascus gave himself a big mental kick in the head. He had spent the morning at the diner nursing his coffee, killing time, focused on practicing his story about what he had *not* been doing—"No, Officer, I did not kill that poor woman's husband"; "No, Your Honor, I did not kidnap that homeless man with intent to injure him with bodily harm"; "No, Lord, I did not obtain that vehicle under false pretenses and then proceed to vandalize it with fire"—that he had failed to come up with a workable story about what he *was* doing.

Then the old man, Ethan Grassman, asked a follow-up question and gave the rev a narrative head start: "Are you on some sort of missionary walk across the desert?"

Thin, but all the help he needed. Rev. Damascus was an inveterate storyteller, able to weave a tale out of the flimsiest of threads. Andrea called it "lying," but then Andrea said a lot of stuff.

Something about the suggestion reminded him of a Bible story Andrea had told him, so Rev. Damascus turned to Ethan, smiled big. "You hit it on the proverbial head, sir. Yea, verily, the Lord has sent me out into the desert to seek his face before I am to be called into the next phase of my ministry."

"How exciting." Pearl Grassman, in the next bucket seat, shrugging in excitement, her arms wrapped around her as if she might fly off.

A glimmer of memory came to Rev. Damascus, Andrea preaching

to him again, something about Jesus going out into the desert to face the devil. Ol' hornhead offered Jesus the world—food, riches, kingdoms—but Jesus turned him down flat.

But you had a different answer, didn't you, he heard Andrea say. *The devil offered you the world, and you took him up on it. Didn't turn out so well for you, did it?*

He was broken out of his reverie when Ethan, eyes on the road, gruffed in a no-nonsense tone, "And what is this next phase of your ministry?"

Rev. Damascus forgot himself, instinctively reached for his cigarettes. He caught himself, smoothly changed it into a search for the photos. His photos. Smiling brown children, under a big banner.

He did not have them. Must have dropped them somewhere in the fields, running in the night, sleeping in the creek bed where he had finally stumbled to and collapsed in the dark. Another clue to his whereabouts. Something else for the State Troopers to find, something else for the dogs to smell and get his scent from.

The long arm of the law would track him all the way to that diner, the only rest stop for miles, the clerk behind the counter would smile at the wanted photo and scratch his head, would tell them to ask Debbie or Wanda or whatever the name of the waitress was.

Then Debbie or Wanda or whatever would furrow her brow, maybe purse her lips, pretending to think deep about it, milking the moment for all it was worth, before batting those big brown eyes and saying, *Yes, officers, he sat right back there.*

She would remember him. Because they had talked. Because he had been charming and likable. But mostly because he'd stiffed her on the tip.

He felt something in one of his pockets, discovered a small pin with a rocket on its face. He must have grabbed it when he was in the truck.

The old man said, "Pearl, what is all that commotion up there in front of us?"

The old woman said, "It looks like some kind of roadblock."

What?

Ethan pulled the Winnebago up to a brown-shirted man, Illinois State Police, who held out a hand for them to stop. Ethan rolled down his window, turned to yell over his shoulder toward Rev. Damascus in the backseat, "Don't worry, Padre, I'm sure we'll be back on the road in a second."

The old man turned to the window as the trooper approached. "What seems to be the trouble, Officer?"

"We're looking for a fugitive."

The old woman, wrapped in her own arms again, lit up. "Oh, how exciting! Did somebody escape from somewhere?"

Brownshirt did not break his grim expression. "Have you folks picked up any travelers, hitchhikers, the past ten miles or so?"

Rev. Damascus held his breath. Tried to remember the Lord's Prayer.

"Not since Macon City, where we picked up Father Damascus here." The old man, Ethan, thumbed over his shoulder toward the back.

Crud.

Crud, crud, crud.

The trooper stepped up onto the running board, looking through the window. Squinted toward the back of the vehicle.

Rev. Damascus had given up on remembering the Lord's Prayer, was now trying to reconstruct the Sermon on the Mount. His mind drifted off into a Monty Python routine before the trooper locked eyes with him.

"Hey!"

At the sound of the man's voice, Rev. Damascus felt his heart stop. "Yes, Officer?"

"Passengers need to wear their seat belts."

Rev. Damascus nodded wobbly, grabbed for his seat belt with rubbery hands. The buckle gave him some trouble and he had to look down, had to jiggle it into place.

When he looked up again, the trooper had stepped down from the running board. "Thank you, folks. Drive safely."

And waved them on.

- 17 -

Charlie manned the phone at his desk, Project 86 rockin' his laptop. Griggs out with some unnamed "source." Charlie distressed he could not take off during lunch for the comic-book store—after all, the new comics came out on Wednesdays.

In the time since the orders had come down from the mountain, the morning had been spent mapping out a plan. The PROJECT: BLAKE task force—what Charlie called it, it hadn't caught on with anyone else—was populated with cops pulled from different divisions, an even distribution of weight and responsibility. Each detective bringing his or her own special expertise, his or her own slant, investigating the Blake situation from his or her own perspective.

The official word was to put this Blake case on top of an already bursting caseload, but the wink-wink expectation was for the detectives to drop everything else and make this media circus go away.

In the other divisions, there were still some detectives left to continue working the normal cases. But for the Organized Crime Division, this meant pretty much hitting the pause button on everything. The resources were already spread pretty thin.

When he thought of the "cease cooperating with the FBI" clause to their orders, Charlie tried to ignore the twinge of hope in his chest, the idea he might finally get a chance to bond with Griggs, now that Special Agent O'Malley would be out of the picture.

He still grimaced at the memory of Sunday night, Griggs and O'Malley bolting out of the car with their guns ready, cowboys ready to head off the cattle rustlers. Leaving him in the car with the radio, a kid with his babysitter.

But Charlie was valuable. Charlie was useful. Charlie was a detective. A detective always connects the dots.

Given the new mandate, he ended up with a lot of desk time, updating current files before setting them aside for now, making calls, chasing sources, trying to find out whether any of their snitches knew anything about the missing billionaire. The intelligence chatter had been relatively quiet.

Which left him at the phone on a Wednesday, lunchtime approaching, still waiting for any callbacks. Although their police-issue cell phones were more or less secure, some of the snitches refused to call in on anything other than a landline.

Pfft. Informants.

Bored, Charlie went through the open files again.

—EDDIE DRAKE. Since his father, Big Ed Drake, had been sent up, the Drake organization had been a shambles. Not much to watch. Had dropped off the priority list.

—SMART TOMMY. Until recently, a major player in St. Louis. Sighted in KC a few times, but not for several months. Once faked out the DA's office by pretending to have Alzheimer's, even fooled the doctors. Once he was let go, had a miraculous "recovery."

Recent chatter was he got whacked, presumably by Evil Duke Cumbee. (And how bad does a bad guy have to be to earn the mob nickname "Evil"?)

—EVIL DUKE CUMBEE. Speak of the devil. Reports of his presence in KC unconfirmed. Keeps a low profile. Does not hang around mob social clubs, avoids mob sitdowns, rarely meets with outsiders, watches himself on the phone, never discusses business at home. Business meetings held in diners or parking lots, a different location each time.

The shooting three nights ago pointed right at his organization, but the whole event came and went so fast—clearly, the bad guys had had a plan before they'd gone in—that there were no positive IDs of any of the shooters. The cars had eluded pursuit, had disappeared, by now no doubt chopped up for spare parts.

He thumbed through other files too, the reports on thugs and low-lifes at various levels on the totem pole in local organized crime.

Charlie, waiting to hear from certain sources, not getting any shiny new comics. Griggs out with his shiny new informant.

He continued to update files and put them back in the "To Do After BLAKE" stack. Fighting the urge to be bitter.

"Hey, Charlie." Detective Croteau, across the room. She was waving him toward the break room. "Come watch this."

He welcomed the break. Maybe this would help him stop sulking.

"Clyde made a bet," she explained when he reached the kitchen area. "I think he's crazy."

Charlie looked over at Detective Clyde Phillips, the oldest and most venerated detective he knew. The two quirks by which most knew Phillips were 1) his running up to detectives at their desks at random intervals, saying, "Listen to this," and thrusting headphones over the ears of the hapless listener, now forced to endure some obscure German folksong; and 2) his challenging the other detectives to unusual bets.

Right here, right now, Detective Clyde Phillips clutched a canister of generic nondairy creamer. His crooked grin meant this was going to be good. "You're just in time."

"What, you're going to chug the stuff dry?"

Croteau said, "He claims that stuff lights up like a firecracker."

Charlie's eyes lit up. "No way."

Croteau laughed. "He's finally lost it."

Phillips winked. "You'll see." He went to the sink, smiling at the growing number of cops at the door. He loved a crowd.

"We start with the playing field..." He reached for the hanging roll of paper towels, yanked off a couple of sheets, stuck them in the sink. "Just add creamer..." Phillips held the canister dramatically over the sink, poured it on the paper towels, and stopped. Charlie leaned in, tentatively, saw a small pile of powder.

Phillips set the canister down, pulled out a pack of matches. "Nothing up my sleeve..." Waved his arms, still working the crowd.

"And then we..." He dropped his voice as he focused on the match, striking it against the book. It lit. Intent, he dropped it over the sink and stepped back, wincing.

Everyone held their breath.

Nothing.

Phillips frowned. Pulled another match, lit it, dropped it tentatively over the sink. Stepped back again, wincing.

Held breath.

Nothing.

The cops at the door starting to drift away, mumbling. Charlie could not hear what they were saying, but he could imagine.

Phillips stepped carefully up to the sink, dared to look in. Nothing happened to him, so Charlie and Croteau followed suit. Charlie saw paper towels, saw the pile of creamer, saw burned-out matches. Hmm.

Croteau grinned. "There is *no way* people would be allowed to ingest something that's flammable."

Charlie thought of an answer, held his tongue.

Phillips shook his head. "It should have worked."

"But it didn't." Croteau beamed. "That was the bet."

Charlie slapped a hand on Phillips's shoulder. "Better luck next time." He left them in the break room, headed back for his desk.

He again tried to wrap his head around the loss of Warren Blake. Considered the possibilities. Skipped out? Kidnapped? Murdered?

He thought of Phillips's failed experiment in the kitchen and chuckled. Maybe Blake had been taken up in a fiery chariot like Elijah.

He wondered what Griggs would think of *that* theory.

- 18 -

Professional thug Nelson Pistek checked the inside of the foil wrapper. STAND TALL. Finally some useful advice. He had dropped Harry Cage off, reported their story to Eddie Drake, driven to a known hangout of Evil Duke Cumbee. An apartment building on the east side.

Mister Cumbee was not in, of course. He rarely risked being out in the open, but Pistek thought he could find work in Cumbee's organization. Hadda be better than working for Eddie Drake.

Pistek parked by the curb down the street, passed the alley. Heard cats fighting. Smelled the stench of the dumpster. Rushed past.

Seemed like a strange neighborhood for a classy guy like Mister Cumbee.

Outside the apartment building, he met up with one of Cumbee's men. Roy Parks had promised to introduce him around. Parks had a way of looking nervous even when he belonged somewhere. "What's keepin' those guys?"

Pistek was almost atwitch. "Who we meeting here again—the Duke?"

Parks shook his head. "No, man, Mister Cumbee is a little far up the chain for you now. You meet Danny and Bobby. Get to know them. If they like you, maybe they introduce you up the ladder, y'know?"

Pistek nodded. He had worked for the Fat Cat organization out on the fringes, spent a lot of time worrying how to worm his way deeper toward the inner circle, how to burrow in toward the center. But his fringe status turned out to be a blessing—he did not get caught in the crossfire when everything went down.

But it also left him unemployed. A more ambitious man would think of this as a business opportunity. But Nelson Pistek was not an ambitious man. He did just enough to get by. He was a non-entrepreneurial, unemployed non-go-getter. A good company man.

Parks was wringing his hands together. "So it's no good working for Eddie Drake, huh?"

Pistek shrugged. "When his old man got put away, it's like it all flew out the window."

"What flew out the window?"

He gave Parks a look. "What do you mean?"

"You said it 'all flew out the window.' What, you mean like somebody left the window open and all the money flew out? Or what?"

How could a man like this be working for Evil Duke Cumbee? Pistek sighed. "It's an expression." He pulled another square chocolate from his pocket. Peeled off the wrapper, crumpled the foil, and dropped it. Popped the candy in his mouth.

Parks, hands clasped, blew into them. "Danny and Bobby. What's keeping 'em?"

"Why can't we just wait inside?"

The other man gave him a startled look. "Look, Pistol, I'm doing you a favor here. Follow my lead." He took to pacing, still wringing his hands.

Pistek nodded as if the exchange had made sense, positioned himself in front of the building, under the cloth overhang. He stretched to full height, threw his shoulders back. Tried to look like he belonged.

Parks stared. "What are you doing?"

"What?"

"You look like some kind of bird."

Pistek saw a woman coming up the sidewalk toward them, carrying a big sack of groceries. She could hardly see over the top of it. Had trouble carrying it. Awkward.

Nelson Pistek smiled big. Knew he should help. Parks did not even make a move for the door, so Pistek grabbed it for her. Once she was almost in, he let go, the door bumping her as it closed. She almost dropped the bag. Good thing he'd held the door for her.

He swallowed the chocolate, realized he had not read his fortune. Knelt and grabbed the crumpled foil off the pavement. Carefully unfurled it. DRINK IN EVERY MOMENT.

No good.

He grabbed another square from his jacket pocket. He offered one to Parks, who declined. He shrugged. "Suit yourself." Peeled foil and read the message inside.

ENJOY THE ANTICIPATION.

Enjoy the anticipation. Good, that's good.

His new life working for Evil Duke Cumbee. This boded well.

Right then, two guys drove up and parked at the curb. Pistek could tell from Parks's body language these must be the guys.

Across the street, Russian mobster Viktor Zhukov watched. Lit up another cigarette, made plans.

BLOG

WHERE IS BLAKE #006
whereisblake.blogdroid.com

"A man is not idle because he is absorbed in thought. There is a visible labor and there is an invisible labor."
—Victor Hugo

Soon (well, not soon enough) a jury of twelve could be considering charges against Blake Media's reigning king and queen, Warren and Evelyn Blake. The two, who started the media empire with a single UHF television station, are accused of stealing $170 million from the corporation by hiding details of their pay packages from the board and pilfering another $430 million by selling shares after artificially pumping up their price. The case will no doubt mention lavish lifestyles and corporate looting.

The <u>Kansas City Scene</u> has reported extensively how the Blakes spent company money on an <u>apartment on Park Avenue</u>; <u>homes in Boca Raton, Fla.</u>; and <u>jewelry from Harry Winston and Tiffany</u>.

Maybe Warren Blake fled to avoid prosecution.

– 19 –

Detective Tom Griggs checked his watch. What was keeping O'Malley?

Griggs at the Hans Doubleman Gallery, surrounded by paintings worth three times an honest cop's take-home. Heck, they were probably worth twice a *dishonest* cop's take-home.

He sniffed some kinda potpourri, wished they had met instead at the batting cages. At least then he would have something to do while he waited.

He kept to himself, floating through the gallery like a phantom, avoiding eye contact with other patrons, pretending to analyze each piece.

The splatters of paint only occasionally made sense to him. A so-so picture of a boat on a lake here. Some lady with an umbrella there. These intermittently popped up among more bizarre works that looked like the artist had tripped over a bucket of paint and was too embarrassed to start over.

By the time Special Agent Martin O'Malley showed up, Griggs was studying the frames. They turned out to be more interesting than the paintings themselves.

O'Malley yelled from across the gallery. "Griggs! How's crime?"

Griggs flinched, annoyed. "Keep it down." Sure, odds were long that anyone in the gallery at this hour would be a spy for the mayor's office. It was still important to be discreet.

O'Malley chuckled, chomping gum like a cowboy. "You think one of these moms pushing a stroller is a spy?" Adjusted a Band-Aid on one of his fingers. "Stop being so nervous."

Griggs motioned toward his colleague's Band-Aid-adjusting action. "What's with the Band-Aids?"

O'Malley held up one hand, Band-Aids wrapped around three fingers. A similar number on his other hand. "I got a habit of picking the skin off my fingers. The Band-Aids keep me from doing that—and let the healing begin."

"And you say you're not nervous."

"This ain't about the job, this is about family stuff."

Griggs didn't know how O'Malley could play it so cool. When word got across town that the KCPD was chasing this case to beat the Feds, it was only a matter of honor for the FBI to respond in kind. Now, bosses on both sides had demanded separate investigations, and never the twain shall meet.

"Calm down, Tom." The agent smiled. "We're fine. Nobody will tattle."

Griggs nodded, flushed. "Tattle" wasn't a word he'd heard since grade school. Sounded like a word Charlie might use.

Of course, O'Malley was probably right. None of the cops Griggs knew would darken the door of an art gallery during the day. Or, for that matter, come at all unless dragged by a spouse or trying to impress a date.

Well, he could see Charlie showing up. He liked stuff like this. But Griggs had left Detective Charlie Pasch back at the station, left him there with a little white lie, a stack of paperwork, and orders to stay by the phone.

Griggs tried not to think about it. Tried to convince himself it was for the kid's own good. It was bad enough for Detective Tom Griggs to disobey direct orders and fraternize with the enemy. He didn't need to drag his partner into it.

At least, that's what he told himself.

— 20 —

As soon as his shift was over, Charlie made a beeline for Randy's Comics Empire. This being new-comics day, the store was thick with traffic. Of course, nobody here knew him as "Detective Charlie Pasch, KCPD, Kansas City, Missouri." This evening, right here, right now, he was just Charlie.

He headed for the front shelves, where the week's new comics were placed in alphabetical order, an assortment of four-color slabs of pop culture, *The Darkness* and *Iron Man* and *Queen & Country.* He glanced through a thick Craig Thompson paperback, put it on his "next time" list.

He bent on one knee to see what was on the lower shelves. Around the front counter, the geek chatter turned, as it did most Wednesday evenings, to another argument about comic books.

This being Randy's Comics Empire, near any opinion was fair game, as long as it didn't lead to fisticuffs. (The one exception being that one brawl over Wolverine's secret origin—some things are a matter of principle.)

The argument today was not about which issue of *Common Grounds* was best, or whether Hal Jordan should have stayed dead, or whether Gwen Stacy should have stayed alive. No, it was something that should have been cut-and-dried. In fact, most assumed it was.

"When was the Golden Age for comic books?" The asker, a snarky guy in an underfitting T-shirt needing to push his glasses back up his nose. Smug, like he was hiding some crucial fact, like he knew the secret reason Bruce Banner got zapped with gamma rays.

Charlie, picking through titles on the bottom shelf, could not help but answer. "That's easy—1938." His leg going numb, he stood quickly to free up circulation. "When Superman debuted in *Action Comics*."

The owner himself, Randy Olson, behind the counter, nodding. "Yeah." Folding his thick arms. "Followed by Batman, Wonder Woman, and near everyone else. Everything today has its roots in what happened then."

Snarky guy grinned, showed bad teeth. "Nope."

Heads all over the store turned toward the front: by the trading cards, over by the collectible statues. Even the guy in the back of the store ogling the poster of Sarah Michelle Gellar turned to look. Charlie casually switched his weight from one foot to the other, hoping to avoid pins and needles.

Snarky Guy had his audience now. "It was the 1800s."

Charlie frowned. "How you figure that?"

"Yellow Kid."

Everyone in the room rolled their eyes collectively. Went back to the trading cards and collectible statues and Sarah Michelle Gellar poster.

But Charlie was stuck. "The character from *Hogan's Alley?*"

"Yeah." Snarky Guy grinning. "It's the 'Golden Age' because he had that yellow shirt."

Charlie suppressed a snort. Didn't want to sound too geek, not even here. "Yellow Kid was in a comic strip," he said. "That's like saying the Golden Age of television started with radio."

"But we're talking about comic books."

Charlie blinked violently, trapped. You can't win an argument with the other guy grinning like that.

"Fine," Charlie answered flatly. Shook his head and walked away. Occupied himself with the rows of back-issues boxes, the "F" section, letting Snarky Guy buy his stash and go on his smug way.

Charlie found some treasury editions, oversized special-edition comics made back in the '70s. By the time Charlie was a kid in the '80s, they had stopped making them. It was hard to find any in good condition anymore—their unusual size made them hard to store flat.

But someone must have brought in quite a set, because here were some classics—Incredible Hulk, Secret Society of Super-Villains, even a big collection of Bible stories. Charlie saw a giant-sized Superman vs. The Flash and glowed.

He grabbed that and the Bible comic, headed for the register. Placed them gingerly on the counter, careful to make sure it was clean. Gave Randy a sheepish smile. "Hey."

The owner nodded a greeting. "How are ya?"

Charlie returned the greeting with a nod of his own. "Good, good." Tapped the enormous collector's-sized comics and smiled. "I cannot believe I found these."

Randy nodded. "Oh, Bible comics. I hadn't seen this before."

"I wonder why there aren't more Bible-type comics. I bet people would buy them."

"We had one book in here. But it was full of mistakes. It's like, if a thing is worth doing, it's worth doing right, you know?"

"That's a shame. It's why I stopped buying Marvel hardcovers. For that kind of money, you'd think they'd take the time to proofread."

Randy nodded. "I know." He started sorting the purchases by price, punching numbers into the register.

"It's like Jacob and Esau, you know?"

"Are they in *The Avengers*?"

"No, they're in the Bible."

"Oh."

"I was just thinking how Esau sold his birthright for a bowl of stew."

Randy stopped with the register, looked up. "What?"

Charlie smiled. "Esau was the firstborn, which meant he would inherit the family fortune, so to speak."

"Yeah?"

"So his younger brother, Jacob, fixes this stew, and Esau comes in from a day of hunting, and he's tired and he's hungry, and he wants some stew. Jacob says, 'I'll trade you the stew for your inheritance.' And Esau is so focused on the moment, he says, 'Sure,' and takes the food. And he has to deal with the ramifications of that impulse decision for the rest of his life."

Randy furrowed his brow. "What does that have to do with comic books?"

"Some of these companies are focused on the short-term, on their shock-value plot twists, on catering to a shrinking audience," Charlie said. "But they're sacrificing their long-term profitability. If you alienate your future prospects, then you have no future."

Randy nodded, did not seem sure how to answer. He returned to ringing up the comics.

Charlie said, "Hey, you expecting any back issues? Especially any Irv Novick on *The Flash*?"

Randy, without looking up. "Who's that?"

"Irv Novick is one of the great unsung artists of the Silver Age." Charlie slipping into his lecture tone. "He penciled *The Flash* in the '70s and '80s."

Randy chuckled. "Before my time."

"Yeah, my uncle had this whole trunk of 'em at my grandma's house. Some of the first comics I ever read." Charlie grinned stupidly, remembering what it was like for a ten-year-old to discover a treasure. "Those issues of *The Flash* were awesome! Novick had this dynamic, kinetic art matched to these great clockwork scripts by Cary Bates."

Randy rang up a couple more comics, stopped, and looked up. "Hey, you're a cop or something, right?"

"Yeah." Charlie nodded. "A detective."

"Know anything about Eddie Drake?"

Charlie held his breath a second. "Why do you ask?"

"Some guy came in the other day, said Eddie Drake wants to buy the store."

"What?" Charlie furrowed his brow. "This store?"

"I remembered his name from that big story in the papers. When his old man was arrested." He shrugged. "Thought maybe you could shed some light."

"I can't really comment regarding an ongoing investigation," Charlie answered with a sideways smile, giving an answer without giving an answer. "Big Ed was sent up for racketeering, that's public knowledge. There wasn't much to convict Eddie. Which left little Drake behind to run the family business."

Randy leaned in, lowered his voice. "I was thinking he probably don't wanna sell comics. You know?"

Charlie nodded slowly, thinking. His gaze drifted around the store. Shelves of comics, rows of boxes, statuettes, all manner of collectibles.

Charlie thinking about Eddie Drake.

- 21 -

The Good Right Reverend Doctor Damascus Rhodes watched the rhythm of the telephone poles passing his window. Still in the Winnebago with Ethan and Pearl Grassman.

They'd hit a dead spot in the conversation about thirty minutes earlier, the old couple out of questions, comments, and suggestions of a religious nature. That was all they seemed to want to discuss with a man of the cloth, fake or otherwise.

That was one downside to hiding behind a clerical collar: People were uncomfortable discussing anything other than sacred matters with a man of the cloth. Never baseball. Never rock music. Never motion pictures. (Unless, of course, it was a movie you were about to picket.)

When his brief burst of conversation with the old couple had ended, the old woman, Pearl, had decided to sing "Blessed Assurance." She knew only the one verse; when she'd finished, there was another block of silence, just the road passing under the wheels, before she'd sung the same verse again.

Then silence. Again.

If Rev. Damascus had the energy, he would have put more effort into the relationship with the Grassmans. But it had taken everything he had in him to talk his way into the Winnebago in the first place.

Following the stressful events leading to his harrowing escape, he was desperate for a quick exit, a getaway, get as far away as fast as he could from the scene of his horrible crime.

Desperate to get away from the sheriff and his deputies, from the state troopers, from the *dogs*, before they sniffed out his trail. Caught him. Put him away. Sent him to the chair.

The death penalty would be bad. The Good Right Reverend Doctor Damascus Rhodes was reasonably sure he was not ready to meet his Maker.

No, if the Almighty were anywhere near as cantankerous as he sounded, if he should ever be alerted to Rev. Damascus's activities, it would not be pleasant.

Not unlike, perhaps, the prospect of again crossing paths with Evil Duke Cumbee. Rev. Damascus—under another name—had invoked Evil Duke Cumbee's name while collecting "alms" in St. Louis.

You'd think a guy with a name like "Evil Duke Cumbee" would appreciate the good publicity. Would appreciate being associated with a charitable undertaking. After all, as far as those people knew, a portion of the money might actually reach the less fortunate. Brown-faced kids smiling under a banner of goodwill.

But was Cumbee *grateful?* Was he *appreciative?*

Not on your life. Cumbee's men had come after him. He'd barely made it out of St. Louis.

So if God was anything like Evil Duke Cumbee, the Good Right Reverend Doctor Damascus Rhodes did not want to attract any attention. The Big Guy had already taken the heart of Andrea. Had broken up the act.

But then there was the miracle. The Miracle of the Blessed Roadblock.

What was *that* about?

A state trooper, bless his heart, had poked his head in the window, had looked directly at him, the fugitive from justice, had looked directly at him and allowed him to pass. On to freedom. Anywhere from here on was the Promised Land.

How did the bureaucracy of miracles work, anyway? Were they the products of some God-set mechanism, set in motion at the dawn of time, perhaps when God finished his creation and walked away?

Or a conscious act of some sentient force for good? Angels? Aliens? The ghost of Abraham Lincoln?

Rev. Damascus continued to mentally peel away the ramifications. Started nodding to himself. Humming "Street Fighting Man."

Then a new thought struck. What if it was a coincidence? What if no one up there was paying attention at all?

Rev. Damascus considered the dark blackness of space, the prospect of an empty, anonymous universe ruled by chance. He shivered.

Imagine. No karma. No retribution. No consequences.

Maybe it was the "Santa Claus" principle. God the kindly old man working with benevolent workers—elves, angels, whatever—weighing the good against the bad. Deciding in the end to reward little Billy's so-so behavior with a toy rocket. Rev. Damascus had never heard of any children really getting coal.

A shaky theory, sure. But enough to bolster Rev. Damascus's spirits.

He started humming more confidently. The old lady, Pearl, noticed and turned to look at him. She must have thought it was some hymn, because she smiled at him and joined right in.

– 22 –

Jeff Guy Bill was in the hospital. Twenty miles outside Belt Falls, Illinois. Following the sucker punch from that town-to-town preacher, he'd gotten up and walked away with barely a scratch.

Had been so preoccupied with the whole incident that he got into a head-on collision the following day.

Had no idea how the other guy in the wreck turned out. Who has time to check? It must have been pretty bad, though, because Jimmy Bodean, in his fresh deputy shirt and shiny badge, kept stopping in to check on him.

Jeff Guy Bill was not in the mood to talk to Deputy Jimmy Bodean. Jimmy was a goodie-goodie before he got the brown shirt and the shiny badge. Jeff Guy Bill could not imagine the shirt and badge would have brought any improvement. So anytime he heard Deputy Jimmy Bodean talking in the hall outside, he played possum.

Actually, Jeff Guy Bill thought it was referred to as "playing raccoon." Nobody ever corrected him; everyone was either too afraid or did not know the difference.

Of course, Deputy Jimmy Bodean would have been perfectly willing to set Jeff Guy Bill straight. But, ironically, it had never come up in conversation. Mainly because every time he came to the hospital room, Jeff Guy Bill was playing raccoon.

Without a working TV, Jeff Guy Bill was bored. Only a stack of unread newspapers to entertain him. Jeff Guy Bill was not exactly what you'd call a reader.

He looked over at the dresser, saw the styrofoam cup with dandelions in it. Chuckled. Darla Mae was purty enuff to be queen of the county fair, but dumb as one of the show animals.

That musta been how she fell for the town-to-town preacher man. Jeff Guy Bill had no idea why she'd traded good beer-and-poker money for that worthless plaster cross which, even now for all he knew, was prob'ly still hanging over the TV back at the trailer.

"I'm just fixin' up the altar right," she said. Explained that if Jeff Guy Bill was going to spend his Sunday morning prayer time at the "family altar" watching football, she was going to make sure he was reminded of who he should be prayin' to.

So she bought that plaster cross from the town-to-town preacher man. Jeff Guy Bill had thrown a fit. First of all, it had been good beer-and-poker money. Second, he did not appreciate her attitude about his Sunday mornings. After a week of hauling deliveries all over God's green earth, he had a right to blow off some steam with the boys on Friday and Saturday nights. He needed his Sundays to recover before he hit the road again Monday.

Couldn't she understand?

Somewhere during the course of throwing his fit, he had thrown out there, *What else you buy, Darla Mae? What else he sellin'?*

The flushed look on her face gave him answer enough. He stormed down to the town-to-town preacher man's new office, planned to give him a fat mouth full of five-fingered Belt Falls–style what-for.

The town-to-town preacher man got in a lucky punch, that was all, clubbed Jeff Guy Bill with a desk or file cabinet or something. And in front of all the local hens no less, ready to cluck their version of the fight to anyone within earshot.

Jeff Guy Bill was finally bored enough for even the newspaper. Grunted as he looked at the front page: big headline, big photo, big manhunt for some escaped convict. Some guy named "Mad Dog," a man with a giant, shaved head, a hideous scar etched down the left side of his face. Paper said there were roadblocks all over a three-state area.

Jeff Guy Bill belched loudly. Wondered where the town-to-town preacher man had ended up.

– 23 –

Randy Olson walked past the rows of comics toward the front door. He twisted the key in the lock, turned the OPEN sign over. Randy's Comics Empire was closed for the night.

On the way back to the counter, he thought again of his conversation with Charlie. Wondered what his regulars would do if he sold out to Eddie Drake. If he let the mob turn the place into a saloon or a gambling joint or whatever.

He counted up the money in the register, put together his deposit for the bank in the morning. He shut the lights off as he headed for the back exit. Pulled the door closed behind him as he left, testing the knob to make sure it locked.

He heard the crunch of gravel, looked around nervously. Didn't see anything unusual in the moonlight, just his car across the lot. He fumbled with his keys, stepped quickly, listening to the crunch of gravel beneath his shoes.

There. That sound again.

Olson turned. "Who's there?" Felt foolish yelling to an empty parking lot.

Nobody answered. He strode even faster toward the car, fumbled more desperately with the keys, cursed himself for parking in the shadows behind the store.

He had the key in the door when he heard the noise and saw his car rock. He turned and saw a shadow, someone who had slapped his hand on the trunk of the car. "Wh-wh—"

A man chuckled. "Eddie has a message for you."

A second man stepped from the shadows, poking the comic-book-store owner in the back. The man popped something in his mouth, some kind of candy. Chewing, he said, "Yeah. A message."

– 24 –

After ditching the geezers, the Good Right Fair Doctor Reverend Damascus Rhodes hitched with some college kids. At first, he thought it would be a trade up, but they turned out to be activists, talking his ear off about the horrors of the class system in India. "Dalits" seemed to be the operative word, whatever that was all about.

Twitching in the backseat, Rev. Damascus was able to get more involved in the conversation after the topic turned to music. Of course, what these kids had cranked up could hardly be considered "music" at all. "What is that?" He hoped his sour face would guilt them into popping the CD out of the player and switching to something else.

"Project 86," the driver said, eyes on the road, head bobbing. A young man in his early 20s, buzz-cut blond, oversized orange T-shirt with some logo, baggy khaki shorts.

The girl in the passenger seat, a girl who reminded him of Andrea, turned and flashed a friendly smile, showing white teeth. "They're the best."

Rev. Damascus forgot his fake clerical collar for the moment. "Can't you play some real music?" Shouted to be heard. "Got any Rolling Stones?"

The kid behind the wheel shook his head. "Naw, man, all their songs sound alike."

"How can you say that?" Rev. Damascus lunged between the front seats and stretched for the stereo, clicking it off. Something in his back hurt from the move. He put a hand on the driver's shoulder. "In their heyday, the Rolling Stones were the greatest white R&B band that ever was."

"That's your opinion."

"I'm talking about the beginning of true-blue rock 'n' roll, man."

"That was a long time ago, dude."

"Yeah, but while everyone else broke up or blew out or faded into the machine, the Rolling Stones kept rocking, growing and maturing at their craft, absorbing whatever new styles they wanted, but remaining true to their honky-tonk rock 'n' roll selves."

"Honky-tonk?"

"I'm not a music critic, I'm just trying to describe it." Rev. Damascus coughed. "All your modern music is just derivative."

The kid turned, flickered a grin at Rev. Damascus. "Well, maybe it's just me, but all the Rolling Stones songs seem to be about tearing things down. Taking everything you can from the world."

"Every rock song is about that."

The kid shook his head, popping the CD out of the player. "No, dude, some bands are about building up." Started digging for another CD. "About what you can put *into* the world."

The kid found a particular disc, seemed satisfied, popped it in. "Maybe this is more your speed." As the disc started, something called "Switchfoot," the kid had his eyes back on the road, bobbing his head.

Rev. Damascus sighed, sat back against the seat, and tried to nap.

⌂ ▭ ⑦   ⊠

BLOG

WHERE IS BLAKE #007
whereisblake.blogdroid.com

"To avoid criticism, say nothing, do nothing, be nothing."
—Albert Einstein

How did I end up here?

I was a bicentennial baby. Born during the two-hundredth year of this great republic, this great democracy, these great United States of America.

Sixteen years ago, I learned I had been raised by a man who was not my biological father. My mother died when I was eighteen, and my dad thought it was time he told me the truth. It was a weird time, both of us still fresh in our grief, but that is when he decided to sit me down and set me straight.

I don't know what his intentions were, I don't know what he expected this knowledge to do for me. Our relationship had already become awkward by that point. I was daddy's little "puddin'" when I was small and cute, but when I began as a teen to start that process of blossoming into womanhood, he began to distance himself, to lose interest in our daddy–daughter times together.

When he first broke the news—that he was not my "father"—I was shocked. I was hurt. The idea that there was a man out there, a father out there I had never met, left me feeling hurt, abandoned, alone.

Alone.

I don't know why my dad decided to compound my hurt by sharing this knowledge during such a painful time, the memory of my mother's funeral still fresh, loose dirt practically still being shoveled onto the casket.

Soon, I was packed up, shipped off, and living with my aunt because, as he put it, I "needed a woman's guidance" in my life.

I had to spend my senior year in a new high school, barely made any friends. Then it was time for college, a community college in my aunt's town. It was all I could afford, even with student loans and a part-time job. I studied communications by day, flipped burgers and sold soft-serve ice cream afternoons, and spent any free nights and weekends on a quest to find my father.

I had to find him. Had to announce my existence. Had to find out whether my father would care.

As far as I had been told, my mother had never divulged the identity of my biological father—not to my dad, not to my aunt. My mother had taken the secret to her grave.

It took me all the way up until last year to discover the secret of my origins...

– 25 –

Friday. April 28. Detective Charlie Pasch was back at Randy's Comics Empire. The mood in the store was low, dread hanging in the air. Instead of game tables filled with geeks and chatter, only a couple of guys sat in today, one shuffling the deck over and over.

In the back corner, a kid, thirteen at most, fidgeted by the rack of posters. The black frames flipped past, Pokemon, Bride of Frankenstein, some basketball player. Somebody must have bought the Sarah Michelle Gellar poster.

Charlie checked the back issues, the "F" box again. Found a copy of *The Flash* #246, from 1977. Less than five bucks. He grabbed a few other titles off the "This Week's Comics" shelves and placed them gingerly on the counter, checking to make sure it was clean. An employee was behind the register today, Jeevan Kapoor, a guy with a goatee. Stood behind the counter, arms folded. Grim.

Charlie nodded a greeting. "What's up?"

Jeevan, eyes elsewhere, jumped from behind the register. "Hey! Get out of there!"

He crossed the store in three great strides, pulling the curtain for the adult section, grabbing a kid by the arm, yanking him out to the middle of the store.

Jeevan wagged a finger in the kid's face. "Either you have a gland problem, or you're too young to be back there!"

The kid, red-faced, ran for the door.

Jeevan returned to the register. "I always hate to see that."

Charlie asked, as much for conversation as curiosity, "Get much trouble like that?"

"Not if you watch for it," Jeevan replied. "Like working at any book or video store, I guess."

Charlie motioned around the room with his head. "Why's it so quiet today?"

"Randy's in the hospital. Some guys beat him up."

- 26 -

Charlie swung by the hospital, stopped in to visit Randy, the owner of the comic-book store. Randy not in the mood to explain how he ended up here.

Charlie did not have the nerve to push. Made small talk—*Star Trek* and *Jonny Quest* and Stan Lee—anything to circle around why Randy was broken and in a hospital bed.

Charlie should have pressed the matter, but he chickened out.

Changed the subject. "I keep thinking about that guy with his whole 'Golden Age' theory, you know?"

"Yeah." Randy staring blankly, mind somewhere else.

"I mean, there are whole books on this stuff," Charlie prattled. "I did a speech in junior high and everything."

"Uh-huh."

Charlie stayed a few more minutes, looking for some opening to do his job. It never came.

— 27 —

The Good Right Fair Doctor Reverend Damascus Rhodes woke up in hostile territory. He had fallen asleep in the car to the rhythm of the tires on the road, to the blare of the gospel-rock band Switchfoot.

He awoke, blinked himself to awareness, tasted blech. Tried to reclaim coherent thought, tried to remember how he got here.

And now he woke up in the car, outside a convenience store.

Across from a familiar police station.

Catty-cornered from a familiar church.

Where he had made his plea on behalf of brown-faced children from whatever name the orphanage had been called for the purposes of that slide presentation.

It had the makings of a sweet scam before he was found out. Before some kid, one of the congregants' children, a kid with acne and an Internet connection, found him out. Told Daddy. Who told the sheriff.

Who came to the presentation.

Preacher Whatever-Name-He-Was-Going-By-Then barely made it out ahead of the authorities, leaving behind buckets of cash. Eight or ten thousand, by his estimates, counting the local businesses that had gotten in on the act. Not TV-evangelist money, nosiree, but still nothing to sneeze at.

Just left it behind. In that building right over there. Where the charity seminar had gotten out of his control, had turned into a blood hunt, angry villagers bearing torches, scouring the town for him. It had been close enough, that he had vowed to never come back.

Yet here he was.

Here he was.

Here.

Now.

In that crystalline moment, the Good Right Fair Doctor Reverend Damascus Rhodes realized he needed a plan. He had spent four years bouncing around, a pinball bouncing off in scary, herky-jerky tangents, an unwanted rag caught in a wind tunnel, helpless, at the mercy and the whim of the forces of an unkind universe.

Just yesterday, he was sure the universe liked him. Now he was not so sure. And the uncertainty was killing him.

No more.

He had been running away, planless, heedless, and it had led him here. Karma, bad luck, whatever you choose to call it, had led him here to this place, the site of his greatest folly. They would see him, they would grab him, they would send his face and fingerprints across the wires and the Internet and find out he was wanted for murder in Belt Falls, Illinois.

Clearly, the lifestyle was not working for him.

The con man with no vision perishes.

In that crystalline moment, hunched down in the car, waiting for the college kids to return from inside the convenience store, rubbing his eyes to cover his face, the Fair Right Good Doctor Reverend Damascus Rhodes knew he needed a plan.

A plan.

A plan.

A plan.

No "plan" presenting itself right off, Rev. Damascus noticed a police car pulling into the parking lot across the street. Rev. Damascus, feeling like a sitting target, bolted upright, popped open the door, rocketed for the convenience store.

Yanking open the front door, he lurched through and heard the melange of noises: the bell signalling his entry; the microwave loudly cancerfying a hotdog; the bloop-bloop-zang of an authentic arcade game.

He could not have made himself a more conspicuous figure if he had worn a sandwich board and shouted obscenities at passing vehicles.

Plan.

Make a plan.

Need a plan.

"Yo, Reverend!" The kid working the authentic arcade game—what was that, Qbert? Dig Dug?—gave Rev. Damascus a thumbs-up. "Be with you in a minute!" The kid, wiped a hand on his oversize orange T-shirt with some logo, turned back to the flashing screen, pounded the button with one palm, angled the joystick with another.

Rev. Damascus returned the thumbs-up, added a weak smile. The kid missed both in his rush to get back to digging or Qberting or whatever.

Rev. Damascus turned toward the smell of irradiating dog, fighting the urge to retch. He saw the girl who reminded him of Andrea. She did not turn from the glow of the microwave, but stared at it, mesmerized, like she thought it might break out in cartoons.

The Good Fair Right Doctor Reverend Damascus Rhodes did not care. No, the Good Fair Right Doctor Reverend Damascus Rhodes just needed one thing.

A plan.

He saw the sign for the men's room and amended his to-do list.

Ten minutes later, his list back to one item, he glanced across the store, toward the employee behind the counter. A young man of some indistinguishable ethnic background was focused on the college kids at the authentic arcade game and the microwave.

Rev. Damascus, unwatched, saw his opening, yanked open the fridge door, grabbed a plastic bottle of liquid. Ducked with his grabbed treasure behind an aisle of paper goods and auto supplies, twisted the bottle open with a whush and guzzled.

There was a moment of blackness. He assumed it was carbonation pushing the oxygen out of his brain. He blinked away stars.

Refreshed, he recapped the bottle, shoved it behind a row of paper towels on the second shelf. Wiped his mouth with his sleeve. It tasted like he had been wearing the jacket for a year.

He looked across the store and saw it: the rack of newspapers.

Something about it called to him, like the voice of God. He walked across the store, picked up a paper.

Tomorrow, the headline would be about the capture of escaped convict "Mad Dog" Barker.

But the Good Right Fair Doctor Reverend Damascus Rhodes had today's paper in his hands, his eyes on the big 72-point headline: WHERE IS BLAKE?

That's when he had a plan.

⌂ ◻ ⑦   ⊠

BLOG

WHERE IS BLAKE #008
whereisblake.blogdroid.com

"The greatest obstacle to discovery is not ignorance—it is the illusion of knowledge."

—Daniel Boorstin

I have tried asking questions around the office. Get a sense of who would have been the last person to see Warren Blake alive and well in Kansas City. But it is a troubling subject for many people up here.

But are they worried for the fate of Warren Blake? Or are they worried for the fate of those he left behind—under the power of Queen Evel?

Where is Blake?

~ 28 ~

Viktor Igorovich Zhukov was waiting. Waiting for his prey. Ernest Potts. One of Cumbee's men.

Zhukov stewed in his bitterness. Evil Duke Cumbee had betrayed him. But like his name, the man was a *dukh,* a ghost, out of reach.

Which left Zhukov to pick off Cumbee's men. Brutally kill them off one by one.

He pushed aside the memories. His own comrades shot down by common dogs. The cowardice of running for the elevator when he should have stood his ground. The disgrace of hiding out, alone, spattered with blood.

He was haunted by the memory of the hail of bullets. And the blood. Oh, the *blood*.

Zhukov thought of Napoléon again. Those who forget history are doomed to repeat it. Napoléon was banished. He died alone, a frustrated, defeated man. A man who always thought he would return to greatness but never did.

Viktor Igorovich Zhukov would not end up like that. He would learn from history.

Drinking again, Zhukov flashed his eyes around the room. He was alone. After the incident at the garage, he dared not return to the few men they had left. He could not face them. He could not trust them. Could not risk them finding out what manner of man he was.

There was a commotion by the front, a thug making a loud entrance, making a scene as he pushed back the bouncer. On his arm a blonde, giggling.

He was Ernest Potts.

– 29 –

At the station, Detective Charlie Pasch caught Griggs at his desk, a rarity lately. Griggs reading one of the files, eating a sandwich. His "informant" must have been busy.

Charlie cleared his throat. "I have a problem."

Griggs looked up at Charlie. Wiped his face with a paper napkin. "Yeah?"

Charlie told the story, especially the Eddie Drake connection. Griggs dismissed it. Drake was small-time, Griggs said. Besides, they were supposed to be looking for Warren Blake.

Actually, his exact words were "I don't care." He waved the sandwich to emphasize his point. "We already got Big Ed, and that turned out to be a disappointment."

"But if Eddie Drake is causing trouble—"

"If you catch him in a crime, pick him up."

Charlie sassed, "I thought assault was a crime."

"Did your friend tell you Drake roughed him up?"

"No."

"Did your friend file a complaint?"

Charlie looked down. Shook his head. "No."

"Without any testimony, all you can talk about is targeting Eddie Drake for an investigation." Griggs ate the last of his sandwich. Wiped his hands on the napkin. "But building a case—that takes money, that takes equipment, that takes man-hours." He spread his hands apologetically. "We're already spread too thin. We got to be choosy about our targets, Charlie. That's the way it is."

Griggs checked his watch, pushed back from the desk, and stood. "I gotta go meet somebody."

— 30 —

Professional thug Nelson Pistek, sitting at the bar. Saw Ernest Potts entering Zoo Girls, tensed up.

Pistek's visit to the apartment building had yielded bupkus. "We'll get back to you," they'd said. Like he was some punk kid asking for a paper route.

Afterward, he came straight to Zoo Girls. Thought he could work his way into the circle from here.

And Ernest Potts was an important man.

Pistek took a gulp of his drink, regretted it, wheezed. Looked over at Potts again. Trying not to stare, trying to play it cool.

Potts had a girl on each arm, chatting it up. Pistek suddenly felt panic. Was it a bad idea barging in on him here, infringing on his space?

Surely there wouldn't be trouble in Zoo Girls. I mean, come on, we're all friends here, having drinks, meeting broads. It's all jake, right?

Sure, Pistek had heard the stories about this place. Cautionary tales about tangling with the wrong people. About the consequences of forgetting your place, your role in the scheme of things.

Gee, Mister Potts, I would love to work for you.

He turned to face the mirror, thought it would be less conspicuous to watch Potts through the reflection. Potts, in a corner booth, yukking it up with his lady friends. The guy was clearly connected. You could tell by the way the others deferred to him.

Any work, really, I got references.

Potts seemed to turn his direction. Pistek panicked, made a point of rolling his head to pop his neck, rubbed the back of his neck with one hand.

He looked over at the bartender, who also seemed oblivious. The man was watching Potts and the women, a dopey grin pasted on his face.

The big guy by the door was in his own world too, sitting on a tall metal stool, reading an Ayn Rand paperback. Right by the door if trouble tried to get in, a matter of yards away if one of the desperate customers tried to make trouble with the girls.

Pistek looked down again at his drink, braced himself, finished the glass. He needed something clever to say, some way to ingratiate himself to Potts. To the organization. If he ever wanted to get out from under a chump like Eddie Drake, he needed to make a move.

He stole another look toward the booth, toward Potts. A thick man with black, shiny, curly hair. Pleasant demeanor, probably a real pal when he was on your side. But if his manner with the others was any indication, he was a man you don't cross. Be his pal at all costs.

A voice burst the bubble of his surveillance: "Need a refill?"

Pistek jumped at the reappearance of the bartender. He did not want to keep drinking, but could not very well stay inconspicuous if he stopped.

He smiled, his eyes watery. Pulled a handful of bills from his pocket. Down to his last dollars. He peeled off a specific amount and slapped it on the bar. The bartender grabbed the bills, went away, and got the refill.

Pistek noticed out of the corner of his eye that Potts was scooching out of his booth, one of the blondes moving out of his way. He was kissing her on the neck, making his apologies. An object in the man's hand, a cell phone. Potts headed toward the back hall, away from the noise.

Pistek did not notice the other man at the bar. Did not see him set his glass down, jaw set, getting up to follow.

Pistek had his eyes on the stage. Pretending he was a customer, pretending he wasn't stalking for the purpose of employment. Looked back at the mirror again, finished his drink.

He nervously gave Potts a few more seconds head start, didn't want to interrupt his phone call. Didn't want to get caught hovering.

He looked around. Bouncer still had his nose in the book. Bartender now digging through some drawer. The customers and dancers still focused on their own desperate lives.

He breathed in deep, took one last swig for courage, blinked himself back from a blackout, got up, headed for the hall. His best window of opportunity would be as the man was coming back after his phone call. Casual.

Wow, imagine running into you here, Mister Potts.

He reached the start of the hall, looked back to make sure no one was watching. He said a silent prayer to the universe and pushed through the invisible door to his destiny.

He was in it now.

The walls were wood-paneled, with weird placement of red paint along the ceiling and floor. There were a series of doors before you reached the end of the hall. Men's. Ladies'. Exit. Three more, unmarked doors.

As he went deeper into the hall, the throbbing music dulled. Pistek held his breath at each successive door, listened for anything. Hushed voices, a deal going down, whatever.

Then he heard the pops. It took a second to register what he was hearing. Not like the movies.

He put an ear to the door, which suddenly opened. He fell into a man fleeing, and the two collided, both hitting the floor.

A gun clattered down, metal on concrete, death for whoever did not grab it first. The room was dark, light intruding from the hall, casting long shadows as Pistek found himself on the floor with the killer, all knees and elbows, both grabbing for the gun twirling in the shaft of light from the doorway.

Pistek must have had karma on his side—he grabbed the gun first. The other figure was instantly on him, grabbing, clawing, growling with a blood threat, not giving him a chance to breathe or think.

Pistek pulled the trigger.

Up close, like a cannon, the crash of a thousand lost opportunities, a thousand lost dreams, a thousand victims screaming for vengeance.

Pistek kicked back, pushed back, scrambled back until he hit the wall. He slid up the wall until he stood, panting, clutching desperately for breath. Suddenly, he was blinded by a bright light, God raining down judgment.

"Hey!" The bartender, aghast, was standing by the switch.

Pistek's eyes adjusted to the harsh overhead lamp, saw what the bartender was gawking at. Two men down, pools of blood. Ernest Potts across the room, face down, cell phone close to his unclutching hand. The side of his head blown out.

"Ernie!" The bartender was across the room in a leap, down with Potts, checking for life.

Pistek, trembling, bent to one knee. At his feet, a stranger, killed by his own gun.

"You!" The bartender pointing at Pistek, looking at him, tears rolling. "You killed Ernie!"

"No, man, I…" Pistek ran out of words. Realized he was still clutching the gun tightly, the gun that killed Potts, the gun that killed the stranger. The gun that now had his prints on it.

Trembling, Pistek gripped the gun. And ran.

⌂ ⌷ ⑦   ⊠

BLOG

WHERE IS BLAKE #009
whereisblake.blogdroid.com

"With the rich and mighty, always a little patience."
—Spanish proverb (as quoted by Jimmy Stewart in *The Philadelphia Story*)

Evelyn Blake has been lording it over us poor employees (the walking dead) and in front of her beleaguered reality-TV-show camera crew that she is a Published Author. (This despite the fact she is not actually "published." But she's married to the head and namesake of a major media company with the ability to publish books, so I guess we could be gracious and call her "pre-published.")

The word around the office is that she pitched her book to several of the big publishers...and then several of the middle-size publishers... and then members of the small press...

And now her book is being published by the newest branch of the Blake Media organization, our new *book* division.

Coincidence? I think not.

But wait—there's more!

Someone like Evelyn Blake, a professional socialite, a professional homemaker, someone who claims to know more than you about how to decorate your home with old pipe cleaners and how to fix fancy duck dinners—you would think the book she was writing would be a handy how-to guide to strengthen her brand as the next Domestic Diva, wouldn't you?

Or, barring that, a memoir of some sort. Some "true life" account that details her triumph over, well, whatever life tragedies and circumstances she claims to have triumphed over. Some book that sends her poor readers a message along the lines of *I am better than you are.* (Her life mantra.)

Well, one of my co-workers stumbled across the manuscript-in-progress. And it is not a handy guidebook. It is not a memoir.

It is a children's book.

But not just any children's book—this is a fable constructed to teach children the world over that rich people have it tough, too. Apparently, Queen Evel has felt like enough fables have defended the plight of the poor, now she intends to defend the plight of the rich.

(I wonder if she had to get a ghost writer?)

- 31 -

The Right Fair Reverend Doctor Bishop Damascus Rhodes got into Kansas City on a Monday. With a plan.

He came to a newsstand and looked at his choices. *Kansas City Star. Kansas City Sun-Times-Register. Missouri Scene.* He pulled out the appropriate change—the old couple had insisted on giving him money, and he had insisted on accepting it—and bought a copy of the *Sun-Times-Register* because it had what he needed on the front page: a big ol' photo and a big ol' story updating readers on the status of the Widow Blake.

Sure, the paper said her husband was still "missing" and there were still high hopes for his "return." But a man can hope, can't he?

Ducking into a coffee shop just down the sidewalk from the newsstand, Rev. Damascus got himself a white-chocolate mocha and took a chair at a small circular table. Snapped the paper open, followed the story chain inside.

According to the story, Warren Blake had been reported missing two weeks earlier when he failed to show up for an important board meeting to vote on some new channel for their cable system. He was last seen in public two nights before that, glimpsed leaving the office late by security. He had waved goodbye, and that was the last anybody saw of Warren Blake.

Rev. Damascus snapped the paper shut, set it on the table. He smiled to himself, to an empty universe that would soon be eating out of his hand. Took a sip of his white-chocolate mocha, eyes darting around at the other patrons, all wrapped in their own little quiet time. As far as he knew, nobody in Kansas City knew the Right Doctor Fair Bishop Reverend Damascus Rhodes—by any name—but it always paid to be cautious.

He thought again of Evelyn Blake. Rev. Damascus would offer spiritual counsel and comfort to the grieving widow. Sipping the mocha, he sorted through his mental Rolodex of religious-themed con jobs, his own and others he'd researched. The mental exercise kept him sharp.

He went over each gambit, examining it, studying it, poking for signs of weakness. For gambits that had failed, he imagined how they could have been done more efficiently, more successfully.

He remembered one of the last arguments with Andrea. *You got to stop cashing in on God's name*, she said. *God is not mocked—whatsoever you sow, that shall you also reap.*

He considered his first major failure, back in Colorado, the camera crews swooping in on his operations. The memory of barely escaping there still fresh.

The first operation after Andrea had broken up the partnership.

He thought over one con he'd heard about recently. The guy persuaded a town's inhabitants to give him hundreds of dollars each, promising to multiply the cash by making it "fall like rain" from the sky with the help of an angel.

The scam had almost worked. He'd told his clients to cover their faces so the angel would not harm them. The unsuspecting people covered their faces, and the imposter disappeared from the area.

The man's only weak spot seemed to be that he forgot to cover his tracks. He had, for whatever strange reason, accepted plastic—and was soon caught using the credit card numbers in another town up the road.

Pfft. Amateurs.

Rev. Damascus thought of the religious artifacts he had faked in the past, under various assumed names. One had even fooled the experts, right up until someone took it on one of those antiques shows on TV. The hapless owner must surely have come back to the reverend doctor's "office" with a loaded gun—that's how justice happened in the backwoods—but the flim-flam man was long gone by then.

"You still reading that paper?"

Rev. Damascus was startled out of his self-education by a freckled young man in baggy clothes standing over his table. "W-what?"

"Your paper there," the kid replied, pointing to the crumpled *Sun-Times-Register* on the circular table. "Done reading it?"

Rev. Damascus paused a second, trying to understand the kid's nerve. Finally shook his head. "No."

The kid shrugged. "Thanks anyway." The kid wandered off to another table, apparently looking for any other available freebies.

Rev. Damascus nervously folded the paper, pressed out wrinkles with his hands, then stuck it under his arm. Gulping the last of the white-chocolate mocha, he dropped the cup in the trash on the way out.

Time to go comfort the Widow Blake.

— 32 —

Fugitive thug Nelson Pistek, a couple of hours since the shooting at Zoo Girls. He had been hanging around outside his apartment building for nearly half an hour. Making sure no one had followed.

At least, that was what he'd been telling himself. Truth was, he'd been so dazed by what had happened at the club that he'd just driven aimlessly. Finally found himself parked down the block from his home.

He'd waited around, afraid to go in. Watching for cops. Watching for suspicious figures. Watching every passing car, every passing pedestrian, wondering if this was it.

Out of his car now, Pistek shivered in the alley, hiding in the corner. Watching old newspapers fly in the wind, trying to rub imagined blood and dim powder burns off his hands, wishing he had a piece of chocolate.

The mob would be looking for him. He'd been caught holding the murder weapon. The bartender at Zoo Girls had seen him holding a gun over two dead bodies, one of them Cumbee's man. Both dead on the floor and Pistek holding the gun. The bartender had looked him right in the eyes and pointed.

WhatdoIdowhatdoIdowhatdoIdo…

Pistek pulled apart dry lips with effort. "What do I do?" he croaked to no one in particular, God or Kismet maybe. His voice raspy, phlegm building in the back of his throat. He checked his pockets for chocolate, couldn't find any.

No chocolates. No foil wrappers. No fortunes.

Pistek shut his eyes tightly, rested his face on balled fists for who knows how long. Listened to his jagged breathing, listened to his heart pounding, tried to will both to slow down to a normal rate.

Where could he go now?

Run to the cops? (What if they didn't believe him? What if they booked him for murder?)

Hide out with friends? (Who could he trust? What if they turned him in for some reward?)

He knew one thing: He could not stay in this alley. He would run into the apartment, grab a few things, grab a bag of chocolates, and hit the road.

Finally, convinced it was safe, Pistek braved up enough to make a run for it. He stuck close to brick and shadows, holding his breath every time another car or pedestrian passed.

He made it to the front porch. Glanced around nervously, pushed through into the lobby. Where the staircase split to go both up and down, he went to the left, heading to the second floor.

Pistek trudged up slowly, one step at a time, weariness jolting through his knees and ankles with each step. He had never felt more old and useless.

But that was no problem, he told himself. He was now headed to retirement. Just had to get out before the mob's "retirement plan" kicked in. Run inside the apartment, grab some gas money, grab some chocolates and clothes and video games, and hit the open road.

He reached his door, wondering where the open road would take him. Wondered whether it was possible to drive to Rio as he stepped inside.

He was thinking about brown girls on the beach when he noticed the lamp. Had he left that on?

A gruff voice in the shadows demanded, "Where you been, Pistek? We been waiting."

Pistek didn't wait to see who it was, didn't wait to see if the mystery guest had friends. Grabbed the edge of the chair by the door and yanked it over behind him, bolted out and toward the stairs.

He heard the men pile into the hall behind him, heard the rhythm of shoes against tile, heard the labored breathing, heard the shouts, heard the cursing.

Heard his own heart beating in his ears.

At the bottom of the stairs, he reached the lobby, slammed hard into the front door. Cursed, yanked it open, ran into a guy at the sidewalk.

The two tumbled to concrete. Pistek didn't know if the guy was here with the others, didn't have time to ask. Just rolled to his feet and gave the stranger a swift kick in the teeth. There was the sound of the door, and Pistek burst into a run again.

As he heard the men behind him, he ignored the pain in his lungs, ignored the spike in his ribs, tried to focus. Where to go?

He reached the corner. He heard the men behind him. Mobsters. Thugs. Killers.

Thought of that guy at the comic-book store. Failed to see the irony.

Pistek turned left and cut across the street, narrowly avoided being hit by a station wagon, the driver hitting the brakes, tires squealing. He stumbled, fell, rolled on pavement. Reached and grabbed the front bumper of the station wagon, pushed himself up. The broad behind the wheel made a face, laid on the horn.

He glanced over to see the three guys jump into the street, then jump back at the blare of a horn, a big truck swerving and screeching to a dead stop. Blocked from their view by the truck, Pistek flipped off the woman in the station wagon, limped off to the parking lot at a burger joint. He only had a few seconds before the men would get around the truck and be after him again.

Reaching the shadows at the far side of the lot, he gauged the high wooden fence along the back. Knew he could never make it over those sharp points. Decided to take his chance with the dumpster. He limped over fast as he could, gripped the side, used the very last of his strength to pull himself over and fall inside. Held his breath. Couldn't risk making any more noise while the killers were after him.

He heard a collage of noise outside. As he controlled his breathing, kept it soft, kept it slow, he never was able to make out whether the thugs came as far as the dumpster.

When the coast was finally clear, he threw up.

He waited another two hours before crawling out.

BLOG

WHERE IS BLAKE #010
whereisblake.blogdroid.com

*"You know, the very powerful and the very stupid have one thing in common.
They don't alter their views to fit the facts. They alter the facts to fit their
views. Which can be uncomfortable if you happen to be one of the facts that
need altering."*

—Doctor Who, *The Face of Evil*

One of the real challenges of putting together a magazine for someone
like Queen Evel is that her focus is always moving around. But when
she does land on something, she becomes obsessed.

Like the time she was a vegetarian. For about two weeks. One day,
she decided it was trendy—one of her hoity-toity friends must have
been trying it—and Queen Evel did not want to be left behind, so she
decided she was vegetarian too.

As such, she came into the office and made a big stink about how that
was what the magazine was all about now. Not a special issue, mind
you—which would have been problematic enough—but an entirely new
direction for the magazine. All the departments, all the columnists, all
the features—everything needed to be "vegetarian-related." We had to
scrap three entire issues in progress and suddenly turn the ship on a
dime and go off on this new course.

Then there was the time she suddenly decided to go "common"—I
don't know, she was trying to impress her driver or something—and
do pop-magazine stories about celebrity marriages, celebrity breakups,
celebrity pregnancies, celebrity arrests. Stuff like that.

And don't even get me started on the time she got caught up in
Kabbalah.

But lest all the "boo-hoos" and "why mes" get spent on the poor,
beleaguered editorial staff, let's think about the worst victims of all:
those poor souls in customer service and in circulation. They have to

deal with the angry calls, cancelled subscriptions, and obsolete direct-market campaigns.

Not to mention the enormous task of rebuilding a brand-new readership from the ground up. Because each time Queen Evel changes what the magazine is about, it changes the target demographic group that would want to read the magazine. A person who subscribes for the Kabbalah content does not necessarily have any interest in extreme diets or which celebrity is having a baby.

Changes it each and every time.

~ 33 ~

Charlie at his desk, Charlie still going through files and reports. That was the problem with this all-hands-on-deck approach: all the reading. He and Detective Griggs could not very well just go start poking around without knowing what poking had been done already. A bunch of law-enforcement vultures, swirling, swooping down, duplicating questions, duplicating investigations, wasting man-hours, wearing down the nerves of every possible lead, tromping all over the evidence.

That's no good.

Charlie frowned and focused. A stack of reports to write, files to sift through, interviews to conduct. Anything to keep himself from obsessing over Randy's Comics Empire.

He'd played a Hank Williams CD all afternoon, had it set on repeat, barely registered how many times it must have played through before he felt the pencil projectile hit his ear. A detective at another desk asked, "Charlie, do you mind?"

He jumped. "Hmm?"

"Why can't you just listen to a classic-rock station like a normal person?"

Charlie played it casual. "I think I've already listened to my lifetime quota of Lynyrd Skynyrd."

The other detective sighed, rolled his eyes. "Fine. Play something else?"

Charlie clicked open iTunes on his laptop. He started twenty-five hours' worth of songs rotating now, show tunes and Christian rock and Americana. Something to annoy everyone.

Focusing anew on the mysterious case of Warren Blake, he read up on what he could. Scratched down notes in a second notebook in case Griggs should ask. Not that he was around to ask. Just after lunch, he'd taken off again to see his mysterious "informant."

Charlie picked up the scrap of paper Griggs had left him and looked at it again. *Gone*. Really. *Will call soon*. Of course. *Griggs*. How about that.

Charlie sipped from his mug and grimaced—still tasted like coffee. He needed more almond milk and Froot Loops.

Flipped through the files, tried to focus on the work. Tried not to think about Randy at the comics store. Tried not to think about Randy's bruises. Tried not to think about Randy laid up in the hospital.

Rubbed his eyes, forced himself to read again from the file on top of the stack.

—MARCH 15. Ground broken on Blake Library in August Heights.

—MARCH 20. Warren Blake and Evelyn Blake fly to Europe. Broker a deal with a communications company in France.

—MARCH 30. Blakes come home.

—APRIL 3. Remodeling begins on Blake Media Towers.

—APRIL 11. Warren Blake seen leaving office late by security at Blake Media.

—APRIL 14. Warren Blake misses a meeting with the board of Blake Media. Is reported missing.

Charlie set the folder back on the desk, pushed it back. Sighed. Stretched his arms. Rubbed his eyes again. He thought of a man like

Warren Blake, thinks he has it all, thinks he's on top of the world. What does it profit a man to gain the whole world and lose his own soul?

It reminded Charlie of the parable about the rich fool: His land produced a good crop, so he thinks, *What shall I do? I have no place to store my crops.* The man tears down his barns and builds bigger ones to store all his grain and goods. He says to himself, *You have it made. Take life easy—eat, drink and be merry.*

But God comes to the man in the night and says, *You fool! This very night your life will be demanded from you. Then who will get what you have prepared for yourself?*

Charlie wondered again about Warren Blake. As he went through the files, he could see Detectives Kurtz and Carillo had done a thorough job. There were also updates from the others. Booker and Croteau had turned in an especially thick report, pursuing the possibility that robbery or theft had been involved in the man's disappearance.

Nothing had come from any of it, of course. There's only so much you can do when there's no evidence of a crime. If not for the very public tirade of Mrs. Evelyn Blake, and the mayor and the police commissioner crumbling under the weight of her nagging, all these detectives would be working on real cases and fighting real crimes.

Sure, the FBI had missing-persons specialists with training and expertise in this sort of thing. They knew to check credit-card records, phone records...

Wait—where were the credit-card records and phone records?

Charlie flipped through the stack again. Surely the records were here somewhere. It was such an elementary thing. Any recent purchases or calls before Warren Blake disappeared could be a pointer to where he was going. Any transactions or calls after Blake went missing would be a pointer to where he or his alleged abductors were now.

Charlie looked across the room, saw Detective Sammi Croteau at her desk, fiddling with a small object. He walked over to her, saw that the object in question was a toy guillotine.

"Hey, Croteau," he said. "I don't see any paperwork or reports about Warren Blake's credit cards or phone records. Who would have a copy of them?"

"I'm sure the Feds have plenty of copies." Croteau flashed a smile.

It was nice. "We had to file papers to get a new set of records of our own. They're not here yet."

"Why don't we still have copies from before?"

"When the chief said, 'No FBI,' somebody boxed up all the paperwork the Feds had shared with us and mailed it back."

"Is 'somebody' an idiot?"

"It might have been a misguided attempt at making a point to upper management." She looked down, started fiddling again with her toy guillotine. "Don't get me wrong—he is an idiot. I was just offering an explanation of what kind of idiot."

"Well, do me a favor and circulate the records when you get them, right?"

"You know it." She dropped the toy guillotine again, looked up. "Hey, Phillips is still trying to win that bet."

Charlie gave her a crooked smile. "What bet?"

"That one where he lights up the dry creamer."

"He still thinks he can do that?"

She nodded. "He still thinks he can do that."

"Huh. Well, keep me posted."

Returning to his desk, he resumed flipping through the files. Chuckled wryly, thinking about detective work, how it looks on television—all gunplay and car chases and gadgety stuff.

But here was the real deal. Reading a stack of papers and trying to figure out what somebody forgot to file.

He came upon notes about some stink down at Blake Media. The government looking into allegations that Warren Blake committed fraud by creating a dummy company and diverting funds from Blake Media into it.

Maybe the board meeting had something to do with this. Did Blake skip out to avoid the meeting? To avoid being fired to his face?

"Hey, Detective Pasch?"

Charlie looked up from the folder to see a uniformed officer he vaguely remembered. "Yeah."

"You like comics." The man handed Charlie a small, brown paper bag. "These worth anything?"

Charlie went through the selections, random comics from the early

'90s, nothing remarkable, nothing in great condition. A few #1 issues, but that was no guarantee of value. *Captain America* annual from '92. *Star Trek: Deep Space Nine* #1 (still bagged, poster inside) from '93. *Ghost Rider* '82. *Superman Adventures* annual '97. *Futurama* '03. *Fantastic Four* relaunch from '01.

Most comics from the last twenty-five years were so easy to find, anyone who wanted a #1 issue probably had one.

As Charlie flipped through them, he thought of the two main factors that affect collectibility—rarity and condition. None of these scored high in either column. Charlie didn't have the heart to be that blunt with the officer, so he promised to take them to the comics store, have a professional take a look. Pass the blame off on them.

Rather than wait until his usual stop on Wednesday, Charlie thought he could take the bag and swing by Randy's Comics after work. While he was at it, maybe pick up that big Craig Thompson book. Do his part to support the store and indie comics.

He still had a few hours on the clock. Tired of waiting for Griggs to show up, he decided to pay a visit to Blake Media.

⌂ ▭ ⑦   ⊠

BLOG

WHERE IS BLAKE #011
whereisblake.blogdroid.com

"When a true genius appears in the world, you may know him by this sign, that the dunces are all in confederacy against him."
—Jonathan Swift

We still have not gotten the latest issue of Blake Life out the door. It should have gone out last Friday.

But Queen Evel made the staff come in on a weekend—on a Sunday night, no less—and do our final read-through on the proofs. This is not, of course, the appropriate stage to make major structural changes.

Sure, there are emergencies. Every media person with any experience understands when something happens that is out of your control—something sudden, something unexpected, something last minute. Your interview with a major political figure becomes moot when he is caught in a scandal. Your health report touting some new treatment is contradicted when the expert turns out to be a fraud. Your fluff piece on a Hollywood star gets pushed aside by some important news development.

These are genuine emergencies.

Queen Evel's tirades are treated like emergencies, but they are not emergencies. They are tantrums. And Dennis the Jerk lets her do it.

You can't make such major changes that late in the process. No matter how big and important you may be, Ms. Blake, the laws of time and space are constant.

But Dennis the Jerk won't stand up to her. There also seems to be something else: a twinkle in his eyes when he steals a glance at her, when he thinks nobody is looking.

What's up with that?

– 34 –

The Right Reverend Doctor Fair Bishop Damascus Rhodes was at the front desk of Blake Media. In fresh if inexpensive clothes, courtesy of the old couple in the Winnebago. Maybe not a donation this time as much as extra cash lifted from an unattended purse.

Finding an audience with the queen was more difficult than he expected.

"Hello, ma'am," he began when he reached the receptionist at the front desk, "I am—"

She held up one finger for him to wait as she spoke to the air, to someone else, some invisible visitor. Only then did he notice the headset, a petite microphone delicately reaching from her lovely earlobe toward her red lips. He took note of her olive skin, her silky, reddish hair pulled up over her head.

Rev. Damascus mentally shook himself, looked away, ignoring her creamy voice. This was not the time to fall for the receptionist. Not when he was here to comfort the Widow Blake. He needed to focus.

He took note of the activity taking place across the lobby, men and women in white overalls carefully removing framed paintings from the walls along the curve of the front lobby. He was no art expert, but they seemed pretty fancy.

The workers were pulling them down from the inner wall, taking them across the room, and leaning them against the giant wall of glass, where bright light was streaming in. He wondered whether the sunlight was a problem for the paintings. Maybe that was why they were taking them down; some crazy rich-people ritual where they had their paintings rotated.

His eyes trailed past the workers toward the horizon. The front lobby curved around and out of sight. You literally could not see the end of the room from here.

The woman at the desk was still engrossed in her conversation with invisibles. So Rev. Damascus began to wander. Wanting to see where the curve led, watching the growing art collection along the base of the wall.

One smocked worker, a young lady with long, dark hair pulled back into a ponytail, caught Rev. Damascus staring at one of the framed works of art. She smiled.

Rev. Damascus smiled back and gave a light wave. "Taking them out for cleaning?"

"The Blakes want us to put all these in storage."

"And just leave the walls blank?"

"No." She sighed. "We have a whole new collection to put up."

Rev. Damascus nodded and walked on. As he stepped around the curve, he came to a door. A man in a gray security-guard uniform stood by, arms folded. The man saw Rev. Damascus but made no attempt to communicate.

Rev. Damascus gave him a casual salute and turned back toward the front desk. When he reached it, the woman with the headset was still talking to invisibles.

He checked his watch, another gift from the old couple in the Winnebago. Wondered how long it would be.

Looking back again at the desk, he saw a young man with short blond hair. In a suit, holding out a wallet in one hand.

A cop. Showing his badge. The woman at the desk was taking note of him, nodding.

Rev. Damascus decided this was a bad time. Turned and casually headed for the exit.

– 35 –

Detective Charlie Pasch navigating his way through the offices at Blake Media. His badge had gotten him past the reception desk downstairs. Scanning the room, he saw a frenzy of activity, cubicles and desks, a couple of young ladies. Decided to speak with them first. Self-consciously ran his fingers through his hair.

One of them was saying, "I can't believe this."

The other. "What?"

"This. Right here."

"With all that goes on around here, *this* is the thing you cannot believe?"

Charlie heard a phrase in his mind—*eyes have not seen, ears have not heard.*

"Apparently Queen Evel is now refusing an ad."

"What do you mean?"

"An ad. In the magazine."

"What magazine?"

"The magazine. At the printer."

"At the printer?" The first woman checked the date on her watch.

Charlie took the space to try and break in. "Excuse me, but—"

"The issue is supposed to be printed already."

"I know," the woman said. "But she decided this Bible ad did not fit in with the image she wanted to project for the magazine. Never mind that she joins some new religion every three issues and we have to write the whole issue around it."

"But this issue is supposed to be printed and out in the world. On pallets, on trucks, traveling across the country, to be placed in mail-boxes and on newsstands all over America."

"I know."

Charlie hung back, smiled awkwardly. Trying to be patient as the two worked out whatever this was. He could flash the badge and stop them in their tracks—it's what Griggs would have done if he were here doing his job—but Charlie did not want to spook them.

Because, as thorough as the files had been at the station, Detective Kurtz and Detective Carillo had suffered some tunnel vision, to be kind. Had only gotten cursory statements from employees of Blake Media, had been content with the company line, information filtered through management.

But Charlie wanted to see what the employees really thought. Somebody here likely had the truth, whether or not he or she even realized it. Held that key piece of information that would unlock the whole thing.

He knew he would end up with a box full of wild theories, gossip, hearsay. But if he got it all down in his notebook and back to the sta-tion, he only had to sift through it, remove everything that was not the truth, and the answer would be there.

"Can I help you?" The first woman looking at him now, annoyed. The other one had rushed off to accomplish something.

He tried to grin casually, imagined it looked as awkward as it felt. He fumbled with the badge in his suit pocket, pulled his wallet out, flipped it open. "Detective Charlie Pasch. Just came out to ask a few questions."

"Okay." She smiled uncertainly. Less annoyed, maybe. Her eyes seemed to sparkle.

Charlie replaced the badge in one pocket, pulled the notebook out of the other, flipped it open, fumbled a pen out of his shirt pocket, self-conscious, awkward, always awkward. "When was the last time you saw Warren Blake?"

"I don't r—"

"Oh. Wait." Charlie scribbling, intent. "Your name? Miss…?"

"Elsa. Elsa Benitez."

"Okay." Scribbling. Looking up. "So then…?"

"The last time I saw Mr. Blake?" She thought a second, eyes pointing up and left: She was remembering something. If her eyes had instead pointed up and right, that would have meant she was making something up. "I guess sometime in March."

"That long ago?"

"He doesn't come around the office much. The last time I saw him here was for a special staff meeting, to talk about the library."

"I see." Scribbling. Puzzled. "What library?"

"The one in August Heights. Mr. Blake is building it." She paused, smiled wryly. "It was in all the papers."

"So in his absence, how is the project going?"

"Hilariously enough, like gangbusters. Mrs. Blake really picked it up and championed it. Which is weird, because she used to act like it was a big hassle. But after Mr. Blake disappeared, she suddenly turned around and started to push it through, like they can't get it built fast enough."

She stopped and raised one eyebrow. "Does she know you're here?"

Charlie stopped writing. "Who are you talking about?"

"What are you, Columbo? *Evelyn Blake.* Does she know you are here?"

Something resembling a shriek erupted from the back of the offices. Charlie looked over, saw a force of nature headed his way. "WHO LET HIM IN HERE?"

Miss Benitez looked at him, gave him an awkward smile. "I guess that answers my question."

Suddenly the shrieking woman was in front of him. Everyone around the room nervously avoiding watching, stealing glances, rubbernecking. "YOU ARE NOT SUPPOSED TO BE UP HERE!"

Charlie tried to stand his ground. Fumbling again for his badge. "Hi," trying to be friendly, "I am Detective Charlie—"

"I don't care if you're *Gandhi,* you are not supposed to be up here. You should not have been allowed past the front desk."

Miss Benitez took pity on him. Threw him a lifeline. "Detective, this is Mrs. Evelyn Blake."

The force of nature turned and glared at Miss Benitez. "Don't give him any more information."

"It was only your name."

"You know what I mean."

Suddenly, Charlie noticed beefy security guards flanking Mrs. Blake.

He had every right to conduct his investigation, but had so completely lost control of the situation he decided to nod politely and bow out. Mrs. Blake had already thrown a fit with the mayor once. He didn't need her calling him back and dropping Charlie's name. "I apologize for making a scene," he said, hiding the irony in his voice.

Glancing around, he saw looks of pity. Faces that said, *Welcome to the club*. He smiled weakly, his face reddening, turned for the elevator.

Taking the elevator to the lobby, he kicked himself mentally the whole trip down. He hated being the center of a scene like that.

Hated it, hated it, hated it.

When the door opened, he made a beeline for the exit, did not want to make eye contact with anyone. Had no idea how fast word might travel in this building.

Heels clacked on the marble floor, approaching from behind. "Officer! Officer!"

He turned and saw a young woman, one he had not noticed upstairs. "Yes, ma'am?"

"I want to help you with your investigation."

"Um…all right."

"Look, I can't talk to you here. Do you know the Mexican restaurant down the block?"

"No."

"It's called Pedro's." She pointed out through the big windows. "It's down by the corner."

He looked out the window, nodded. "Sure." He looked at her again, taking in her eyes. Big brown eyes. "When?"

"After work? I think I can be there by seven."

Charlie looked away, pretended to think about it. Nodded and locked eyes again. "I can do that."

As she left him, he looked around the lobby one last time. Saw smocked workers moving framed paintings around. What was that about?

Heading for the Blake Media visitor lot, he checked his watch. He had just enough time to swing by the comic-book store.

He drove off, the sack of comics nestled comfortably on the passenger seat. Nearing the turnoff for the store, he thought again about Randy, laid up in the hospital, battered, threatened, too scared to talk.

He was fumbling with the radio when he saw telltale yellow tape stretched across the store entrance. He switched it off as he pulled into the empty parking lot. There was a big sign slapped on the door.

CLOSED BY ORDER OF THE COURT.

⌂ ▭ ⑦   ⊠

BLOG

WHERE IS BLAKE #012
whereisblake.blogdroid.com

"The beautiful thing about learning is that no one can take it away from you."
—B.B. King

There was a detective in the office today. Well, not for long—Queen Evel threw him out.

It was probably just as well. Anytime Her Dark Majesty is around the offices, there's just this cloud of oppression and depression that hangs there. You don't dare cooperate with the police or you're out. And in today's market, jobs with medical benefits are hard to come by.

But as the detective hit the elevator, I took to the stairs, taking them as fast as heels would allow. I made it to the lobby before he was gone, scheduled a meeting. A chance to do my civic duty.

But he was a no-show. And I did not have the nerve to call the police and try to find him.

Too bad he didn't show up.

Because I think I have something to tell him.

- 36 -

Griffin, chief forensics pathologist, came in on metal crutches, bringing Detective Tom Griggs news. "I found a connection between the shooting at Zoo Girls and the incident at the parking garage last week."

" 'Incident.' That's an interesting way to label a massacre. You forensics guys always—"

"Do you want this or not?" Griffin looked around the office nervously. "I don't want Utley to see me talking to you. He would make a stink."

Utley. "So what? I have a right to this information, too."

"It's just easier to avoid the stink."

Griggs sighed. "Okay, what are you trying to share?"

"One of the victims at the club can also be placed at the parking garage. At the, um, 'massacre.' "

"Who, Potts?"

"No, the other one."

Griggs folded his arms. "Really…"

"In the elevator, we found some blood, not much, maybe from a scratch. Fresh enough to take a sample. We had it on file when the other case came through the meat lockers."

"So who is the guy?"

"We haven't made an ID yet. It would make the looking easier if we could get into some of the national files. So if you happen to run into any, say, *federal agents…*" Everything but the wink.

"You can't access the databases yourself?"

"Since this Blake thing turned into a horse race, red tape has gotten worse all around." Griffin was clearly perturbed. "The paperwork is more complicated than I remembered."

"Wow, Evelyn Blake is making life tough for everybody."

"Yup."

"So you may or may not find the guy in the files—weren't there witnesses at the club?"

Griffin shook his head. "Several came in after the fact, said they heard shots and saw a third person standing over these two, holding a gun." He adjusted his weight on the crutches. "They were pretty tight-lipped about what they saw." He smiled knowingly. "It is, after all, a mob bar."

"This third guy...payback for the ambush at the garage? One of the Russians?"

"Both vics appear to have been shot with the same gun. But here is the intriguing thing: The mystery man who left the blood in the elevator also has powder burns on his hands."

"He fired a weapon?"

"He fired a weapon. But no extra gun was recovered at the scene. All the ricochets picked out of the walls seem to have come from the one gun."

"Maybe someone grabbed another gun before the uniforms showed up." Griggs looking at the photos of the two dead men, one of them the mystery man with the blood in the elevator.

"I need to run, Griggs. But, like I said, if you should happen to run into agents of federal law enforcement...?" This time even the wink.

"Sure." Griggs staring at the two pictures.

Three men were at the scene. Something told Griggs they'd better find that third man before the mob did.

⌂ ▭ ⑦   ⊠

BLOG

WHERE IS BLAKE #013
whereisblake.blogdroid.com

"Great minds have always encountered violent opposition from mediocre minds."

—Albert Einstein

I thought I would have had more closure by now. It was a long, long road from home to here, ever since Dad—ever since *Joe*—sent my whole world into a tailspin.

It took a lot of years to get here, a lot of miles to get where I am. To get inside the Blake Empire.

One month ago—maybe two weeks before Warren Blake was reported missing, in fact—I finally had my chance to speak with Mr. Blake, to speak with him privately. To share with him my secret.

You know, coincidence is a funny thing. There is clearly a force beyond our comprehension that binds us all together. That connects total strangers together in ways that would surprise even Kevin Bacon.

I finally get a moment alone with the point of my journey, the very object of my mission, and he takes it badly.

Warren Blake is my father. But when this happy news is brought to his attention, what does he do? Laugh? Smile? Cry with joy and wonder?

No. He turns on a personality dime, becomes angry, suspicious.

If there is any doubt about my claim, I am willing to submit to any test, any investigation into my genetic heritage.

Warren Blake is my father. He took the news badly.

I am not certain what I expected. I spent so much of my recent life to get here that I didn't think much of the results.

Whatever mental energy I spent "imagining" was spent wondering how Dad—excuse me, wondering how *Joe*—has been doing. I have barely spoken with him since I left home.

I sent a couple of cards at first. Birthdays, Christmas, that sort of thing. But it sort of trailed off.

I think I started to shut down the part of me that *feels*. And in the process, I disconnected myself from the past and future. A person with no past can't be followed. A person with no future can't be broken.

Eventually, my past life became this distant image, like trying to see from the bottom of the swimming pool. And my future became an eternally unexpected surprise. My journalism training came in handy.

I used to think the most honest reporting came when you entered the process with no specific expectations. You start with the lead, you dig through the evidence, you let the facts tell the story.

I don't actually believe that anymore, by the way. But my quest to connect with my estranged biological father—who, apparently, did not know I existed—must have somehow tapped that vein. Because when I hear myself say "I'm not certain what I expected," it sounds hard to believe to me too.

But I was just looking for my moment of truth. And he left.

Not that I should be surprised.

Everybody leaves.

~ 37 ~

"And he stood you up?" Elsa Benitez stirred her coffee. Set the cup down on a Pedro's coaster.

Dakota Flynn slurped from a straw. "I guess so. Maybe there was some police emergency." Grabbed a chip and scooped salsa.

"Wouldn't it have turned up on the news or something?"

"What, some headline that says, POLICE EMERGENCY BREAKS OUT, CUTE DETECTIVE MISSES DINNER WITH GORGEOUS EDITOR?"

Elsa chuckled. "That might be overstating it a bit, don't you think?"

"What, the 'cute detective' bit?"

"No, the 'gorgeous editor.'"

"*Gracias.*"

"I'll grant you 'attractive editor.'"

"*Muchas gracias.*"

Elsa sipped from her coffee, set it back down on the coaster. "Why did you want to talk to him? Cruella D'Evelyn won't like that."

Dakota grinned. "Maybe I think he is cute."

"We covered that. But there must be something more to it than that."

"I can be as shallow as I want to be." Dakota slurped from her straw again. "So what happened with that ad?"

"What ad?"

"The Bible ad. What's up with that?"

"The ad department sold it, fair and square. Sent us their film, we got it to blueline, and somehow Cruella D'Evelyn gets hold of it—"

"Somebody *showed* it to her?"

"I don't know how she got hold of it. All I know is she was flipping through the bluelines and she got to this ad for this Bible and freaked out."

"Freaked out about what? Freedom of speech?"

"Apparently. She started shrieking that it was against 'policy.'"

"*Policy?* What policy? There's no policy."

"I know there's no policy, but she tells the advertising director to call and tell the advertiser we have a policy and to cancel the ad."

"After it's already in blueline?"

"Yep."

Dakota finished her soda, looked around to see where the waiter might be. "So what did the printer say?"

"They have other magazines waiting in line, so they had to put us aside until we had our act together."

"So how far behind does that put us?"

"Another two weeks."

"Arrgh."

"I know."

"*Policy.* She sees someone at a Hollywood party wearing a Kabbalah bracelet and suddenly we have to cancel whatever we're working on and dedicate an entire issue to Kabbalah."

"And alienate a third of our subscribers, who just want to read a nice magazine with human-interest stories and some recipes."

"Then she yells at the circulation department because the numbers are dropping. She has no idea how brilliant they are to build a brand-new subscriber base from scratch every time she does this."

"Remember that week when she thought she was vegetarian?"

"Yeah, the circ department loved that. Especially when they sent out that direct-mail piece and the next week D'Evelyn finally figures out vegetarians can't eat steak."

"*Policy*. The only policy here is that she is the queen, lording it over her serfs. It's like she does this stuff to us for the thrill of it—to prove she can!" Dakota posed, fists on her hips, and said in a dramatic and unnaturally deep and musical voice, "Ho! Ho! Ho!"

"What is that? Santa?"

"No—it's the Jolly Green Giant." Flynn felt her face redden. "You know, 'Ho! Ho! Ho!' Giant green guy stepping on all the helpless villagers, kicking over their horse carts."

"I don't think the Jolly Green Giant would do that."

"I was making a point."

"And defaming, like, a national treasure."

Their co-worker Aubrey Burke showed up at the table. "Hey, you guys—Dennis the Jerk is looking all over for you two to proofread the new pages."

Dakota slurped the remainder of her soda. "Yeah, I knew this oasis wasn't going to last." She grabbed the check and got out of her chair. "Well, let's go."

The chair vacated, Aubrey took it, then grabbed Dakota's glass and sampled the beverage. Dug out a handful of chips and shoved them in her mouth. Chomping, she said, "You go ahead. Tell Dennis the Jerk I'm in the ladies' room. That should buy me another ten minutes."

Dakota shook her head and headed for the cash register. "Well, back to the bloodbath."

– 38 –

Professional thug Nelson Pistek, at the end of his rope. Wandering, lost in thought, finally ending up at the trailer park, at the home of his sister, her husband, and their daughter. The door opened, and Pistek was face-to-face with his brother-in-law. "Hi, Jesse."

The man nodded. "Nelson."

It was awkward. Jesse Hart was a man who worked with his hands, something Pistek never quite knew how to discuss. They stood, staring at each other through the doorway, each waiting for something. Pistek waiting for Jesse to invite him in. Jesse apparently waiting for him to ask.

Trying to make Pistek ask.

Trying to force Pistek to ask.

Well, Pistek was not going to ask. It should have been obvious to even the lowest common denominator that a man does not show up on the doorstep of his sister and brother-in-law and niece for the express purpose of getting into a staring contest with his dirt-under-his-fingernails brother-in-law.

As the rain fell in the darkness outside the canopy, Pistek's mind flashed on the dark world out there. The back room of the club. Blood on the concrete. His own fingerprints on the murder weapon. A witness with the wrong idea.

The mob, no doubt, looking to gun him down in the street. The cops, no doubt, anxious to lock him up forever. Running out of options, he blinked first. "Jesse, I need your help."

His brother-in-law looked him up and down uncertainly. In the harsh porch light, he must have looked a mess. He certainly smelled.

Finally, Jesse rolled his eyes. Held the storm door out for him. Walked away.

Pistek entered, glancing nervously at the dark street. Trying to see if the night was watching.

He would not feel safe for a long time.

Inside, his sister, Darva, offered him instant tea—Jesse would not allow alcohol in his home. "You need to go to the police with this," she said over a cup of wildberry.

Pistek whimpered into his hands. "I can't. I can't."

Suddenly, there was a noise in the hall, and the three grown-ups turned to see little Janice. Darva left her chair and went to the little girl, done up in her jammies. "You need to go to bed, honey."

As little Janice left for her room, Pistek was amazed how big she had gotten. Wondered if she even remembered her uncle.

Jesse grunted, shifted in his lounge chair. "I don't understand why you got involved with the criminal element in the first place."

Pistek raised his head. Probably looked like a madman, but it was a mad, mad world. "I. Did. Not. Get. *Involved.*"

Jesse leaned forward, elbows on knees, and gave an indignant look. A man with stubble on his face and oil under his fingernails. "Then what do you call it?"

"What do you...?" Pistek stopped and looked over at Darva, but she averted her eyes. He looked back at Jesse, put on a serious face, his most serious face. "I was following a lead on a job and—"

"No!" Jesse rocketed to his feet. "You were at a bar, hanging out with these Mafia. And your friends got rough."

Jesse looked over at Darva, who was nervously bouncing her gaze back and forth between her husband and her brother. He poked a thumb in Pistek's direction. "I don't think he should be here."

Pistek was so rattled, his head so full of images of what had happened, of what could happen, that he was fresh out of words. He watched Jesse storm out the living room and down the hall. Darva, on the verge of tears, raced after him.

Through interlocked fingers he saw shadows in the hall, heard hushed voices both pleading their side of the case. Saw Jesse's posture soften. Heard a loud sigh. Jesse's silhouette leaned and kissed Darva's on the forehead.

The two came back into the living room, and Jesse offered Pistek his hand. "You can stay." Gripped his hand tightly. "For now."

Jesse turned back to glance at a grateful Darva, then looked square at Pistek and pointed. "Tomorrow, you go to the police."

Pistek clasped his hands again, looked down, nodded vigorously. Fought a frog in his throat, may or may not have succeeded in uttering a gruff thanks.

Jesse left the room again. Darva got some sheets so Pistek could stretch out on the couch for the night. She apologized for the lack of an extra pillow. He grabbed her wrist at one point, made a more concerted effort to say thanks. She left him for the night, offering directions to the kitchen and the bathroom.

He took the throw pillows from around the room, bunched them up together at the head of the couch, finally got comfortable.

Heard the car.

Bolted upright, hand jerking open the blinds at the picture window. Nothing. Nothing.

He leaned back down on the stack of throw pillows, tried again to find the posture combination that was most comfortable.

No, he would not feel safe for a long time.

⌂ ◻ ⑦   ⊠

BLOG

WHERE IS BLAKE #014
whereisblake.blogdroid.com

"Learning without thought is labor lost; thought without learning is perilous."
—Confucius

It has become increasingly clear to any observer that Evelyn Blake does not miss her husband. I wonder what their last conversation was like.

Did they part on good terms? Did they fight? Did they get along?

That last night, did they have a fight? Did they have a night of married passion?

Does she know where he went? Did she send him there? Did she drive him there?

Did he mention the appearance of a long-lost child? Did she take the news even worse than he did? Did Her Highness, Queen Evel, feel like her empire was threatened?

Did he mention to her it was one of her own employees? (I hope he did not mention me by name.)

Queen Evel does not strike me as mom material.

I have a pleasant memory of my mother from when I was young. My mom and dad—I'm sorry, my mom and Joe—took me to some farm to get a puppy. I was five or six maybe, so the memory is all distorted. But there were lots of puppies.

I remember this little bundle of fur and spunk, floppy ears, brown-and-black coat. Claws. I remember claws. Poor fella had no idea of the ferocious power in those claws.

He smelled, too, of puppy breath and puppy sweat and grass and fresh air.

In the car, my parents put the little guy in a cardboard box on the floor by my mom's feet. I remember stretching up to see between the car seats, straining to see the newest member of the family.

My parents asked what I wanted to call him. Naturally, I said, "Lassie." He was the only dog I remembered seeing on TV.

They didn't think that was a good name for a beagle. Eventually, somebody in the car—I don't remember who, it may have even been me—suggested "Poncho." I thought I was naming him after a fun kind of coat, but apparently it was also the name of the Cisco Kid's sidekick. So that made my dad happy. *Joe*—it made Joe happy.

I remember this one sweet, brilliant moment: my mom turning to look at me, brushing my hair back. Smiling.

That was a great moment. I felt loved.

I like that memory.

– 39 –

By the next morning, Detective Charlie Pasch, officer of the law and comics fan, had ascertained two things: 1) Randy Olson, owner of Randy's Comics Empire, had been released from the hospital, was now home, and would not take visitors; 2) employee Jeevan Kapoor was sitting in a jail cell, arrested for selling adult materials to a minor.

This did not sound right. Charlie had seen for himself how diligently Jeevan kept children out of the back section.

Discreetly getting a copy of the arrest report, Charlie found the official story. An undercover vice cop went into Randy's Comics Empire on Monday. Entered, as an adult, into the curtained "adult section" of the store. Purchased, as an adult, one comic book, entitled *Angel McCoy*, labeled "For Mature Readers" due to graphic violence and sexual themes. Arrested a store employee, one Jeevan Kapoor, no priors, for selling adult materials to a minor.

Charlie couldn't believe what he was reading. He had read *Angel McCoy*. A little rough for his personal taste, but certainly not pornographic.

The arrest report did not even pretend to include evidence to support the charge. It was entirely based on the lie that "comics" was an art form exclusively for children. Therefore, the loopy logic ran, their very existence somehow proved that the store was selling mature titles to kids.

Charlie returned to Griggs's office. He found the older detective eating a portable breakfast, poring over an assortment of mobster photos.

"Vice made a bust a couple of days ago," Charlie said, stammering. "I think there's something fishy to it."

"Why would you say that?"

"They arrested a guy at a comic-book store for selling adult materials—"

"Wait right there." Griggs put the breakfast bar down, pushed aside the photos to keep them from getting messy. "If this is somehow geek-related, then you are already way too close to this."

Charlie fought the urge to sulk. "I could work this on my own time."

His partner sighed a good-natured sigh, leaned back in the wooden chair. It creaked with authority. "When I was a kid, I worked as a stock boy." Locked fingers behind his head, elbows out. "You know what my boss would always say?"

"What?"

"If you have time to lean, you have time to clean."

"And what does that mean?"

"If the chief finds you're devoting time to yet one more case, he'll say that means you have more time for the cases you already have." Griggs smiled. "I know cartoons are important to you—but you have to understand they are not important to everyone else."

Charlie sighed dramatically. "Not cartoons, comic books."

"Whatever. Comic strips." Griggs grunted, rubbed his eyes. "Why can't we ever talk about normal 'guy' things, like the Kansas City Chiefs or cars or something?"

That again. Charlie generally did a better job of not acting annoyed. But this was important. "This is about a man arrested for something that is not a crime. This is about a man arrested because of the lie that 'comic books are for kids.'"

"We're going to have to circle back around to 'I don't care.'" Griggs stopped. Smiled sympathetically. "C'mon, Charlie, this is simple. A guy was selling a comic to some kid—"

"Why would you assume that?"

"Assume what?"

"You said he was 'selling to some kid.'"

"Comics are for kids. No offense."

Fighting the urge to pace, Charlie sat on the edge of the desk, awkwardly, but he was in the middle of it now. "Comic books achieved their widest circulation during World War II, when troops overseas looked forward to packages with cigarettes and copies of *Superman*." He stood. "Detective Griggs, the comic book is just another art form. A vehicle for narrative."

"Your words are starting to get big again."

Charlie nodded a couple of seconds, thinking. Then his eyes went wide. "When you were a kid, did you watch TV?"

"Sure."

"Does that mean 'TV is for kids'?"

"Of course."

"No, I mean, that TV is *just* for kids, and *nobody else?*"

"Oh. Then, no. I'm not an idiot."

"So we're not going to arrest the guys at NBC or the cable company for giving a grown man the right to watch material targeted for his age group?"

"Of course not." Griggs shrugged. "That would be crazy." Then he caught on, pointed cautiously at Charlie. "You can't mean the guy buying the comic was a grown-up?"

Yahtzee.

"Surely they had some kind of evidence—"

"Nope. In five years, there has only been one complaint." Charlie flipped open his file. "And that was two years ago. Some woman dismissed as a crank." He looked up. "A few days ago, the owner refuses to sell to Eddie Drake—and Vice suddenly decides to follow up on a two-year-old complaint?"

Griggs was silent now, elbows on desk. Finally he looked up. "Okay, Charlie, maybe you have something."

— 40 —

The Right Fair General Doctor Bishop Reverend Damascus Rhodes, sitting in a small park situated across from Blake Media. Stymied. Hanging around, wondering how to get past the moat of employees and security.

The queen locked up safe in her high tower, unapproachable by the masses. No doubt grieving the loss of her husband. Vulnerable. Lonely. Seeking spiritual direction.

Queen Evelyn Blake was protected, but cast adrift spiritually in a broken world without a—

"Judge Gideon?"

He turned toward the voice, using one hand to shield his eyes from the sun. "Um, yes?"

A young lady approaching. "You're Judge Gideon Judge, aren't you?"

Calling him by an alias from his past. As small as the world had gotten, it was surprising this sort of thing had never come up before.

He imagined Andrea's voice again. *It's your past come to haunt you.*

He regarded the smiling woman, a young lady in her twenties with dark red hair. He still had to shield his eyes. "Hello, child." Friendly, vague. In case he was supposed to know her. *Judge Gideon Judge. Judge Gideon Judge.* Where had he used that one? "How are you this fine day?" Hoping she would say something that would give him more context.

She beamed at him. "You know, my mother still cherishes that vase she got from you."

No help.

He smiled. "It makes my heart glad to hear that, child." Keep the answers simple. Hope she goes away.

No such luck. She sat down next to him on the bench. "What brings you here?"

He was not comfortable sharing his message at hand, even with a good spin. He had no idea who this stranger was; any shred of truth could backfire. He licked his top lip. "I am following the Lord's leading. He led me...to this new place."

Her eyes lit up. "Like Philip and the Ethiopian eunuch?"

Sure. Whatever. "Yes, child. We are often led in the spirit of things to a new place, for a work we have not yet discovered."

"That's awesome." She adjusted her purse on her shoulder. Grinning now.

He grinned back. "So...what brings you here...to this place?" Let her interpret "here" however she wanted. Maybe it would finally give him a clue where she was from.

Might she be some sort of cop or agent or detective, someone who had not just stumbled onto this bench, but someone actually trying to trap him into a confession?

With that hair. With those lips. With that curve of her chin.

"After college, I didn't want to hang around Webster Groves, so I came out here to Kansas City to get a job."

Webster Groves. Wait a second—that's near St. Louis.

"So while you're here, I guess your television show is in reruns or something?"

Bingo.

Rattled now, playing it cool. "That season of life is over now. The Lord said it was time for me to move on."

She looked astonished. Spoke in a hushed tone. "Wow, if God told me to stop being a TV star, I don't know that I would be willing to give that up."

He smiled, kept his next thought to himself. That he had not had much choice in the matter. Evil Duke Cumbee's men had seen to that.

"...So, anyway," she was saying—she must have been talking this whole time, "I ended up in Kansas City. I work at Blake Media."

"Really?" He continued nodding, had been nodding even during the part where he'd been pretending to listen. "How interesting."

"In fact, I work for Evelyn Blake."

Really. How very interesting. "Tell me more about your job."

– 41 –

Detective Charlie Pasch at the August Heights Library, a construction project still in progress. A few minutes before the press conference at three PM, when things would start hopping. Assorted citizenry milling about, clustered, huddled, chatting. Some, no doubt, members of the press, while others were, no doubt, local royalty, so to speak.

The library was not quite finished, not quite ready to open to the public. But Evelyn Blake was still pushing the contractors ahead, snapping the whip, full steam ahead, to mix some metaphors. Charlie was still kicking himself for missing his meeting with the woman who worked at Blake Media. He had gotten so worked up over the comic-book store closing that he had forgotten about the meeting until much too late.

He was too embarrassed to try to get in touch with her again. He didn't know the young woman's name, was afraid to call the front desk and try to ask for her, unsure how to explain himself.

He was hoping to run into her again. Maybe if he acted just casual enough, he could try and charm her, flash his smile and his "little boy lost" look, which seemed to work. His days with that routine were numbered; soon it would pass from cute to just sad.

Hopefully, today it was still cute.

"Ladies and gentlemen of Kansas City and members of the press: We wish to thank you for coming out today." A man at the front of the crowd, raising his voice. Most of the crowd chatter began to die down. Not quickly enough. It annoyed Charlie when audiences ignored the people speaking up front. I mean, if you didn't want to pay attention, you could have gone anywhere for that. You didn't have to come here.

"And now, I would like to present the lady of the hour"—dramatic pause, a wave of his arm toward the small group standing behind him—"Evelyn Blake!"

A smattering of applause, growing as the members of the crowd caught on. Eyes turning front to the woman herself, Evelyn Blake, as she appeared stage left and came before the crowd. A camera crew following her, cataloging her every move.

"I want to thank you all for coming out today," she said, putting on a smile. It looked a little practiced, but that was to be expected, given the circumstances. The weather was not great for holding an event outside an unopened library: gloomy, wind blasting at irregular intervals. It felt like the skies would crack open any second with a deluge to scare Noah. "If the children would come forward, please."

Charlie craned his neck, trying to see who she was motioning to the front. A group of kids, young, maybe first- or second-graders, came up from the side and were instructed by a lady with glasses and bun hair to sit in a semicircle around a metal folding chair. Mrs. Blake picked up something off the chair—what looked like an oversize picture book—and sat.

With everyone sitting, it was hard to see. What was this all about? Who had put this event together?

Charlie could not hear well, the members of the crowd murmuring among themselves again. He strained to hear what Mrs. Blake was saying to the kids. They weren't paying attention, either. Another blast of wind pulled the book out of Mrs. Blake's hands. She enlarged the forced grin, made panicked eyes to one of her assistants, who ran and grabbed the book, returned it to her.

Charlie tried to listen as she tried to read to the kids, who were sitting in the grass, fidgeting but not listening. He could hardly hear, barely see what she was doing. His attention wandered, looking for the young lady from before, the one who had been willing to talk. He did not see her, but he did see some of the others from his disastrous visit to Blake Media. He recognized the two women from the other day, including Miss Benitez. There was a man with them who looked familiar. For some reason, Charlie thought the man reminded him of a televangelist, but he couldn't place who.

— 42 —

The Right Reverend Fair Bishop General—

No!

The *former* Bishop Right Fair Good Doctor Reverend Damascus Rhodes was at the August Heights library-in-progress.

Judge Gideon Judge, he told himself. *Your name is Judge Gideon Judge.* Again.

So far, the event at the library had been a disaster of near-biblical proportions. It could not have gone worse if Evelyn Blake had turned to a pillar of salt right in front of the assembled media, a feat Judge Gideon Judge always attributed to Noah's wife, if only because he assumed it was supposed to explain why oceans were salty or something.

Not that he had paid much attention to the failed media event. While the Widow Blake was courageously struggling to read to the children sitting around her in the grass, his mind was focused on his current predicament. Gauging the risk of reusing an old alias, particularly one that had gotten so much play in the media.

It would only take one person to dig up his past. And not necessarily through any complicated detective work, either. With an alias as distinctive as "Judge Gideon Judge," it would only take one Internet search to do him in. With a name like that, he would pop up at the top of the search results. Bring all that bad karma crashing down around his ears.

All these years, he had followed the philosophy of creating the most outrageous names possible. Over the top. He had found the outrageous names were like a lightning rod for the gullible; they also did a superb job of pushing away those with whom he should not waste his time.

But the alias only worked if you shucked it at the end of the job, shed it like a snake's skin, never to be used again.

In his wide travels, he had never expected this: to be recognized, locked into an old name—but by someone he needed. Nine times out of ten, if a stranger in a crowd played a round of, "Hey, aren't you...?" the conversation always ended with Judge Gideon Judge—by any name—making an exit and going far away.

But this. Here. Now. His best chance of finally connecting with Queen Evelyn Blake in her high castle was through happenstance. Meeting one of her insiders, one of her employees, who just happened to know him as "Judge Gideon Judge."

And just a few hours' drive from St. Louis, from Evil Duke Cumbee. Wearing an old alias that Cumbee would remember.

God is not mocked, Andrea told him. *Whatsoever you sow, that shall you also reap.*

If he believed in anything, he would have taken it as a sign he should abandon his current course and go far away.

But this was the plan. Become a confidant of the queen. Get within arm's reach again of the good life. He could taste it.

This was the plan.

After the event, Miss Benitez took Judge Gideon Judge up front to meet Evelyn Blake. She seemed excited, star-struck at being able to introduce her boss to a person who was something of a local celebrity from back home. If he hadn't been so nervous, he would have thought it was sweet.

Although Miss Benitez had gotten him into the Blake Media building after their meeting in the park, they had missed the queen there. But here she was now, and Miss Benitez apparently did not want to miss the opportunity.

Nor did (cough) Judge Gideon Judge.

He stuck a hand in his jacket pocket, feeling for the fresh set of prints of the photos of brown-faced children. He pulled them out, checked the name on the banner in the pictures.

He mentally worked himself up, worked up his shtick. This was his chance to finagle his way into the graces of Evelyn Blake, the queen.

His ticket.

He did not want to blow this.

As Miss Benitez led him through the crowd around the queen, he heard a commotion. Evelyn Blake distressed about something.

"I WANT TO KNOW WHO PUT THIS TOGETHER," she was shrieking. Her voice carried over the wind like you wouldn't believe. She was sweeping her hand toward the camera crew behind her. "I DO NOT NEED THIS KIND OF THING HAPPENING ON TELEVISION."

Miss Benitez pulled at Judge Gideon Judge's elbow, pulled him closer to the front.

The queen continued her tirade. "I DON'T KNOW WHO INVITED THESE CHILDREN."

He was within a few steps of her now.

The queen shrieked, "THE NEXT PERSON WHO EVEN MENTIONS CHILDREN TO ME IS FIRED."

Uh-oh.

~ 43 ~

Call the cops. That is what he had promised. Intermittent thug Nelson Pistek, staying with his sister and brother-in-law and niece, had promised to call the cops. The price of rent, of staying at his sister's trailer home.

All told, it was probably the wisest course of action. At least, that's what he told himself all morning. As he washed his face. Tried to clean up. Tried to shave with a borrowed razor.

He went to the kitchen, where he found his sister, Darva, and his niece, Janice. As Darva began to make breakfast—he decided on the blueberry filling with the glittery frosting—he got a chance to catch up with Janice. When the little girl came to the small circular table—how old was she, four? five?—he greeted her with a dopey grin. "Do you remember your Uncle Nelson?"

She hid half her face behind long blonde strands. Smiling sheepishly, somehow shrugging and nodding at the same time.

He wasn't sure how to follow such a noncommittal gesture. He tried again. "I'm your Uncle Nelson." Tried to give it a little lilt, pretending he was actually somehow clarifying his earlier question. "I'm Darva's—" Started over. "I'm your momma's brother."

The girl just kept staring at him. Her mother, coming in from the next room, went to the counter and poured juice into a glass. "Don't stare at your uncle, sweetheart." She set the juice and a plate of Pop Tarts in front of the little girl. "Eat your breakfast."

Janice folded delicate hands over her breakfast, closed her eyes, and moved her lips silently. It took Pistek a second to figure out what she must be doing: praying. Sweet.

Following the ritual, she opened her eyes with a satisfied nod and reached for her breakfast, taking a bite. Judging from the stain at the corner of her mouth as she chewed carefully, hers had some sort of red filling.

He tried connecting again. "How old are you?"

Still chewing, she breathed impatiently through her nose, set the toaster pastry down, and held up her hands, exhibiting two fingers and two fingers.

He raised his eyebrows playfully. "So you're four now?"

She nodded. Grinned, showing Pop Tart in her teeth.

So young. So innocent. So many years before she would be old enough to get into a jam like her Uncle Nelson.

Darva poured him black coffee into a cup with some kind of smudge on it. "So, you driving out to see the police, I guess?"

"Yeah." He dipped his Pop Tart into his coffee and took a bite, chewed thoughtfully, nodded. Who would he talk to? He could not very well walk in off the street and talk to anyone in a uniform. Who knew where that could lead?

He strained to think of a cop. One he knew. And was on speaking terms with. Who wasn't on the mob payroll.

He wasn't anxious to go see the cops. For that matter, wasn't anxious to be out in the open, where he might bump into some mob soldier. Who knew what the word was on the street? Were they kicking up stones looking for him? Was there a price on his head?

Stalling for time, Pistek went into the living room, plopped in the easy chair, thumbed the remote. After flipping through a few channels, he grumbled, "There's something wrong with this connection."

He went across the room, knelt down, and pulled the entertainment center from the wall. "Well, here's the problem," he said, yanking some of the wires and reinserting them according to their color code.

— 44 —

Detective Charlie Pasch visited the comic-book employee, Jeevan Kapoor, at his home. He argued with himself in the hall of the apartment building, repeated Griggs's warning to himself, was still debating his actions even as he reached the man's door.

Then he knocked and the debate was over. Jeevan kept the door mostly closed, just cracked it open as far as the chain would allow. "What do you want?"

"Hi, Jeevan, it's Charlie Pasch." Not sure how to play this. "I buy comics from you." Nothing. "I just wanted to see how you were doing."

"Okay. I guess." Jeevan looked past him into the hall. Made eye contact again. "How do you know where I live?"

"Oh—it was in the police report."

"What, are those public now?"

Charlie hesitated, coughing into his fist. "No." Wasn't sure how to break this, finally just came out and said, "I'm a cop."

He reached for his wallet, flashed his badge. "See?"

Jeevan's eyes narrowed, dead. "Oh." Pause. "Haven't you guys done enough?"

"I'm here to help." He pocketed the badge, held out empty hands. "May I speak with you?"

Jeevan hesitated, closed the door. There was the sound of the chain, then the door opened again, wider. Jeevan not saying a word, just waving Charlie in.

Charlie, nervous, made small talk at the kitchen table. "Hear about that guy at the store the other day?" He tried to look nonchalant. "Jawing about 'When was the Golden Age for comic books?'"

His host leaned one elbow on the table. Smiled polite. "Why, what'd he say?"

"He claimed it started with The Yellow Kid. Can you imagine that?"

Jeevan dropped the smile and nodded, thoughtful. "I don't know what that is."

"You work in a comic-book store and don't know the history?"

"I just know what I like." Jeevan went to the cabinet, pulled out a couple of drinking glasses. "Water?" Charlie nodded, and Jeevan filled both glasses from a pitcher in the fridge. "So he was the first comic strip?" He set the frosted glass in front of Charlie.

"No, but he was a major star. He was so popular that Joseph Pulitzer and William Randolph Hearst fought over him." Charlie took a drink. "Apparently, his presence in Hearst's papers is why their questionable tactics came to be called 'yellow journalism.'"

"Huh." Jeevan sipped his water, set it down. "You have a lot of stuff in your head, don't you?"

Charlie felt his cheeks redden. "I read a lot as a kid. It gave me a sense of empowerment."

"I see." His host shrugged. "So when do *you* say the Golden Age was?"

Charlie tried not to snort. "The late '30s—"

"I don't know." Jeevan took another sip.

Charlie stopped breathing. "What? But—"

"Naw," Jeevan smiled. He leaned forward, a twinkle in his eye. "I think the Golden Age for comics is ten."

"What do you mean?"

"You know, whatever you connect with as a ten-year-old, that's your personal 'golden age.' It's the benchmark you carry in your head for the rest of your life."

Charlie didn't know how to answer that. Changed the subject. "You want to tell me what happened the other night?"

The sudden shift caught Jeevan off guard "Oh." Dead eyes again.

Charlie tried to encourage him. "It would really help me to hear your side of it."

Jeevan sighed, sat back in the chair. "There's not much to tell." He started sliding his glass in a little circular pattern, pushing around condensation on the plastic tablecloth. "I was minding my own business. Next thing I know, I'm handcuffed and hauled off to jail."

"I know it must be painful to think about, but—"

"Do you? Do you know what it's like to be handcuffed in front of your customers and shoved out the door in front of your neighbors?

Shoved in the back of a car like some robber or murderer?" Jeevan stared at his glass a second, stopping his circular pattern. "I came to this country to get away from that kind of thing."

"Please, Jeevan, let me help."

The other man stared off into some private space for a long moment. Eyes closed, he breathed through his nose several times. Finally, he relaxed his posture. Turned to Charlie with kinder eyes. "What do you need, Officer?"

"Call me Charlie. I need you to walk me through what happened. Step by step."

"I already had to do this down at the—"

"I know, Jeevan." Charlie kept saying his name, a way to control the course of the conversation, a way to keep his interview subject focused. "But—please."

Jeevan sighed again, more relaxed this time. "I was working alone in the store. I was behind the counter."

"What were you doing?"

"I was updating our inventory records in the computer."

"Okay. Then what happened?"

"This...man came in. The cop."

"Did he identify himself as such when he came in?"

"No." Jeevan shrugged. "He looked like a regular guy."

"What did he look like?"

"Tall, I guess, football-player shoulders. Had this tan jacket. Big red moustache."

"What did he do when he came into the store?"

"Sort of wandered around, I guess. Like he was browsing."

"Did he seem suspicious to you?"

"I was working on the inventory. So I just said hi, and he went on browsing, and I went back to the computer."

"That's all you said to him?"

"Well, a few minutes later he came up and asked me where the porn was."

"And you said...?"

"I told him we didn't have any. Randy doesn't carry that stuff. So he asked if we had any adult stuff—that's what he called it, 'adult stuff'—and I told him we kept the restricted stuff in the back, so kids couldn't get to it."

"You told him that?"

"Yeah."

"That kids couldn't get to it?"

"Yeah."

"Then what?"

"I don't know, he went back there for a while. Then he came back out, and he bought a comic. And he arrested me."

"Arrested you for selling a comic?"

"Yeah."

Unbelievable. "What was the comic?" Charlie knew the answer from the police report, but wanted to help Jeevan focus on the moment.

The other furrowed his brow, closed his eyes. He opened them again. "I think it was *Angel McCoy*."

Charlie reached for his glass of water, took a sip, sat back in the chair. He realized he had been subconsciously moving closer and closer to Jeevan during the recounting, infringing more and more on his personal space.

Relax, Charlie, relax.

He smiled. Playing it cool. Everything is cool. "Okay, so he came out of the restricted area there and started to talk to you about *Angel McCoy*."

"No, he just bought it."

Charlie frowned. "He must have commented on it or said something."

"No." Jeevan shook his head. "He just bought it. I rang it up, he gave me the money, I gave him the receipt, and he arrested me."

The detective leaned forward again. "Jeevan, think very carefully." Put a hand on the man's arm. "When the undercover officer came to the register, did he make any effort to engage you in a conversation before he purchased it?"

"No." Jeevan sipped some water. Shrugged. "Does it matter?"

"It might." Charlie did not want to pursue the thought any further right now. Grabbed his glass of water and sipped. He set the glass down and gave a satisfied sigh, smacking his lips. "You know, I was hoping to write some comics. Do you get a lot of guys at the store who want to make comics?"

"Like ninety percent of comics fans think they can make them too."

"Really?"

"Sure. Although the fact that eighty-nine percent of them have never actually made anything proves they're wrong. It's not enough to have an idea—everyone has ideas—you have to do something with it."

Charlie grinned. "I have an idea."

"Yeah?" Jeevan seemed mildly interested. Maybe he was just being polite.

"I want to pitch a series to Marvel Comics about Quicksilver."

"They can never seem to make him work. Nobody can keep the continuity straight anymore."

"Yeah, but that was my idea—do a series where all the weird and contradictory stories are part of the deal."

"Yeah? How do you do that?"

"Up to now, Quicksilver has been a lot of things," Charlie said, counting off on his fingers. "A mutant terrorist, a supervillain, a superhero, and a government agent. Each time they try to give him this 'new direction,' it looks like he can't make up his mind who he is."

"Sure."

"But what do these personas have in common?" Charlie let the question hang a second. "He's trying to change the world. He just can't decide how to do it."

"And your book would be different because...?"

"I'd have him run for office." Charlie grinned, like it was the greatest idea in the world. "For mayor or governor or something."

"Okay."

Charlie, eyes lit up like a kid, gestured to make his point. "Suddenly, all this baggage is vital to the story—because the press would really have a field day with a guy running for office who is an ex-terrorist / ex-criminal / ex-superhero / ex-government agent. Now, instead of ignoring his awkward and complicated past, we embrace it. Therein lies drama."

Jeevan pursed his lips and nodded. "Could work."

The detective made small talk a little while longer. Eventually realized he was just imposing.

Left Jeevan's apartment feeling like a failure.

🏠 🗁 ⑦　　　　　　　　　　　　　　　　　⊠

BLOG

WHERE IS BLAKE #015
whereisblake.blogdroid.com

"Great minds discuss ideas, mediocre minds discuss events, small minds discuss personalities."

—Eleanor Roosevelt

What a couple of weeks! Just a short time ago, Evelyn Blake was more worried about wreaking havoc on the magazine than the whereabouts of her missing husband.

Of course, the roses that have started appearing on her desk could be a clue. At first, the buzz around the office was that she ordered them herself. After all, who would send Queen Evel flowers?

But over the course of a few days, the flowers have shown up like clockwork—including this morning. And she has this look on her face, a mix of surprise and secret hope.

It must be from a lover. Ew.

Maybe they are from Warren Blake, sent from wherever he's hiding out. Maybe they are from a secret admirer.

Ew.

— 45 —

"What's wrong with this TV?" Jesse Hart, back at his trailer home after a hard day at work. Plopped in the easy chair, duct tape covering a big tear in the vinyl. Armed with the remote, targeting the television, hammering the buttons with his thumb.

Darva came into the living room, the scent of aloe following her. "What is it, hon?"

"Dang-darn-doodle TV here ain't working like it did when I flicked off *Good Morning America* and left for work."

Darva lowered her eyes, said nothing.

"Did he do something?" Jesse jerked his head toward the hall, as if his absent brother-in-law was standing there.

Without waiting for her answer, he struggled out of the comfortable chair, paused to check the stripe of duct tape. Hit the floor in sock feet, hobbled across the small living room to the pressboard entertainment center.

Bent awkwardly on one knee, cursing loudly despite his wife's presence. Grabbed a corner of the furniture, heaved it out from the wall. "What did he do?"

Jesse checked the wires running between the DVD player and the VCR, between the VCR and the TV. He looked at the connections. Sure enough, there was a dangling, disconnected cable of some sort. "Uh-huh."

He unplugged all the cables from the color-coded hubs, re-inserted the left half of the split stereo-compatible cable into the mono audio jack, jammed the right half of the split stereo-compatible cable into an irrelevant video jack.

There. All the cables were plugged into *something*. That felt right.

Jesse grunted, heaved the entertainment center back against the wall. Struggled to stand up again, hobbled back across the room in sock feet, dropped hard into the easy chair, sending a tremor through the trailer.

He tried the remote again. Nodded and grinned at the results.

When that no-good brother-in-law comes back, he was going to give him whut-for.

Darva said nothing, returned to the kitchen.

– 46 –

Next morning. Detective Charlie Pasch was headed for his desk with a cup of coffee and Froot Loops when Detective Sammi Croteau stopped him in the hall. "Phillips is going to try again." She motioned for him to follow.

"Try what?"

"You know, prove powdered creamer is like fireworks."

"Oh. Right."

In the break room, the scent of microwaved sausage hung in the air. Made Charlie wish he'd had more for breakfast than Fritos out of the vending machine.

Detective Phillips mugged it up for the room of doubters, once again making a big show of nothing up his sleeves. *Dah-dahing* some sort of theme music, he grabbed the nearby canister of dry creamer. "I take the magic ingredient, an ordinary container of nondairy creamer—"

"And make an idiot of yourself again?" One of the cops, mocking. "I lost money last time."

Phillips flashed a showman's grin, waved the can again. "I have it all worked out."

Charlie watched him pour a little powder out in the sink, presumably on another paper towel. He wondered whether the experiment would work this time.

But why would a powdered beverage be flammable? Did it share common elements with, say, gunpowder? The possibility made Charlie glad he used almond milk instead of creamer in his daily cup of coffee and Froot Loops.

Phillips, *dah-dahing* again, set the canister down and reached for the matches on the green countertop. Charlie wondered what kind of bacteria lived there.

"And now, gentlemen," Phillips said, adding in Croteau's direction, "and *ladies*, I light a simple match"—he lit a simple match—"I hold it over the sink"—he held it over the sink—"and I drop it on the nondairy creamer."

He took a dramatic pause, then dropped the match.

Nothing.

The crowd laughed. Phillips scratched his head, started to retrace his steps.

Charlie rolled his eyes and headed back to his desk. A stranger was waiting for him. When did this guy show up?

The man jumped to his feet as soon as he saw Charlie. "Are you Pasch?"

Charlie nodded, sipping from his mug of coffee and Froot Loops. "And you are?"

"I'm Barnes—Detective Dan Barnes, Vice." Charlie recognized the name from the report. "When Vice pulls a piece of scum off the street, it's not your job to get involved."

Charlie sipped again, frowned as he set the cup down. "Actually, it's normal for departments to cooperate when their cases intersect. Aren't we all after the same thing?"

"If you wanted to co-operate"—Barnes said it just like that, *cooperate*, like it was two words—"you would have asked."

He grabbed the file off Charlie's desk, waved it in his face. "Keep your nose out, Detective," he growled in a low voice. "Or it gets bit off."

Charlie nodded, said nothing as the vice cop walked away. Sat down in his desk chair, grabbed his mug, and sipped. The vice cop was playing belligerent, covering up something. Otherwise he would have complained through normal channels.

He thought of the woman in the report, the crackpot who had filed the original complaint against the comic-book store. Reached into his jacket pocket and pulled out the address.

⌂ ▭ ⑦   ⊠

BLOG

WHERE IS BLAKE #016
whereisblake.blogdroid.com

"Names is for tombstones, baby."

—Mr. Big, *Live and Let Die*

Evelyn Blake runs Blake Media like an authoritarian state. Her recent decrees include banning makeup. She also has made it mandatory to read her autobiographical pamphlet and take a written test on it as part of our annual employee evaluations.

She has more than once complained about the art displayed around the Blake Media offices. Of course, she has no taste.

Her husband, however, has excellent taste in art.

But while Warren Blake might allow Queen Evel the run of the kingdom—to the regular frustration of us poor serfs who cannot afford to leave the health benefits—one thing about which he has remained steadfast is the *art*. Mr. Blake has certain expectations concerning the fabulous works of art decorating the hallways and offices, and he will not allow Queen Evel to make changes.

With Warren Blake missing—kidnapped? murdered? escaped?—she has been making changes. For days now, a team has been taking down all the art, cataloging it. No doubt preparing to replace the works with monstrosities chosen by Queen Evel herself.

I would not be surprised if she put up portraits of herself.

(As for the makeup thing, this is just another one of those rules she hands down but does not follow herself. Word around the office is that the purpose of the directive is to help her feel more beautiful than anybody else.)

~ 47 ~

Judge Gideon Judge with a problem. Sitting in the young lady's cubicle, at her desk, staring at the computer screen. Lost.

Back at the library, when Evelyn Blake had started yelling about how much she hated kids, Judge Gideon had panicked. Sweaty palms on pictures of brown-faced children in his pocket, he'd had to come up with a brand-new ministry on the spot.

He'd thought of those college kids, the ones he'd hitched with. Between gospel-rock songs from a band called Switchfoot they had talked about the plight of these "Dalits."

In that panicky moment in front of Evelyn Blake, Judge Gideon had cobbled together the few words he could remember from the college kids' earnest speech. And suddenly he was lecturing Evelyn Blake on the plight of these "Dalits."

Apparently, he must have bluffed his way through pretty well, because the Widow Blake had sort of blinked at him, had not shrieked, had told him to meet with her on the topic in the morning.

A meeting that was now just minutes away with the Widow Blake. Still no idea how to bluff his way through a pitch regarding the circuitous class system of India.

Wait—was "circuitous" the word? Or "byzantine"?

He did not know whether it was more appropriate to call it "circuitous" or "byzantine." Or maybe "complicated." What if he just called it "complicated"?

Just one more thing to figure out before his meeting. In forty-five minutes. With the queen.

He heard a voice behind him. "How are you doing? Okay?" The young lady from the park. He glanced at the stack of business cards on the desk. Elsa Benitez, ASSISTANT EDITOR.

Judge Gideon looked up from the computer screen, blinking. "I'm not good with this technology."

She nodded. "Give me a second and I'll be back to help you."

While she was gone, he randomly pointed and clicked for several minutes. In fact, he pointed and clicked and opened several different boxes on the computer screen.

The one in front here looked interesting. A big page of text, some sort of essay or diary entry, banner across the top, "Where Is Blake?"

When Elsa Benitez, ASSISTANT EDITOR, returned to help, her jaw dropped when she saw the open window. She lunged for the device known as the mouse, clicked the Web page shut. "You don't need to bother yourself with that."

She looked at Judge Gideon, broke into an awkward smile. "S-sorry. I can help you search the Web."

In about fifteen minutes, she had helped him find and print out several pages. Apparently, she did not think it odd he was so ill-prepared for his meeting with Evelyn Blake on the topic of these "Dalits," despite the fact that these "Dalits" were supposed to be his passion.

Not that he had time to explain any of this to Elsa Benitez, ASSISTANT EDITOR. He now only had about twenty minutes to read the materials and pretend they weren't just printed off the Internet.

Now what about these "Dalits"?

> *One of the mysteries of India, the caste system has existed for thousands of years. The system seems to have been developed by the priests to maintain their superiority.*

I see.

> *Eventually, the caste system was formalized into four distinct classes: 1) "Brahmins," priests and arbiters of what is right and wrong in matters of religion and society; 2) "Kshatriyas," soldiers and administrators; 3) "Vaisyas," the artisan and commercial class; and 4) "Sudras," farmers and peasants.*

> *Beneath these is a fifth group, which has no caste. They are "Dalits" ("the untouchables"), a downtrodden and exploited social group.*

Judge Gideon Judge checked the clock on the desk. Ten minutes. He had no idea how he was going to remember this.

> *The term Dalit in Sanskrit comes from the root "dal"—literally "to break." As an adjective, it means "crushed." The term describes the outcastes as the oppressed and broken victims of the Indian caste-based society.*

"Judge Gideon?"
He looked up from the printout. Hoped the panic did not line his face. "Yes, ma'am?"
Elsa Benitez, ASSISTANT EDITOR, smiled. "It's time to go see her majesty now."

– 48 –

Detective Charlie Pasch spent the whole drive over to the complainant's address stewing, festering. Who did "Detective Dan Barnes" think he was? The *nerve* of that guy.

By the time he reached the crackpot's house, he was pretty worked up. The visit did not go well. Maddie Nicholas was smug, she was righteous, she had a big Jesus statue in her living room. The house was dingy, a wreck, with dust everywhere.

Barely a few minutes passed before Charlie lost his temper, got off track explaining that comics were like any expressive medium, they could speak to any age group they pleased. Only an idiot ropes off an entire art form for a single demographic.

She wouldn't listen. "I know what a comic book looks like, Officer," she preached in a special voice.

"Detective," he corrected, but she didn't seem to hear.

"I would read them to my little boy."

Fighting to level his voice, he asked, "Did you read books with your little boy?"

"That's what I just—"

"No, *books*," he snapped. "Regular, normal books. Did you read books to your little boy?"

"Oh, sure."

"So did you pick books that were age-appropriate, or did you read him *Brave New World*?"

"I don't—"

"Perhaps *Slaughterhouse Five*? Or maybe *The Last Temptation of Christ*?"

"I would never read that to my child."

"I see. So you exercised discernment." His words coming out in clipped, flat tones. At least he wasn't yelling. "And when did you picket the bookstore?"

"What?"

"Every bookstore in town carries those books." He was pacing the living room now. "Do you picket them like you picketed the comic-book store?"

"I don't really—"

"Did you picket Blockbuster for carrying R-rated movies?"

"No, I—"

"Because if you're going to say a parent has the right to be too lazy to distinguish what is age-appropriate, only a hypocrite stops with the comic-book store."

"I don't understand."

"No, ma'am." He shut his eyes tightly, then opened them again and glared. "You don't."

Charlie, clenching and unclenching his fists, looked on the mantel and noticed the framed picture of a smiling boy. A whole collection, dusted recently. The rest of the house layered with dust, yet these frames were clean.

Charlie softened. Pointed. "Is this your son?" In one picture, the boy was smiling, holding a trophy. In another, he was racing in a track meet. At the instant the picture was snapped, he seemed to be doing pretty well.

She spoke softly, in a different voice. "My little boy." Her whisper trembled. "He would have been twenty-two come October."

Charlie's throat went dry. He had to lean against a chair. "I'm sorry." Silence hung in the air for a few minutes. Then he whispered hoarsely, "He was ten. Wasn't he?"

"Going on eleven."

"What happened?"

"He got sick and the Lord took him home."

Charlie held his tongue. This was not the time to get into a theological debate. Then something occurred to him. "Can I see his room?"

Puzzled, she nodded, led him to the stairs. As they went up, he rubbed his finger on the banister. Dust.

They reached the top of the stairs, third door on the left. Inside, his suspicions were confirmed. The room was immaculate. The rest of the house a sty, but this room cleaned every day.

On the nightstand by the bed were knickknacks and action figures. On the dresser a trophy, the one Charlie has seen in the photo downstairs.

A shoebox peeked from under the bed. He inched over, turned to Mrs. Nicholas. "May I?"

She folded her arms, shivering, and nodded. The detective, on his knees, pulled the box out gently, opened it to reveal a stack of old comics. *Classics Illustrated. Batman. Fantastic Four.* Nice condition. Not perfect—shoeboxes weren't the best way to store comics—but still nice. They also looked well-read.

Suddenly, he knew. She still pulled out the comics from time to time, read them to the empty room. Pretended she still had her ten-year-old.

Two years ago, she'd gone to Randy's to buy some comics, a way to stay connected with the memory of her son. A way to remember what it was like, reading to him. She had been confused by all the modern options.

Charlie didn't ask. He just knew.

He politely excused himself, with the promise not to bother her anymore.

⏤ 49 ⏤

Judge Gideon Judge, in the office of the queen. Evelyn Blake. Herself. He'd had a tough time finding the room—apparently, she had recently moved into this office. A nameplate had been recently pried off the wall outside the door.

As he walked up the hall, trembling (what was wrong with him? he had never been this nervous in his life), he noticed more framed paintings along the baseboard. On the walls, rectangles of faded wallpaper betrayed the former location of each and every framed piece.

Somewhere in the back of his mind, a question flickered about the paintings. It was a big project across the Blake Media campus.

In the meeting itself, he was a nervous wreck. He had never felt this off-balance. Wondered what could have happened.

Maybe it was desperation. His desperate need to get out of the nickel-and-dime business and back into style.

Maybe it was the sudden shift in "ministry" focus. In a moment of panic, he had stupidly jumped from a sales pitch he knew inside and out, to a topic he'd only heard about a few days ago.

Maybe it was because he could not stop thinking about what Andrea had said. About Jesus in the desert with the devil. What she had said about his own choices.

As he stumbled through his presentation (one he was still sort of making up as he went along, hoping she thought this was his usual spiel, not something he had printed out off the Internet and stuck in a loose file folder on the way to her office), he was hit with an epiphany:

It was *her*. Evelyn Blake was the reason he was so rattled, so off his game. Had to be.

She had this sheer force of presence about her. Like a force of nature, a dark cloud that could bring much-needed rain...or wash you off the map forever.

He could see why Blake would have left her.

In the office, he was led to a chair facing the big oak desk. Taking in his surroundings, he noticed boxes of things against the wall. Left by the office's previous occupant?

The TV crew was setting up.

TV crew.

"Good morning, Reverend," Evelyn Blake said, far more cordial than her behavior at the library had led him to expect. "I'm glad to see you this morning."

He had to lean hard to his right to see her around the big vase of roses. "Th-thank you," he said, trying to catch his breath. He gestured nervously toward the T-shirted group across the room, adjusting the lights, setting up the tripod. "Are they going to be televising this meeting?"

Evelyn Blake smiled. She could be pleasant when she wanted. "They are a documentary crew," she said. "They are going to film everything, and then it's going to be edited together for my new television series."

Judge Gideon licked dry lips. Television show? What if the wrong person saw this? What if Evil Duke Cumbee was watching?

One of the guys approached him, a heavy-set man in a smudged white T-shirt. "Hi, I'm Derek." The man offered his hand. Judge Gideon shook it with a sweaty palm. "I don't want you to be alarmed or uncomfortable. This is all going to be edited before broadcast."

Broadcast?

The heavy-set man turned to Evelyn Blake. "Now, what is this meeting about?"

She beamed. "The reverend here is going to be sharing about his humanitarian ministry."

"Oh?" The man's face fell. He turned to Judge Gideon. "And that would be...?" He waved his hands in a *help me out here* kind of way.

"Mrs. Blake and I are going to discuss the fact that some 240 million people in India are oppressed."

The heavy-set man nodded. "I see." He turned to Evelyn Blake. "This actually is not going to play well on TV, so we're going to take a break."

Evelyn frowned but nodded. "If you think so."

The man signaled the others to cut the lights, to set the camera aside for later. As they headed for the door, he turned. "We'll touch base with you later, Mrs. Blake. Don't fire anyone without us."

With the crew gone, it was just Judge Gideon and that force of nature known as Evelyn Blake. He tried to calm himself by reading off his notes.

"In India, one in four people—almost 250 million people—are 'Dalit.' In the strict caste system, these people are considered 'outcaste' or 'untouchables.'"

Avoiding eye contact, he stumbled through the reading:

> *Theoretically, everybody in India has the same rights and duties; however, in practice it is quite different.*
>
> *A Dalit is not considered to be part of human society.*
>
> *The Dalits perform the most menial and degrading jobs.*
>
> *Dalits don't have access to enough food, health care, housing, or clothing.*
>
> *Dalits don't have access to education and employment.*
>
> *If a higher-caste Hindu is touched by an untouchable or even has a Dalit's shadow across them, they consider themselves to be "polluted" and have to go through a rigorous series of rituals to be "cleansed."*
>
> *Their social backwardness and lack of basic resources keeps them in bondage to the upper castes.*

When he finished his awkward presentation, he looked up from the folder into Evelyn Blake's cobalt eyes as she sat behind her desk.

This was all wrong. The presentation, the atmosphere, the way they had met—only now, in this horrible moment, did he realize he was still caught up in the flood, carried against his will by the Fates or God or whatever.

This had been his chance to get back in. And he had blown it. Looking at her across that big desk, he could not for the life of him read the expression on her face.

⁓ ⁓ ⁓

Later, outside the office, down the hall, back at the row of cubicles, Elsa Benitez, ASSISTANT EDITOR, beamed at him, clasping her hands together. "How did it go, Judge Gideon?"

He returned her beam with a blank stare. His knees wobbling, he grabbed the wooden arm of a chair and sat down.

Looking up, he blinked at her. "She...made me an editor."

⁓ 50 ⁓

Fugitive thug Nelson Pistek, at the police station. Well, outside the station, across the street, pacing, squinting at the sun, trying to blend into the crowd while he considered his next course of action.

Gauging his ability to handle this himself. Without involving the cops. Without risking a lot of unfortunate questions. Wondering whether he was sweating from the heat or from the predicament.

Maybe he would be all right. Maybe the mob did not know where he was. Maybe they had no idea. Why would they?

Pistek looked across the street at the entrance. Watched cars passing on the street between them. Watched folks from all walks of life entering and exiting. He looked at the various people and imagined their needs, wondered how they stacked up against his own predicament.

Excuse me, Officer, my cat is up a tree again.

Jiminy-jillikers, Mr. Policeman, my skateboard ended up on the other side of the fence inside Old Man Winter's yard.

I was involved in an altercation at a known mob hangout, at least two mob associates appear to be dead, and I—

Pistek felt his shoulders sag with the weight of recent events. Scuffed his shoes on the sidewalk, found his way to a bench. *Did the mob know where he was hiding out?*

He did not know. Had spent the past few days pretending they didn't, pretending his sister and her family were not in any danger.

But the truth was, he did not know.

Did. Not. Know.

He looked across the street toward the entrance of the police station. Imagined a host of questions.

If you're not guilty, why did you hide the gun?

Would you wait for us to check on other outstanding warrants for your arrest?

Could you step into this jail cell, please, and wait for your murder trial?

He thought again about Zoo Girls. Tried to estimate his relative safety.

He ran for the car and drove back to his sister's trailer. Eyes darting to the rearview mirror the whole way. Just checking.

─ 51 ─

Associate Editor Dakota Flynn with co-workers Aubrey Burke and Elsa Benitez—Pedro's again, for frozen margaritas and chips and salsa.

Elsa slurped margarita. "So they're still trying to find whoever is writing all those blog entries, huh?"

Dakota tensed. Focused on her own drink.

Aubrey said, "Yeah, Dennis the Jerk got his fingerprints all over my computer screen. If he's going to search our computers, he needs to at least wipe his hands first or something. And not touch them so much."

Dakota smirked. "Ew."

Elsa looked at her. "So your cop friend hasn't called you back?"

Dakota slurped. "How could he? He doesn't even know my name. I was just a lady in the lobby." She set her glass on the coaster. "Besides, he's afraid of Queen Evel."

Aubrey snorted. "Can you blame him?" She tilted her head. "Why'd you want to talk to him? Got a hot tip?"

Elsa leaned across the table. "Maybe you had some way to break this whole missing-person case wide open."

Dakota stirred a straw in her drink. "If it *is* a missing-person case."

Aubrey made a face. "Again with the big conspiracy theory?"

"It's not just my theory. It's whispered all over the office."

"Then why hasn't there been some mass exodus to the unemployment office?"

"Because the angel of death would hunt them down and kill them."

"Angel of death?"

"Queen Evel. If everyone was scared before, how much more so now that she's a murderer?" Dakota, chip in hand, scooped some more salsa, continued as she crunched the chip down. "If a person leaves now, it would raise Queen Evel's suspicions."

Elsa nodded. "And where are you going to go that she can't find you? She has a major media empire at her disposal—she'll find you and she'll dump your body wherever she dumped her poor husband's."

Aubrey raised eyebrows at Elsa. "You don't believe that, do you?"

Elsa shrugged. "One good thing—in death, you would finally solve the mystery of the missing Warren Blake."

Dakota didn't say anything.

~ 52 ~

About eight PM, Charlie went to the comic-book store to regroup. It was dark, police tape flapping in the breeze, empty parking lot like a graveyard. The strip mall closed for the night.

He walked in a big circle, getting a feel for the neighborhood. Past the flower shop, past the salon, past the dry cleaner.

Under a flickering streetlight, you could see the big gas station two blocks down, shining against the night. The other direction, the middle school was a boxy shadow huddled in moonlight. At the end of the block, turn right and you have a row of family restaurants and churches.

He thought again about Eddie Drake. This was not an ideal location for his sort of business.

Turning the corner, stepping in shadows, Charlie reached the back door. He still had a key from the time he'd helped with Free Comics Day, his annual day to pretend he worked at a comic-book store.

Fumbling with the key in the moonlight, he saw that someone had broken the lock. Pried it open with a crowbar, by the looks of it. He held his breath, listening. Heard nothing but the rustle of dead leaves.

Charlie pushed in. A stale smell enveloped him as he shut the door. He stabbed the blackness with his flashlight before venturing further into the store.

Two open windows faced an empty field. *Hmm. Empty field.* Maybe Drake got a tip about some developer headed this way, planning a new mall. Expecting property values would soon shoot to the sky.

Then he saw the mess. Some thug—or a herd of them—had torn the place apart. Posters ripped from the walls, display cases smashed, tables overturned, comics strewn across the concrete floor.

Charlie headed for the corner door leading to the basement. He stepped carefully over shiny, flat slabs of pop culture, horrified to leave them on the floor, but he did not dare tamper with a crime scene.

Downstairs, his flashlight found the stockroom in a similar shambles. Stranger still, there were several holes in the dirt floor, buckets and shovels pushed to the side. Someone had been digging. He looked at the tools and came to a conclusion.

Someone was coming back.

A hunch, of course, but all he had at this point.

～ ～ ～

Charlie parked in the darkness across the street. Checked his reasoning. During the day there were open businesses nearby, witnesses up and down the short sidewalk. Whatever was going on, the miners did their whistling after store hours.

He spent two hours, three hours, in his car, waiting. Clinging to the belief some crime was still in progress.

During the long wait, he found himself thinking about powdered nondairy creamer. Maybe Detective Phillips was doing it wrong. Charlie found himself calculating different ways to conduct the experiment, different variables to try. He would have to check the ingredients when he got back.

Finally, around midnight, the stakeout paid off. A beat-up Dodge pulled into the gravel lot, drove around back. In fractured moonlight, Charlie saw two guys enter.

Ten minutes passed. It appeared safe, so he snuck over from across the street on foot. He did not risk going in, could not exactly call for backup.

Couldn't see much from outside the window. Caught snatches of dialogue as the men stumbled toward the basement door.

One said, "We done everything but bust up the cement bricks in the walls."

The other replied, "Then we bust up the walls, okay? As long as Eddie says it's here, we keep looking, okay?"

"What if it ain't here?"

"As long as Eddie says it's here, we keep looking, okay?"

Charlie went back to his car, watched the Dodge from across the street. Fought fatigue until about three AM, when the Dodge emerged from the darkness. He trailed it, unseen, until the driver dropped the passenger off in front of an apartment building.

Charlie parked across the street and went into the building. Hearing noises up the stairwell, he took the stairs two at a time. Heard someone tromping down the hall on the fifth floor. He peeked around the corner, saw the man entering an apartment.

— 53 —

Four AM. The Blake guest house. Judge Gideon Judge was living the high life.

When he'd been suddenly hired onto the magazine staff, he'd

mentioned his lack of lodging. He'd dropped a small hint, just hoping to get an advance of some sort on his new salary, whatever it was.

But Elsa Benitez, ASSISTANT EDITOR, had picked up the baton and run with it for him. She had filled in the rest of the story—as she understood it—on how he had been on a wilderness journey, lo, these past forty days (give or take a few), had sought the will of the Lord without the aid of any conveniences, just the clothes on his back.

The young lady rattled it off so well, it was like tumblers clicking into place. His quest to get close to Mrs. Blake had gone from being the most impossible thing to suddenly being the easiest. He'd merely been hoping for some kind of advance; he was now a guest at the Blake residence and had an expense account.

He was set.

He moved in with a brand-new wardrobe and a case of liquor. The guesthouse out back turned out to be a fine residence in its own right, with its own appliances and plumbing and everything.

And thanks to the clerical collar—a real one this time, freshly bought from the uniform store—the house staff was too flustered or superstitious to block his access to the main residence. He went to examine what manner of lifestyle these pagans—these lucrative, famous pagans—lived in the privacy of their own castle.

Inside, he ogled the fancy carpeting. The exotic tapestries. The statues.

But there was something about the paintings. All the paintings had been pulled down and set along the baseboards. Waiting for something.

And now, at four in the morning, he was sitting pretty, had the central air going full blast, had popped open a bottle of something strong and cold, had pulled out a cigar. Spent the last several hours flipping from channel to channel. Because he could.

He had met with the devil, in her own office, and come out ahead. What would Andrea have to say *now?*

— 54 —

Detective Charlie Pasch, in the hall outside the man's apartment. The man who had left Randy's Comics Empire. Who had left all those precious slabs of pop culture spilled out on the floor.

Charlie had his badge in one hand, weapon in the other. He knocked, stood away from the door. There was a stirring inside. He knocked again, stood away.

Finally, the guy came to the door. He cracked it open, croaked in a weary voice, "Hello?"

Charlie jumped hard against the door, slammed it against the guy, knocked him to the floor. "Police! Stay down!"

There was a brief struggle, an end table pushed over, figurines smashed on the floor. The guy, whose name turned out to be Harry Cage, folded pretty quickly. At four in the morning, after a night of manual labor, the guy was just too exhausted and disoriented.

As the man slumped into a chair, the detective glanced around the room. Saw all sorts of toys and ceramic collectibles. On the coffee table, on the kitchen counter, on the TV. A framed movie poster over by the hall, *The Wizard of Oz.*

He played hard with the suspect, but careful not to cross the line. This needed to stay off the record. "Why is Eddie so desperate for that store?"

"He needs money."

"For what?" He kept his hand close to his gun. Kept checking to make sure they were alone.

"When the Feds grabbed Big Ed, there were legal costs. Eddie got into hock with some other family."

"How did you get Barnes to co-operate?" Charlie realized he had split it into two words. Realized the ceramic figurines close by were Munchkins and a scarecrow.

"Who?"

"Barnes, the vice cop."

"Oh—Eddie got the guy on film," Cage croaked, throat full of dust. "He showed up one night and tried to shut down a porno shoot." He tried to chuckle, but it turned into a cough. "It got complicated."

Charlie wasn't sure how to process that. "I don't get it. What's the comic-book store got to do with anything?"

"We been looking for Johnny Brown's stash."

Charlie knew about Johnny Brown. Longtime resident of the Gray

Bar Hotel. Died last month. His last big haul, a million bucks, never recovered. "Where does that fit in?"

"Big Ed met him in the stir. Johnny knew he was dying, told Big Ed where he'd unloaded his fortune."

"In the comic-book store?"

Cage nodded, coughing.

━ ━ ━

Charlie drove back to his apartment in the wee hours, hoping to catch a few minutes' sleep before heading in for work. Spent the whole drive, spent the remainder of his fevered, sleepless night, sorting through the facts.

1) Johnny Brown told Big Ed he had unloaded his fortune in that comic-book store.

2) Eddie Drake tried to muscle into the store himself. Denied.

3) Eddie had dirt on a cop, called in a favor. Got the place closed down, giving free access to rip and dig.

4) The treasure wasn't in the wallpaper, wasn't in the floor.

Charlie was awake when the alarm went off. Was brushing his teeth when the tumblers in his head finally clicked into place. He thought of Jacob and Esau.

Of course.

Charlie slapped his forehead. It hurt.

⌂ ▢ ⑦   ⊠

BLOG

WHERE IS BLAKE #017
whereisblake.blogdroid.com

"When you appeal to the highest level of thinking, you get the highest level of performance."

—Jack Stack

A new directive from the Office of Evelyn Blake: Effective immediately, white orchids are the only flowers allowed in the office. In the reception area, in the cubicles, *anywhere*.

(This, of course, in direct contradiction to the deliveries of red roses that keep showing up on Queen Evel's desk.)

She is also showing off for her camera crew. She has been creating fake copy corrections on older rounds of proofs, then claiming she "asked for this three times." To make us look incompetent, to make her look like the only one making the magazine.

Sigh. Without Warren Blake's presence to rein in her tyrannical nature, Evelyn Blake is out of control.

~ 55 ~

Six AM. Fugitive thug Nelson Pistek struggling to fall asleep on the couch in the trailer home of his sister and her family. He awoke to see Darva setting up the breakfast table. Somewhere out of sight was the sound of morning-news chatter.

Darva noticed he was more or less awake. "Come on, Nellie-Bear," she said playfully, like they were still twelve and eight. He didn't like it, but held his tongue.

He ignored creaking bones, rolled off the couch and onto bare feet. Stumbled toward the table.

His sister was placing steaming bowls of this-and-that in the center of the table. He was not a fan of this-and-that.

He turned toward her. "What's going on?"

A gruff voice from behind him. "It's something called *breakfast*." His brother-in-law. "In this house, this is what we do." Using that tone of voice. Stomping over to turn off the TV.

Pistek did not want to push his luck, did not want to antagonize his host any more than he seemed to do with any act beyond breathing.

They took hands to say grace. Another awkward moment for him. Heads bowed, Jesse mumbling something worn from repetition. Pistek's mind drifted.

Once the eating commenced, there was not a lot of chatter. Just a lot of chomping. Pistek avoided the full-mouth puffy-cheeked glare of his brother-in-law, kept eyes down on his plate. Some kind of grits maybe.

Without TV, he found himself bored, looking for something to hold his attention. He looked at his water glass, grabbed it, held it up to the light. Were those greasy fingerprints his? Or were they on the glass before he got it?

"So what did the police say?" Jesse, chomping, eyed him distrustfully.

Pistek smiled. "They said I should talk to a particular detective."

"Who, Chad Everett?" Jesse sort of hee-hawed through a mouthful of grits.

Pistek did not get the joke. "Anyway, he wasn't there. They told me to come back later."

Jesse stopped chomping, glared again, the mirth draining from his eyes. He did not say anything.

Pistek returned to the grits. And his worry.

What was he going to do?

⌐ 56 ⌐

At the station, Detective Charlie Pasch yawned. Sipped his coffee and Froot Loops, checked his watch. Hoped to connect with Griggs, update him on the case.

Eventually, he gave up. Griggs was a no-show. Again. No doubt out with his shiny new "informant," whatever that meant anymore.

Charlie went to Detective Sammi Croteau and spilled his story up to this point. She was impressed.

He laid out all the details for her on the way to the suburbs, Croteau driving, Charlie filling in the blanks. "So this mob guy in prison has hidden all this stolen money, admits on his deathbed he 'unloaded a fortune in that comic-book store.'"

Croteau nodded. "The bad guys assumed he meant somewhere on the premises."

"Right." Charlie grinned. "They must have missed *Charade*."

"Oh, right," she said, turning the corner. "Cary Grant, Audrey Hepburn."

"Right," he replied, nodding. "Anyway, what they were looking for wasn't under the floor."

Croteau drove a bit further in silence. Eyes on the road, she said, "Hitchcock, right?"

Charlie frowned. "What?"

"*Charade*. That was directed by Hitchcock, right?"

"I don't think so."

She laughed. "I think it was."

"No, it was directed by Stanley Donen." Charlie trying not to slip into his lecture tone. People hated that. "The same guy who directed *Singin' in the Rain*."

They reached the house in twenty minutes. Croteau shifted into park. Turned to him. "Are you sure?"

"Yeah, this is the house."

"No, about the movie."

"Pretty sure."

They walked up to the front door and knocked. Johnny Brown's sis, Amanda Flowers, opened for them. The two detectives showed their badges, explained the events that led them to her door, how they had determined Johnny's personal effects would be in her possession.

The woman, shriveled and brown from a lifetime of smoking, did not ask for a warrant, simply allowed them in. They passed yellowed wallpaper as they headed to the hall. She pointed to the ceiling, to the square door leading to the attic.

The two detectives looked at each other. Croteau, hands in her overcoat, said, "This is your show, Charlie-boy."

He sighed and grinned stupidly, jumped and grabbed the knob on the end of the short rope. Pulled with his weight, opened the door. The ladder slid out. He climbed, and Croteau followed, Mrs. Flowers staying below.

Based on shouted directions, they went to the far corner of the attic, balancing carefully on wooden beams. They reached the pile, opened the trunk. Found an old camel-hair overcoat. A beat-up, moth-eaten hat. Assorted junk—paper clips and twine and electrical adapters—a collection only a bachelor would throw in a trunk for safekeeping.

Charlie dug, pulled, searched. Sat back on his heels. Looked at Croteau, pained face. "I don't see them."

"It's just that it seems so much like a Hitchcock film, you know?"

Charlie made a face. Threw out his hands. "Do you mind?"

She shrugged. "Are the comics stuck somewhere in the lining? A false bottom, maybe?"

Charlie rapped knuckles all through the inside, checking every surface. "No," he grumped.

The two climbed down from the attic. Charlie held tightly to his patience, used as calm a voice as possible. "Mrs. Flowers, I don't think what we're looking for is up there." He made gestures as he spoke, more than usual. "Did your brother leave anything else? A suitcase, maybe?"

The shriveled woman pursed her lips in thought, shook her head. "No, sir, I can't think of anything else."

Charlie deflated. "He didn't maybe have comic books?"

The old woman lit up. "Oh my, yes!" She grinned, baring crooked teeth. "I had those out for the grandchildren."

⌂ ▭ ⑦   ⊠

BLOG

WHERE IS BLAKE #018
whereisblake.blogdroid.com

"Spoon feeding in the long run teaches us nothing but the shape of the spoon."
—*The Observer*, "Sayings of the Week," October 7, 1951

I guess in her own private Blake World, Queen Evel is accustomed to the laws of physics and time and space bending to her own perfect will. When she comes out to play with us mere mortals, this presents a problem.

(I wonder if this issue will ever make it to the printer.)

⁓ 57 ⁓

Mobster fugitive Nelson Pistek drove around for hours. Not going to the police. Not going to the mob. Not going to his friends.

Mid-afternoon, when he thought he might not have to deal with any of the family, he pulled into the trailer park where his sister lived, dust rising from the gravel road. He drove past the trailer, past his usual spot, and parked a few trailers away.

Eyes focused on the strange car parked out front.

Who would be visiting? The cops?

Maybe. Maybe brother-in-law Jesse got tired waiting for him to make good on his promise to talk to the authorities. Maybe he thought he was helping.

But did that car look like it belonged to a cop?

Hiding behind a second trailer, Pistek squinted across the lot at the strange car. Would a member of the mob have a car like that?

He didn't know. He was bad with cars. Had no idea what make or model it was. All he knew was "brown."

It was clean, more or less, just a layer of dust from driving into the trailer park. Before that, it probably looked freshly washed.

Pistek hesitated. Debated whether or not to tiptoe to the trailer, step onto a cement block, and peek in. He heard a crunch of gravel behind him, a crunch of gravel and a voice. "Well, what do we have here?"

He jolted, eyes wide, struggled to retain control of bodily functions as he regarded the shriveled little old lady. He tried to speak, croaked, cleared his throat, tried again. "Um…"

"You're not another one of those salesmen, are you?"

"Salesmen?"

"Yeah, saw 'em knocking on a few doors of the trailers along this row. Came to my door, but I just held my peace and waited for them to leave."

Pistek nodded.

She continued. "At first I thought they might be Mormons. I woulda opened for them. I like to give 'em a hard time."

Pistek nodded again.

"But those men were dressed too fancy for Mormons."

— 58 —

"All that, and then they turn out to be worthless." Detective Charlie Pasch, back at Randy's Comics Empire. Still a shambles. A work in progress before it could open again for business.

Randy in a wheelchair, behind the counter, his black eye less swollen now. "What did he have? Reprints or something? Sometimes speculators don't know what they're looking for."

Actually, Charlie explained, the haul turned out to have once been worth almost $900,000: *Looney Tunes and Merrie Melodies* #1 (1941), less than 200 copies of which are thought to exist, purchased for $15,000; *Amazing Fantasy* #15 (1962), introducing Spider-Man, purchased for $42,500; *More Fun Comics* #52 (1940), the first full appearance of the Spectre, $78,000; *Detective Comics* #27 (1939), the first appearance of Batman, $350,000. Topped off with the most valuable comic book in existence, *Action Comics* #1 (1938), $400,000, which launched Superman into the world. And started a golden age.

"He bought all those?"

"Didn't you know?"

Randy shook his head. "He didn't buy them from me. Some grandpa came in here, looking for rare comic books. I turned him on to one of the big auctions, where a lot of the Golden Age stuff turns up."

"Johnny must have been the hit of the ball."

"Yep." Randy chuckled. "So how could a stack like that be worthless?"

"What do you always say are the two main factors that determine the value of a comic book?"

"Easy. Condition and rarity."

"There you go."

Randy made a face. "What happened?"

"Grandkids." Charlie nodded, pained mirth crinkling his eyes. "One of the kids took a magic marker and made alterations to the artwork. I guess another one glued all the ad pages together so the stories would flow better."

Randy swallowed dramatically. "I gotta sit down."

"You are sitting down." Charlie laughed, glancing around at the bustle around him.

A lot of kids were helping with the fix. Still a lot of work to go.

~ 59 ~

An hour later, Detective Charlie Pasch pulled into the parking lot of Pedro's. A block from Blake Media headquarters.

The lady had called the Mexican eatery a local hangout. He did not know her name. Did not know where she worked in the Blake Media building.

All he knew was she had told him to come to Pedro's. Of course, he was several days late. And a little embarrassed.

Once he'd decided to get back on track, he had come by this place two, three times. Did not see her. Did not see any familiar faces from his brief visit to Blake Media, no familiar faces from the disaster at the library.

He didn't relish the idea of trying to reconnect with the young lady at her office, him out of his element, her surrounded by co-workers. Not to mention the horrifying thought of another run-in with Evelyn Blake.

Each time Charlie came to Pedro's, he reminded himself it was a long shot he would show up right when she was there. He did not have time to wait around. He had things to do. Reports to type. A complaint to file against a certain vice cop.

He had excuses.

Of course, he finally admitted to himself what this was all about. He was afraid.

Yes, Detective Charlie Pasch—whiz kid of the KCPD/FBI Organized Crime Joint Task Force, a man who had been shot in the line of duty and had a medal to show for it, a man who could face down a mob killer—was afraid.

Of a pretty girl.

But he had a job to do. An apology to make. A case to solve.

Just not in front of an office full of co-workers. Under the evil eye of Evelyn Blake.

He had been parked for a couple of hours when she drove up. She was alone.

Charlie figured others were coming to meet her for a late lunch—if they were not already waiting inside. He decided this was his best chance to speak with her alone.

He walked up briskly, came up behind her on the sidewalk, said the first thing that came to mind. "You're a hard woman to find."

The woman, gripping the door handle, turned. Gave him a wry smile. "You tracked me down. Some detective."

"By the way, I'm Detective Charlie Pasch, KCPD."

"Dakota Flynn." She paused a second. "BMP."

He reached past her and got the door. "BMP?"

"Blake Media Publishing."

"Ah." He put hands in pockets, felt the *aw, shucks* expression come over his face. "You mentioned this place was a regular hangout. I've been by a few times, but this is the first time I've found you here." He glanced around for the hostess. "Would you mind if we sat and talked?"

"I'm meeting some friends. I guess we can talk until they get here."

The hostess led them to a booth, someone—a waiter? a busboy?— quickly came by with bowls of chips and salsa. Asked for their drink orders. Charlie ordered a Diet Pepsi, Dakota ordered a margarita.

Charlie said, "I'm sorry I missed our appointment the other night." Dakota shrugged. "No big."

"So what sort of information did you have for me?"

"What? No preamble, no getting to know me?"

"I'm sorry, but it's been a weird couple of days for me. My partner has been running off and doing his own investigations without me, and it…" he stopped. Sighed. Why was he telling her this?

The drinks came. He took a sip of Diet Pepsi through his straw.

Smiled. "Let's try this again, Miss Flynn. Maybe you can tell me what you think about the mystery of Warren Blake."

"What mystery? He's buried under the library."

— 60 —

First, Pistek went back to his car. Had to decide whether his intention was to flee. It would be so easy. Just drive out of town, shake the dust off his heels, head off into parts unknown.

Just drive until he was out of gas. He would know where he was going when he got there. All he had to do was get in the driver's seat, turn the key in the ignition, hit the gas, and be gone.

That was all he had to do.

Opening the door, he reached toward the dash, pressed the button, listened for the telltale click. Going around to the open trunk, he dug through the blanket, through the sleeping bag, wrapped his fingers around the gun. Felt the cold metal, courage coursing through him.

Closing the trunk, Pistek zig-zagged behind trailer to trailer. Work or grocery shopping or whatever had everybody out at this time of day. Everybody but a nosy old lady and whoever had that brown car. He came up from the far corner of Darva's trailer. Wanted to stay out of sight of any of the windows.

He reached the trailer, leaned his back against its vinyl siding, panting from heat and nervousness. The dust in the air made him want to cough.

He inched over. If Darva and Jesse had visitors calling, they would all be sitting in the living room.

He shouldered past the bathroom window, careful to keep out of sight. He reached the next corner, was about to turn, changed his mind, decided to come at the picture window from the opposite side. He took three steps toward the middle of the trailer, pulled open a gap in the vinyl skirt, and ducked under the trailer.

He crawled underneath in darkness, on his belly, elbows and knees scooting in damp gravel and dirt, dragging himself to the other side. Gun gripped tightly.

The whole time listening, listening for voices, listening for clues that this was all a big mistake, that he was crawling around in the mud like an idiot for nothing.

Twice his head clunked against something hard, probably pipes hanging from the underbelly of the trailer. Finally, he reached the far side, his head again brushing the vinyl skirt. Gripped the gun more tightly, reached the far side and a hole where the vinyl skirt had torn.

He peeked through. A car was driving by on the road behind the trailer, on the other side of the fence and vines. He waited until it passed.

The coast clear, Pistek pushed out into the sunlight. Mud on his shirt. He pressed his back against the trailer, scooted toward the picture window.

He was now at the metal steps leading to the front door. He dared not risk them. He took one of Jesse's cement blocks and set it upright under the window. Pistek tested it with one foot, put his weight on it, pushed himself up. He carefully peeked in the window.

He immediately dropped to the ground, the image blazed on his brain forever. His sister, Darva, shivering on the couch, holding daughter Janice close. His brother-in-law, Jesse, slumped on the floor, out cold. A couple of mugs in suits, one sitting by the door holding a gun in his lap, the other thug pacing.

Bad, very bad.

His family in danger, gun in hand, Pistek did the only thing he could think of.

He ran.

- 61 -

Already afternoon. Judge Gideon Judge deciding he should put in an appearance at his new office. He was, after all, the new religion editor.

He would "take a car" to Blake Towers. Mrs. Blake's "personal driver" would chauffeur him.

He wished Andrea could see him now. See him living the high life.

As he was driven through the swanky neighborhood, on toward the city, he started to plan his next move. Should he stay or should he go?

If he stayed in town, in the Blake guest house, he could start to work his charms on Mrs. Blake, on the neighbors. Cement his place in high society. Finally live the life of an old Cary Grant movie.

But the longer he stayed, the greater the risk of someone digging up his past. What had happened back in St. Louis.

If he hedged his bets and took off, he needed the easiest, most convenient way to grab as much as he could and take it with him. Liquidate it all as quickly as possible.

Maybe one of those paintings. They were just lying around, who would notice if one of them was misplaced? Given the lavish Blake lifestyle, any one of those paintings could be worth thousands. Maybe hundreds of thousands.

Judge Gideon smiled to himself as he watched passing trees become passing telephone poles, then passing telephone poles become passing buildings.

He was barely through smiling when the limo pulled into the semicircle drive in front of Blake Media. The driver looked at him through the rearview mirror. "Here we are, sir."

Judge Gideon Judge was thrown off balance. He had expected the man to have a British accent. "Thanks," he said, leaning forward and patting the driver on the shoulder. He exited the limo into a world of sun and concrete.

As the limo pulled away, Judge Gideon sauntered toward the front entrance of his new place of work. Out of the corner of his eye, he saw a man headed in his direction. He turned and started to offer a greeting. His face fell when he saw the dead expression on the thug's broken face.

The man jerked a thumb toward a beat-up car now pulling up to the semicircle curb. "Come with us and there won't be trouble."

Something about the man's demeanor encouraged Judge Gideon Judge to go quietly. But he could tell there would still be trouble.

He was glad Andrea could not see him now.

⌂ ▭ ⑦   ⊠

BLOG

WHERE IS BLAKE #019
whereisblake.blogdroid.com

"Man's mind, once stretched by a new idea, never regains its original dimensions."
—Oliver Wendell Holmes Jr.

Anyone notice how uninterested Evelyn Blake was when her husband launched the major library building project? When Mr. Blake broke ground on it, she did not seem to give the project the time of day. He made it clear it was a bid to enrich the lives of the children of Kansas City. She made it clear she hates children.

Anyone notice how when her husband disappears, she suddenly becomes very interested in his library?

Anyone notice how they added an extra wing to the building, the foundation of which was poured the very same morning he was reported missing?

Am I the only one who finds this suspicious?

– 62 –

In the trailer home of the Hart family. In the living room, a mobster named Al was pacing. It was getting on the nerves of the mobster named Karl. "Can you stop that?"

Al stopped, pulled the toothpick from his mouth. "What?"

"That pacing. Can you stop that pacing?"

"It calms my nerves."

"Find a different way to calm your nerves."

Al went to the big lounge chair—the sleeping guy wasn't using it—and plopped down. Found the remote, tried it on the TV. After a few minutes, he frowned. "There's something wrong with this TV."

Karl sighed. "What now?"

He got out of the chair, went across to the entertainment center. Got on one knee, yanked it out from the wall. "I see what the problem is." He turned to his partner. "These wires are color-coded, you know."

"Whatever." Karl went to the window, looked out, saw a car going out of the exit to the road. Otherwise, nobody around.

Al, finished with rewiring the entertainment center, checked his watch. "What if this guy don't show?" He shoved the cabinet back against the wall.

"Yeah, I guess it has been a long time." Karl checked his watch. "We gotta be gettin' back."

Al replaced the toothpick in his mouth. "Yeah, I guess you're right."

Karl sighed. He stood, pointed the gun at Darva and little Janice. "Let's drop these three and get out of here."

~ 63 ~

Detective Tom Griggs checked his watch. Found himself nervously glancing around, looking for familiar faces here at Science City, in the middle of Union Station, looking for familiar faces at the front door, at the emergency exits, in the crowds, at the cafeteria.

Whenever he and FBI Special Agent Martin O'Malley had one of their secret meetings, he did not want to run into anyone from the department, anyone who might report back to Charlie.

O'Malley, as usual, was late. Sometimes he toyed with the idea of just allowing for O'Malley's lateness. Showing up late himself.

But he liked keeping the game where it was—O'Malley and Griggs set a time, O'Malley shows up late, Griggs gains a few karma credits. Something he can bring up in the future. *Hey, O'Malley, you know how you're always late and making me wait?*

When the FBI agent finally did show up, Griggs made a show of tapping his watch. "You're late."

O'Malley, out of breath, stuck a Band-Aided thumb toward the entrance behind him. "Parking."

Griggs just nodded, and the two walked deeper into Science City. He leaned toward O'Malley and murmured, "I like it better when we meet at the batting cages."

"That seems a little careless," O'Malley said, louder than Griggs liked.

"I thought you weren't nervous about getting caught."

"I'm not nervous," O'Malley said, chomping gum, pointing out a direction for them to walk. Moving, always moving. "But I'm not *careless*. It's good to change it up."

They walked past interactive exhibits, past waves of small children and parents with strollers. The FBI man clutching a big envelope under his arm. "Besides, this is a good place for us. Not too many adults here. The odds of running into the wrong person are pretty remote."

Griggs nodded. "I haven't been here in years." Pointed as they passed the entrance to the Dino Lab. "I guess that's new."

"The dinosaur? Yeah, I read about that. The bones were dug up in Wyoming."

"Then why don't they have the bones in Wyoming?"

"It was the University of Kansas dug 'em up."

"Then why don't they have the bones in Kansas?"

O'Malley shrugged. "That'll be our next case."

"You sound like Charlie."

"You shouldn't be so hard on him. He's a good kid."

Having determined they weren't being followed, the two men took the spiral stairs to the second level. O'Malley pulled a file out of the big envelope, handed it to Griggs. "Look at this—we finally have some transcripts with Evil Duke Cumbee on them."

The detective raised an eyebrow. "How'd you manage that? He's a ghost. He never stops moving."

"He finally landed somewhere."

"Where?"

"The Blake residence."

Griggs squinted this time. "You...put a bug in the Blake residence?"

"Why not? It's an ongoing investigation, and Blake's wife has not exactly been acting grief-stricken, if you know what I mean."

"And you got a judge to sign off on the electronics?"

O'Malley smiled. "I didn't say this was admissible." He tapped the file. "But you've forgotten the point—we found Evil Duke Cumbee on these transcripts."

Griggs looked down at the papers in his hands. "Yeah...what's *that* all about?"

"Based on these conversations, it sounds like Evil Duke Cumbee and Mrs. Evelyn Blake are having an illicit relationship."

"An affair?"

"Sounds like it."

"You aren't sure?"

O'Malley rolled his eyes. "Well, neither of them has actually said, 'As you know, we are both having an affair.' But yeah, we're pretty sure."

"So we now have another motive for a possible homicide."

"That we surely do."

Griggs smiled broadly. "I don't suppose either of them said, 'As you know, we both killed Warren Blake.'"

The agent shook his head, mock sadness. "I'm afraid not."

"Any mention of Cumbee's interests in Blake Media itself?"

"Not really. As you read through the transcript, there is a lot of her talking, and a lot of him saying *mm-hm* and *uh-huh,* stuff like that. In fact, it doesn't sound like they're lovers, it sounds like they're married."

"Very funny." Griggs flipping through the transcript. "Still, this ought to give us enough probable cause to—"

From nearby, a familiar voice said, "I've got more."

Griggs looked up, and his blood went cold. It was his abandoned partner, Detective Charlie Pasch.

"Charlie, what are you doing here?"

"I got tired of waiting for you to come back to the office." He turned to O'Malley. "Hello, Special Agent O'Malley."

"Charlie-boy! How's it going?"

Griggs could not quite pinpoint his partner's facial expression, but he knew it was some shade of hurt. Charlie spoke softly. "I know where Warren Blake is."

O'Malley nearly jumped out of his chair. "And how do you know that?"

Charlie looked at Griggs. "A detective always connects the dots." He stepped closer, trying to hide his hurtness, hiding it poorly. Reaching into his jacket pocket, pulling out a folded sheet of paper, handing it to Griggs. "I think you want to see this."

Griggs, unfolding it, starting to skim. "What is this?"

Charlie said matter-of-factly, "I know where Warren Blake is buried."

O'Malley grinned. "Hoo-boy!" Chomping gum, he elbowed Griggs. "You certainly taught the kid well!"

Griggs frowned, started reading Charlie's report in earnest. He thought of the dinosaur bones nearby, wondered what the University of Kansas would think about *this?*

– 64 –

Fugitive thug Nelson Pistek, at the edge of the trailer park, huddled in a drainage ditch. Hiding. Waiting. Shivering. Chiding himself for being a coward. Imagining the blood on the walls inside that trailer.

He heard shots. Cannons rattling inside the trailer.

BLAM. BLAM.

– 65 –

Speaking of the house trailer, this was Al's mistake: He did not simply lean down and shoot this guy in the back of the head. BLAM. That would have been the end of it. BLAM BLAM BLAM, three dead, father-mother-daughter, what a shame. No witnesses, so far as the thug named Al and the thug named Karl knew.

But he didn't do that. Al leaned in close to the man lying on the floor. For whatever reason, decided to check whether the man on the floor was unconscious.

If only he had not held the gun loose.

If only he had not gone down on one knee.

If only he had not gotten within arm's reach.

If only he had not reached out, put a hand on the man's shoulder.

If only this guy had still been unconscious.

In the bedroom, the second thug, Karl, heard the two shots ring out, echoing through the hall from the living room. He winced at the noise, at the way it echoed and rattled through the house trailer. Peeked out the curtain. Could only imagine what it must sound like outside.

He did not think any of the neighbors were around to hear it. He and Al had knocked on several doors before they'd found the right trailer.

But would passing drivers hear it from the road?

Gun held ready, he hesitated. Adjusted his grip on the pistol, kept it leveled at the woman and the girl, both huddled in the corner, clutching each other and sobbing. A shame to kill them, but this was business.

He started to think about ways to muffle the sound. Looking around the room, he considered his options. Pillow? Blanket? Mattress?

He walked over to the small bed, yanked off the blankets, tugged at the mattress. Behind him, he could hear Al clomping down the hall in his boots. It was not enough he shot up the place to wake the neighbors, now he had to clomp around—

Wait. *Boots?*

Before he had a chance to turn, he heard a pop, saw blood spatter across the wall. His own.

His last thought in this world was wondering when Al had started wearing boots.

BLOG

WHERE IS BLAKE #020
whereisblake.blogdroid.com

"Education is the ability to listen to almost anything without losing your temper."
—Robert Frost

Some of Evelyn Blake's put-upon staff have gone to disgusting extremes to exact revenge. For example, some editorial assistants added some special "ingredients" to a meal Queen Evel ordered them to pack up and send home in a company car so she could eat it later.

"She is just so horrible to so many people," one of my co-workers said, justifying herself. "You can't blame us."

Maybe you can, maybe you can't. Without the tempering presence of Warren Blake these days, his wife has taken the opportunity for all it's worth, demonstrating the full force of her presence on us poor serfs.

You could say she has blossomed.

If our previous publisher were here, we might have a chance. She always stood her ground with Queen Evel. Of course, that is probably why she was eventually fired.

Her replacement, Dennis the Jerk, has been a more compliant underling for Queen Evel.

You should see the way he looks at her when he thinks nobody is looking. (Is he the one secretly sending the flowers?)

Ew.

- 66 -

Judge Gideon Judge, driven by his captors out to a row of warehouses. Judge Gideon meeting his host. The man nervously pacing the length of the big metal warehouse, smoking like three cigarettes at a time. The man occasionally lunging for a big bottle sitting atop a crate, taking a heavy swig, and slamming the bottle down to resume pacing and smoking.

Apparently, things were not going well for him. Not that Judge Gideon could really brag about his own life at the moment. Maybe Andrea was right.

The man with the cigarettes had flinched when he'd seen the others at the door. Recognizing two of them, he'd grinned, pointed a cigarette straight at Judge Gideon, and spoken to one of the thugs. "This the guy?"

One of them must have nodded, because the man had dropped the cigarette and leaped across the room. "That's big!" He'd started pumping Judge Gideon's hand. "Thanks for agreeing to come see me, Your Holiness."

Judge Gideon, rattled, did not know which part of the sentence to correct first. Instead, he said, "Um, fine."

"I'm sure you already know about my trouble."

Judge Gideon nodded sympathetically, hoping the man would elaborate.

Unfortunately, the man just turned to light yet another cigarette. Judge Gideon had no idea what the man had done with the previous cigarettes. It was like a magic trick.

The man took a puff on his fresh cig and continued talking. "I am in a serious bind, Your Holiness. You see, Your Honor, I owe a very powerful gentleman a lot of money." He took another nervous puff. "This is big."

Judge Gideon, flailing, still not sure where he was or what this was about, heard his own voice again. "But if this is about money—"

The man kept right on talking. "So I've exhausted every avenue I can think of." The man chuckled to himself. "I even sent some of the boys out to dig for buried treasure. In a comic-book store, of all places."

Judge Gideon nodded. Still had no clue.

"So now I've turned in all directions for counsel. Saw a palm reader. Been reading my horoscope." He reached in his jacket pocket, fiddled a second, pulled out some monstrosity on a chain. "Even got one of these."

"But I don't understand—"

The man made a dramatic gesture, flicked his cigarette to the concrete floor. "It all came to nothing." He pulled another cigarette, lit it, took a puff. Coughed. "Nada."

The man came close to Judge Gideon, put a smelly hand firm on his shoulder. "Which is where you come in. I need you to call down the power of God."

Judge Gideon felt himself growing paler by the second. "How do you mean?"

The man resumed pacing, took a series of puffs on his cigarette as he jerked from one side of the floor to the other. "I don't know how it works. You're the expert."

"But I just—"

"You know, do the chant or break out the wine or whatever it is you holy joes do to get the Big Man's attention." He whirled on Judge Gideon, pointing the cigarette again. The fiery end glowed in the dark room. "I don't care whether you call down good luck for me or bad luck for him, I just need the odds to change. I need fire, brimstone, the works."

The works?

The man took another puff, pleased with himself, eyes in a faraway place. "That's big!" The man came back and faced Judge Gideon, blowing smoke out of the side of his mouth. "I need you to get all 'Left Behind' on Evil Duke Cumbee."

Judge Gideon Judge felt all the blood rush out of his head. The room spinning. The walls pressing in. He'd never needed Andrea more in his entire life.

Judge Gideon Judge needed to sit down. "I-I need to sit down."

His host seemed to soften, concerned. "Of course, Your Honor." He put a hand on Judge Gideon's arm, leading him to a crate. "You can have yourself a seat here."

Judge Gideon could not even articulate his shock at the mention of Evil Duke Cumbee's name. So he said, "If you don't mind, could you start at the beginning?"

The man lifted a foot, stepping on the corner of the crate. Looking down at Judge Gideon. Cigarette dangling from the corner of his mouth. "Sure. How far back do you want me to go?"

"Could you start with your name?"

The man stiffened, eyes flashing rage. He pulled the cigarette out of his mouth and whirled, lunging toward one of the men standing behind him. "You monkeys!" He threw the cigarette, the man on the right flinched. "You had that entire car ride over here, and you don't tell the priest where he's going?"

The man on the right shrugged. Said nothing.

The man on the left made an apologetic face. "It din't come up, boss."

"Didn't come up? The entire purpose of the visit didn't come up? Not when you introduced yourself, not when he got in the car, not during the entire drive over here?"

The two men looked at each other, shrugged.

The man shook his head, sighed. Turned back to Judge Gideon, who was still sitting hunched on the crate, wishing he could breathe into a paper bag.

The man grinned. "My apologies, Your Honor," he said, putting out a hand, which Judge Gideon took. The man's handshake was firm. "I am Eddie Drake."

- 67 -

The trailer home of Jesse Hart. The dead bodies of the two mob killers on the floor, in the living room and bedroom, where they had fallen. Jesse and Darva walking through, looking over the damage. Their little daughter, Janice, at the neighbor's.

"What are we gonna do?" Darva, sniffling, trembling.

"I guess we call the cops." Jesse looked around. Then turned and, noticing the Mrs. had not snapped into action, furrowed his brow. "So *call* the *cops*."

She nodded, went to the stand by the easy chair. Grabbed the phone, hesitated, then punched some numbers.

Jesse walked over to her softly. She looked at him and braved a trembly smile, until she realized he was not coming to comfort her but to plop in the recliner.

While she talked with 9-1-1, he grabbed the remote. Started flipping channels. She thanked the person on the phone and hung up. "They'll be here in a few minutes."

He frowned. "Hey, what happened to my picture?"

- 68 -

The judge signed the necessary papers by eight AM. Detectives Tom Griggs and Charlie Pasch had arranged for the earthmovers to be out at the Blake library by ten. The library was not yet open to the public, but there was a crowd nonetheless; someone had leaked the grisly purpose of the dig to the press, who had come out *en masse*.

When Charlie had found Griggs and O'Malley back at Science City, surrounded by screaming kids and interactive exhibits, he laid the whole case out for them. The next morning, Griggs laid it out for the judge: An employee in the Blake organization had tipped them that Warren Blake was buried under the newest wing of the Blake library.

Based on that tip, Charlie had done some digging—no pun intended. Had discovered that the last time an employee of Blake Media had seen the big boss alive was April 11, 11:42 PM. He was reported missing April 14, 10:17 AM, when he had not appeared at an important meeting.

Charlie had checked the construction records. The foundation for most of the building had been poured March 20, 8:12 AM.

But there had suddenly been a request from the Blake organization to expand the unfinished library, and a new wing was added—with an additional foundation. According to the work order, the new concrete was poured April 14, 6:00 AM. Conveniently during that narrow window of time after Blake was last seen alive and before he was reported missing.

The construction company was owned by Evil Duke Cumbee.

The judge read the paperwork, occasionally adjusting his glasses, nodding grimly. He signed the papers quickly.

Of course, it was no help when Griggs and company showed up at the site and discovered the Feds had beaten them to it.

Griggs stormed over to Special Agent O'Malley, who was surrounded by clones in suits and dark glasses. Charlie thought Griggs was going to pop him in the mouth. "Where do you get off?"

O'Malley grinned from behind reflective lenses, chomping gum like a cowboy. "I guess I get off right here."

"This is *our* dig," Griggs shouted, flailing his arms. Men in yellow hard hats circled, hoping to see a fight. "We did the work, we got the papers signed—"

"I beg to differ, Detective Griggs." The FBI man adjusted his sunglasses with Band-Aided fingers. He was still enjoying his gum. "This is now a federal investigation."

One of the other agents stepped forward, but O'Malley held out a hand. "I'll allow the two of you to observe," he said, glancing from Griggs to Charlie and back, "but you have no—"

"Hey! Marty!" Another Fed, over by a guy with a hard hat.

Griggs and Charlie followed the agent over, where they were introduced to the main construction guy, Joe Brice. The other agent said, "Joe here says we have a problem."

Brice nodded and waved for the men to follow him to the corner of the new wing. There was no way to get the big tractor with the scoop inside the building—they would have to tear out a wall to make room.

"As I was telling the other guy," Brice said as they followed, "I don't see any evidence this wing of the building is any newer than the rest of it."

O'Malley shrugged. "It's all new—just some of it is newer than the rest. How would you tell the difference?"

"Look, this is what I do." Brice spit on the ground. "I don't fight crime, you don't build things, right?" He pointed at the wall. "If these were two different jobs, there should be seams. Laymen like yourselves would not see it, but a professional would."

Charlie and Griggs looked at each other. Both looked at O'Malley, his face blank. Griggs said, "So what are you telling us?"

Brice held his hands out. "Look, I got a court order says I gotta dig this corner up, so I'm gonna dig this corner up." He pointed to the brick wall as he spoke. "But since this wall is already up and the interior already plastered and painted, there's gonna be a mess."

O'Malley nodded. "Okay."

"I just thought you should know."

The FBI agent rubbed his chin with Band-Aided fingers. Nodding again. "We got no choice." He looked at Charlie, who shrugged.

"Everything points here."

Brice shook his head. "All right." He walked away, pointing to his men and barking orders over the roar of the yellow tractors.

Brice was right—it was a mess. By late afternoon, there was a growing cloud of dust and a growing pile of debris. They found brick and concrete and plaster and fabric.

But no Warren Blake.

– 69 –

Dakota Flynn asked, "Was he mad?"

Detective Charlie Pasch struggled to hear her over the noise of the arcade. Their second date. Well, not "date," exactly, but—well, what *do* you call something like this, exactly?

"Pretty mad." He stopped at the change machine in the middle of the dark room, put in a five. He listened for the telltale whirring and clicking, watched it drop tokens in the slot.

He pulled them out and headed for the pool table, passing a series of beeping, zapping, blinking videogame shoot-'em-ups, karate fights, and oddball novelty games. Nervously shuffling tokens in his sweaty palms the whole way.

He would have loved to stop, try his skill at any one of those games, anything rather than pool. But you couldn't split your attention between exploding zombie invaders and an ongoing interrogation. Well, not "interrogation" exactly, but—well, what *do* you call this, exactly?

At the pool table, Charlie carefully set the spheres in the wooden triangle. Flashed Dakota a sideways smile as he took the white cueball, placed it on the dot at the far end of the table. He motioned for her to go first.

She gave him a playful frown and went to remove the wooden triangle. He had left it on the table.

He winced.

She lined up her stick, smoothly shot the white ball across the table, snapping the spheres in every direction. "So did you get in trouble with the government or something for digging up the library?"

Charlie saw both stripes and solids dropping into pockets. She had her pick. He was glad they weren't playing for money. "Actually, the irony is that the Feds tried to steal our thunder." Getting comfortable, he leaned on the stick. "Since they beat us to the scene, they also get the fallout."

"The FBI?" She took another shot, a solid red into the corner pocket. Already eying her next shot. "When did they come in?"

Charlie was glad nobody was watching him get shellacked here. A man has his pride. "When I finally caught up with my partner, Detective Griggs, I found him with an FBI agent of our acquaintance. When I laid the story out for him, the Fed got the whole story too."

"You 'found' him with the FBI agent?" She glanced over and smiled. Turned back to her next shot. SNAP. Two more solids in the side pocket. "Something about your choice of words sounds like there's more to it."

He leaned harder on his stick. "I'd rather not talk about it." He looked at the table. Was he ever going to get a turn?

"I see." Another solid. Was that all of them? "What *do* you want to talk about? Comic books?"

"We don't have to." He sighed with relief when she missed a shot. He finally had a chance to get some of the stripes off the table.

Stepping back from the table, Dakota took a gulp from a glass of cola. "Here's a question. What's the deal with Batman?"

Charlie, eyeing his shot, stopped and stood. Frowned thoughtfully. "What deal?"

"You know, his deal. What powers does he have?" She nodded toward the table. "You taking your turn?"

Charlie's brain locked a second. Then he slowly leaned over the table, started sizing up his shot again. "He's just a guy."

Missed.

Dakota smoothly set her next shot; clearly, she had it already figured out. "He can't be 'just a guy,' he's got a mask and a comic book and stuff."

"Sure, but he doesn't have magical powers or anything. He's a human being who trained his body and his mind. He's in peak condition."

She dropped the last solid in the corner pocket, started setting up for the eight ball. "I thought he was bit by a bat or something."

"Nope."

"Huh."

She dropped the eight ball, and the game was over. Charlie fumbled for change for another game. "I wrote a story when I was a kid where Batman teams up with this Green Lantern from outer space. Not the regular Green Lantern, but an alien one."

She blinked at him. "Green what?"

"The Green Lantern Corps is like this intergalactic police force." He dropped the change in the slot and started setting up for the next game. Filled the triangle. "Anyways, this particular Green Lantern comes to Earth looking for this intergalactic criminal, and he looks up Batman for help because Batman is like famous throughout the universe."

He removed the triangle from the table, motioned for Dakota to shoot first. She was still giving him a look, so he shrugged. "Hey, I was ten years old."

She lined up her stick. "Why would he be famous throughout the universe if he's just a guy?"

"He's in the Justice League."

"Ah." She clipped the white sphere hard, and once again the rest snapped in all directions. Great.

"And he comes to Batman for help because he thinks Batman has all these great batlike super powers. And he's all disappointed because it turns out that Batman is just a human being in a mask."

"He's got that belt."

"Well, sure, he's got the gadgets. But he doesn't have superpowers."

"I see." She started dropping stripes left and right. "You're about to get blinkered again."

"'Blinkered'?"

"You know, beat bad."

"I thought 'blinkered' meant 'drunk.'"

"Not where I come from." She dropped the last of the stripes, then went after the eight ball. "So how does the story end?"

"Batman catches the intergalactic criminal and the alien cop has to admit he underestimated him."

"And you wrote that story when you were ten?"

"Yep." He suddenly felt embarrassed. "Dumb, huh?"

Dakota snapped the eight ball into the side pocket. Game over. She looked over at Charlie and smiled. "I think it's cute."

His cell started ringing. He checked the number. Griggs. He flipped it open. "This is Charlie."

"We got a call here regarding Evelyn Blake."

"What, is she suing us for destroying the library?" Wouldn't be surprising. Charlie was relieved the Feds had stolen the dig.

"No, she's in the hospital."

Did he hear that right? "Hospital?"

"Yeah. Sounds like she's been poisoned."

⌂ ▱ ⑦　　　　　　　　　　　　⊠

BLOG

WHERE IS BLAKE #021
whereisblake.blogdroid.com

"It is the mark of an educated mind to be able to entertain a thought without accepting it."

—Aristotle

The authorities tore up the floor in the what-was-almost-finished library project. They apparently went digging for the remains of Warren Blake. No luck.

Where is Blake?

I am caught in a sort of limbo here—the uncertain future mocks me. Have I come all this way for nothing?

Did he skip town? (What was the motive?)

Was he kidnapped? (Where is the ransom note?)

Was he murdered? (Where is the body?)

Did Warren Blake leave because of me?

— 70 —

Detective Tom Griggs at the counselor's office. It had been a few weeks.

"It's not usual for you to come here alone," the counselor said. "Did you want to talk about Carla? Is that why you aren't here together?"

"No." Griggs fidgeted in his chair. "Actually, the wife and me talked about this. Thought it might be worth a visit."

The counselor sat back in his counselor chair, had notebook and pen ready. "What did you want to talk about?"

"You know, I've really been working to focus during our sessions here."

"I've seen that. You've made a lot of progress." The man made some sort of scribble. What in the world could he be writing down already? "I remember our early sessions together. Many times you were here in body, but rarely in spirit."

"Right." The detective glanced out the window. Took note of the Kansas City Power and Light building on Baltimore and 14th. He shook off the urge to be distracted, turned back. "But I want to make it work. The marriage, I mean."

"That's good to hear." The other man made another scribble. "But that isn't why you're here today, is it?"

"No." Griggs fidgeted again. The vinyl chair squeaked. He hated that. "Things have gotten kind of weird at the precinct."

"The police station."

"Yes." He nodded. He started to speak, but nothing came out. After a few moments of nonspeaking, he laughed. "This is hard."

"Why? You've been here many times, Tom."

"I know, but it's always with Carla. Sharing is easier when it's tag-team, I guess."

The counselor smiled. "We have time."

There was a long silence. Griggs became aware of the hum of the air conditioner. "Someone I trusted betrayed me."

"I see." Counselor made a scribble. "How does that make you feel?"

Griggs pursed his lips. "Mad." He glared at the coffee table. "Furious." He looked up, held his hands out. "Would it be all right if I walked around?"

"If it helps."

"It would." He pushed himself up against the arms of the chair. Started for the window, decided he would be less distracted if he focused on the room. Started pacing. "This guy was sort of my partner, I guess. And we shared a lot of information. Secrets and stuff, you know?"

"Sure." The counselor nodded, scribbled something.

"And then he betrayed me. Took all that trust, all that friendship, just chucked it for personal gain."

The other said nothing.

Griggs glanced over to make sure the man was still listening. He found himself talking just to fill the nervous space. "Charlie says I have some sort of 'forgiveness' issues."

"And who is Charlie?"

"He's my partner."

"So when Charlie betrayed you—"

Griggs waved a hand. "No, Charlie wasn't the one."

The counselor consulted his scribbles. "So then you are referring to...?"

"O'Malley...Marty."

"And Marty was your previous partner?"

"No, Marty is in the FBI." He grunted. "My previous partner was Jurgens. And he can rot in hell."

⌂ ▭ ⑦   ⊠

BLOG

WHERE IS BLAKE #022
whereisblake.blogdroid.com

"People learn something every day, and a lot of times it's that what they learned the day before was wrong."

—Bill Vaughan

Evelyn Blake is out of the office—sick. Joy!

Apparently, she is a victim of "food poisoning." Regular readers of this blog may draw their own conclusions.

~ 71 ~

Detective Charlie Pasch and assistant editor Dakota Flynn, having lunch at the Mexican eatery near Blake Media. The place filled with the sound of sizzling fajitas and the smell of spices. Charlie was saying, "I challenge the automatic gratuity."

"What, you don't tip?" She raised an eyebrow at him.

"No," he said, pointing to the fine print on the menu. "This says that for parties of more than eight, they automatically add eighteen percent to the bill. I challenge that."

"But you need to tip your waitress." Dakota popped a salsa'd chip in her mouth, crunched. "Or waiter, as the case may be."

"I do tip my waitress. I'm a great tipper. That's not what this is about. When you boil it down, the automatic gratuity means I'm automatically grateful."

"But you should be grateful. They're serving you. They're bringing you stuff."

Charlie drank more soda. "A tip is supposed to be matched to the quality of the service. If someone gives me excellent service, I give them an excellent tip. If they give me sloppy service, less so."

"What do you consider an excellent tip?"

"I don't know, twenty percent and up, I guess." He grabbed the straw in his Diet Pepsi, slurped to the bottom. "I usually gauge the quality of the service by whether I get thirsty." He set the glass at the edge of the table, started glancing around for the waiter. "Like here, I'm ready for a refill. If this guy comes by soon and fills me up, then we're on track for a good tip."

"So, twenty percent, huh?"

"One time, I gave a really small tip. My friend got mad, but the waitress got our glasses mixed up."

"How do you know?"

"Because when she came back with our refills, I still had my straw, and his straw was in my glass."

"Ew."

"I know." He slurped the last drops of his soda. "One time, I gave a one-hundred-percent tip. Of course, the meal was only five dollars, but she never once let me get to the bottom of the glass. So I tipped her five bucks."

"Big spender." Dakota scooped more salsa. "But the deal with the automatic gratuity is to protect the waitstaff. Big parties tend to stiff big time. Big parties and church people."

Charlie was relieved when the waiter showed up with a second glass of soda, traded for his empty glass. The man took their lunch order and left.

While Charlie slurped his soda, Dakota asked, "So, you been a fan of Batman for life?"

"I wanted to be Batman when I was in first grade."

"Don't all first-graders?"

"No, I mean as a career choice. My first-grade teacher, Miss Reineke, had us all do this thing where we were supposed to act out our future occupation. I did this thing where I'm racing in a circle, holding this air steering wheel."

"Really?" She sounded amused.

"And the kids are all, 'You're a race-car driver?' And I shake my head and keep driving in a circle. 'You're driving a police car?' Nope. 'A fire truck?' Nope. Finally, they're like, 'Then what?' And I say, 'It's the Batmobile. I'm going to be Batman.'"

"How cute!"

Charlie felt his cheeks redden. "And Miss Reineke said, 'You can't be Batman. And I said, 'Sure, I can.'"

"What did she say then?"

"I don't remember. I think she gave up and went to the next kid."

Dakota broke a chip in half and scooped more salsa. "Look at you, Charlie, you wanted to be Batman when you grew up, and now you're a cop. You're living the dream."

"I don't know about that."

"Dude, you're fighting crime."

"It's not the same."

"Dude, you fight crime."

"Okay, it's not *quite* the same." He smiled quietly to himself. He wondered when his flautas were coming. "The car isn't as cool."

"You ever shoot anybody?"

"Once." Charlie's eyes clouded a moment, remembering a life-and-death struggle in a hospital room. He had saved the life of Detective Jordan Hall, but took another life to do it.

He shivered, came out of his reverie, smiled weakly. "I got a date out of it."

"A date?"

"Well, not really a date. But she went to a comic-book store with me."

"Every geek's dream."

"I don't know. I felt awkward. You know, I got trapped in that weird mental space where I don't know whether what we did is a *date*. And, more importantly, whether *she* thought it was a date."

"Did you ask her?"

"That would have been logical." The waiter arrived and set steaming plates of food in front of them. "Besides, she's long gone. She was suddenly engaged to some guy I didn't even know existed, and then she transferred out of the department altogether."

He grabbed the bowl of salsa and poured some on his flautas. A little more plopped out than he intended.

Stabbing items for her fajita with a fork, Dakota nodded toward his pile of flautas and salsa. "Want some flautas for your salsa?"

"I have condiment issues." He grinned stupidly. "So who is *your* hero?"

She stopped mid-chew. Eyed him warily. "What do you mean?"

"You know, I had Batman when I was a kid, who was your hero? Polly Pony?"

"When I was a kid, I watched James Bond, thank you very much."

"Ah."

"What do you mean, 'Ah'?"

"My mom didn't let me watch James Bond. Thought he was a corrupting influence. I guess she was afraid I would grow up to be a spy."

"So it was okay to grow up to be Batman?"

"She couldn't fight fate. So why did your mom let a little girl watch James Bond?"

"I watched it with my dad." She set her fork down, her eyes staring off into some faraway place. "We haven't done that in a long time."

From that point, Charlie felt like Miss Flynn never really came back to the table. Her mind still on that faraway place.

~ 72 ~

A trailer home full of detectives. A cop taking pictures of the scene. Tape outlines in the living room and bedroom. CSU forensics team members going about their business, picking, scraping, collecting. The homeowners, a man and wife and little girl, taken down to the station to make a statement and then be placed in safe housing.

"Some mess, huh?" One detective, Boyett, giving the what-do-ya-know elbow to another detective, Volkman. While the rest were keeping busy, the two found themselves standing around.

Volkman shrugged. "I guess."

Boyett leaned in and winked. "How do you think something like this will set back Cumbee?"

Volkman shook his head thoughtfully. "Dunno. I guess the Duke will have to get some new hired hands."

"You really think the guy whacked these mobsters all by himself?"

Volkman glanced around at the investigation going on around them. "That was the story."

"Surely he had some kinda help. I mean, these are professional killers here, and he's, what, a mechanic? Maybe there was another shooter."

"What can I say? Hired killers ain't what they useta be."

"Maybe someone pops out of the closet?" Boyett waved his hands. "Or—wait, wait—someone is peeking in from the outside, shoots through the window?"

"Nothing to indicate that. So far, it looks like just the guy and his wife and kid were the only ones here. Besides, the man was protecting his home. A guy in that position can surprise ya."

"Yeah?"

Volkman leaned in, spoke in a low tone. "There was this one lady. Her kid gets pinned under this car, she freaks out and lifts it up so he can crawl out. Like, lifts the car right over her head."

"That true?"

"I heard about it."

"Even so, I don't know that lifting a car is the same as getting the drop on a couple of cold-blooded killers."

"Same principle."

"I'm not so sure it is."

"Same principle."

Boyett shrugged. "Fine."

Volkman wandered off to see how Griffin and his forensics team were doing.

Boyett stretched his back, checked to make sure his shirt was still tucked in. The investigation going fine around him, he took to the easy chair in front of the TV. For a moment, he pretended he was sitting in the chair for investigative reasons, searching for some vital clue that would break the whole case wide open.

He eyed the room around him, slowly, as if he might see something. He sniffed. Smelled like someone had broken a jar of mustard nearby. He looked over the side of the chair. On the wall, saw a telltale yellow stain. Probably not the clue to break the whole case wide open. Just a mustard stain.

He pulled out his handkerchief and carefully grabbed the remote, careful not to smudge any prints. It was not long before he discovered it was one of those picture-in-a-picture sets. "Hey, cool."

As he thumbed some more buttons on the remote, though, there was a problem—the smaller picture didn't seem to work. "Well, that's no good."

He pushed out of the chair, went across the room. Grabbed the corner of the entertainment center and pulled it out from the wall. This should only take a second. After all, the wires are always color-coded.

- 73 -

Judge Gideon Judge, back in the Blake guest house. Pacing. Fretting. Cursing. Wondering how his life had ever come to this. How he'd come to be trapped in Kansas City with a previous—and risky—alias. How he'd come to be the good-luck charm for an illiterate chain-smoking mobster.

How he'd come to be in the same vicinity as Evil Duke Cumbee. The man he'd pilfered from. The man who'd ordered him beaten or killed or worse.

Judge Gideon took stock of the situation, decided there was really only one recourse.

Run.

Take a bus, take a train, take a plane. Get as far away as possible.

Away from Evil Duke Cumbee. Away from Eddie Drake. Away from the Blakes. Away from Judge Gideon Judge.

Find a new name, find a new mission.

Yeah, that was it.

Judge Gideon found himself hankering for a cigarette. The curtains in the guest house smelled of nicotine and ash. A previous occupant must have been a smoker.

He began digging through the drawers, the dresser by the door, the nightstand in the bedroom, the cabinet out by the living-room window. Somebody, at some point, had cigarettes in this guest house. If there was a Lady Luck, he would find a pack left behind.

Nothing. All the drawers pulled and askew, Judge Gideon slumped against the far wall and slid to the floor.

He grabbed the curtain, an ugly aqua number with green flowers, took a whiff. It did not help.

He began to calculate his next move, began thinking of where he might go. *Mexico?* He wondered whether they had running water. *Canada?* Wondered what moose tasted like.

He could really use a Rolling Stones disc right now, something to just crank up and rock away the blues. He began to hum "Emotional Rescue," was alarmed to discover he could barely remember the words. Something about being your "savior," something about being your "knight in shining armor."

He was more rattled than he thought.

His mind drifted to those college kids again, the ones who had given him a ride. The nerve of somebody dissing the greatest rock 'n' roll band in the world.

He thought of the kid's pet cause, the plight of the—what were they called?—Dalits. Tried to imagine the hopelessness of such a life. Wondered what one lowly man could do about it.

His own dilemma rushed back to him. If he did not get out of here quick, he would be in no condition to help himself, much less anybody else.

Judge Gideon put on a clean set of clothes. Once he hit the road, who knew how long he might be wearing this same outfit?

He looked around for something he could use to carry things. When he'd bought these clothes on the company card, it hadn't occurred to him to tack on a suitcase or bag for good measure. He thought he had it made. He thought he knew what he was doing.

It pained him to admit to himself he didn't know what he was doing at all. He had expected to get back his old swagger through sheer force of will. But his charisma, his slick mastery of the language, was wheezing out of him like helium from a balloon.

He had no control over his life. Fight as he might, he really was just a piece of flotsam on a sea of doubt and uncertainty, at the mercy of an indeterminate universe.

Is this what the end of your rope looks like?

He was desperate. Found himself mumbling. Found himself praying. Making promises to whomever might be listening. Hoping he wouldn't have to see those two thugs again—he didn't know their names, he just remembered them as Mister Banner and Mister Grimm.

He stuffed clothes into a garment bag, wadded it under his arm, went for the front door. Flipped out the light, cracked open the door, peeked outside. Nobody on the walkway to the house, no faces peeking out lit windows. This might work.

Outside, he pulled the door shut, listened for the click. He turned and headed for the dark part of the sprawling yard, for the trees.

He was in the middle of breathing a prayer of thanks to whomever might be listening, when he heard the crackle of a twig. He turned and saw the lit end of a cigarette, floating in darkness. A gruff voice said, "How ya doin', Father?"

His eyes adjusting to the moonlight, he saw the gradual form of Thug #2. That would be Mister Grimm. When Judge Gideon failed to reply, Mister Grimm stepped forward a bit. "Need a ride somewheres? Mister Drake put us at your disposals."

Judge Gideon sighed, tried to upgrade his appearance to confident. "No, thank you, my son." Could not think of an explanation for the wrapped garment bag tucked under his arm. Hoped it would not come up in conversation. "I was just—"

Going for a walk?

Stepping out for a drink?

Making a break for it?

"—headed for the house." He pointed casually, as if that were where he'd been headed all along.

Mister Grimm took a drag on his cigarette. Nodded toward the house. "Must be a nice joint."

"A man of the Lord does not make such judgments of material things. It is all the Lord's." He hoped the shtick did not sound as flat to the thug as it sounded in his own ears. "I was just hoping to get a lemonade and find something to read."

He turned toward the house, now committed to this unexpected path, trying to play it cool. Don't walk too fast, don't walk too slow. Play it cool, play it cool.

He breathed another silent prayer to whoever might be listening. If he was going to be stuck, at least he hoped not to run into any of Evil Duke Cumbee's men.

He reached the back door and knocked lightly, lightly enough to hope nobody would hear, so he could believably shrug and turn back for the guest house and start a new plan.

He did not expect the door to open. The maid or somebody dressed in black stood there. Before she could speak, a voice from the next room said, "Is that the reverend? Send him in, there's someone I want him to meet!"

Judge Gideon was ushered into a large and gaudy room. The lady of the house, Evelyn Blake, was sitting on a gaudy couch. She saw him and motioned him over. "There he is!"

She turned to the man sitting across from her, a man in an expensive silk suit. Gesturing toward Judge Gideon, she said, "This is our guest, Reverend...?"

She trailed off, gestured for Judge Gideon to finish it. Recognizing her guest, he said in a disheartened voice, "Reverend Gideon." A slight change in alias in the interest of self-preservation.

The man stood. Judge Gideon knew this man well. The man offered his hand. The man said, "Hello, Reverend. I'm Duke Cumbee."

☖ ▭ ⑦   ⊠

BLOG

WHERE IS BLAKE #023
whereisblake.blogdroid.com

"Let's be sure we'd be acting perfectly right in bustin' that there door open, a
door onbust is always open to bustin', but ye can't onbust a door once you've
busted en."
— Mr. Sandy Wadgers, from *The Invisible Man* (by H.G. Wells)

Evelyn Blake is still out of the office. However, that does not stop her
from causing trouble.

Now her lawyers have shown up. Apparently, with Warren Blake
missing, there is some sort of contention with the board of directors
about whether she is in control of Blake Media. After all, there is a
cable television show on the line.

The camera crew is always underfoot, documenting everything in the
office. When you see this sort of stuff on TV, you wonder how people
could act like that on camera.

But I gotta tell ya, you get used to the cameras. Maybe the crew
goes to ninja school or something, because once they set up, they
eventually fade into the walls and you're just going about your
business. Scrambling to make deadline.

But Blake Media controls the cable network. Blake Media could even
pull the plug on Queen Evel's new television show. In fact, if the board
of directors can prove Warren Blake is permanently out of the picture,
can prove she is not running the show, they could shut her down
altogether.

Oh, happy day.

I am torn: If the board loses, the reign of terror continues. If the board
wins, it means Warren Blake is really gone.

Did he leave because of me?

~ 74 ~

Professional thug Nelson Pistek, huddled in the alley, shivering in the rain. A block over from the apartment building from before, where he had met some of Cumbee's men. Ignoring the smell of the dumpster.

He found himself imagining the horrible fate of his family, his sister, his brother-in-law, his niece. The goons he saw through the window had to have been Cumbee's men. Had to have been looking for him, coming after him because of the shooting at the club.

Pistek knew the sorts of atrocities mobsters were capable of. Mutilations and murders in the name of "business," committed with tools that could whap and chop and gouge.

Even watching from the fringes of Fat Cat's organization, Pistek had gotten more of an education in the mob than he could ever have expected. He was not afraid to muscle somebody, not afraid to drop somebody from the fire escape—but some of those guys were just sick.

Some of the guys got to where they were almost competing to see who could think of the most gruesome thing they could do. Sometimes it was running chatter in the back of the bar, sometimes it was guys experimenting in the field and bragging about it afterward.

If you were lucky, they just shot you and you were done.

Pistek thought again of his sister, his brother-in-law, his niece. The mob should leave a man's family out of it. Should keep it man-to-man. This wasn't how it worked during the glory days. The old guard kept to a kind of code, if only to keep life simple.

But the new guys, they were just crazy.

Covering his nose with one hand to block out the stench of the dumpster, he felt his pockets. In his left pocket, the gun, still that gun from the club. The one that had gotten him in all this trouble. In the other pocket, a wadded bag of candy.

He pulled out the gun. Flexed his grip on the handle, working up courage. Droplets shined. He pretended to draw it from an imaginary holster, pointing the barrel toward the dumpster.

See here, Mister Cumbee, I had nothing to do with any of this. You got no call to gun down my family.

How would Cumbee react? Would he be impressed that he was being confronted in his own territory? Would Cumbee offer him a job? Offer to make him a capo, a trusted soldier in his army?

Pistek practiced aiming for the high windows at the end of the alley, squinting one eye. Had to blink rain out of it periodically. Glanced toward the open end of the alley—it would do him no good if Cumbee's men walked by and caught him from behind.

He felt his other pocket again, retrieved the plastic bag of chocolates. Worried about the candy getting wet, worried about pollution. He'd heard about that acid rain.

Deciding the foil would keep his prized candy safe, he risked opening the bag. Unwilling to let go of the gun, he awkwardly peeled the foil from the chocolate, fumbled, dropped it into a puddle. *Blech.* He let go of the wrapper, felt in the bag for another piece. Awkwardly peeled foil from this one, popped the chocolate in his mouth.

Ah. Sweetness. This was the life. He took a second to savor the moment. The smooth chocolate melting in his mouth, in his soul. He ignored the cold rain, ignored the smell of the alley, ignored the friction of the brick wall against his back.

He pulled the wrapper taut to read the fortune inside. LIVE TO RUN.

Seriously? The wrapper was telling him to hightail it to parts unknown? Just turn his back and get on with his life?

Remembering the other wrapper, he dropped to his knees on wet concrete. He needed a second opinion.

He felt the cold water seeping into his pants. He wiped his nose again to fight the smell of the dumpster, for all the good wiping did. He could not just cover his nose, he needed one hand free to keep his balance, and he was not letting go of this gun for anything.

The wrapper was near the chocolate he had dropped. Both soaking in a puddle. He grabbed the chocolate, made an angry fist, threw it as far as he could.

Shifting his weight for balance, he fished the wrapper out, wiped it against his shirt. Still a layer of crud on the wrapper. He wiped again, held it to the light. He had to angle it right to read it.

LIVE TO RUN.

- 75 -

Detective Tom Griggs and Detective Charlie Pasch, at Blake Media for a round of interviews. While Croteau and Booker quizzed some of the other media divisions, Griggs and Charlie were left with talking to the magazine staff.

On the drive over, the two detectives mapped out their strategy. "I need to warn you, they may not be forthcoming," Charlie said, watching trees pass by.

Griggs turned at the corner. "Everyone has something to hide?"

"Not necessarily. Just...afraid to get caught cooperating with someone from the outside world." Checking for his notebook and a working pen. "Of course, with Mrs. Blake still out of the office, it can't possibly be as bad as my last visit."

Not much chatter after that. There was still a strain on the partnership. Charlie wished he could say something to the older detective that could mend the awkwardness between them. He came up empty.

Finally, Griggs pulled into the front parking lot reserved for visitors. Inside, they found that even in Evelyn Blake's absence, there was still a cloud of fear and uncertainty. No matter who they pulled aside, no one wanted to be caught sharing any useful information. At least, not in front of the others.

The detectives passed out a few business cards, offered a few assurances. They split up, took names, took notes, asked questions. Charlie got into an argument about the Bible with the magazine's new religion editor.

Later in the morning, Griggs and Charlie connected again, compared some notes. Only one important interview left: Dennis Jung, publisher, the man left in charge in Evelyn Blake's absence.

Jung had been tied up in meetings all afternoon. But now they got past the man's assistant, into the office, saw Jung nervously shuffling papers at his desk.

When the man looked up, he seemed to grow more nervous. "Yes, gentlemen?"

Griggs and Charlie flashed badges, just needed to ask a few questions. While the man paused to articulate a reply, the two detectives each took a seat across from his desk.

Griggs consulted some notes. "So, Mr. Jung, you are a recent addition to the staff here?"

The publisher now seemed more agitated than nervous. "Pardon me, but we already talked to the authorities. And I don't believe Evelyn would appreciate your being here."

Griggs raised an eyebrow. "Evelyn?"

"Ms. Blake."

"Uh-huh. We are in the middle of an investigation. And I would think you'd have a vested interest. After all, your boss, Warren Blake—"

"I was under the impression no one had found a body yet."

Charlie wrote the word BODY on his notepad and put three question marks next to it.

Jung continued, "Besides, haven't you people done enough damage already? That library is going to be way behind schedule now."

Griggs smiled, oozing politeness. "That wasn't us." He glanced at Charlie, then back at Jung. "The reason we are doing these follow-up interviews is to get a clearer picture."

Charlie spoke up. "It's like that movie *Citizen Kane*. You ever see it?"

"No." The man behind the desk shook his head carefully. "Evelyn has mentioned it."

"Well, the film is the life story of an eccentric billionaire—and the whole thing is told through the interviews with other people."

"Even so—"

Charlie held a hand up. "At the end, the viewer is limited to this fractured portrait, because it's patched together from all this anecdotal evidence. So we are doing these follow-up interviews to get a clearer picture of Warren Blake and what may have become of him."

"I see. Well, make it quick."

Griggs sighed, started over. "What is your impression of Warren Blake?"

"I'm not sure I have an opinion. He was always out of town working on some new deal. I never spoke with him directly."

"You *never* speak with him?"

"I report directly to Evelyn. There is no reason for me to speak with Mr. Blake."

Charlie checked his notes. "Someone else mentioned Blake was always traveling on business. Do you know what sorts of deals he was working on?"

Jung shrugged again, shaking his head. "He was out running the cable network and media operations." He looked furtively toward the office door, then leaned forward and said in a low voice, "I think he was involved with organized crime."

Griggs regarded the man. "Why would you say that?"

"I saw Mr. Blake talking with Duke Cumbee."

"You saw this yourself?"

"Yes. I saw them in the parking garage."

"Can you tell me about that?"

"It was maybe a month ago. I was working late. I went out to go home for the night and saw the two of them in the garage. They were having this argument, and Cumbee was sort of shoving Mr. Blake. Cumbee was shouting something like, 'I'll kill you.' "

Charlie nodded and scribbled. If Cumbee was making threats, they needed to follow that up. Griggs asked, "Was there anyone else with them?"

The man shook his head. "I didn't see anyone. When they were done, Cumbee got in his car and drove away. Mr. Blake got in his car and left, too."

Charlie scribbled, CUMBEE ALONE. Something to consider later.

Griggs asked Jung, "What did you do then?"

"I didn't do anything. I went home."

"You didn't feel the need to report this to anybody?"

"No."

"I see." The older detective looked over at Charlie, then seemed to think of something. He turned back to the publisher. "What is your impression of Mrs. Blake?"

Jung hesitated. His cheeks seemed to redden. "She's a strong, vibrant woman with fresh ideas. She is often misunderstood."

Griggs leaned in, smirked. "Got some kind of crush on her, do ya?"

The man gritted his teeth, jumped to his feet. "That is completely inappropriate!" He shoved a finger toward the door. "Get out!"

Griggs didn't know how to follow that up. He looked to Charlie to see whether he had any additional questions. Charlie shook his head. The two detectives thanked Jung and excused themselves.

By the elevators, Griggs stopped Charlie. "What do you think?"

"If Blake is in it with Cumbee, that could explain a lot. And if he was making threats…"

"Yeah, we should investigate Cumbee, all right." Griggs pursed his lips. "But there's something about Mr. Jung's story that doesn't sit right with me."

"You mean, other than his taste in women?" Charlie grinned.

Griggs nodded. Smiled.

Charlie. "What do you want to do now?"

"We need to visit that garage."

- 76 -

The detectives got directions, were pointed to the indoor garage, a gray tomb. The security guard was more helpful than on Charlie's previous visit. Griggs had a force of presence about him. Charlie needed to learn how to do that.

Inside the garage, the older detective put his hands on his hips and took stock of his surroundings. He gazed for a long moment, taking in ceilings, walls, floors, rows of cars. Gray concrete, colored stripes to indicate the level.

Charlie felt lost without a book or spreadsheet. "If Blake is getting thick with the mob, anything could have happened." He began walking down the slope to the level below. "Maybe he ran for his life. Maybe he was kidnapped."

Griggs shook his head. "They may have been arguing about a woman."

"Why would you say that?"

Griggs nodded, descending the concrete slope again. Looking around the walls, the cars. "Because the FBI says Cumbee and Evelyn Blake—" Griggs glanced at his partner, rethought his choice of words—"have gotten very friendly."

Charlie listened for cars. It would be no good to be standing in the middle of the lane if someone drove through. "You mean, Special Agent O'Malley says."

Griggs stopped. Turned, showed a sour face. "Yeah." He started walking again.

Charlie regretted the dig, tried to move the conversation forward again. "He would have sent muscle."

"What?"

"When Cumbee has a problem with someone, he never gets personally involved. He would have sent someone."

"Yeah." The other stopped again, looked around. For places to hide, for exits, for security cameras. Getting a sense of how easily a person could watch what happens here. "But some of the other interviews suggested there was a partnership in the making."

"I heard that too. Like Blake and Cumbee were planning something." The two continued walking down the slope. Charlie frowned. "What business would bring them together?"

"Cumbee has been looking to expand his porno operation. Blake has a cable empire. You do the math."

Charlie snapped his fingers. "Cumbee has the content, Blake has the distribution."

"Like I said, do the math."

"But if Cumbee was alone, that would indicate something more amiable than a muscle operation." He turned to Griggs. "You think Blake was a willing partner?"

"Maybe."

"And then he got in over his head."

Griggs stopped again, hands on hips. Gazing at the ceiling. "Maybe."

"You know, we're working off the word of one man."

"You think he got the facts wrong?"

"Maybe Cumbee's men were there." Charlie pointed at some of the nooks and crannies around them. "Maybe off to the side. We don't know Jung's vantage point. Maybe he just didn't see them."

"Maybe Cumbee's goons stuffed Blake in a car and took off."

Charlie checked his book. "No, they left separately. And shortly after that, Blake and his wife took off on their international junket."

"It would be helpful to lock down the exact time of this meeting."

"Blake and Cumbee?"

"If that meeting happened right before Blake left for his trip," Griggs said, "maybe he was running for his life."

"If so, why come back two weeks later? Why come back at all?"

Griggs smiled. Touched his nose. "That would be the sixty-four-dollar question."

They walked around the circumference of the garage, spiraling down toward the exit. They reached the booth, a uniformed man sitting inside. They approached the booth, flashed badges.

Griggs asked, "How do you keep track of all the cars that come and go through here?"

"The pass cards keep track for us." The man pointed to the gray box. "They swipe 'em. Like a credit card."

"What if someone doesn't have a pass card?"

"If you don't use a pass card, you can't get into the garage," the uniformed man said. "The computer keeps track of the time you use the card to get in, and when you use it to get back out."

"What about visitors?" Griggs squinted. "You know, guests?"

The guard shook his head. "Guest parking is out front. No visitors park in the garage."

Griggs looked around. "Is there a pedestrian entrance and exit here?"

The guard pointed toward the elevators. "You can enter and exit the garage from the building inside." He turned and pointed back toward the big open air exit. "But the only way to get in from the outside is to walk past me. And there are emergency exits on every level—but you don't want to use those, because they set off the alarm."

Charlie pointed across the garage. "Like that door over there?"

"No, that's the utility room. The emergency exit is over there, where you see the big sign saying, 'Don't open this or the alarm will go off.' And then you have those exits that go back into the building."

Griggs raised an eyebrow. "Is there some way to exit through the utility room?"

"Not in this world."

"What do you mean?"

"The only door inside there is to the incinerator."

Griggs nodded. "And is there someone stationed here at all hours?"

"During business hours, yeah."

"And after business hours?"

The guard shrugged. "The computer keeps track of anyone using their pass key to get in or out." He jabbed a finger toward the back corner, where a camera sat high on a tripod bolted to the wall. "And we have security cameras on every level."

"How do we get a copy of the records of comings and goings?"

"Talk to my supervisor."

- 77 -

Judge Gideon Judge, at the Blake Media offices. Back at his desk after his third trip to the coffee machine.

His mind aswirl with recent events, he found the only way to keep his brain from shutting down was to focus on the machine. Right there, among the packets of Swiss Miss and Equal, amid the canisters of powdered creamer and sugar, stood the miracle coffee machine.

Choose a small, sealed individual serving of coffee from a selection of boxes; pull the drawer on the machine and place your selection inside; set your Styrofoam cup under the spout, press the blinking button, listen for the *whoosh*, and then hot liquid coffee trickles into your cup. In seconds.

A dumb thing on which to focus your attention. But when you're trapped in a web with organized crime and equally trapped in a new job that makes no sense, sometimes all you can do is wonder how the coffee machine works.

He still could not believe he had survived his meeting with Cumbee. Somehow, he made it through the whole evening without saying his entire name. Without saying the name he had used back in St. Louis, without saying the name Cumbee would no doubt remember.

Because if Cumbee had figured him out right then and there, Judge Gideon knew his brains would have been splattered all over the carpet.

No, Mister Cumbee was too classy for that. He would call aside some of his loyal soldiers, have them follow Judge Gideon to some quiet spot.

But Cumbee had not placed him. So there was no point in going there.

And then there was the appearance of the police earlier. Even after they told him they were investigating the disappearance of Warren Blake, it was a long while before his heart slowed back to a normal rhythm.

And the nerve of that younger detective, correcting him about the Bible. For all he knew, the kid was right. But it was still rude to correct him like that.

Judge Gideon returned to his desk with a steaming cup of Belgian Chocolate Walnut. He smelled the sweet aroma, sipped the warmth. It was delicious. For a brief, wonderful moment, he was able to forget Eddie Drake, forget Evelyn Blake, just focus on the magic aroma of his Belgian Chocolate Walnut coffee.

Reaching his desk, he was again confronted with the mystery that was his new job. He had no idea what he was doing. He had been awarded the title of "Contributing Editor, Religion" whatever that meant. No one had bothered to explain it to him. He wasn't sure what he was supposed to contribute. And nobody had brought him anything to edit.

He wondered what sorts of articles he should write. "Your Guardian-Angel Horoscopes"? "The End-Times Rapture Quiz"? He could bluff his way through one or two columns, but his shtick was not really designed for repeat business.

He thumbed the weathered Bible. It had turned up somewhere in the office, but no one had claimed it, so they figured it was his department and left it on his desk. Judge Gideon wasn't sure what to look for, so he set the book down and tried to figure out the blank screen staring at him.

The computer guy had set him up with a computer, explained a lot of gobbledy-gook about passwords and printers and things. His desk out here in a sea of cubicles, he could not very well nap. So to look busy—hoping he might eventually feel busy—Judge Gideon began clicking around. Just randomly clicking items on his desktop, seeing what opened.

Eventually he poked his head around the cubicle wall and saw a young man in the next space. "Excuse me, could you help me?"

The young man, clicking and tapping away at some document, turned suddenly and pulled back headphones. Rock 'n' roll came pounding out in little tinny bursts. "How are ya?"

Judge Gideon flashed his million-dollar smile—although, the way things had been the past few months, it was at best a thousand-dollar smile. He hoped it was enough. "I am sorry for bothering you, son, but I have recently been installed here." He offered his hand. "I am Judge Gideon Judge."

The young man gripped his hand firmly. "Tony Reed." He yanked the headphones off entirely and set them on the desk. Rolled his chair to Judge Gideon's cubicle. "What do you need?"

"I still have a few questions about my machine."

"Sure, what do you want it to do?"

"How do I engage the Internet?"

"We're all plugged in through the network. All you have to do is open your browser and go."

"I don't know what that means."

"You know, just open the program and you're already online."

"And that gets me on the Internet?"

The young man faltered, apparently baffled at the question. "You just open your browser."

"And where do I find that?"

Reed reached for Judge Gideon's computer, moved the mouse smoothly, the cursor moving to the bottom of the screen. "You have several downloaded, it looks like. FireFox, Internet Explorer, Safari. Do you have a preference?"

Judge Gideon gave the question more thought than *I did not recognize a single word in that sentence* required, finally shrugged. "What do you suggest?"

The other moved the mouse again, clicked a little picture at the bottom of the screen. "I like FireFox." He glanced up, the goodwill draining from his face. "Anything else?"

Judge Gideon did not want to push his luck. "You have been quite helpful. Thank you."

The young man shrugged. "Sure." He started to roll back to his own cubicle but stopped. "What is it you do here?"

"I'm an editor."

"You're the editor?"

"No, 'an' editor. I am a contributing editor."

Reed nodded doubtfully. "You're a contributing editor, and they have you stuck back here in a cubicle?"

"This is temporary. Mrs. Blake has not told them where she wants me placed yet."

"I see." Reed smiled and nodded, disappeared into his own cubicle again. The tinny rock music disappeared, indicating he had replaced the headphones on his ears.

Turning to his computer screen, Judge Gideon now had the much-vaunted World Wide Web at his disposal. But he didn't know where to go.

He thought about Andrea. Could he use the World Wide Web to find her? It was possible she was right there, somewhere, waiting to be found. Waiting to share her Jesus.

But Judge Gideon was not ready for that.

It was time to get another cup of coffee. He went to the kitchen, played with the machine one more time, fascinated with the sounds of the inner workings, trying to imagine what it was doing inside that charcoal-colored metal casing.

Slurping from his cup of Belgian Chocolate Walnut, he found himself wandering. He ended up back in one of the halls, where the art was still placed along the baseboards all the way down.

A young woman with a clipboard was looking at each individual piece. She would write something down about that particular piece, attach a little slip of paper, then move on to the next one.

Judge Gideon, still stalling before returning to work, asked, "What's with all the paintings on the floor here?"

"We're taking them all down, cataloging them, and putting them away."

"And then there will be nothing on the walls?"

"My understanding is that the Blakes have requested we put a whole slew of new works in their place."

"But all these pieces laid out on the floor—why are they sitting around like this?"

"Yeah, it's not the way to run a railroad. But Mrs. Blake keeps making this more complicated than it needs to be. She wasn't satisfied with us doing this the right way, so now we have them all down on the floor all over the place. All told, there's something like three hundred different pieces being cataloged. If we lost something, it would serve her right."

"I see."

As she resumed her work, she wrote something down on a pad, then attached a yellow slip to the frame of the next piece. He nodded and left her to her work.

He started thinking about Eddie Drake. Maybe he had a solution to their troubles.

- 78 -

Instead of returning to the office, Detectives Tom Griggs and Charlie Pasch dropped in at the batting cages.

When Griggs made the suggestion, Charlie was incredulous. "In the middle of the day?"

"The smack of the bat helps me think."

As long as they were stopping, Charlie got some hot dogs and a couple of Pepsis. When he got back to his partner, he found the man in a batting cage, in position, bat at the ready. The pitching machine rumbled, sounded to Charlie like a lawnmower, ready to burst forth stitched projectiles.

The first ball rocketed toward Griggs, who connected with a loud CRACK. He wobbled the bat in hand, placed it on his shoulder, yelled back toward Charlie. "So tell me what's going on."

Outside the cage, Charlie, mouth full, could not answer. He could feel mustard on the side of his face. Holding the dog and Pepsi in one hand, he fumbled for a paper napkin with the other.

When he didn't answer, Griggs turned. The next ball whizzed past him. Strike! "Hey! Whiz Kid!"

Charlie finished chewing, swallowed with a dramatic gulp. "I'm trying not to choke here."

"Want some hot dog with your mustard?" Griggs was now inching toward the fence, bemused look on his face.

Charlie felt his face redden. "I have condiment issues."

Griggs offered him a quick smile, stepped back to the plate. The next ball shot out. Griggs swung, connected with a loud CRACK, the ball shot up into the net.

Charlie self-consciously wiped his mouth again. "Would that have been a home run?" He took another big chomp.

"Nah, more like a base hit. Might have got me to second."

The machine spit out another ball. Griggs swung. A line drive. He prepared for the next pitch. "Look, Charlie, if you're not going to talk shop, then we're just playing hooky."

Charlie swallowed hard. "I thought we *were* playing hooky."

"No, we're working." The next sphere rocketed toward Griggs. He connected awkwardly, the ball went wide and into the net. The machine sputtered to a stop.

He turned, looked through the chain-link fence. "If you can't talk business out there, then you need to come in here."

Charlie gulped down the rest of his Pepsi, set the can down. He grabbed the other can off the bench, handed it to Griggs as the detective came out the swinging door.

Charlie stepped into the cage, donned the helmet. Felt weird. Following Griggs's instructions, he got the machine rumbling, felt the weight of the bat in his hand. While he was getting himself settled, a baseball whizzed past him and smacked into the backstop.

Griggs held up his Pepsi. "Strike!"

Charlie frowned. Ground his heel into the dirt. Leaned forward. Heard Griggs yell, "Straighten your arm!" He straightened his arm. Heard Griggs yell, "Step closer to the plate!" He stepped closer to the plate. The ball whizzed toward him, he swung awkwardly. Missed.

"Strike two!"

For the rest of the session, the older detective kept shouting tips, Charlie kept following them badly, kept swinging awkwardly. He connected with the ball once, a solid foul ball that rocketed off into the net. When the baseball-throwing monster finally rumbled to a stop, he was thrilled it was over.

Pulling off the helmet, he exited the cage. "Well, that was fun." More sarcastic than he intended.

His partner was sitting on the bench now, staring off glumly.

Charlie said, "What are you thinking about?"

Griggs worked up a slight smile, a sideways number that held sadness. "Just thinking."

Charlie grabbed his Pepsi can off the bench, hoping to find even a couple more ounces. It was dry, but he didn't want to go back to concessions. There was something in the air here, like he and the elder detective were connecting. He didn't want to risk breaking the circuit, didn't want to risk losing the moment. "This is what you and O'Malley do, huh?"

Griggs flashed anger a second, looked away. So that was the score.

"You can't stay mad at him forever."

Griggs looked back at Charlie, incredulous. "He stole our dig away from us."

"What's the point getting sore? It didn't pan out anyway." Charlie slurped at the edge of his Pepsi can again. Set it on the dirt and stepped on it, crushing it into a flat circle. "Besides, the Feds saved us the trouble of looking stupid."

He leaned forward, picked up the flat circle of aluminum, tossed it into the nearby receptacle. "When you look at it that way, they did us a favor."

The older man was silent a moment, looking at the ground, nodding. Finally, he sighed. "I guess."

"This way, Blake Media is suing the federal government and not us. Think about that."

Griggs looked at him, smiled slightly. "How can you stay so upbeat about all this? O'Malley did this to you, too."

Charlie shrugged. "It's not really my place to be mad, I guess."

"What, you never get mad?"

"It's not that I never get mad," Charlie said, slowly, mulling over each word before sharing it. "It's that I have to regularly remind myself I have to forgive."

"Why is that?"

"Because Jesus said if we don't forgive others, then God won't forgive us."

Griggs nodded. Thoughtful. "That so?"

"That's what it says in the Bible."

"Huh."

The two were silent a few minutes. Griggs thinking, a cloud still hanging over him. Charlie wondering if they could get back to work. Still not wanting to ruin the moment.

Finally, Griggs stood. "Well, if you're going to waste a perfectly good batting cage," he smacked his palms together with a loud whap, "I guess we need to get back to the station."

– 79 –

Professional thug Nelson Pistek spent all day not busting in on Evil Duke Cumbee. Shivering outside, around the corner from the apartment building, in the alley. Waiting. Waiting for an opening. Waiting for the right moment. Waiting for courage.

Not that it ever came.

Finally, consulting the chocolate, he knew it was time to try another direction. Seize the reins of his life, take control. Up to now, he had been simple flotsam on a sea of doubt and uncertainty, at the mercy of the harsh waves of circumstance.

(Not that he could have articulated it so handsomely, but that was the gist of it.)

He considered going back to Eddie. Maybe Eddie would take him back. Maybe all would be forgiven. Maybe everything would be jake.

If maybes were horses, it would still bite him in the end.

Nelson Pistek thought of Evil Duke Cumbee. Gritted his teeth. Decided to go for it.

Wiping grime and rain out of his eyes, ignoring the stench of the dumpster, he marched to the front of the apartment building. Opened the front door, pushed past some old man on a walker.

Heading up the stairs, Pistek heard a clatter and a whump behind him. Wondered whether the old man was okay. Did not stop. Who has time to check?

When he got to the second floor, he stepped into the hall, looked dully toward the other end, staring at a row of look-alike wooden doors. Faded carpet held some creepy design, yellowed wallpaper held smoke and history. Was this the right floor?

On his previous visit, he had been on the elevator, he had been ushered, he had been nervous. Sure, he was nervous now, but a different nervous. It had been a hopeful kind of nervous before, the nervous that points to a happy future of sunflowers and puppies.

Now he had the nervous of imminent death, the nervous that points to a future of black roses and maggots.

(Not that he would have articulated it so handsomely, but that was the gist of it.)

He could not go back to Eddie—that bridge was burned. He could not go to the cops—why should they protect a nobody like him? He could not go back to his sister—by now, she and her family were being hauled off to the morgue.

Nelson Pistek felt like a man without a country. Without a home. Without options.

He reached for the gun in his belt, the same gun he'd inherited after the killing back at Zoo Girls. He gripped the handle tightly. This would be his bright and shining moment. It had to be. It was all he had left.

No, this can't be the right floor. He remembered being in the elevator longer than this.

He stepped back onto the stairs, hand on his gun, taking it a step at a time, holding his breath, listening. Third floor looked identical. Fourth floor looked identical.

Reaching the top floor, he decided to try this hall. Door by door, he tried to remember the previous trip, tried to remember the number of doors. Tried to remember which one served as one of the many hangouts for the Cumbee gang.

Looking at the place now, it seemed like a bit of a dump. Why would a classy guy like Cumbee set up in a dump like this?

Pistek, gun in the air, ready, reached the end of the hall. None of the doors had spoken to him.

There was a window. He pulled back the curtain slightly, peeked down five floors at concrete and weeds below. Maybe this wasn't the floor.

Halfway back to the stairs, he heard a deadbolt unsnap. Held his breath, stepped back from the door. An old woman appeared, pulling one of those little square baskets on wheels.

He whipped the gun behind his back. Offered a grim smile. The woman barely made eye contact, shaking her head. Apparently accustomed to seeing thugs and guns in the building.

Turning away from him, she started pulling the basket up the hall. Headed for the stairs or the elevator. Given the basket on wheels, he guessed the elevator.

Pistek grunted at the thought. You wouldn't catch him on the elevator. Not in enemy territory. Not inside a box like that.

He could imagine the scene: You're in the box.

The doors open. They're standing there, waiting. You're in the box.

They shoot you. You can't run. You're in the box.

Then you're dead, and then you're in the ground. In another box.

He walked slowly behind the old woman. Not passing her, not wanting to rush the process. His adrenalized stupidity starting to fade. Realizing how deep in it he was.

What if he *had* found the right door? What if he *had* knocked? What if he *had* kicked it in? What then?

Stepping lightly on creepy red carpet, gun clutched tightly behind his back, Pistek finally noticed the voice of reason whispering from the edge of his brain.

> *You don't gotta rush in like a cowboy.*
>
> *Hide in the shadows.*
>
> *Shoot Cumbee from a window.*
>
> *Stick a bomb in Cumbee's tailpipe.*
>
> *Creep into Cumbee's home when he's sleeping and wrap piano wire around his neck and pull.*
>
> *Be sophisticated.*

The old lady pressed for the elevator. Pistek heard another door behind him, stopped and turned nervously, holding his breath. Some fat idiot in a numbered T-shirt, locking his apartment behind him.

He turned back just as the elevator doors opened. Looking dead in the eyes of two made thugs in unseasonable overcoats. Their eyes lit up—they knew him.

The moment slowed to a crawl. Crystalline dust sparkled in the window. The scent of old paint and Bengay wafted in the air. Nelson Pistek on the outside of the box.

Two of his targets inside the box. Wrapped and ready for him.

He was here. His opening. His moment. Gun clutched tightly in his hand. He locked eyes with the enemy and knew what he had to do.

He ran.

He hit the stairs running, jumping down two and three steps at a time, yells and loud curses behind him, the old woman shoved and screaming bloody murder. He couldn't stop to think. Couldn't stop to plan. Couldn't stop to consider.

They were a matter of steps behind him.

Fourth floor.

Third floor.

Second floor.

He hit the ground floor hard, pain shooting through his shins, heart thumping loudly in his ears. Stumbled and dropped his gun.

No time to stop.

No time to pick it up.

No time for anything but to run.

The grunts and yells and pants of large men barreling down the stairs behind, he hit the front door hard, shoved it open—

—and met more of Cumbee's men. They had all arrived together.

One ogre reached instantly, popped him one, knocking him flat down.

Pistek on his back, room swirling. Gasping desperately for air.

A heel pressing against his chest. A large man leaning hard. Saying, "We been lookin' for you."

🏠 🗔 ⑦   ⊠

BLOG

WHERE IS BLAKE #024
whereisblake.blogdroid.com

"To be conscious that you are ignorant is a great step to knowledge."
—Benjamin Disraeli (1804–1881)

I am so confused.

Before I left home, I spent my whole life knowing who I was. Knowing where I belonged.

And then my mother died and everything changed. I became someone else. I belonged somewhere else.

All I had was the word of Joe—the man I spent most of my life assuming was my dad. We were so close when I was younger. Buddies. Pals.

But I guess I grew out of that. As a teen, I caused my share of troubles. That's what teens do. But I always felt loved. Like I knew who I was. Like I knew where I belonged.

Then my mother died, and the man I always called "Dad" pulled me aside after the wake and changed everything. I was devastated.

But I put together a plan. I went to school. I studied. I investigated. I came to Kansas City to find a place to belong. I came to Kansas City to find someone to be.

I was actually at Blake Media a while before I made my move. Before I had the nerve to speak to Warren Blake in person. Before I had the nerve to speak to him privately.

I watched him from the edges, from the fringes. Watched to see what kind of person he was. How he treated his employees. How he carried himself in public.

It took a while. Although Mrs. Blake is a publicity freak, seeking attention wherever she can, Mr. Blake tries to be private. He only comes to the office on infrequent occasions.

In fact, none of us here in the office even saw Warren Blake for weeks before he disappeared. He and Mrs. Blake went to Milan for two weeks. After they got back, it was only a few days later when he went missing.

Shortly before he left for Milan, I met with him, shared my secret with him. He was agitated, to say the least. But he seemed to grow into the idea. He e-mailed me later and asked me to meet with him again.

I don't know what he was planning. Maybe he was going to test me somehow. Maybe he was going to try to pay me off. Maybe he was going to tell me to get lost.

But he was suddenly off to Milan, and now I will never know.

While he and Mrs. Blake were on their trip, he must have said something to her. Something about me. About the secret. About the surprise. About the possibilities.

How did she take it? Did she spend the entire trip fuming? Plotting his murder?

The revenge of a wife scorned? Or a plot to take over the media empire for herself?

Bet she didn't expect the board of directors to stand in her way. Bet she didn't know the board of directors *could* stand in her way.

What will she do now? Kill the rest of the board of directors?

— 80 —

Judge Gideon Judge got the painting out of the office and down to the car pretty easily, more or less.

Sure, it had taken all afternoon to work it out. All afternoon to hatch the plan, all afternoon to work up the nerve, all afternoon to make sure the coast was clear.

He had milled around the Blake Media offices for hours, pretending to sip his Belgian Chocolate Walnut coffee. Had successfully ducked engaging any of the other employees in direct conversation. At occasional intervals he went back through the maze to his cubicle, pretended to tap out something important on the computer-machine keyboard.

Killed time. Waited until most of the other employees had escaped for the night. Until no one seemed to be watching.

Found a row of artwork in one of the back halls, a line of framed works still unlabeled, still uninventoried. This project had been going on for days now, so there was no danger that some smocked worker was planning to wrap this up tonight.

He looked around for something to carry it in, happened upon someone's portfolio case valise in an empty cubicle. As he emptied the contents out on the desk, he grunted a prayer under his breath that the owner of said portfolio case valise would not notice him with it.

He quickly buzzed through his artistic choices, trying to distinguish one painting from another. Determined which frame could come closest to fitting in the portfolio, more or less.

The framed work was not a perfect fit, but he cleverly draped his jacket over everything. Carried the whole suspicious bundle under his arm. Locked his face into an expression of *I know what I am doing.* Headed for the exit.

No one stopped him by the cubicles.

No one stopped him at the elevator.

No one stopped him in the lobby.

No one stopped him at the exit.

Judge Gideon Judge exhaled in relief when he made it out to the front concrete, gasping at the cold night air, looking around for his ride. For the first time he was glad to see his keepers sticking close, his getaway car. Headlights came on, the car easing up the semicircle drive to pick him up.

He squinted at the car windows, saw the now-familiar mugs of Mister Banner and Mister Grimm. Glancing both directions to make sure nobody was watching, he grabbed the back door and shoved the package into the seat. Stepped in, slammed the heavy metal behind him.

Inside the car, he sat back, felt like the man in charge. "Boys, take me to see Eddie. I think I got it worked out." He was starting to feel like a gangster. It was wonderful.

He heard Andrea's voice again, remembered that bit about *It is appointed unto men once to die, but after this the judgment.*

I hate to break it to you, baby, but I ain't dying anytime soon.

What shall it profit a man if he shall gain the whole world, and lose his own soul?

What good has my soul ever done for me?

The oaf behind the wheel, the one he affectionately called Mister Banner, said, "Worked it out, huh?" The man glanced out the window, started driving toward the exit.

As the car pulled out into the street, the other guy, Mister Grimm turned and said, "What's up, Father?"

Judge Gideon grinned big and put a hand on the package. "Once Eddie gets a load of this, his money troubles will soon be over."

Mister Grimm chortled. "What? You got a bag fulla money there?"

He guffawed, looking to the driver for confirmation that he was the funniest man in the world.

Judge Gideon was unflapped. "Near enough." He sat back, locked fingers behind his head. The car stank of old cheese and beer. But that did not bother him. He felt good. Felt in control.

Maybe this was his new life. Maybe this was his new place in the world. He could drop the religious racket altogether.

Thinking of the untold riches hiding under his jacket, he leaned forward and grabbed the frame jutting out of the portfolio. Slipped the painting out—carefully, carefully—and held it up to take a look.

He turned the frame around to show the painting. "This is worth a fortune."

Mister Banner glanced at the reflection in the rearview mirror. Ever his eloquent self, said, "Yeah?"

"You better believe it. Eddie puts this in the hands of the right collector, and he's got a bucket of cash for his trouble."

Mister Grimm nodded thoughtfully. Did not seem to have an answer.

Mister Banner, glancing from the road to the mirror, squinted in the reflection. "It don't look like no fortune to me."

Judge Gideon felt his confidence go down a notch. "Sure it is." He looked out the window, watching streetlights and headlights pass in the night. He looked back toward the rearview mirror. "This is a priceless work of art. It's priceless."

"It looks like a buncha splotches. My nephew does stuff like that, and he's six."

"Ah, you're crazy." Judge Gideon turned the frame back to gaze at the painting. Streetlights pulsed in the darkness as they whizzed by. He angled the painting to get a better look. "You don't know good art."

Mister Banner had a point. They did look like splotches. Maybe he should have been choosier.

Mister Grimm furrowed his brow. "If it's priceless, how can it be worth a fortune?"

Judge Gideon blinked at him. "What?"

"I mean, if you buy a thing, it has a price. But if you can't buy it, then you can't sell it." He looked over at Mister Banner for support. "Am I right? Isn't that why it's priceless?"

Judge Gideon did not answer. Watched headlights and streetlights out of the car window. Clearly, these guys had no real class.

Philistines.

— 81 —

Detective Tom Griggs left Detective Charlie Pasch back at the station. The kid was still back there connecting dots between today's interviews and the folders of info the team had already gathered. Waiting for the faxes that would show them the pass card history for the past month at the garage.

Griggs looked at the flowers on the passenger seat. Smiled. Eyes back on the road, he was heading home to his wife. The plan was to surprise her with flowers, whisk her off somewhere to dinner. Carla would be thrilled.

As he navigated through traffic, he again thought of his day with Charlie. The kid had seemed to be okay, but there was still something unspoken between them, an awkwardness. He thought taking the kid to the batting cage would square things—that one big act, you know—but somehow it didn't seem like enough.

He knew he had betrayed his partner. He knew he was as guilty as Special Agent O'Malley. Well, almost as guilty—when Charlie showed up out of the blue with what seemed like such a compelling lead to break the case, at least he let the kid pursue it. He hadn't done like the Feds and cut the kid off at the pass.

Sure, the excavation had turned out to be a major public-relations and legal disaster. But that wasn't the point. O'Malley took the kid's theory and stole it. Tried to steal the whole case from them.

Griggs reached over and switched on the radio. Didn't want to think about his own culpability. Didn't want to think about all the times he'd ditched Charlie. As he pressed the buttons, he kept hitting commercials.

Finally, he gave up on the preselected stations and turned the knob and ended up on some familiar squawking: an opera singer. He had no idea if he was listening to some fancy French guy or some fancy German guy.

Charlie had tried to teach him about opera. Trying to find something for them to bond over. U2 hadn't worked. Burt Bacharach hadn't worked. Sometimes the kid drove him nuts.

He reached for the knob again, found some country music. The real stuff, too—cowboy singers weathered by a life of cheatin' and drinkin'. None of that freeze-dried pop music in a cowboy hat.

Reaching the suburbs, he was almost home. As George Jones wailed "He Stopped Loving Her Today," Griggs reached his street. Barely noticed the growing number of cars parked along the curb.

Then he got home and knew something was wrong. Lots of cars out front. Lights in the living room. People.

Grabbing the nondescript bouquet off the car seat next to him, he stomped to the front door. Batting off some bugs flying around the porch light, he tested the knob. Unlocked.

Inside, there were groups of women, clusters of them throughout the living room and dining room, chatting. None of them seemed to notice him.

Bouquet clutched tightly in hand, he scanned the crowd, trying to see Carla. Giving up on that, he turned for the kitchen. White light streaming out, maybe she was in there.

As he headed that way, he heard snatches of dialogue.

"Looks almost as real as..."

"Well, sometimes people are so unhappy, they think that's the only way they can solve their problems..."

"...he never saw it coming..."

"It's the age-old question, isn't it? How much do we really want to know about our neighbors?"

"Like I needed any encouragement..."

When Griggs reached the kitchen, he found Carla by the microwave, watching something rotate on the carousel inside. The air smelled like cinnamon. He said, "What gives?"

Carla turned and jumped, surprised he was suddenly standing there.

"Oh, hi, sweetheart." She smiled and put arms around him, kissed him lightly on the mouth.

He grunted, awkwardly extricated himself from the hug. Shoved the flowers toward her. Nodded toward the living room. "What's going on?"

She said "ooh" at the flowers, set them aside, and went to the cabinet for something to put them in. "It's the book club. We're meeting here tonight."

"Some last-minute thing?"

She shook her head thoughtfully. "No. We've known about this for a couple of months."

The microwave beeped and went dark. She popped open the door and pulled out a plate of cinnamon rolls. She smiled and said, "Ooh." The same "ooh" she said at the flowers. Which, he noticed, were still on the counter.

"So when were you going to spring this on me?"

She set the plate down and reached for a packet. "Spring what, honey?" She began squeezing white frosting onto the rolls, where it began to melt.

Griggs realized he was starving. "When were you going to tell me you had your knitting meeting tonight?"

"I told you several times. I told you this morning."

"But what about dinner?"

"I made something for you." She moved toward the stove.

He stopped her. "No, I mean, I was going to take you out to dinner." He made a face, meant to be sincere and earnest. "You know, surprise you."

She stepped up and kissed him on the cheek. "That's sweet, dear." She patted him on the chest. "Well, it would have been sweeter if you'd remembered I had my book club tonight, but this was sweet, too."

This was not happening. He lunged over, grabbed the flowers off the counter, re-shoved them in her direction. "Here. Don't say I never do anything for you."

She did not seem to know how to respond. After a hesitation, she smiled gently and said, "I love you."

He breathed loudly through his nose. "Yeah—well, actions speak louder than words." He threw the flowers on the floor and stormed out.

— **82** —

Out in the car, driving aimlessly, Griggs cursing himself for being an idiot. A big, dumb, stupid idiot. A brute who brings his wife flowers and then throws them on the floor. A brute. An idiot. A big, dumb, stupid, brute idiot.

Worse still, back there he'd heard the voice of his father. Out of his own mouth. He wasn't turning into his father, was he?

That was one reason he'd finally agreed to the marriage counseling. Somewhere in the back of his mind lurked the fear of turning into his father. Every stubborn word out of his mouth, every obstinate position held against the oncoming wave of facts and truth and reality, just reminded him more and more of his father.

The man who had tormented his family, treated them like second-class citizens, blamed them for every stupid mistake of his own. Classic blamer. Never took responsibility for his own actions.

Griggs yanked the turn signal, turned at the light toward the city. A drizzle coated the streets with a shiny film.

He thought about the time he almost lost Carla. Griggs and the joint task force closing in on crime boss Frank "Fat Cat" Catalano. And the fat man sent killers after Carla.

Carla Griggs.

His wife.

He could have lost her.

Before those events, Tom and Carla Griggs had been seeing the counselor. Both clinging to their pain over the death of their daughter. Each blaming the other for the vacuum left in their home, in their lives, in their hearts.

Until that night at the abandoned church. Tom and Carla and a group of mob killers. Only two people walked out alive.

Carla had tried to talk about it with him since then, wanted to talk through their "feelings." But he was not comfortable sharing. His father's example was that a man can only show his feelings in a damaging way. A man can only show his feelings to torment those unfortunate enough to love him.

But something else had happened back at that abandoned church. A moment of truth, a fatal error. Griggs shot the man who was saving his life.

Horrible, horrible thing.

Many times since then, he'd shuddered awake in the middle of the night. That man's face in front of him. Those eyes.

The scene played out again and again in his mind: Detective Tom Griggs and professional killer Solomon Long. Guns drawn, ready. The hit man shoots, Griggs shoots. Griggs hears the whump of the body behind him. Turns and sees the last of the mob killers dropping to the floor.

Long had saved Griggs's life.

Griggs had fatally shot Long.

He replayed the final moments between them. Rushing over to the man slumped on the floor. The look of relief in the man's eyes, the hand pulling an object from his coat and pressing it into Griggs's hands, the whisper...

"I forgive you."

Griggs had never told anyone about that moment. Not Carla, not Charlie, not the commission that had to decide whether Detective Thomas A. Griggs was going to be dismissed or penalized for rescuing his wife from mob killers.

Nobody else knew how it ended.

Griggs yanked the turn signal again, pulled to the shoulder of the road. Headlights rushed past him as he parked.

He sat for long moments. Gripping the steering wheel. Staring into the flow of headlights and the rhythm of windshield wipers fighting drizzle.

He looked at the glove compartment. Reached over, snapped it open, pulled out something.

A Bible.

The object Solomon Long handed him before he died.

All this time, Griggs had been afraid to confront it, afraid to acknowledge it, afraid to...

What? Afraid to what?

Tom Griggs was not a complicated man. But he was a man who

clung to his decisions, no matter how wrong or harmful. Like his father. A man who, once committed to a course, followed it with unswerving focus, even after the course was proven to be one that would take him over a cliff, followed by a long, fatal fall to the rocks below.

Like his father.

This weathered Bible was proof Griggs did not have it all figured out. He found the swirl of memories and thoughts and feelings more than he could deal with right now. Every instinct, every ingrained intuition told him to wall off all doubts and keep driving.

Carla had made him mad, he should fight to stay mad. He had stormed out, he should fight to keep storming. He had driven away, he should fight to keep driving.

Griggs shoved the Bible back into the glove compartment. Slammed the compartment door shut.

Gripped the steering wheel tightly again, breathed hard through his nose. Thinking. Trying not to think. Feeling. Trying not to feel.

He glanced into the rearview mirror, turned, glanced over his shoulder. Yanked the turn signal, checked traffic again, pulled the car out onto the road. Rain picking up. He adjusted the wipers to do their job faster.

He reached the corner, turned. Headed back home.

⁓ 83 ⁓

At the house, Griggs ran from the car through the rain. Brushed back wet hair out of his eyes.

Got inside. The lights were all on. The chattering not as loud as before. He found the women in the living room, seated in a circle of chairs, listening as one of the women spoke. Maybe she was "sharing her feelings."

Feeling his resolve fading, he forced himself to stand in the hall, waited for Carla to notice him. He felt his cheeks redden.

The woman sitting next to his wife saw him, turned to tell her. Carla made a face, one he could not place, stood, and set her book down on her chair. Came to the hall, looking embarrassed and a little afraid.

Griggs suddenly wished he had waited until after her party. But he was in too deep now.

She pulled him deeper into the hall, whispered, "What is it?"

He hesitated a second. Whispered, "I love you too."

Carla's expression melted into confusion. "What?"

"I was wrong. Before, when I stormed out like that. I'm sorry."

"O-okay." She had a trembly smile now, eyes misting up. "Thank you."

"You have your meeting and your friends and everything, so I'm going to head back to the station." He leaned down, kissed her on the forehead, on the nose, on the lips.

Carla grabbed him by the shoulders, turned it into a tight hug, kissed him full on the lips.

They both let go, slow, tender. She was grinning.

He smiled. "I'll see you later."

When he got to the car, he turned and saw her in the doorway. She waved a little wave, shut the front door.

As Tom Griggs turned the key in the ignition, the car rumbled to life. He checked for traffic, pulled out into the street again. He felt much better about the world.

He had apologized to his wife.

Let's see his father try *that*.

— 84 —

At the station, Griggs found Charlie working late. In fact, several detectives were there, an impromptu meeting of the "We Were Pulled Away From Our Real Work And Put On This Blake Case" support group. Booker, Croteau. Phillips, MacKenzie, Gainer. Trading notes, comparing stories.

"What's up?" Griggs trying to sound light. Like he hadn't almost had a meltdown just an hour or so ago.

"Griggs!" Booker waved. She motioned for him to come over. "Join the party!"

He pulled a chair from behind someone's desk, dragged it across linoleum to join the circle. "You guys got it all figured out?"

Charlie was glowing. "We seem to be getting there." He pointed to Croteau, who held a stack of spreadsheets. "Tell him what you got, Sammi."

Croteau flipped through the thick stack. She said, "We have confirmation here that Warren Blake and Evil Duke Cumbee had phone conversations."

"Phone conversations?"

"Several times a week, right up until a month before Blake disappeared."

"Who made the calls?"

She glanced down at the spreadsheets again, pointed at something. "Both directions. Blake called Cumbee, Cumbee called Blake. The duration ranged from a few minutes to," she pointed at something else, "almost forty minutes."

Charlie burst in. "So the two might have been talking business in the garage together that night."

Griggs nodded thoughtfully. "Maybe. If the Blakes' sudden business trip gave Cumbee the wrong signal..."

Croteau frowned. "What signal?"

Griggs shrugged. "The Feds discovered that Mrs. Blake and Evil Duke Cumbee had a...'thing.' Warren Blake suddenly grabs his wife and leaves town. Maybe Cumbee took it the wrong way."

Booker remarked, "They went to Italy. I'd like to go to Italy."

Charlie said, "Was it a sudden trip? I mean, Warren Blake works up business deals all over the world—wouldn't this have been scheduled?"

Griggs put up a finger. "Wait a second." He stood, walked down the hall to his office, found the notepad on his desk, the one from his interviews at Blake Media. He returned to find the group chattering, something about powdered creamer.

He sat down and began flipping through. "Here it is." The others were still chattering, so he looked up and said, "At the risk of getting back to the topic at hand..."

The others stopped. He smiled. Looked down at his notes. "When we talked to the employees at Blake Media, I actually heard from more than one person that the trip to Italy was quite unusual."

Croteau said, "In what way?"

"It was unexpected. But what seemed to shock most people was that Blake took his wife along."

The other detectives went silent, sat back in their chairs to consider this information.

⌂ ⌷ ⑦   ⊠

BLOG

WHERE IS BLAKE #025
whereisblake.blogdroid.com

"Curiosity is one of the most permanent and certain characteristics of a vigorous mind."
—Samuel Johnson

Now there is a color code for Evelyn Blake's coffee. She has put a Pantone color swatch in the kitchen to make sure whoever is making her coffee can mix in the correct ratio of cream.

Ever since Blake Media launched the magazine, there has been back-and-forth concerning editorial decisions. Warren Blake made it clear he wanted a big-circulation magazine, one that would be accessible to a wide number of supermarket shoppers. Very Middle America.

But Queen Evel acts like the magazine is some personal platform for her whims, change as they do from day to day. She proposes stories on convicted murderers and alleged members of organized crime. And not some angle that would make sense to supermarket shoppers in Middle America—she wants to do the *mobster's* side of the story. She wants to give them a platform to make excuses for their criminal behavior.

Needless to say, stories like those would be extraordinarily inappropriate for the delicate mix of a mass-circulation women's

236 — Chris Well

magazine. It is almost like she is trying to prepare for something...as if she knows it will come to light what kind of woman she is, and is creating an environment in which her exposed secrets will not seem like such a big deal.

How long was she planning the murder of her husband?

~ 85 ~

Amateur thug Nelson Pistek woke up in a chair. His arms tingled from lack of circulation. He tried to adjust his wrists, but the phone cord held them tight. He checked the inside of his lip with his tongue; it was swollen. He tasted blood.

Squinting through a black eye, he checked his surroundings. A small apartment, presumably inside the building where he'd gotten caught. Drab decor, only necessary furniture.

Three guys at the card table, one dealing. Pistek croaked through dry lips. "What's the game?"

The three looked over and laughed. First guy went back to dealing cards. Second guy said, "Hey, Sleeping Beauty done woke up!" Third guy turned back to examine cards in hand.

The three each took a turn, shoving chips toward the middle of the table, trading in cards with the dealer. Finally, one pivoted toward him again. "We're playin' to see who gets to kill ya."

The men bellowed with laughter. Pistek struggled to breathe, fought the cord around his wrists just to get some circulation in his arms again. Didn't know whether they were joking.

Of course, if they wanted him dead, he'd be popped and dropped in a ditch somewhere, right?

Right?

Memories of grisly stories percolated in the back of his brain, stories of random acts of torture and violence. If you were lucky, they shot you dead and left you alone.

Many were not so lucky. Mobsters were known to commit cruel and inhuman acts. To prove their manhood. To make a point. To pass the time.

One of 'em said, "Hey, Rox, what do you call a guy who sees you in the elevator like that and then runs like a little girl?"

The guy called Rox seemed to think a minute, then yelled at the man bound to the chair. "Hey! What's your name?"

"P-pistek." His voice cracking with fear and uncertainty.

"Pistol, huh?" Rox turned to the first guy. "I guess I'd call him 'Chicken Pistol.'" He chuckled like he'd made an actual play on words.

The first guy said, "So how would you kill Chicken Pistol?" He shoved more chips toward the middle of the table, traded in another card.

Rox set his cards face down. "Let's see, something poetic." Lit a cigar thoughtfully, carefully, like a professor. Finally, he turned to the first guy and shrugged. "Pluck him, maybe?"

"He ain't got no feathers."

Rox shook his head. "No, I mean I'd skin him." Added more chips to the pot, kept his cards.

"Yeah?"

"I always wanted to try that. Read about it in a Japanese book."

The dealer stared at Rox. "You can read Japanese?"

"It was translated."

"Oh."

Rox pushed away from the table, holding his cigar with two fingers. Walked over to the trembling seated captive. He turned and spoke to the others, pretended Pistek could no more understand him than a turkey before Thanksgiving. "You see, what you do," he jabbed a finger into the side of Pistek's head, "you stick the knife in around here, right behind the ear. Start carving." He began running his finger down the side of Pistek's head, neck, shoulders, arm. "If you do it right, it's one continuous line, until the skin comes right off."

The second guy at the table says, "So is he alive for this?"

Rox chuckled, tousled his captive's hair. "For most of it." He walked back to the table. "And we make hats out of him and throw the rest out."

The guys bellowed again. Pistek fought the urge to scream or cry.

Trembling, he bit his swollen lip. The pain gave him something to focus on. Keep it together, keep it together.

Rox said, "Alton, how would you kill him?"

The one called Alton said, "I would go for one of the classics. Bury him in cement, maybe."

The dealer said, "Aw, he'd smother in a couple minutes."

Alton pointed at the dealer. "No, you stick him in a hole that's narrow and deep." Took his cigarette, motioned around his chest area. "So he's standing straight up. You pour the concrete in slowly."

The man looked over at their captive, replacing his cigarette in his smirk. "The cement globs around the ankles, then the knees, then the chest...if you do it slow enough, he's watching it harden around him before you top it off."

Pistek couldn't hold his terror anymore, started sobbing. Felt his pants grow wet. His deteriorating composure only egged the mobsters on.

Rox turned to the dealer. "So, Hokie, how would you do him?"

The man they called Hokie sat back in his chair, chewing on a toothpick. He regarded the sobbing man. Grinned. "I think you boys are going too easy on him."

Alton chuckled. "Yeah? If you're so tough, what would you—"

A pounding on the door cut him off. Rox got up, Alton and Hokie sat forward, hands on their guns. Rox made sure the other two were ready, walked gingerly to the door. Pulled the cigar from his mouth, said in a harsh voice, "Yeah?"

"It's me."

Rox and the others traded alarmed looks. Rox began undoing the deadbolts.

Pistek blacked out again.

− 86 −

Judge Gideon Judge, doubled over on the grimy floor of the warehouse. Low-grade mob boss Eddie Drake kicking him while he was down.

Eddie Drake grunting, "I do not like being treated like a common thief." Eddie Drake grunting, "I am not a fence for stolen goods."

Judge Gideon, face on concrete, twitched an arm where Eddie's toe had connected. He looked over at the stolen painting, tossed carelessly, angrily, across the room, leaning crookedly against a crate.

He hoped they hadn't damaged it. It could still bring him a fortune. If he lived long enough.

Suddenly, Andrea's Jesus-talk didn't seem so bad right now.

Rough hands gripped his arm like a vise, jerked him up from the concrete floor. He was almost dangling next to Mister Banner. "W-what do you expect me to do, Eddie?"

Drake flashed eyes to the thugs. One of them slapped Judge Gideon. The thug said, "You speak with respect to Mister Drake."

Judge Gideon, room swirling around him, somehow extricated himself from the grip of the first thug. He motioned to the painting. "This is not some stolen CD player out of somebody's car. This is a work of *art*."

Eddie Drake paced a few steps, turned, and pulled the cigarette from stupid lips. "Yeah?" He cocked his head sideways and regarded the crooked piece. Took a couple tentative steps closer. Looked back at Judge Gideon, smiled like he hadn't just kicked the guy in the ribs. "Yeah?"

Judge Gideon nodded vigorously. "Oh, sure. *Sure*." Rotating his shoulder to try and make it pop. The pain was driving him crazy.

Drake took another couple of steps closer to the piece, which was still looking unloved against the wall. He took some puffs on his cigarette, deep in thought.

Finally, he turned back to Judge Gideon again. Motioned toward the painting with the cigarette. "Show me."

Judge Gideon squinted. "What do you mean?"

Drake stabbed toward the frame with the cigarette, wild ashes flying through the stale air. "Show me how this is a piece of work."

Judge Gideon took a halfhearted step forward. Looked nervously toward the goons on either side. Stony faces ignored his plight.

He looked at Eddie Drake and spoke carefully. "I don't understand what you are asking me to *do*."

"You know so much about this stuff." Drake took another drag off his cigarette. "Tell me about this one."

Judge Gideon nodded, more to convince himself than anything. *How hard could this be?*

All he had to do was bluff. He'd been bluffing for years. Spent years bluffing about the Bible. The beauty in that is, most people have no idea what the Bible actually says. You can make up anything you want—who's going to know the difference?

It stood to reason that art criticism would hold to more or less the same principle. He hoped.

He wiped his hands on his jacket, for all the good it did. His palms were still filthy, still felt oily. He coughed into his fist, the dusty air making his eyes water. Or was it the cigarette? Or the sore ribs? Or the imminent death by gangsters?

He limped across the concrete floor toward the stacks of crates. Leaned painfully, slowly—grabbed the painting by the frame. Picked it up. It was heavier than he remembered.

He held the frame in both hands, regarded the painting inside. His eyes scanned every square inch, looking past the art and into the craft, the components, the physical oil and the canvas underneath, trying to determine whether the manhandling had damaged it. He had no idea what the painting was worth, but he didn't think a horrible gash would help with its value.

He heard Eddie Drake breathing behind him, right on his shoulder. Judge Gideon held the painting out at full arm's length and made a show of examining it like he knew what he was looking at. "Oh, *yes*."

Turned and made accidental eye contact with Eddie Drake, who was standing uncomfortably close. "The swatches of color match the emotional state of the panorama." That's it, just stitch some words together. Watch low-rent mobster Eddie Drake look thoughtful, furrow his brow, nod like he understands.

Drake pointed with a cigarette, ash flying again. "It's a barn."

Judge Gideon nodded vigorously. "That's called 'pastoral.'"

"Heh. Like you, Padre."

It took Judge Gideon a second to make the connection. "No, here the word 'pastoral' means, um, 'farm.'" He nodded to look like he knew what he was talking about. "The shade of green there indicates the emotional state of the farm community."

He handed it off to Drake. "It's chock-full of meaning."

The mobster looked at the work doubtfully. "But you said something about it being rich."

Judge Gideon began massaging his shoulder. Wondered if it would ever feel right again. "Collectors pay through the nose for that kind of thing."

Drake gazed at the painting silently—long, wordless moments—like he was gonna buy it. Finally, shook his head and shoved it in Judge Gideon's direction. "Not my thing."

"B-but—"

"Too much work. I didn't bring you here to make work for me. I brought you here to get me in good with the Big Man upstairs."

"But God helps those who help themselves."

Eddie Drake smiled. "Now, c'mon, Padre, you can do better than that." He turned to Mister Banner and Mister Grimm. Made a savage motion toward the preacher man. "Take him back. Don't bring him again unless he's got something good."

He glared at Judge Gideon Judge and pointed, a cigarette dangling between two fingers. "Do right by me. Or I'm gonna send you on to see your Father in heaven ahead of schedule. Got it?"

Judge Gideon Judge could do nothing but nod. And try to figure out how to pray.

⌂ 🗀 ⑦   ⊠

BLOG

WHERE IS BLAKE #026
whereisblake.blogdroid.com

"It is not the answer that enlightens, but the question."

—Eugène Ionesco

I have been seeing a cute detective. Well, "seeing" may not be quite the right word for it. I mean, let's not kid ourselves here—this is an officer of the law who is, of course, investigating the disappearance of Warren Blake.

And, despite my sending him on what turned out to be a wild-goose chase, he seems to think I am a worthwhile source of information to help him navigate the churning waters that are Blake Media.

For my own part, I must confess a vested interest. I have secrets. (Most longtime readers of my blog will no doubt guess.) I want to know how much the authorities know about me.

A girl can't be too careful.

My new detective friend is funny. He sure loves his comic books. In fact, when we were first going to meet, he stood me up—for what turns out to be a case that is somehow comic-book-related.

He also seems to be something of a *Star Trek* geek. He has this whole spiel about how the sixties TV series was like Joseph Conrad's novel *Heart of Darkness*.

I read *Heart of Darkness* in college, of course. It never occurred to me I could have saved myself a lot of time and just watched a bunch of space jockeys running around in tight red shirts and those black pirate boots.

Ah, well. Such is life.

For my part, I guess I can't talk—I am a fan of the old James Bond movies. But I have an excuse: They remind me of when I was a kid, watching them with my dad—with Joe, that is.

Sure, I could be like my detective friend, make up some highfalutin excuse, cloak it in a lot of college termpaperspeak. I could talk about how the Bond movies of the Cold War era serve as sociopolitical time capsules, showing us a glimpse of the world as it was when the films were made. Yada yada.

But let's be honest: When I pop in *Diamonds Are Forever*, I am not a grown woman, an award-winning magazine editor, a journalist. No, when I pop in *Diamonds Are Forever*, I am ten years old again, sitting on the couch with my dad, listening to the sounds of my mom making snacks in the kitchen—popping corn, pouring chips into a bowl, fizzing soda into plastic tumblers.

Every scene from that movie comes to me through the prism of a child's perspective—the moon-buggy escape, the car chase through the Las Vegas parking lot, Jimmy Dean locked away while the bad guys impersonate him. I think of these scenes and I have to smile.

You might laugh. But that's my childhood.

─ 87 ─

Detective Tom Griggs checked his watch. What always kept that guy?

He heard a familiar voice by the front desk, greeting the cops by the door. He marched over and stood before Special Agent Marty O'Malley. The two eyed each other for a few silent moments, then both fell into sly smiles and clasped hands.

Griggs said, "I'm glad you came."

O'Malley shrugged. Chomping gum like a cowboy. "I'm glad you called."

The detective motioned for O'Malley to follow him as he headed for the captain's office. They reached the nameplate, CAPTAIN TROY HICKMAN. Griggs knocked fast, pushed the door open before they had a chance to be turned away. "Captain, we need to speak to you."

Captain Hickman looked up from his paperwork, harried expression on his face. "Yeah?"

"Yes, sir. We're putting the joint task force back together."

Captain Hickman looked from Griggs to O'Malley and back. Shrugged. "Okay."

─ 88 ─

Someone threw a mug of liquid in Nelson Pistek's face. It stung his skin, the vapor burned his eyes.

His head bobbed, he blinked hard, he forced himself through strength of will back to consciousness. He saw an unfamiliar man staring too close into his face. Breathing greasy onions and stale cigar.

The unfamiliar man chuckled with malice. "Well, what do you know? Snow White wakes up."

One of the thugs behind the man spoke up, somebody out of Pistek's vision. "Hey, that's what he said before. Except he din't say 'Snow White,' he said that—"

The man turned away. "Shut up!"

The room was silent. The man leaned in too close again, looming large in the tied-up man's vision. "What are you doing here? Who do you work for?"

Pistek's head was swirling. His heart was pounding in his ears. "W-what?"

The man slapped him. He tasted blood again. The man said, "Who sent you? Duke? Huh?" He glared hard. "Did the Duke send you?"

The question didn't make sense. Pistek fought to stay conscious. Fidgeted with the cord around his wrists, fighting the numbness in his arms. "I…I came here…"

Throat dry. Lip swollen. Surrounded by killers. "I came here looking for…a job." Don't mention the niece. The sister. The brother-in-law.

Get out alive. Got to get out alive.

Come back for revenge later.

Pistek repeated hoarsely, "I came here looking for a job."

He began sobbing. Imagining the blood on the walls of the trailer home.

The man pressing him with weird questions stood up straight. Eyed him warily.

The man stepped back. Turned to the others. Mumbled something Pistek didn't catch. The group of men then walked across to the other end of the room, formed a huddle.

What were they talking about? What were they planning?

Pistek tried to stop sobbing, tried to listen. There was more mumbling over there. There was laughing. There was planning.

He struggled against the cord, but his arms were too numb. He was too weak. Had been beaten too badly.

Finally, the man who had questioned him came back close. Pistek wanted to say something, say anything, came up with nothing.

The man motioned to one of the others, the one they called Alton, who came over, grinning. Alton stepped with vigor, he stepped with purpose. He stepped behind the chair. What was he going to do?

Alton circled around in front of him again and pulled a big knife. Grinned as he waved it in Pistek's face. Which one of them had talked about skinning him?

Alton went behind him again. Pistek was sobbing. Felt the sharp tip of the knife against the side of his head. Felt it caress his ear.

He shut his eyes tight, braced himself for the worst. Tried to remember how to pray.

Then he heard an odd sound, a chuckle. The leader. Their leader was chuckling. He said, "We apologize for the misunderstanding."

What misunderstanding?

"Clearly, you are an upstanding citizen," the man said. "You came here with good intentions, and we took them wrong."

The sliced telephone cord fell to the floor. Pistek felt his arms spreading involuntarily. He shook them to try to get the circulation going again. There were pins and needles. He started shaking them more vigorously.

The men laughed. But were they laughing *with* him, or were they laughing *at* him?

Rubbing his wrists, each in turn, he looked at the man who seemed to be the leader. "W-what are you saying?"

The leader paced the length of the room, lighting a cigar. He took his time. He turned back to the seated man, all smiles. "You're free to go."

Pistek squinted. He must have heard wrong. "I can get outta here?"

—— ——

Pistek stumbled out the door, all crooked grins and waves.

After he was out, Smart Tommy smiled. Went over to the kitchenette and poured something into a mug. Sipped. Took his time.

The others stood silently, waiting. Finally, Smart Tommy turned to the other men. "Now, I guess we see."

Alton said, "So what do you think, boss? Did the Duke send him here for you?"

Smart Tommy shook his head. "Cumbee don't know I'm here." Took a swig from the mug. Laughed. "Cumbee don't know I'm alive." He set the mug down. "All right, you know the drill. See where he goes."

The three men nodded. Alton, looking out the window. "Whatever you say, boss."

⚊ 89 ⚊

Outside the Blake home, FBI agents in an unmarked van. Watching, listening.

Special Agent Gareth Hunt engrossed in a magazine. Special Agent Ian Hendry engrossed in watching the banks of screens and listening through the headset.

Agent Hendry said, "How's the magazine? Keeping up with all the latest celebrity gossip?"

"This is research." Agent Hunt looked up from his issue of *Wired* and grinned. "Gotta keep up with the latest tech."

When the man in the suit showed up, Hendry was watching. The man in the suit was dropped off by a late-model Honda, was carrying a large, flat, unidentified object under one arm. The car disappeared around the corner. The man in the suit with the large, flat, unidentified object under his arm limped across the enormous yard, under the looming trees, around the corner of the gigantic house. Disappeared around back.

In the unmarked van, Special Agent Hendry checked his headphones. Turned to Special Agent Hunt. "I wonder what that's about."

Hunt didn't look up from his *Wired.* "What *what's* about?"

"That." Hendry pointed to one of the screens, a black-and-white image of the front yard. "There."

Hunt did not look up. Licked a finger, turned to the next page. "You'll have to be more specific, Ian."

"There was a car. It dropped off a man. He was carrying something."

Hunt sighed dramatically. Made a show of closing his magazine and looking up. "Fine. What man?"

Hendry waved a hand at the black-and-white screen. "Well, he's gone now."

"You made me lose my place for that?"

"I didn't ask you to lose your place. I just said there was a guy."

"Well, I don't see anybody."

"I didn't say there was a—" Hendry held up a hand, other hand on the headset. "Hold on. I'm hearing something."

This is what he heard:

MALE VOICE (later identified as Judge Gideon Judge):	I didn't expect to be so—
FEMALE VOICE (later identified as Evelyn Blake):	That's quite all right. My doctor has ordered me to stay here at home a few days.
SECOND MALE VOICE (later identified as Evil Duke Cumbee):	Orders? I don't think you've ever taken orders in your life.
EVELYN:	What is that supposed to mean?
CUMBEE:	I didn't mean any harm. I was just saying that you don't do anything you didn't choose for yourself.
EVELYN:	Well, I don't know about that.
CUMBEE:	So, what do we have here?
EVELYN:	Surely, you remember—

JUDGE: We met the other night, Mister Cumbee.

CUMBEE: Right, right. Reverend Judge. I still feel like I know you from somewhere before.

JUDGE: I don't think so.

CUMBEE: Somewhere.

JUDGE: I can't imagine where, sir.

EVELYN: Tell him. Tell Duke. He needs to tell you about this, Duke.

CUMBEE: Tell me what?

EVELYN: About this charity.

JUDGE: About the—

EVELYN: Duke, he needs to tell you about this charity.

CUMBEE: I'm not one for—

EVELYN: Tell him about the charity, Judge Gideon.

JUDGE: Well, there was this... orphanage...in Mexico...

CUMBEE: Really.

JUDGE: Um...yes...His Mercy Children's Orphanage.

EVELYN: No, no. I mean the *charity.*

JUDGE: But...

DUKE: Orphanage...

EVELYN: You know, the one about the Indians. Duke, this is important. Get out your checkbook.

DUKE: Do what?

EVELYN: Your checkbook, get out your checkbook. This is going to be good.

– 90 –

Inside the Blake residence, Judge Gideon Judge wished desperately for a hard drink. Facing Evil Duke Cumbee and Evelyn Blake, feeling the ice beneath him threatening to crack. Wishing he had listened to Andrea.

Rattled. Tentative. "I'm not sure what you want me to say, Mrs. Blake."

If only he had a drink. But he dared not ask. Dared not risk loosening his tongue. Not here.

Evelyn Blake said, "You know, what you told me at Blake Media. About those unnamed people."

Judge Gideon was looking at Evil Duke Cumbee, right there. The man who would kill him if he ever connected the dots. If he remembered that scam from back in St. Louis.

"Yes," Cumbee said. His tone cryptic. "Tell me about the unnamed people."

Judge Gideon grinned. Hoped it was charming. He really was losing it here. "Actually, what Mrs. Blake is referring to is the, um, plight of the Dalits."

Evil Duke Cumbee offered a strange smile. "The plight of the what?"

Evelyn Blake helpfully added, "They are the unnamed people."

Judge Gideon ignored her. "It's a group of people in India who are considered the bottom of the heap. The lowest of the low."

"Oh." Cumbee nodded. He began feeling his pockets. "The 'Dalits.'"

"Yes." How had he pronounced it before? "It's a horrible situation."

"These people can't get jobs," Evelyn Blake interjected. "Can't do lots of things."

The crime boss harrumphed. "It's the way of the world. Lots of people are at the bottom of the food chain." He pulled a cigar out. "It's how a man like me stays in business."

Cumbee stood. Walked across the living room to a silver tray with a bottle of liquor. Poured himself another drink.

Judge Gideon watched dryly. Studiously refused to ask for a drink of his own.

Cumbee turned, set the drink down. He pulled out a match, was in the process of lighting his cigar when Mrs. Blake said, "Don't you dare light that in here, Richard Cumbee." The mobster paused a moment, then shrugged and dropped the match on the silver tray.

When he sat down, she said, "Now, make out a check for the Indians."

"What?"

"We need some good karma. Write out a check."

"Why me?"

She slipped into the tone again: "Richard."

Cumbee rubbed his chin, as if he were considering his options. Finally, he called out toward the other room. "Larry!" A large man with a blank face entered the room.

Judge Gideon sank a little lower into his chair. Who was *this* guy now? Was this someone else who might finger him from his time in St. Louis?

The crime boss snapped fingers. "Checkbook."

The big man reached inside his jacket and retrieved a rectangular folder. Handed it to Cumbee, who filled in an amount. Then glared at Judge Gideon. "Who do I make this out to?"

Judge Gideon froze. How to answer? How to hold fast to his remaining shred of undiscoveredness? "Um..."

Evelyn Blake jumped in. "This is not nearly enough."

Cumbee frowned. "What?"

She snatched the check from him, ripped it in half. "Make it for a larger amount."

Judge Gideon watched crime boss Evil Duke Cumbee grumble and scribble. Judge Gideon felt the room tilt, move, sway.

Evelyn Blake said helpfully, "Just go ahead and make it out to him. You can trust him." She turned and smiled. "Can't he, Reverend?"

Judge Gideon somehow managed a nod.

She leaned over and said, "Write it out to 'Judge Gideon Judge.'"

The name. She said the full name.

He watched Evil Duke Cumbee start to make out the new check. He watched Evil Duke Cumbee speak as he wrote.

"Judge...

"Gideon...

"Judge."

Cumbee raised his head. A look in his eyes. "Judge Gideon Judge."

"Yes."

"You were in St. Louis."

"Yes."

He knew.

The crime boss narrowed eyes. "I see."

Evelyn Blake helpfully added, "So you boys know each other after all?"

At her voice, Cumbee's face changed. Hiding his growing fury.

Judge Gideon smiled awkwardly. "It was a long time ago." Met eyes with the other man. "I just assumed you wouldn't remember me."

"It took me a while." Cumbee now seemed jovial. "But it's come back to me now."

Evelyn Blake helpfully added, "Well, hand him the check, Richard." She took the check from Cumbee's clenched fist, oblivious to the crackle in the air, handed the crumpled paper to Judge Gideon.

Judge Gideon folded it best he could, put it in his shirt pocket. What else could he do? "I must be going."

Cumbee said, "Let me show you to the door."

Evelyn Blake helpfully added, "He knows the way, silly, he's staying with us."

Judge Gideon nodded awkwardly, looking at the carpet as he made a quick exit from the room. Behind him, he heard Cumbee say the name of the thug, the big guy with the stone face.

He did not wait to see what would happen. He was out the door.

⁓ 91 ⁓

Out in the van, Special Agent Ian Hendry was still listening to the Blake residence. Heard Judge Gideon Judge make his exit. Heard Evil Duke Cumbee pull his thug aside. Heard Evil Duke Cumbee's instructions.

Turned to Special Agent Gareth Hunt. "There's going to be trouble."

🏠 🗀 ⑦   ⊠

BLOG

WHERE IS BLAKE #027
whereisblake.blogdroid.com

"Education is a progressive discovery of our own ignorance."
—Will Durant

My fault. My fault. If I had never started this blog, never started spilling company secrets, never come to Kansas City searching for my past, for my future, none of this might have happened.

But now a human being is dead. As dead as if I had aimed the gun myself and pulled the trigger. And now they're coming for me.

They're going to find me any minute. I know it. I must have been crazy, but then, that's how it always is, isn't it? You feel the thrill of secrets, the thrill of sharing from behind an anonymous mask, the power—and then you are caught. Napoléon was caught. Hubris, I think it's called.

DELIVER US FROM EVELYN — 253

Icarus. I would log onto a <u>dictionary site</u> and check the definition but I don't have the time.

Because they're coming for me. When my adoring fans log onto my blog tomorrow morning, I wonder whether my secrets will still be here. I wonder whether my "crazy theories" will have been proven.

I wonder whether I will have paid for my part in the death of <u>Warren Blake</u>.

But they're coming. These are not people who forgive. These are not people who forget.

All I can think is how it must have been for Warren Blake when his time came. Nobody deserves to go like that.

How will it be when my time comes? A shot to the heart? A knife to the back? A push into an open elevator shaft? Can a person ever know how it all ends for them?

– 92 –

Failed thug Nelson Pistek at the end of his rope. No idea what had happened back in that apartment. No idea how he'd survived up to this point. No idea where his sudden good luck had come from.

No idea he was being followed.

Freshly released from the clutches of mobsters, he found himself wandering, dazed, through the grimy side of Kansas City. Sticking to the alleys, sticking to the back roads, sticking to the side routes.

Trying to lay low. Trying to think. Trying to plan.

He needed some chocolate. He needed to unwrap it from its foil, needed to let the chocolate soothe his nerves, melt slowly in his mouth. He needed to see what the message in the wrapper said, needed some advice real bad right now.

He checked his pockets, came up with nothing. Those mudheads back there must have taken his wallet.

Two blocks from the apartment building, Pistek stumbled upon a small store, looked like it might have what he needed. He was feeling wobbly, but he could still lift a bag of chocolate from a little mom-and-pop store.

Inside, he glanced around and saw an old woman behind the register. Not doing much. She saw him and smiled. Said hello. No matter. Even if she saw him, even if she spoke to him, he needed the chocolate.

Around the back, he saw a boy, a teen maybe, pushing a broom. The boy saw him and smiled. Said hello. No matter. Even if the boy saw him, even if the boy spoke to him, he needed the chocolate.

Pistek stumbled through one aisle, two aisles, three aisles, before he found the candy. Breathing heavy, he examined his options. Plastic bags of all sorts of candies, hard candies, soft candies, chocolate candies with nuts, chocolate candies with caramel, jelly beans, all sorts of candies.

Not his brand.

Looking both ways, he saw the coast was clear, grabbed a bag of something, not sure what it was, tore the bag open right then and there. Pulled out a small candy, something chocolate with a cream filling, ripped off the wrapper and popped it in his mouth.

Mmm, good.

Ahhh…

Before he tossed the wrapper, he checked the inside just to be sure. No message.

He was on his own.

He pulled a handful more out of the bag, dropped the bag to the floor with a rattle. He stuck the handful of wrapped chocolates in his pocket.

Behind him, the old lady shrieked. "Hey! You can't do that!"

Pistek turned and sneered. Didn't answer, just headed for the exit. He heard the quick steps behind him, probably the kid, maybe bringing the broom to clobber him. He felt a hand on his shoulder, heard a squeak, "Hold on, Mister," turned and clocked the kid with a solid right to the jaw.

Nelson Pistek had been bludgeoned by a room full of mobsters who'd threatened to skin him alive. A punk kid with a broom was nothing.

The woman shrieked behind him, threatened to call the cops. Pistek stepped out into the new day. The theme from *Town Without Pity* playing through his head, he looked for his car.

— — —

Pistek considered his options as he drove. Considered finally going to the cops. Come clean, explain the whole ordeal. Maybe he could turn state's evidence or something. Maybe they could bring him in as a star witness.

Problem was, he had nothing of value to offer.

Then he thought of his ol' pal Harry Cage. Harry, with his *Wizard of Oz* collectibles and his touchy attitude if you tried to have some fun with his beloved movie. They hadn't touched base in a few days, not since they'd leaned on that one guy and Pistek dropped him off the deck.

Cage was the only person Pistek trusted. The only guy left in this crazy world he could tell what's what and not be judged. Cage knew the score.

The whole drive over, Pistek pulled stolen chocolates from his pocket, unwrapped with his teeth while he drove, nibbled. He hated the waxy taste. But it was all he had.

Reaching the building, he parked a block over to be safe. Went in, oblivious of the car pulling up across the street, the eyes watching.

He went upstairs, found Cage's apartment. Pounded on the door. Listened. Heard nothing.

Pounded and shouted. Listened. Heard nothing.

Felt around the frame for a key, got on his knees and felt around the baseboard, around the welcome mat in front of the door.

Heard his knees pop as he grunted and stood. He looked around, walked to the end of the hall, and grabbed the big silver fire extinguisher off the wall. Hefted it back to the door.

Shifted it from one hand to the other, gauging its weight, then lifted and brought it down hard on the knob. A couple times, noise racketing up the hall. Nothing.

Pistek gasped for air, the events of the day taking their toll. Finally he gave it one last try, rammed the extinguisher into the door itself. The lock gave way and the door swung open.

Inside, he dropped the big can to the floor with a PTANG, stumbled to a chair. Fell into it, panting.

He was too exhausted to switch on the light as he came in, so all he had was moonlight from the window. He considered just collapsing into a coma right here in this chair. Cage wouldn't mind.

As his eyes adjusted to the dark, Pistek saw the shambles. Saw the *Wizard of Oz* junk strewn about the table, littering the floor at random angles.

There had been a fight here. Evil Duke Cumbee's men?

What if they were coming back? What if they were watching the place now?

Exhausted beyond all reason, Nelson Pistek pushed himself out of the chair. Braced himself against the table, knocking another Cowardly Lion off with a crash, fragments of porcelain flying. He could barely stand on his own strength.

But Nelson Pistek had to go somewhere safe.

Had to go see Eddie Drake.

Eddie would make this all okay.

Good ol' Eddie.

- 93 -

Outside the Blake residence, Judge Gideon Judge wasted no time. Evil Duke Cumbee's check in pocket, he immediately headed toward the guest house, following the brick walkway in the glow of the moonlight. Heard his shoes scuffing on the rough surface.

Once he reached the front, he stepped off to the left and headed for the woods behind. Hoping to run into Mister Banner or Mister Grimm. Hoping the check in his pocket was his ticket to sanctuary.

Evil Duke Cumbee had finally placed him. There wasn't much time.

It took Judge Gideon a few minutes to find his thugs in the dark woods, a few minutes of eternity, tromping, crunching dry grass and leaves underfoot, afraid to speak up too loudly, realizing he did not remember these men's actual names, could only whisper with desperation, "Hey! You back here?" Hoping he didn't run into any of Evil Duke Cumbee's men instead. If they weren't back here already, they'd be coming soon enough.

Finally, he saw a tiny glow floating in the air. His mind played tricks on him, he imagined it was some magical creature flying about, some agent of the Fates, until reason tapped him on the shoulder. It was someone taking a drag off a cigarette.

Judge Gideon's heart stopped in his chest. "Is that you?"

He waited forever and a day before he heard a gruff, "Yeah?"

He hoped it was one of his thug escorts. He never expected he would want to see them so badly. He pressed one hand against his shirt pocket, afraid the wind or God might pull the check away from him. "I got what Eddie needs this time."

In the darkness, the glow of the cigarette came closer, some hideous, hulking thing of moonlight and shadow forming in front of him. Giant feet crunching up the dry grass. It was hard to gauge distance in the dark, but he was sure the man was close enough now to strangle him if he felt the need.

The man said, "Are you sure this time?" It seemed to be Mister Grimm.

Judge Gideon nodded vigorously. In the dark, he had no way to know whether the man even saw him. "Yes. It's a can't-miss."

Of course, he had to be sure. He had to see Eddie Drake and make the sale of his life. And then hit the back door and leave Kansas City forever.

The man finally said, "All right then." Led Judge Gideon back to where the car was parked.

Neither of them saw Evil Duke Cumbee's men following.

− 94 −

Thug Nelson Pistek, failed thug Nelson Pistek, out-of-chocolates Nelson Pistek, forced-to-choose-his-own-destiny Nelson Pistek, outside a row of warehouses. He parked in the gravel by a broken streetlamp, oblivious to the set of headlights that had followed him up the road.

Which warehouse? Which door to Eddie Drake? Which door to sanctuary?

Pistek felt his pockets again, in vain. Without chocolate, he was all alone in the world.

He passed one dark warehouse. Nothing.

Came to a second warehouse. Grabbed the edge of the big door and yanked, but it didn't budge. He walked around the side, out of the moonlight, feeling for the side door in the blackness. Tripped on something in the dark, something that banged his shin something awful.

Face down in gravel, Nelson Pistek cursed. He could smell oil, felt ooze on his hands. Ugh.

Head pounding, palms scraped by gravel, he crawled in darkness toward the shadow of the big black wall, pushed against it to force himself up. He stood for long moments, panting, trying to get his bearings again. Finally, he inched forward more carefully, shoulder against the wall. Something scraped his arm, but he ignored it.

He finally found the door, gripped the knob, but it only rattled in his hand. Locked.

Maybe the next building.

Pistek inched carefully toward the moonlight, dragged his feet to keep from tripping again. He got to the front of the third building, came to the big door. Held his breath and listened. He heard voices.

Pistek reached for his gun—and remembered he was unarmed. No chocolate, no gun, just living by his wits and his charm.

But he knew if he could only find Eddie Drake in there, his problems were over.

He came to the big door. Placed a grimy hand against the edge and yanked. Got nothing for his trouble but a splinter. The voices had stopped now, but he was sure this was where he'd heard them.

He stumbled awkwardly around the corner, leaned against the building for support the whole way. He kept close to the building, did not want to risk another fall as he slipped from pale moonlight back into darkness. Felt his way along the wall with one hand, located the small side door. Felt around for the knob, found it.

Gripped the knob, turned—success—and pushed the door open. Inside, Pistek waited for his eyes to adjust to the naked lightbulbs. He debated whether to announce himself (what if it wasn't Eddie?), decided to wait and check the place out first.

He held his breath and listened. No voices. No nothing. He pulled the door shut behind him, stepped carefully behind a row of crates. Planned to make his way circuitously toward the big center of the space.

Every few steps, he stopped and listened. He heard something behind him, sounded like the door he had entered. Maybe someone in the warehouse was leaving.

He was turned around, lost in the maze of stacked crates. He remembered a trick he'd heard somewhere: When you're in a maze, you put one hand against the wall and just keep it against that wall the whole way. Eventually you had to find the way out.

He placed his left hand purposefully against a crate. Blinked sweat out of his eyes, wiped an arm against his brow. He had the worst headache of his life.

He just had to find Eddie. Then everything would be okay.

Pistek reached a gap in the crates, lost several minutes debating whether to remove his left hand from the previous crate or risk getting lost. It was getting harder to think.

When he felt the barrel of the gun pressed against the back of his head, it made the decision a lot easier. A gruff voice said, "Take it easy, partner."

He licked dry lips. Croaked a greeting from a dry throat. "I got no trouble. I'm just looking for Eddie."

Pistek clenched his fist once for luck, clenched it again, whirled, swinging. He drew upon images of his murdered family for rage, missed the guy by a mile, got smacked in the face with the pistol, and fell to his knees. He held up his hands in surrender. "I got no problem."

"I thought so." The other man motioned with the gun for him to stand, pointed a direction for him to walk.

Hands raised, arms aching, head throbbing, Nelson Pistek was marched through the gap toward the large opening in the center of the room. A wide, smooth concrete floor tapered down to a small circular metal drain in the middle. They were surrounded by stacks of crates, a couple of forklifts parked off to the side.

He was relieved to see Eddie Drake leaning quietly against a stack of crates, lighting a cigarette. Pistek grinned and dropped his hands. Almost cried with relief. "Mister Drake!"

Drake acted annoyed, pointed a cigarette at him, said to the man with the gun, "This all you found?"

The other man shrugged. "Yeah." Held the gun squarely pointed at Nelson Pistek.

"What about the other car? I heard two cars."

"He's all I saw."

Drake came close, angry face. "You bring anybody?"

Pistek's heart fell. Not the homecoming he'd expected. "No, boss. Just me."

Drake's face loosened a bit, a sort of smile. He took a couple puffs on his cigarette. "All right, then." He began to pace, puffing on the cigarette. "You know, I never thought I'd see you again, Pistol. Not after Cumbee's men came by looking for you." He stopped and stabbed the air with the cigarette. "You got the meat, boy, getting away from Cumbee like that and coming back here for me."

"I don't understand."

"Sure you don't." Drake spoke to the other man. "You got his piece, right?"

"I didn't see one."

He glared at the other man. "Did you check him?"

"What do you mean?"

"I mean, *did you check him?* Maybe he's got a knife in his pants or something." He smiled at Pistek. "He wouldn't be stupid enough to come after me empty-handed."

Pistek's world was spinning. "I don't understand, boss." He felt the bigger man now patting him down for a weapon. "Ain't I one'a your boys?"

The boss chuckled, puffed the cigarette. "Not after you offed one'a Cumbee's men like that. Him and that Russkie."

No, no, no. "I had nothin' to do with that, I swear! I din't…" Pistek stopped. Wait a second. "What do you know about it, Mister Drake? Did someone come here spreading stories?"

"Stories? They came here thinking it was my idea to send you." Drake puffed. "Trouble like that I don't need. When I gave 'em your sister's address, I thought that was the end of it." He laughed. "I do gotta thank you for one thing—in all the craziness, I got an extension from Duke on my loan."

Pistek felt rage growing in his belly, thoughts of his little niece rushing through his head. His sister. Even his brother-in-law. Unspeakable acts committed against them.

He clenched his teeth, growled as he leaped forward. "You sold me out?"

Before his hands reached Drake's neck, everything went black.

- 95 -

Judge Gideon Judge sitting in the back of Mister Grimm's car. Being chauffeured to Eddie Drake's hangout. He could get used to this.

If only he weren't one bullet away from dead. And Evil Duke Cumbee's gun being loaded even now, so to speak.

Judge Gideon nervously felt for the paper in his shirt pocket. Whew. Still there. His ticket. His escape.

There is a way that seems right to a man, but in the end it leads to death.

Not now, Andrea, not now.

Judge Gideon looked out the car window, watched headlights passing. Mumbled, "I wonder what Cumbee will do now."

"Whuzzat?" Mister Grimm behind the wheel, answering the reflection in the rearview mirror. "I couldn't hear what ya said."

Judge Gideon shook his head. "Nothing. Just thinking out loud." He watched more headlights, counting them off as they passed. "What do you know about Evil Duke Cumbee?"

The thug gruffed, "Sorry. I ain't s'posed to fraternize."

Judge Gideon nodded silently. Whatever. Watched the headlights again. Counting them off as they passed.

He thought of Andrea. Tried to remember how long it had been since he'd last seen her, how long since he hollered at her and stormed out. He had to count backward, month-by-month, and eventually realized he couldn't figure it out.

It had been too long. It had not been long enough.

Judge Gideon recalled their last few conversations, chuckled at the thought of her preaching to him like that. All they had been through, all the scams they had pulled, and in the end someone had still clobbered her with religion. And she tried to pass it on, foolish enough to think he would come along for the ride.

Well, no thank you, Missy. I got my own road, baby.

He missed Andrea more than he could reckon. Missed the homemade lemon-drop cookies. Missed the hot chocolate, a mint stick melted in it just like he liked it.

What was Andrea doing now? Was she still dating Jesus? She'd hated it when he phrased it like that.

Another few minutes, and Mister Grimm pulled into the gravel road. Judge Gideon breathed a sigh of relief. Just a few more minutes and he could endorse this check over to Eddie Drake. And his job was finished.

Then Eddie could cash it and use it to pay back Evil Duke Cumbee.

He laughed to think of it. Eddie's problem solved, Judge Gideon's problem solved. The only one poorer for the transaction would be Evil Duke Cumbee. "As long as Duke doesn't stop payment on the check."

"Whuzzat?"

"Nothing. Thinking out loud again." So what if Duke stopped payment? Judge Gideon would be long gone.

The car stopped. Mister Grimm said, "Here we are." As they got out of the car, the thug said, "And I hope you got something good this time."

They walked on gravel past the first, past the second, toward the third building. No clue about the series of cars that had followed them here, pulling even now into the gravel drive.

– 96 –

Out on the highway, one car held Detective Tom Griggs, Detective Charlie Pasch, and Special Agent Marty O'Malley. The other held two more federal agents. They reached the turnoff and pulled in.

Called in by the Feds who had been out in the van listening to the Blake house, the task force had followed two carloads of Evil Duke Cumbee's men, who in turn must have followed someone else here.

All following the preacher man, whoever he might turn out to be. Someone for whom Evil Duke Cumbee had been pressured into writing a huge check. Someone from whom Cumbee wanted the check back.

In the first car, O'Malley, chomping gum like a cowboy, rubbed his jaw with Band-Aided fingers. "You ever get bad feelings?"

Griggs smiled. "Every time we get together."

Charlie said, "What's with all the Band-Aids?"

O'Malley replied, through chomps on gum, "It's a long story."

Griggs frowned as he continued driving. Wherever this preacher guy was going, he had trouble on his tail. And if Griggs and the Feds didn't get to the scene in time, the man was done for.

No matter how the hammer fell, there was gonna be blood.

They drove up the gravel drive.

– 97 –

Judge Gideon Judge and Mister Grimm passed the big warehouse door in front. Grimm made a fist and pounded the door twice to announce they were coming.

They walked around the corner into the dark. Then reached the side door and Mister Grimm pushed it open, light streaming out. He stepped aside, motioned for Judge Gideon to go first. "After you, sir," he said, putting on airs.

Judge Gideon patted his shirt pocket again for luck and nodded as he passed the thug and entered. Remembering his previous visits, he went straight for the gap in the crates and headed for the big open area with the drain. Every time he visited, he wondered if blood ever went down that drain.

He thought again about Andrea.

When they reached the big circular area, Eddie Drake was standing there, smoking, perplexed look on his face. Some guy was face down on smooth cement. To Drake's left, Mister Banner was in some strange posture.

But Judge Gideon gave it only a flicker of thought. Judge Gideon thought of the threat of death coming for him and launched into his speech. "Eddie...I'm sorry, *Mister Drake,* I think I have the answer to your problems."

Behind him, Mister Grimm started to say something, and there was a whap. Turning, Judge Gideon saw Mister Grimm slumping to the floor, unconscious, dropping his pistol near his head.

Judge Gideon looked at the other man standing there, a stranger with a gun. "What is this?"

The man grinned, waved his pistol. "Oh, you don't know?"

"I'm afraid I don't." He noticed another man come out of the shadows, behind Eddie and behind Mister Banner.

The first stranger said, "You're what, the vicar or something, right?"

"Something like that."

With his free hand, the man brushed the hair out of his eyes. "Well, vicar me this, Batman, why are you meeting Eddie Drake in the middle of the night?"

Judge Gideon realized his hands were raised. The man had not asked, but it always paid to be careful. "I had some business."

Yea, though I walk through the valley of the shadow of death, yea, though I walk through the valley of the shadow of death...

"I see." The man with the gun worked his jaw, thinking, weighing things in his mind. "So this wouldn't have anything to do with Smart Tommy?"

"Smart Tommy?"

"You know the name?"

"Perhaps." Judge Gideon calculating as he went. *Shadow of death, shadow of death*…trying to think of some angle to get him out of this alive. "I knew him back in St. Louis." A lie, but a calculated risk. All he had.

As long as this man didn't turn out to be Smart Tommy himself.

Judge Gideon added slowly, deliberately, "Why, is he here? Can I talk to him?"

The man opened his mouth to speak, and then another voice shot out from the darkness. "What're you sissies doing here?" A man stepped up to the light. The ogre from back at the Blake house. Cumbee's goon. He must have followed.

The first stranger said, "This is private business."

Then the shooting started.

- 98 -

Outside the warehouse, the members of the KCPD/FBI joint task force were barely getting themselves situated when they heard the gunfire. Multiple weapons, by the sound of it.

They ducked behind cars and barrels and whatever was handy. Did not want to catch stray bullets punching through wood or metal siding. Griggs sent Charlie to call for additional cops—for backup or cleanup, depending on what they found when they got here.

And then came the silence. After one, two, three long minutes of it, O'Malley looked at Griggs in the light of the parking-lot lamp and shrugged, headed for the door, weapon ready. He reached the big front door, put a hand against it. Pushed.

Nothing.

Griggs joined Charlie at the car, opened the passenger-side door. Popped open the glove compartment. Pulled out the worn Bible, set it on the vinyl seat. Reached for the flashlight.

Armed with gun and flashlight, Charlie following, Griggs led the charge around the side of the building. Behind him, O'Malley made hand gestures for the other two agents to break off and follow him the opposite way.

Reaching the side door, Griggs switched off the flashlight. He and Charlie stood on opposite sides of the door, waiting for one of them to push it open. In the dark, he nodded to Charlie. In the dark, Charlie nodded to him.

Finally, he sighed. "I'll do it." Reached carefully and felt for the knob. Pushed the door open. Whispered a three-count and dropped to his knees and swung to point his gun inward. Charlie swung around and pointed his gun high.

Nothing.

The question now was whether everyone was dead, or whether they were all slinking around in the warehouse, playing some cat-and-mouse game.

Or had escaped out some other side door.

They heard footsteps running in from outside. O'Malley and the other two Feds had circled the entire warehouse the long way around. O'Malley shook his head. Whispered, "No other exit."

Griggs nodded. He turned to Charlie. "Go watch the front."

Charlie nodded and darted off. The two other agents followed O'Malley and Griggs into the warehouse.

After long, careful minutes of stepping lightly, making hand signals, and aiming guns in all sorts of directions, prepared for mobsters to come swooping at them from all angles, they finally reached the open center of the building.

Littered with bodies.

Wait, one of them moving. Griggs walked over briskly and pressed the muzzle of his gun to the man's head. "Freeze."

Shivering, the man stretched his hands out away from him. Trying to demonstrate his willingness to cooperate.

Griggs put a hand on the man's arm. "Are you hurt?"

His face pressed against the cement floor, his voice was muffled. "I-I don't think so."

Griggs put his other hand under the man's arm. He yelped as the detective yanked to help him up. "Can you stand, sir?" Griggs asked.

The man seemed to be taking stock of his aliveness for a moment. "Yes." Surprised. He felt for something in his shirt pocket.

The FBI men were checking the eight or so others at the scene for signs of life. O'Malley finally called out, "Here's another one." Shook him. "But he seems to be unconscious."

He looked at Griggs. "I guess at least one ambulance." He glanced around at the scene. "And some meat wagons."

— 99 —

The next night. Detective Charlie Pasch and *Blake Life* magazine assistant editor Dakota Flynn at Pedro's. Enjoying the chips and salsa, waiting for their dinner.

In the intervening time, Charlie filled her in on the previous night's events. "And there was a big, old-fashioned shootout among competing gangs."

"Bullets whizzing past your ears? The whole deal?"

"Not exactly. By the time we got into the warehouse, all we found were men lying on the floor."

"What's a big gangster shootout like?"

"I don't know." Charlie occupied himself with a chip and salsa. "When you're in the middle of it, you don't have time to think about it."

Dakota pointed to his forehead. "Is that how you got the scar?"

He blushed. "What?"

"That scar, right there."

"No, I've had that...a while."

"I know that—I mean, did you get that scar fighting crime?"

Charlie sighed. "There was this major drug deal. We swooped in to make the arrests and I got shot in the head."

"Oh, my. How bad was that? I mean, was there damage?"

Charlie shrugged. "I don't think so. I mean, I was already reading comic books, if that's what you're asking."

"So what does this tell us about Warren Blake?"

"What, me reading comic books?"

"No, the gangsters. Last night."

"We don't know yet. We rounded up Evil Duke Cumbee and Evelyn Blake for questioning. As for the warehouse, there were only three survivors." Charlie nibbled another chip. "One was unconscious during the whole shootout, a small-time hood named Nelson Pistek. Another is shot up and in critical condition, a guy named Morton York. Oh, and the third guy turned out to be your religion editor."

"Who?"

"Your Judge Gideon."

"He's not *my* Judge Gideon. The man leers at anything in a skirt. I can't stand him."

"Some religion editor. He didn't know much about the Bible." Charlie slurped through his straw. "Anyway, we questioned Pistek and Judge and are now waiting to see if York's condition improves."

The waitress came with their dinner. Charlie got the chicken flautas, Dakota got the veggie fajitas.

Dakota took a hot tortilla, piled it with sautéed onions and beans and rice. "What did y'all find out?"

Charlie stirred up sour cream and guacamole and refried beans. "Apparently, Smart Tommy came to Kansas City to give Evil Duke Cumbee trouble. And Eddie Drake got caught in the middle."

"Smart Tommy? Evil Duke Cumbee? Where do they get these names?"

"Smart Tommy is a crime boss in St. Louis. Evil Duke Cumbee, one of his lieutenants, tried to take over. When that didn't work, Cumbee came here to Kansas City to try and make his mark. Smart Tommy came west on I-70 to make trouble."

He took the bowl of salsa, applied it liberally to his plate. "You remember that shooting with the Russians a few weeks back? That was Smart Tommy's work. He was trying to set up Cumbee, get him dragged into a gang war."

"But what does this tell us about Warren Blake? How was he caught up in all this?"

Charlie stabbed one of the flautas with his fork, sliced it open with his knife. "We're still working on that." He took a bite, chewed, and swallowed. "We did finally get to the bottom of that library deal."

"What do you mean?"

"That hard hat was right—there was never a second foundation. Cumbee faked up all the paperwork."

"Why would he do that?"

"He was cheating on his wife with Evelyn Blake. Apparently, one of his explanations for being out of the house all hours of the night was that he was working on a construction job overnight."

"His wife believed him?"

"That's where he got himself in hot water. Mrs. Cumbee, being a bright lady, didn't believe him. So he doctored up some fake work orders just to show her. It never occurred to him it would backfire like that."

"Huh." Dakota started working on another fajita. "But Evil Duke Cumbee and Warren Blake were working together on some business deal, right? I mean, if Cumbee's company was building the library—"

"Your publisher saw them arguing in the parking garage. Maybe arguing over Mrs. Blake, maybe arguing over business details. Cumbee ain't talkin'." He stabbed another piece of flauta. "You know, if this were one of those old movies, we'd put everyone together in a room and finger the culprit that way."

"*Thin Man*, right?"

"Sure, sit everyone around a big dinner table and get everyone talking. Wait for someone to slip up and give themselves away." Charlie ate some more of his flauta. Then slipped into his best William Powell impression. "*The murderer is right in this room. Sitting at this table. You may serve the fish.*" He smiled. "I really need to have another one of my famous DVD parties."

"What's that?"

He chewed another bite, swallowed. "I like to put together movies that have some connection. Maybe the same director or some thematic link."

Dakota nodded. "I see." Finished off the rest of her current fajita. "Sounds like fun."

"What movies would you put together?"

She had to think about it. "I guess you could do *Citizen Kane* and *Diamonds Are Forever.*"

"I don't get it."

"You know, *Citizen Kane* is this—"

"I know all about *Citizen Kane*. This whole Blake investigation is *Citizen Kane*. But what does that have to do with James Bond?"

"The first movie was based on William Randolph Hearst, who the screenwriter knew personally. And the screenwriter's son is the guy who wrote the script for *Diamonds Are Forever*. Which has a character based on Howard Hughes."

"Never saw it."

She assembled another fajita, rolled it up. "You know, it could make good research for finding Warren Blake."

"How's that?"

"Jimmy Dean plays this reclusive billionaire no one ever sees. So nobody notices the difference when the bad guys lock him up somewhere and set up shop in his penthouse suite."

"And then what?"

"And then they pretend to be him. You know, when no one ever sees the real billionaire, all you need to fake is the voice on the phone—"

Her purse burst into music. She groaned and reached in, grabbing her cell phone. "This is Flynn. State your biz."

Publisher Dennis Jung. "Miss Flynn, I'm afraid you need to come to the office."

"What, tonight?" She put a hand over the mouthpiece and mouthed to Charlie, "It's my boss."

The voice on the phone said, "Did you think we wouldn't find out what you were doing?"

Oh, no. "What are you talking about, Dennis?"

"Your online Web log. You have broken company policy and shared trade secrets on the World Wide Web."

No sense playing dumb now. She sighed. "I guess I can clean out my desk in the morning."

"No, we need to take care of this tonight."

She considered pressing the matter. Decided it might be better to cut the ties after hours like this, without the prying eyes of the entire office looking on. "Fine. I'll be right there."

Dakota flipped the phone shut. "I have to go to the office and get fired. Come with?"

Charlie gave her a puzzled look. "Sure."

He settled the check. As they reached the parking lot, he said, "Wait, wait, control-alt-delete...tell me more about how one pretends to be a missing billionaire."

— 100 —

In the car, Dakota Flynn driving the two blocks from Pedro's to Blake Media. With her, Detective Charlie Pasch on his cell phone, trying to reach Griggs.

Finally he left a message. "Detective Griggs, this is Charlie. We need to rethink this whole Blake investigation. It's Jacob and Esau all over again. I'll fill you in tomorrow."

He hung up, shoved the phone in his left pocket.

Dakota was still watching the road. " 'Jacob and Esau'? What was that all about?"

"In the Bible, there were these two brothers. Esau was the older brother, and Jacob was the younger one. When it came time for their father to bless the oldest son, Jacob pulled a switcheroo."

"How could the dad not tell them apart?"

"He was old, and his eyesight was poor. So while Esau was out of the house, Jacob put on Esau's clothes and put goatskins on his arms and neck."

"Why would he do that?"

"Apparently, Esau was a hairy, hairy man."

"And...what does this have to do with Warren Blake?"

"The last time he was seen in person was that night he left the office late. But what if that was someone else? What if the security guard saw someone else from the back, who he *assumed* was Warren Blake?"

She made a thoughtful face. "All right."

"And if you back up from there—Warren Blake was reported as leaving on his private jet for Italy. How do we know it was Warren Blake who came back?"

Dakota nodded, catching on. "Or even went in the first place?"

"That's what I'm saying." Charlie got out his notepad and pen, started scribbling some notes. "We need to go back to those reports and re-check them. Wire photos to Italy to see whether the man they knew as Warren Blake was actually Blake himself."

He looked out the windshield, saw the Blake Media Towers looming. "While we're here, I can ask a few questions too. Your publisher was the last person to see Blake in the office before the trip to Milan. Maybe he can shed some light."

The car bounced as it entered the visitor lot. Charlie looked at Dakota. "We're parking in the visitor spaces?"

She pulled into the space. Shifted into park. Turned and grinned. "What's the worst he could do?"

They walked across concrete, reached the front entrance. Charlie, ever the gentleman, reached and tried to get the door for her. He yanked hard, rattled the door. Locked.

Dakota laughed and flashed the pass card for him. "I think you need one of these, Detective." She waved the card in front of a gray box on the wall. A green light beeped on, and the door came open.

Charlie blushed, held the door for her.

They passed the empty front desk—the security guard was away, must be walking a patrol—and headed right for the elevators. Charlie pressed for the elevator and, wouldn't you know it, the button ignored him.

Dakota smiled wryly. It reminded Charlie of Myrna Loy. "Allow me, Detective." She went up to another gray box, waved her pass card in front of it. A green light beeped on, and they could hear the sound of the elevator approaching.

The doors opened. She sighed as they entered and she pressed for their floor. "I guess I won't have this pass card after tonight."

He patted her on the back. "You'll be okay."

"Is this the level of moral support I can expect? Couldn't you amp it up a little?"

"I'll work on it."

They reached their floor and the door opened. It was dark. Dennis Jung standing there. Pointing a gun. "I've been waiting."

Reflexively, Dakota put her hands up. "I'm not sure I expected this."

Jung said, "And who is this, Miss Flynn? You were supposed to be alone."

Charlie said, "Um, sir? Apparently, you have some sort of…issues… but you really want to give me that gun. My partner knows I'm here."

"Wait a second." Jung squinted at Charlie, moving the nozzle of the gun in a little circle. "You're that cop." He shifted his weight from one foot to the other. "Toss your gun over here."

With Dakota so close to the line of fire, Charlie had to oblige.

Jung held his weapon steady, bent to one knee, and got Charlie's gun off the floor. Pocketed it. "Huh. So how did you find me out?"

Charlie, hands in air, started calculating in the back of his head how to take this guy down. In the meantime, of course, the trick was to keep him talking. "Actually, sir, we did not find you out. Until…well, now. When you were holding that gun."

Dakota huffed, "Come on, Dennis, what are we doing here?"

"Oh, like you don't know. Broadcasting all over the World Wide Web like that. Telling everybody about me, about Evelyn. About you and Warren Blake."

"Okay, Dennis, this isn't helping. Lots of people do blogs about their co-workers. They get reprimanded. They get fired. None of them get shot."

Charlie frowned. "Mr. Jung, what do you think you read on her blog?"

"How that floozy mocked Evelyn. Stole her husband. Tried to frame her."

It was Dakota's turn to frown. "What do you mean 'stole her husband'? How am I supposed to have done that?"

"You were his mistress."

She made a face. "*Ew*. I was *not*."

Charlie said, "Mr. Jung, I don't think you read the blog closely enough. Miss Flynn thinks she may be Warren Blake's *daughter*."

Dakota looked at him. "You read my blog?"

He shrugged. "Of course."

Jung raised the gun and narrowed his eyes. "Well, whatever the case, you're about to meet him." He motioned with the gun for them to start walking down the hall. "Go."

Dakota and Charlie, hands still raised, started down the hall, Jung following. "Where are we going?" she asked.

Charlie answered, "The parking garage." Remembering the conversation he and Griggs had with the security guard. He turned, yelled over his shoulder. "You're taking us to the incinerator, right?"

Jung said, "How did you know that?"

"Evil Duke Cumbee was never here in the parking garage." He turned and explained to Dakota, "Mr. Jung here made the whole story up." He yelled over his shoulder. "You were the one who had an argument with Warren Blake, right? You killed him and you dumped his body in the incinerator."

Dakota wanted to vomit. "That's horrible!" She turned on Jung. "How could you do something like that?"

Jung threatened her more forcefully with the gun. "Because he didn't deserve her. He wasn't worthy of her." He motioned with the gun again. "Over there. Take the stairwell."

The pair walked over to the door. As they got closer, Charlie knew this was his chance. Get inside the stairwell door, slam it shut, hold Jung outside while Dakota ran away. There would be shots fired through the door.

The trick was to survive.

Jung ordered, "Okay, you two, down the stairs."

Charlie motioned for her to go through first. Tried to give her a reassuring smile.

Dakota offered a brave smile of her own. Pushed through the door.

He watched her, wanted to make sure she was going to be safe. He listened to her heels echo in the stairwell.

He wasn't listening to Jung behind him. In that fraction of a second, the other man ran up, body-checked Charlie through the door. The detective grunted from the impact, fell against the iron railing.

Fell over.

Fell.
Fell.
Fell.

~ 101 ~

Pain. Charlie woke in a world of pain and darkness, in the flicker of an EXIT sign. Head throbbing, he moved slow, aching in every joint, every bone, every muscle.

He carefully flexed his fingers, slowly, checking for broken bones. Stretched his legs, slowly, checking for broken bones. Stretched his arms, slowly, checking for—

Ow.

Left arm. Probably broken. His left hand numb.

Ow, ow, ow.

Stairwell. He was in the stairwell at Blake Media. Had been pushed over the rail.

Dakota. Dakota Flynn. Dakota Flynn was in danger.

Man with gun. Making her go to the incinerator. Where he'd murdered Warren Blake.

Dennis Jung. Dennis Jung had killed Warren Blake.

Head start—how much of a head start did they have? How long had he blacked out for?

Charlie gritted his teeth, crawled to the wall. Pressed his back against it, grunted, pushed himself up. Tasted blood. Salt in his eyes.

Dear Jesus…

Cell. Cell phone. Call for help. Maybe he could call the front desk, try to reach the security guard.

He blinked, adjusting his eyes to the dim light of the EXIT sign. He apparently hadn't fallen all the way to the bottom. At some point, he must have bounced off the rail, ended up on one of these middle floors.

Trying not to jostle his left arm, he used his good hand to try to reach his left pocket. Reach his phone.

Dear Jesus, help me…

Ow, ow, ow.

He couldn't do it.

Had to remember how to get to the utility room. He shuffled up the stairs to the nearest door, tried the handle. Locked.

The EXIT sign was one floor above. Hopefully, that meant that door would be open.

Dear Jesus, help me do this...

Charlie grunted, shuffled up and around the circular rail to the next level. Put his right hand on the handle and pushed down. *Click.* The door opened.

He stumbled and fell into the hall. Yelped. Bit his lip to stop. He had no idea where the others were; the last thing he needed was to call attention to himself.

He squinted, trying to see in the dark hall. There were dim lights here and there. He started walking, started reminding his legs how to work.

Faster, Detective Pasch, faster. A woman's life is at stake.

Lord Jesus in heaven, help me do this...

He reached a big opening in the wall, what seemed to be a room. Felt around for a switch and turned on the lights. It was a kitchenette.

Salt burning his eyes, Charlie stumbled over to the big stainless steel sink and reached painfully for the faucet. Cold water poured out, which Charlie threw in his face. He grabbed a paper towel and soaked up cold water, wiped his face.

He looked around the kitchen, tried to find something sharp. Something blunt. A kitchen knife, a big wooden spoon. Seriously, at this point, any weapon would do.

Forcing himself to think through the haze, he grabbed something off the kitchen counter, was sticking it under his arm when he heard a gruff voice from the door. "Hey! What's going on in here?"

The security guard.

⁓ 102 ⁓

Dakota fought the urge to sob. She was not going to give Dennis the Jerk the satisfaction.

He shoved her across the parking-garage floor. "That way!"

She kept walking. "You do realize we're going to show up on the security cameras?"

"They only check this in replay, sweetheart, and by the time it occurs to someone to call up the tapes, you and your boyfriend will be long gone. And I will be in Milan with Evelyn."

"You can't be serious."

"Oh, yes. I am very serious."

He pointed to the metal door at the end of the garage. Motioned with the gun. "That's where we're going."

She wondered how to possibly get out of this. Gauged the likelihood of him actually shooting her if she made a move against him. Tried to imagine whether she would come across some blunt object she could chuck at his head just before she tackled him and beat him senseless.

They reached the door. She went for the knob. Locked. She turned and shrugged dramatically. "Well, Dennis," she announced in her most plucky voice, "I guess we'll have to come back in the morning."

Dennis the Jerk faltered, did not seem prepared for the possibility that someone locked the door. "Let me try that. Step back."

He threatened her with the gun as he went for the door himself. He tried the knob, rattled it, rattled it again. "This can't be happening."

Suddenly, a gruff voice echoed in the garage. "Hey! Get away from there!" Dakota turned and saw a man in a uniform—security guard. There was the crack of thunder, and the man fell, holding his arm where he was shot.

Dennis the Jerk, gun still trained on Dakota, inched toward the fallen man. "Give me your keys."

The guard, face pale, shocked from the gunshot, released his grip on his wounded arm, pulled off his key ring, tossed it over.

Dennis gripped the ring, cackled—Dakota could not believe it, the man actually cackled—and returned to the door. He turned and handed her the keys. "You find it."

She felt her lips tremble. This was too much, now. Asking a woman to find the key to her own murder. But she took the ring, flicked through the idea of whether it might work as a set of brass knuckles, decided to go ahead and try to find the key. If she got inside quickly enough, she might be able to shut the door behind her before he got in.

Or maybe there was something inside. Something big, something metal. At this point, any weapon would do.

She tried one key. She tried a second key. A third key.

She heard another crack of thunder behind her, turned and saw the security guard now slumped on the parking-garage floor, Dennis standing over him.

Trembling, sobbing, she tried the keys faster.

Fourth key. Seventh key.

The tenth key did it.

She popped the door open, jumped through, but Dennis was too close, too ready, he pushed her in, made her stumble and fall.

There was a big metal box across the room.

Dennis, waving the gun, got between her and the incinerator. "This thing heats up to something like three thousand degrees." He unhooked the cover, raised it up. "All that was left of Warren was the ashes."

Dakota glanced around, tried not to be too obvious about it. Saw odds and ends lying about, tools, junk. A shovel standing in the corner. She looked back at her boss, waiting for her chance.

He was motioning now for her to walk to the chute. She started backing up. He *tsked-tsked* her. "Don't give me a hard time, Miss Flynn. After I'm done with you, I need to drag that guard over here, then I have to go back and drag that cop all the way over here. I have a busy evening ahead of me."

She heard a wonderful voice. "Let me save you some trouble." It was Charlie, now waving a canister in Dennis's direction.

White powder flew between her captor and the heat source. As the cloud of creamer expanded, the heat ignited the particles, and there was a *whoosh* and a burst of fire.

Dennis stumbled backward. Fell. Started shooting wildly. On the ground, he wiped his eyes with his sleeve, pointed the gun at Charlie. "I see that you—"

He was cut off by the large shovel to the face.

ONE WEEK LATER.

~ Epilogue 1 ~

The batting cages. Detective Tom Griggs. Special Agent Marty O'Malley. Detective Charlie Pasch.

Charlie with the arm in a cast. Chomping on a hot dog, triple mustard. "It's ironic how it all went. Evelyn Blake thinks her husband skipped out on her. She's afraid it will mean losing her show, so for the first couple of weeks, she and Cumbee try to fake Warren Blake still being around, pretend to be man and wife in Milan."

O'Malley in the cage, swinging. A miss.

Griggs yelled, "O'Malley, I do believe you're the worst batter I've ever seen!" He turned back to Charlie. "So why didn't they keep the masquerade up?"

"Well, the first time Warren Blake was missed was when he didn't show up for a board meeting—one that Mrs. Blake and Cumbee didn't know anything about. If they had, they might have found some way to keep the charade going." He shook his head. "We might never have figured out he was even missing."

O'Malley's time was up in the cage. He handed the bat to Griggs, who went in the cage, started the machine.

The FBI man turned to Charlie. "So what's the deal with the exploding powder?"

Charlie explained how Detective Phillips had tried to prove powdered creamer is flammable by dumping it on a paper towel and dropping a match. "As I thought about it, I realized the creamer is only flammable if it is airborne."

"Why is that?"

281

"I guess it's because you're not just lighting the chemical, you're lighting the oxygen too."

O'Malley remarked, "Charlie, I think Mr. Spock would have been proud."

In the cage, the machine pitched. Griggs swung. Connected. O'Malley cheered.

Charlie was on top of the world.

~ Epilogue 2 ~

Dakota Flynn was ready to begin her journey. Car packed, ready for the drive. Directions printed out off Yahoo. A cooler full of bottled fruit juice and Snickers.

She thought about her long-distance call of the night before. The surprise in Joe's—no, the surprise in her *dad's*—voice.

He'd said he missed his little girl.

Dakota Flynn was packed, fueled up, ready for the open road. Ready for home.

~ Epilogue 3 ~

The bus station. Judge Gideon Judge checked the schedule. Thought about his life up to this point. About his home. About his name.

His real name.

Years of fakery were shellacked on him like so many bad coats of varnish. It was hard to remember the real him.

Hard to remember the real Dan Block.

He thought of Andrea again. About when she'd gotten religion. Him thinking it was some angle. Her telling him it was time to stop thinking of God like he was a monkey in a circus act.

Dan Block in a bus station, waiting for his departure time. Waiting for his new beginning. Waiting for his new life.

He patted his shirt pocket. The check was still there. A sizable contribution for the Dalits, courtesy of Evil Duke Cumbee.

He picked up the weathered Bible. The unclaimed Bible that someone had left on his desk. Began to thumb through it. Yes, he and Andrea would have a long talk.

— Epilogue 4 —

Randy's Comics Empire was open again for business. While Randy signed Charlie's cast, Charlie took note of the walls around them. Ripped posters were taped back together, broken shelves nailed into rough shape. "You got everything up in record time."

"It's still a work in progress." Randy finished signing, put the pen down. "And I had help from the kids." He smiled. Even with his lip mostly healed, it looked painful. "Thanks for calling some of the moms and telling them I was innocent."

Charlie shrugged. "Just wanted to help straighten things out." He nodded toward the door. "Well, I gotta go, Randy. Glad to see you back in business."

"Hold on a minute." Randy carefully wheeled around to a box against the wall. He pulled a single flat item out, wheeled back to the broken glass counter, set the item on top of the wooden sheet. "I found something for you."

Charlie gasped: a pristine copy of *Flash* #268, four-color magic in a slick, shiny plastic bag, kept flat by a thin white sheet of cardboard. "I can't believe it!" He held the find gingerly, gawking at bright colors shooting off the cover.

Randy laughed. "What's with you, detective man?"

"What do you mean?"

"You had all those rare books in your hand before, *Action* #1 and all those others, and you go gaga over this? It's not even a landmark issue—no deaths, no origin stories, nothing special."

"This was the first comic book I ever saw."

"Ah." Randy nodded. "That explains it."

Charlie looked at the comic again, transported back to his tenth summer, transformed into that little boy with the wide eyes. The comic was printed in 1978, but he'd discovered it years later in a trunk at his grandma's. It had opened up a whole new world for him. One from which he'd never recovered.

And then Charlie suddenly understood. Jeevan was right. The Golden Age of comic books is ten.

— Epilogue 5 —

At the house trailer. Jesse Hart, his wife, Darva, and their little girl, Janice, were back home from visiting Darva's brother, Nelson, in jail. His lawyer said if he cooperated with the authorities he could get a reduced sentence.

It was their first night back home since that horrible ordeal. Darva came into the living room, found her husband kneeling by the entertainment center. "Hey, Darva." He was reaching for something behind the cabinet. "These wires are color-coded!"

She smiled. Said nothing.

— Epilogue 6 —

The Griggs home. Detective Tom Griggs arrived, and Carla met him at the door with a kiss.

He thought about his life up to this point. The walls he'd spent years building up around him.

Carla went to the kitchen. Began working on dinner. Singing.

He went to the dining room. Grabbed a box out of the closet, set it on the wood table. The box full of unopened letters and packages from his father.

Griggs spent a long moment staring at the box, breathing heavy through his nose. Bracing himself.

He reached in, pulled out a letter at random. It was postmarked six months ago.

He ripped the envelope across the top. With trembling hands, he pulled the letter out.

Began reading.

— — —

NEWS

EVELYN 4 LIFE TV BACK BY POPULAR DEMAND
May 12, 2007.

Blake Media's new hit reality show, *Evelyn 4 Life TV,* will return during the 2007–2008 television season for an additional thirteen episodes. The second season order of the breakout success is an increase over the first season's eight-episode run.

"At first, we were worried about the negative publicity surrounding the Blakes after recent events," said producer Herman Benson. "But it turned out to drive the show to huge ratings."... <click for more>

＊ ＊ ＊

MEMORANDUM

TO: All employees, Kansas City Police Department
FROM: Captain Troy Hickman
DATE: May 31, 2006
RE: Igniting powdered creamer

IT HAS COME TO MY ATTENTION THAT THE HORRIBLE SMELL IN THE OFFICE IS THE RESULT OF SOMEBODY REPEATEDLY IGNITING POWDERED NONDAIRY CREAMER IN THE KITCHEN AREA.

CUT IT OUT.

＊ ＊ ＊